Praise for

TRACEY ENERSON WOOD

THE PRESIDENT'S WIFE

"Tracey Enerson Wood once more paints a vivid portrait of a woman whose remarkable role and achievements in history have largely been relegated to the shadows. Rich in historical detail and impressively researched, *The President's Wife* gives the reader a rare peek through the lens of Edith Wilson, from her courtship with a president to her decisions over matters ultimately leading to world wars. A fascinating read!"

—Kristina McMorris, *New York Times* bestselling author
of *Sold on a Monday* and *The Ways We Hide*

"Lush, lyrical, and riveting, with exquisite detail that brings alive the courageous determination of one of America's First Ladies, *The President's Wife* will charm and astonish you while holding you tight in its intriguing grip."

—Jennifer Rosner, award-winning author of *The Yellow Bird Sings* and *Once We Were Home*

THE ENGINEER'S WIFE

"This important work of historical fiction brings to life the strength and resolve of a nineteenth-century woman overshadowed by men and overlooked by history books."

—*Booklist*

"Well researched with great attention to detail, *The Engineer's Wife* is based on the true story about the exceptional woman who was tasked to build the Brooklyn Bridge. Though the great bridge would connect a city, it would also cause division and great loss for many. Tracey Enerson Wood delivers an absorbing and poignant tale of struggle, self-sacrifice, and the family transformed by the building of the legendary American landmark during the volatile time of women's suffrage, riots, and corruption. A triumphant debut not to be missed!"

—Kim Michele Richardson, *New York Times* bestselling
author of *The Book Woman of Troublesome Creek*

"*The Engineer's Wife* is just the sort of novel I love and—I hope—write. Against all odds, a dynamic, historic woman builds a monument and changes history as she and her surrounding cast leap off the page. What a life and what a beautifully written and inspiring story!"

—Karen Harper, *New York Times* bestselling author of *The Queen's Secret*

"*The Engineer's Wife* is historical fiction at its finest. Tracey Enerson Wood crafts the powerful and poignant story of Emily Warren Roebling, the compelling woman who played an instrumental role in the design and construction of the Brooklyn Bridge. This is necessary fiction for our time—paying tribute to women's overlooked contributions and reminding us of the true foundations of American history."

—Andrea Bobotis, author of *The Last List of Miss Judith Kratt*

"Who really built the Brooklyn Bridge? With its spunky, tough-minded heroine and vivid New York setting, *The Engineer's Wife* is a triumphant historical novel sure to please readers of the genre. Like Paula McLain, Tracey Enerson Wood spins a colorful and romantic tale of a storied era."

—Stewart O'Nan, award-winning author of *The Good Wife*

"Wood's satisfying historical feels true to its era yet powerfully relevant to women's lives today."

—*Publishers Weekly*

"Tracey Enerson Wood raises Emily Warren Roebling from the historical depths, bringing to vivid life the story of the woman who saved the Brooklyn Bridge."

—Anne Lipton, MD, PhD, coauthor of *Putting the Science in Fiction* and Harlequin Creator Fund recipient

THE WAR NURSE

"Tracey Enerson Wood achieves two particularly difficult things with this novel: a fictionalization of a real person's life, which is always a challenge, and the feat of writing a character from a century past who is accessible to a modern audience but still entirely of her era. In *The War Nurse*, based on the true story of pioneering WWI nurse Julia Stimson, we are transported to early-twentieth-century France, where a band of medical professionals struggles to meet the ever-changing demands of a war zone. You will smile, shed a few tears, and learn alongside Julia in this impeccably researched, well-drawn, based-on-a-true-story tale, written by a former RN. As our collective interest in WWI is reawakened, *The War Nurse* shines an important light on a woman whose story was, until now, lost to time."

—Kristin Harmel, *New York Times* bestselling author of *The Book of Lost Names*

"*The War Nurse* is a vividly rendered, moving tribute to one woman's determination to make a difference in the world. Tracey Enerson Wood sets us down in war-ravaged France and immerses us in the lives of a band of courageous nurses braving battles both physical and moral. A riveting and surprisingly timely story of courage, sacrifice, and friendship forged at the front lines."

—Kelly Mustian, author of *The Girls in the Stilt House*

"An incredibly well-researched historical fiction novel with a sympathetic heroine… Any readers who enjoyed the mix of romance, intrigue, and medical accuracy of *Call the Midwife* would love *The War Nurse*."

—*New York Journal of Books*

"*The War Nurse* is a fascinating, intimate look at the true story of Julia Catherine Stimson and the incredible work she and her nurses did to save lives during World War I. Through careful research, this book shows the incredible bravery and compassion of women who find themselves in extraordinary situations."

—Julia Kelly, international bestselling author of *The Last Garden in England* and *The Light Over London*

"Based on a true story, Wood's latest highlights Julia's quick thinking, organizational skills, and endlessly caring heart, bringing life to a brutal era. Fans of Patricia Harman will love Wood's treatment of medical expertise in a historical setting."

—*Booklist*

"*The War Nurse* is a rich, gripping history of one woman's lifelong battle against systemic prejudice. As Tracey Enerson Wood's heroine says of herself, 'I wasn't a man, for whom the things I wanted to do would have been easy. I was meant to break down the wall in between.'"

—Stewart O'Nan, award-winning author of *The Good Wife*

"If you've read *The Engineers Wife*, Tracey Enerson Wood's debut, you are already aware of her talent for merging fact and fiction into a story that will make your heart hurt and hold you captive until the very last page. She doesn't disappoint with *The War Nurse*. I LOVED, LOVED, LOVED this book!"

—Barbara Conrey, *USA Today* bestselling author of *Nowhere Near Goodbye*

"Once again, Tracey Enerson Wood, with her impeccable research and evocative prose, kept me glued to the page. Wood has a talent for bringing strong, yet lesser-known women from history to life. Her fictionalization of WWI nurse Julia Stimson, as well as the supporting cast, transported me back in time and had me smiling, crying, and learning. Fantastic!"

—Linda Rosen, author of *The Disharmony of Silence*

"If you, like me, are a voyeur of historical drama that unfolds as if the kitchen window flew open and the characters were caught in action, then *The War Nurse* is for you. Tracey Enerson Wood's storytelling verisimilitude—the detail, persuasive dialogue, and twinning of history with a hidden love story—prove her skill at immersion but also that rarest of traits: a big and generous heart that roots for the unsung heroines and heroes of the time. This author shines a light for us all to see our past anew."

—Diane Dewey, author of *Fixing the Fates*

ALSO BY
TRACEY ENERSON WOOD

The Engineer's Wife

The War Nurse

Homefront Cooking: Recipes, Wit, and Wisdom from American Veterans and Their Loved Ones (coauthor)

Life Hacks for Military Spouses (coauthor)

the
PRESIDENT'S
WIFE

A Novel

TRACEY ENERSON WOOD

Published by Sourcebooks Landmark, an imprint of Sourcebooks
P.O. Box 4410, Naperville, Illinois 60567–4410
(630) 961-3900
sourcebooks.com

Library of Congress Cataloging-in-Publication Data

Names: Wood, Tracey Enerson, author.
Title: The president's wife : a novel / Tracey Enerson Wood.
Description: Naperville, Illinois : Sourcebooks Landmark, [2023]
Identifiers: LCCN 2022061961 (print) | LCCN 2022061962 (ebook) | (hardcover) | (epub)
Subjects: LCSH: Wilson, Edith Bolling Galt, 1872-1961--Fiction. | Wilson,
    Woodrow, 1856-1924--Fiction. | Presidents' spouses--Fiction. | United
    States--Politics and government--1913-1921--Fiction. | LCGFT:
    Biographical fiction. | Historical fiction. | Novels.
Classification: LCC PS3623.O6455 P74 2023 (print) | LCC PS3623.O6455
    (ebook) | DDC 813/.6--dc23/eng/20230105
LC record available at https://lccn.loc.gov/2022061961
LC ebook record available at https://lccn.loc.gov/2022061962

Printed and bound in the United States of America.
LSC 10 9 8 7 6 5 4 3 2 1

To all the spouses working quietly behind the scenes, unknown, unpaid, and untrained, yet without whom little would get done

ONE

W aiting in line at the reception desk of perhaps the grandest and
most elegant hotel in Virginia, Edith grew impatient as the
young couple in front of her quizzed the clerk about teatime
and tee times and proper dress for each, as if they were important matters
of state.

The carved walnut reception desk stood at one end of the long Grand
Hall of the hotel, which was lined with comfortable chairs arranged in
intimate conversation groups. Sunshine poured in from the Palladian
windows that fronted the building, giving her the feeling of standing in a
Renaissance master's painting.

The sights and sounds of tea being served, newspapers turning, brass
luggage carts rolling, the exchange of greetings echoing against the cool
white marble floors and columns were real and tangible, yet Edith felt
estranged from it all. She stood amongst it, flesh and blood, but it seemed
her true self was present only in the reverie of decades past.

The man and woman holding up the line were fresh-faced, brimming
with the same innocence and exuberance that Edith once had, thirty-one
years ago, when she stood in that very spot next to her new husband. Her
nose detected the floral and spice scent of Shalimar, the modern version of
Jicky, an old French perfume and yet another reminder of her past life. She

wondered if the pair appreciated how glorious each day together was, how special each and every moment was.

Eventually the young couple trotted off, with their pearls and feathers and heavy leather trunks carried by four bellboys in red uniforms. Edith stepped up to the desk and gave the clerk a sympathetic smile. "You must tire of answering the same questions over and over." She set the huge brass room key on the desktop with a *thunk*, so as not to carry its weight on her morning walk.

"Good morning, Mrs. Wil...er, Ignatz. The Homestead welcomes all questions." He turned to hang the key on a hook behind him. "Is everything to your satisfaction in the Presidential Suite?"

Was it? Perhaps it had been exactly what she needed, but the trip had left her feeling empty, the warm welcome of the familiar hotel now faded into eeriness. "Yes, of course. It just makes me think of the president, and I miss him so. What I wouldn't give to have that time back."

"I imagine so." He leaned close, as if to share a secret, but then asked a most difficult question. "If I may ask, Mrs. Ignatz, why the assumed name? Do people bother you for autographs and such, because we can..."

To others it would seem an innocent question, asked by a young clerk who couldn't have known the depth of the crevices that held the truth. Flustered, she didn't have a ready answer. How could she explain the cataclysm and consequences of a love story that had changed history?

Edith realized with a start that the young man was probably still in his twenties, too young to grow a decent beard and not even born when she and Woodrow spent their honeymoon at this very hotel. He wouldn't know of Ignatz, the cartoon character from back in the silent-movie days. Her husband had dubbed her with the pet name, as he fancied himself to be the top-hatted Krazy Kat, always trying to win over Ignatz the mouse.

She adjusted her hat, with its netting that she hoped made her face less recognizable, and leaned in. "Dear boy, it's not that." She took a breath. How could she put it in a few words? "You see, we all seek to understand the horrific war we've been through and try to find the root causes. It's not enough to blame Hirohito, Hitler, and Mussolini. Who and what set the stage for this evil to grow and nearly take over the world?" She waited to hear if he had any answer, but he just scratched his ear and took on the pained look of avoidance she had witnessed on so many faces.

She continued anyway. Both world wars needed to be thoroughly examined, and she needed to come to terms with her part. "Some say that if you boil it all down, trace back in history to decisions made in the decades previous, all signs point to one person. One person who could have intervened, who had the opportunity, the moment, the power to change the course of events so a different path could have been taken. And that person is little ol' me."

The clerk dismissed her notion with a small laugh, his eyes already falling on the people behind her in line. "Oh, Mrs. Ignatz, you're such a jokester."

She raised an eyebrow and nodded, a pleasant smile fixed to her face, even though the unfathomable burden of responsibility she had borne was hardly anything to joke about. Admitting her culpability to the young man felt as if the hard shell she had built around herself had been torn off, exposing her like an opened oyster.

As she exited the Grand Hall through the yellow pools of sunlight, her heels clicking against the hard floor, she felt the slight hush that fell over each conversation as she passed. The guests were older and wiser than the clerk. They had lived through the horror of both world wars. She studied their faces, trying to discern their thoughts. What did they think of her? For Edith—in her lowest moments—would forever believe she was at least partly to blame.

TWO

Washington, DC
March 1915

She should have suspected the setup the moment Altrude lost interest in the tour books and maps spread across the dining room table. They were in Edith's comfortable rowhouse in the heart of the District. Three stories high, but so narrow that a sofa and two side tables barely fit across the parlor's width, it suited Edith's sense of order and usefulness.

She and Altrude sat in the comfortable wooden chairs Edith favored for the simple lines of their Eastlake design, so calm in comparison to the carved cherubs and curlicues of her childhood home. Twenty-three-year-old Altrude Gordon was a frequent visitor, but Edith lived happily alone. Her dearly departed—well departed anyway—husband had left her enough financial stability to travel in style, and her home was her nest to return to between adventures.

"It doesn't matter; just pick someplace. But let's not be gone for more than a week or so," Altrude said. She was as close to a daughter as Edith could hope for. The girl's father, a dear friend of Edith's, had raised her alone, and just before he passed away a few years ago had asked Edith to watch over her. Since then, they had tried to squeeze a decade of adventures into every year and spent the past few summers traveling Europe and New England.

Before Edith could object to Altrude's suggestion, the jangle of the telephone interrupted them and Altrude sprang into action, disappearing for a chat with the Grayson boy, who was occupying more and more of her time. Eventually she floated back into the room like one of the dreamy ballerinas in *Swan Lake*, pausing now and then to peek between the curtains at the front window.

Even though Edith had introduced the couple, she couldn't help feeling adrift. Of course, adult children must flee the nest, but Edith had not yet had enough time. She glanced at a blurry photograph of a tiny infant in a silver frame perched on her desk. That and a blue knitted layette set he had never gotten to wear were the only evidence her son had existed, other than the permanent hole in Edith's heart. Was Altrude about to be taken from her as well?

"That Grayson fellow has reduced your mind to a bowl of Jell-O," Edith said. "Am I to trek the Alps on my lonesome?"

Altrude stopped flitting long enough to stab a finger on one of the maps. "There's a war going on, for heaven's sake. And so much still to see in the States."

"Exactly. We must get over there to see what's left before it's all destroyed. But if you're truly worried about it, I've always wanted to go to the Orient."

Altrude was back at the window. "He's coming! Come on out with me?"

"No thank you. I'll leave you two lovers to it." Edith shoved the travel brochures back into their folder. "You may have your head in the clouds, but I'm not giving up on my dream to see the world."

"He doesn't have time to stop. He's just motoring by." Altrude was beaming and already halfway out the door.

"Oh, for goodness' sake." Edith followed her out the door, just in time to see a huge black Pierce-Arrow limousine turn the corner toward them, its top folded open and the gold presidential seal adorning the rear door. Small American flags attached to the front bumper flapped in the wind. She recognized Altrude's beau, Dr. Cary Grayson, in the back seat, looking sharp in his navy uniform. Dark blue with a stand-up collar and a matching brimmed hat, it befitted the distinguished wearer and the fine motorcar.

Seated next to him and smiling and waving like a movie star was his only patient, President Woodrow Wilson.

Having lived in the District since her marriage to Norman Galt in 1886, Edith had glimpsed several presidents and many congressmen. She never felt that was anything special and failed to understand the fawning attention political leaders garnered wherever they went. Nevertheless, her heart lifted as the magnificent motorcar and its smiling, waving passengers floated by, bookended by the nondescript Secret Service automobiles, as if in their own tiny parade.

Altrude was grinning from ear to ear, and Edith couldn't resist ribbing her.

"He's handsome all right. And a doctor to boot. But isn't it pretentious to ride around with his manservant like that?"

"What? That's the pres..." Altrude took in Edith's smirk. "Oh, you're impossible."

Several days later, it became apparent that the tiny parade had a purpose. Altrude came bouncing into the bedroom while Edith was still in her dressing gown, her dark, wavy hair not yet put up.

"Oh, I've seen you worse." Altrude waved off Edith's shriek as she bent to the mirror to smooth her own light-brown waves. "Listen. Cary is concerned about the president's cousin, Helen Bones. She's been lonesome for female company since the First Lady died—she's been rattling around the White House like Marley's ghost. They've invited you to tea."

Edith sorted through her dresses, looking for something comfortable to wear for a walk in the park. "Tea at the White House? That doesn't sound like me at all. What have you told him?" She had known the doctor as an acquaintance for several years, but they weren't close.

Altrude planted her hands on her hips. "Just that you're a pleasant conversationalist and a wonderful hostess. She's had to do that too, you know, at the White House, and maybe you can help. She doesn't know a soul in town besides her cousin Woodrow, and society dictates you can't refuse an invitation there, so..."

"You fail to recognize my distinct lack of interest, dear girl. I'm sure there are dozens, if not hundreds, of women who would claw out their own right eye to do it. People who haven't slithered out of the backwoods of southern Virginia." She went extra heavy on her usual drawl. "So don't be using that social etiquette on me."

Edith opened a drawer of her jewelry dresser and poked through several diamond chokers and necklaces to find her favorite string of pearls. Pride washed over her, not because the jewels represented wealth but because her own hard work had saved her late husband's jewelry store during hard times. She slipped on her Cartier watch. Polished to a high sheen and sporting large Roman numerals, it had been a gift from the late Mr. Galt.

"Oh yes, you simple backwoods girl." Altrude cast a disparaging look at the watch and necklaces.

"You know what I mean." Edith slid the drawer shut. "The other day—when the men drove by—was that some sort of test…or inspection? Because I don't care for it."

Altrude shrugged. "Who knows? And who cares?"

Edith turned for Altrude to fasten her necklace. "You know how I feel about the role of government in private lives."

Altrude sighed. "I know. The big bad government took away everything your family had worked for, leaving them penniless. The War between the States has been over for what, fifty years? And you weren't even alive during it."

"I was alive to see them struggle. And I grew up with a healthy sense of distrust for politicians."

"What are you really afraid of? That you won't fit in? That they'll see you as something less? Because Cary's not like that, and this cousin and the president himself are Southerners."

"Nothing of the sort." Edith smoothed the lamb's wool collar of her chosen smart, fitted suit. "I'm no less than anybody, even if my schooling was at my grandmother's knee."

"So that's it." Altrude's voice softened. "They are a well-read bunch. I've heard Ellen Wilson, God rest her soul, could quote any author, any poet at just the right moment. But listen." She gently laid her fingers on Edith's arm. "It's just tea with a lonely woman. Please don't embarrass me by refusing."

The plea in Altrude's eyes caused Edith a pang of guilt. She realized for the first time the awkward position in which she was placing her darling companion. And if Altrude was forced to choose between loyalty to Edith and her budding relationship with the doctor, Edith would surely lose. No, she couldn't bear that.

Where was the harm in having tea? Especially if she could manage a compromise. Edith felt the muscles ease in her shoulders. "Perhaps I doth protest too much. You can tell Miss Bones I would love for her to join me for tea. Right here in my home. Do you think that will suffice?"

Altrude's face brightened, which warmed Edith's heart. "I'll tell Cary straight away."

~

Helen Bones turned out to be a slight woman with a quick wit, and a delightful companion. Tea turned into lunch, which led to many more visits to Edith's home. Edith would drive them in her electric car to nearby Rock Creek Park and park in the shade of a tree. They took long walks, full of conversation about books and travel and their mutual love of food and music. Edith felt her long-held prejudices against anyone and anything related to political power begin to melt around the edges like cold butter on a warm day.

One morning, Helen showed up with a surprise, a young woman in unfashionable but sturdy walking shoes. The woman took Edith's hand and fairly pulled her out the door, eager to get the walk underway. "Good morning. I'm Eleanor McAdoo, but everyone calls me Nell." The tall, dark-haired and rather sternly featured woman, perhaps just a bit older than Altrude, became so engaged in conversation with Helen that they were halfway down the block before Edith managed to inquire as to their relationship.

"Why, first cousins once removed, isn't it?" Helen answered, with a wink toward Nell.

They seemed to be enjoying Edith's bewilderment. Refusing to succumb to their teasing, Edith waited until she was home alone to plow through old newspapers to find Nell's name. Finally, she found a year-old wedding announcement. Nell was the youngest of the president's three daughters and had married the secretary of the treasury in a ceremony at the White House.

Thereafter, the twosome often became a threesome for walks in the park. Nell seemed to enjoy gossip and always knew the latest exploits of people like Alice Roosevelt. "She set a new record, over a thousand society events in a year. Oh, and Father has banned her from the White House," she reported with glee. "Again. This time for telling raunchy jokes about him."

Although Edith loved a joke as much as anyone, and could tell a few herself, Nell's rumormongering only served as a warning not to tell Nell anything she didn't want circulated at the next party.

Fashion was one of Helen and Edith's common interests. On a raw March day, they walked on paths muddied from recent rains, which soiled their boots and hems. Afterward, they stood in Edith's drawing room, warming their hands at the fireplace. "Who's your favorite designer?" Helen asked as she admired Edith's simple yet elegant morning dress.

"Jean-Philippe Worth," Edith replied, with all the modesty she could manage.

"You mean *the* Worth, in Paris?" Helen ran her finger along the lacy deep-blue fabric of Edith's dress. The skirt draped in three tiers, which Edith felt balanced her rather buxom top. "Is this one of his?"

"No, but I have several evening gowns, which I have little use for." She felt guilty of the sin of pride. Her mother had taught her to always look and act her best yet professed it unladylike to enjoy any attention good style brought.

"You must show me right now. I have nothing of the sort. I'm afraid a Parisian fashion house like that wouldn't know what to do with bony little me."

"Au contraire. You're built like a French woman. With my build, I always felt like an American amazon in Paris."

The rumble of a motorcar engine and the thump of its door diverted their attention.

"Sadly, it sounds as if my ride is here," Helen said. "But we haven't had time for our tea. Why don't you come back with me? It's about time I played hostess."

"Oh no, my clothes and boots are a disaster, and it wouldn't be kind to ask your driver to wait while I cleaned up."

"Then don't change. No one will be there. Dr. Grayson is out golfing with Cousin Woodrow, and we'll just sneak in the service entrance."

Edith peered at her dirt-spattered dress. "You must be joking. My first visit to the White House, looking like this?"

Helen waved at her own equally soiled self. "I insist. It will be our little secret adventure."

"Oh, you evil woman. You know I can't resist an adventure."

"Not to mention a secret. Let this be the first of many."

They climbed into the motorcar, which swiftly whisked them down Pennsylvania Avenue. It was challenging to hold a conversation on the stretch from the West End all the way to the Capitol building, with the rattling street cars and tires rumbling over the patchy asphalt that failed to cover the sett stones beneath. The sweet earth smell of horse dung was still there, but Edith had to seek it out amidst the more powerful fumes of the trucks and automobiles.

"Fewer horses every year," Edith said.

Helen nodded, likely not even hearing her.

Finally, they passed through the wrought-iron gates, and the road became as smooth and quiet as if they sailed on a windless lake.

"I wonder if the grass will be ready. Easter is early this year," Helen said.

Edith glanced at the expansive lawn, just beginning to green up. It took her a moment to realize Helen was referring to the annual Easter egg roll for the children.

But Helen was already onto something new, telling the driver to stop at her preferred entrance in the East Wing.

"I feel like a burglar, about to climb in a back window," Edith said.

Helen laughed. "Well, not through a window, but we will sneak in the back way to the elevator."

As they strolled down the ground-floor colonnade, lined with windows looking out to the garden on one side and huge framed portraits in between closed doorways on the other, Edith began to relax and even enjoy the adventure. As much as she told herself that politicians weren't nearly as important as they thought they were, a thrill ran through her like an electric current. She was inside the White House!

It seemed the building itself had not yet been fully electrified. Gas lamps flickered in wall sconces on dark wallpapered walls, giving a rather eerie feel, like a haunted house. This was a pleasant surprise, as Edith had envisioned stiff formality and gold-encrusted everything, like the palaces she had seen in Europe.

She forgot all about her muddy shoes and mussed hair as she waved to friendly staff with their bemused smiles. Helen and Edith giggled about the wide-eyed stare of a housekeeper carrying a stack of linens as they exited from the tiny service elevator. Thankfully, Helen knew how to operate it, as there was no space for an attendant. They had only taken a step or two when they were confronted by two men coming around a corner.

Helen, just ahead of Edith, gasped. "Oh, we didn't expect…"

"Ladies." Dr. Grayson, dressed in a baggy white golf sweater and plaid trousers, tipped his head in greeting.

As Helen moved aside, Edith saw the man next to him was the unmistakably tall and stern-looking President Wilson, also wearing a sweater and rather bright and ill-fitting knickers. Edith repressed a chuckle.

"So sorry." Edith tried backing into the elevator, but Helen quickly gripped her arm.

"Dr. Grayson, I believe you know Mrs. Edith Galt. Mr. President, please excuse us. I implored Mrs. Galt to join me here for tea." She then nodded for Edith to politely retreat.

"Are you in a hurry?" asked the president. "Would you be terribly bothered if we joined you?"

Edith had heard him speak once before, when he was campaigning in Philadelphia. He had struck her as eloquent and measured, but somehow that didn't prepare her for the warm and personable aura he presented. His warm gray eyes gazed at her as if she were a long-lost friend. Edith rarely lacked for words, but at that moment she was spellbound.

Helen quickly agreed, and before Edith could object, they were offered slippers by house staff and went to Helen's room to tidy up. Dramatic blue velvet curtains adorned the window, which offered a view of the North Lawn. A tall double bed dominated the room. Edith couldn't help wondering if that was where a president's child had been born, or died. What was it like to sleep with the ghosts of history?

As Edith did her best to look presentable, she tried to think of a way to politely excuse herself from the tea. She preferred to prepare herself for the big events in her life, but the sudden invitation hadn't given her time to look up things any well-informed citizen should know. She knew the president was born in Virginia, not far from her own birthplace, but not where he grew up or attended college. What was his position on important issues like the economy and women's suffrage? "It is so kind of the president, but I feel like an interloper. Surely he has better things to do..."

"Nonsense. You can't back out now. Off we go." With that, Helen led Edith down the hall of the residential floor.

Countless elaborately framed portraits featured former presidents and their families, and quite a few horses and dogs. Furniture that may have been set in place nearly a hundred years before seemed less than welcoming. Edith wouldn't dare have settled her ample frame into any of the delicate chairs.

"Dolley Madison was surely more petite than me." Using humor helped settle her nerves, and poking fun at themselves was common between herself and Helen.

"Oh, I don't think those furnishings survived the fire set by the British," Helen said, not unkindly.

But Edith got the message along with a twinge of embarrassment. She needed to brush up on her American history.

The president and Dr. Grayson were waiting for them in the oval sitting room. The arc of windows showcased the budding trees of the South Lawn, but a foggy haze prevented a view past the stone-and-iron fence. A lovely china tea service had been set out, and the soft aromas of Darjeeling and lemon greeted them. The president waved away the white-coated help after they had set out some tiny triangle sandwiches, and the four of them proceeded to have a lively discussion about Southern accents, of all things.

"I love your lilting drawl," Helen said. "I'm glad living in the cosmopolitan District hasn't forced it out of you."

"And I admire yours as well," Edith responded. "But I can get at least two more syllables into a word like 'y'all.'" For emphasis, she overpronounced it "yoo-all-le."

The president laughed. "Ah, I do miss the music of the Southern vernacular."

"Yes, what happened to yours, Mr. President?" Edith nodded toward him. "Weren't you born a Southern gentleman?"

Helen chuckled. "He had to dispose of his accent when he moved to New Jersey. That's the law there, you know."

"Too much time with the upper crust of Princeton." Dr. Grayson sniffed the air like a disdainful king. He also spoke with a Virginia accent, but of a more refined, northern Virginia sort.

Dr. Grayson's and Helen's gentle teasing helped Edith feel less awkward. She eased the choke hold of one hand over the other and felt her heart calm its rhythm.

The president asked Edith if she enjoyed poetry, and when she said she did, he selected a well-worn book from the shelf and settled back into his chair. He removed his pince-nez eyeglasses and replaced them with a pair that made his large gray eyes seem even bigger, then proceeded to read out loud. He had the perfect voice for it, clear and strong when needed, while softening at the right moments. Edith thought she could listen to him for hours.

A knock on the door disrupted their pleasant gathering, and soon the president rose to get back to work. "I'm so enjoying our chat, but I must go." He took Edith's hand in his. "Won't you please join us for dinner?"

With her hand firmly in that of the president of the United States, she was so flustered that nothing would come out of her mouth. Instead, she tried to remember if a lady stood or remained seated in this situation. Helen remained in her chair, so Edith followed suit. Fearful of overstaying her welcome, not to mention the discomfort of her inappropriate attire, she sought a graceful way out. After the awkward pause, she blurted out, "You've been so gracious, and I've had a most lovely time. But I'm afraid I must decline."

Undeterred, the president invited Edith to dine with Helen and him the next week. "No big state dinner, just a small family gathering of twenty or so."

A part of Edith wanted to say *no, thank you*, even though a week would give her time to prepare for the visit. But this was not her world. Surely the president was just being polite. Yet there was something about him, a certain charm, a graciousness that drew her to him. Her heart pounded against her ribs. Was it because of who he was? She thought not. She had met plenty of well-known and important people. Or was her body responding to an innate attraction to a sympathetic soul?

Maybe they were just kindred spirits and could be friends. After all, they had both been widowed (although he much more recently than she), so there was a certain level of loneliness that only people who shared that experience could understand. If that was the reason, she could hardly say no. "I'd be delighted." She stood, thinking she must consult Emily Holt's book of etiquette for such things.

To her great surprise, the president kissed her hand and said softly, "Until next week, then."

THREE

Riding in the presidential limousine with Altrude beside her, Edith adjusted and readjusted her hat, her gloves, the poofiness of her sleeves, until Altrude finally demanded, "Stop!"

"This is a mistake. I know it. Let's just get through the evening; then I'll go on my way, like Mary Magdalene." Edith knew she was being overly dramatic, but Altrude, of all people, understood her distress. Her week of reviewing American and White House history had only multiplied Edith's qualms. "I don't belong there. I'm as out of place as a streetwalker."

Altrude huffed and rolled her eyes. "For the umpteenth time, Mary Magdalene wasn't a prostitute and didn't abandon Jesus. She was pushed away by Peter. And you're not going to abandon a kind and lonely man who seems to enjoy your company. He isn't aware you have a habit of comparing yourself to the lady apostle."

"It was just once before this," Edith sniffed. "And it rescued me from an improper dalliance with that Frenchman."

"Is that what you're worried about? An improper dalliance? For heaven's sake, it's just dinner among twenty or so witnesses."

Edith gazed out the window.

"So there is something else. What haven't you told me?"

It was still so new, so raw, that Edith didn't know what to make of her feelings. "There's just something about him. Do you feel it? I don't mean because of his position." She lowered her voice to a whisper; the driver was about six feet away. "I'm a little afraid of what I would do if left alone with him."

Altrude faked a cough behind her gloved hand. "No, I don't 'feel it.' I only have eyes for Cary."

But Edith needn't have worried about being alone with the president. Along with Helen, Altrude and Cary, Nell and William McAdoo, and Woodrow's eldest daughter, Margaret, there was an odd fellow from Texas named Colonel House, a congressman or two with their wives, and some friends from Princeton at the dinner. Woodrow formerly introduced Edith as a friend of Helen's and a new friend of his own.

They dined in the State Dining Room at a single long table set for twenty that was still dwarfed by the room's expanse. Floor-to-ceiling curtains festooned enormous windows, now black with night. A fireplace dominated one wall, with a portrait of Abraham Lincoln above it.

The table was set with white and gold china and more glasses and silverware than it seemed could possibly be used for one meal. Small tented note cards with each guest's name written in beautiful calligraphy were perfectly aligned at each place setting. No doubt their order reflected some pecking order, with the most important political persons closer to the president. Edith was at the far end, anchored by Margaret, Helen, and two Princeton professors.

She alternated between being amazed at the grandeur of it and longing for a simple meal at home with Woodrow, where she could get to know him without all the trappings and people vying for his attention. Edith imagined just the two of them enjoying an after-dinner drink. She'd love to chat with him about what this life was really like, what *he* was really like. Now *that* would make an interesting evening.

Margaret sat directly across the table. Her resemblance to her father was striking, both in looks and vocal cadence. She seemed to eye Edith's every move, and politely asked impolite questions. Just when Edith managed to scoop up a forkful of petite peas, Margaret loudly said, "So I hear you're a tradeswoman. How do you deal with being around so many men?"

Nell, sitting next to Margaret, apologized for her. "You don't have to answer my rude sister."

Edith dabbed her lips with the starched napkin and ran her tongue across her teeth to ensure nothing was embedded in them. "I don't mind. It's a fair question. Yes, I'm a successful businesswoman. After turning around a nearly bankrupt company, I put more competent men in charge. Now I just attend board meetings and collect my share of the profits."

"Hear, hear!" The professors surprised her by raising their glasses to her. The president, seated at the head of the table, caught her eye and smiled with the slightest of nods.

Course after course appeared, and Edith found her usually robust appetite constrained by the knot in her stomach and the need to carry on a pleasant conversation with the unfamiliar men on either side of her. It wasn't that she was nervous or timid, as she felt she could hold her own with people from any walk of life. It was the formality of the setting, the unsaid words somehow louder than the actual conversations, and the feeling of being examined like a bug under a magnifying glass that made her uncomfortable.

As the evening came to a close, Edith seized her chance to escape with the excuse that her wrap had been placed in the ground-floor cloakroom. After saying her farewells, Edith was making her way toward the doorway when an appealing voice stopped her.

"Allow me to accompany you," Woodrow said as he caught up with her. "I could have sent someone, of course, but thought we both could use a stroll."

They walked down the colonnade toward the East Wing, the same place Edith had entered that first day with Helen. He opened the wide, tall door to a darkly paneled room that seemed about the size of an entire floor of her rowhouse.

"Well. There it is." Edith nodded toward her wrap, hanging forlornly by itself in the long room that was somehow designated as a closet. She felt about as awkward as her statement.

"Ah yes." He retrieved the wrap and placed it on her shoulders. "Mrs. Galt, my apologies for neglecting you as a guest. It was selfish of me to try to squeeze in some time with you when time is what I have least to share."

"Please, it's Edith. And do not apologize. It is a thrill to be here. A thrill to be in the same room with you."

"Many feel that way. Until they get to know me." He chuckled.

There was something sweet and completely endearing about him. So different from his cool, detached reputation. She fought an impulse to give him a big hug. "I'd like to get to know you."

They took small, halting steps toward the cloakroom door, neither one of them in a hurry.

He opened the door, letting in the brighter light from the passageway. "Would you? Myself as well. You must come back another time when fewer people are about."

That dinner led to another and another, and soon Edith was dining at the White House three times a week. Each time, she would leave thinking it would be the last, for after all, the president had proposed only one more get-together. But there was always one thing or the other that Helen or Woodrow (for they were now on a first-name basis) wished for her to join.

Margaret treated them to an a cappella concert, as she was studying voice. Secretly, Edith didn't much enjoy her warbling soprano, even though it was the current style. She preferred the deep swaying tunes of the hymns sung in the little white chapel just steps from her childhood home.

When Helen took a weekend trip to New York, Woodrow had no one else with whom to dine, or so he claimed. He invited Edith to dinner, as well as his sister so as not to appear improper. His personal secretary, Joseph Tumulty, also joined them at the last minute, and it turned into a lively affair.

This was the first time Edith had had a chance to get to know Tumulty, whom she had seen only briefly before. She felt it was important, because he was the president's closest confidant and political ally. Tumulty had met Woodrow when he was running for governor of New Jersey. There, the young attorney and legislator had attached his star to Candidate Wilson.

She thought him to be several years younger than herself, but his fair hair was already receding, and he had the softness about his face of a middle-aged man. His northern accent was so pronounced that Edith sometimes asked him to repeat or spell out his words for her. It became a game of sorts, with both of them using colloquialisms or pronunciations they knew the other wouldn't understand.

At dinner, this time in the smaller family dining room, the president, a preacher's son, rose for a short prayer. "Let our hearts not be troubled, have faith in God and Jesus, Amen." He raised his wineglass. "A toast to the lovely ladies: may their days be bright, and their worries few."

"Hear, hear," said Tumulty. "Mr. President, I have some good news. Your request for the *Mayflower* has been scheduled, with all those here invited guests."

"The *Mayflower*?" Edith could only think of Pilgrims.

Tumulty replied, "She's a steamer yacht with a colorful history. She served in the Spanish-American War, was the site of Teddy Roosevelt's successful peace negotiations between Japan and Russia, and now serves as the presidential yacht."

Edith cringed. Somehow her review of history had missed this.

"And she's a beauty," the president added. "I'm scheduled to review the Atlantic fleet in New York next month, and I thought it would be grand to sail there on the *Mayflower*. It would give several days of relative peace. And I would like for all of you to come."

Edith's bewilderment must have shown in her face.

"Sorry, I should have checked with you first, Edith. Will you join us?" Woodrow asked. "And of course Helen and Dr. Grayson and Altrude. There are six staterooms, so plenty of space for all to be comfortable."

"Oh my. Just how big is this yacht?" Edith asked.

Mr. Tumulty replied, "Over two hundred seventy feet. I can get you schematics if you like."

The conversation went on, with much enthusiasm regarding the upcoming trip. Edith wasn't sure how she fit in with all of them, or what the press would have to say if she should go. It seemed too big a step to make so casually. Just where did she stand with Woodrow? Was he seeking a clandestine sexual relationship? If so, how did she feel about that? She desperately needed some time alone with him to sort this out. She smiled noncommittally but didn't join in the bubbly discussion.

A few evenings later, Dr. Grayson showed up at Edith's door unannounced. The big Pierce-Arrow was parked on the street, its top and windows rolled up despite the warm temperature. Cary stood on her doorstep, dress uniform hat in hand as if he were a hired cab driver coming to fetch her.

"If you have spare time, Mrs. Galt, could you join Altrude and myself?" He looked this way and that down the street. Edith and Woodrow had taken pains to keep any hint of a relationship out of the public mind. It had been less than eight months since the death of Ellen Wilson, and it would be unseemly for the president to even give a hint of involvement with another woman so soon.

Edith let Grayson in and closed the door. A knot developed in her stomach. She had already decided that becoming Woodrow's secret mistress was not for her. Yet she couldn't deny her attraction and caring for him. "What is this about? Is the president ill?"

"No, no. Ease your mind. This is a happy occasion." He worked the edge of his hat, and his long facial expression seemed to contradict his words. "You see, the president hadn't been himself since Mrs. Wilson took ill. When she passed, he was understandably devastated."

"Of course." The knot in Edith's stomach remained.

"For months, he has been doing his duty, yes. Superbly in fact. But his heart was not in it. It was as if his soul died right along with Ellen, and he was just waiting for the Lord to take him to be with her."

"I'm so sorry. I'm a widow myself."

Grayson nodded. "So you understand." Finally a smile crossed his lips. "I've never seen a man so dependent on a woman for happiness. And it seems that is what you have brought him."

Maybe the invitation for the *Mayflower* sailing wasn't casual or, worse, came with an expectation of a tryst. She made Woodrow happy, at least according to Grayson. Her heart lifted with a joy she hadn't felt in a long while.

Altrude, apparently aware of the plan, popped down the stairs wearing a sparkly dress and gloves up to her elbows. She was singing a popular song with enthusiasm, "Goodbye, Piccadilly. Farewell, Leicester Square. It's a long way to Tipperary, but my heart's right there."

Edith had nothing else on her schedule that evening. Buoyed by Grayson's comments, and intrigued by the mysterious plan and Altrude's song, Edith decided to join them. "I'll fetch my wrap."

Cary opened the back door of the motor for Edith, but as she climbed in, he said he would ride with the Secret Service in another car. Altrude waved goodbye, and the door was closed over Edith's startled protest.

"Champagne?" Next to her, Woodrow sat with a self-satisfied smile and two flutes of bubbly wine.

"We're fooling no one," she said as she accepted the glass. "But a toast to your scheming effort."

Woodrow parted the curtain that divided the driver from them. "Up the river then. Slowly." The car was so long, he had to shout the instructions to the driver.

Edith wondered again what his intentions were. She had to know, yet needed a polite way to ask without being too presumptuous. This was no ordinary banker or lawyer. *Learn to ask the hard questions sideways*, her mother had always advised her.

"Your time is so precious," Edith said. "I hope I have not been too demanding of it."

"My dear little girl, you have it all wrong. I can barely get through a day in which I don't see you. You are the light that helps me endure."

So it seemed Cary had been accurate in his judgment, if these were Woodrow's true feelings. She gazed at his dear face; he seemed earnest enough. This was all happening rather quickly. She had been preparing herself to turn down an offer for a different kind of relationship and wasn't sure if her own emotions matched Woodrow's.

But it was clear that he was still deep in mourning for his wife—too soon for him to know who or what he truly needed. She vowed to prepare herself for heartbreak.

They followed along the river to the northwest, the city fading behind them. Woodrow slipped closer to her on the seat, and when Edith had finished her wine—drinking a little too quickly—he laid his hand over hers. She could feel something changing, despite her vow of just moments ago. It was in the air, which was seemingly charged with the electricity now making its way into the last corners of the country. It was in the touch of his hand, warm and strong and tender at the same time. It was in the flash of the trees in the glowing pale-green of spring, and in the deep, smooth leather of the seat.

He wrapped his arm across her shoulders, and she leaned in toward him, at once fearing she was on a scary path and thrilled at his solid, warm, and masculine presence. It had been so long since she felt that, and maybe not ever. Was the champagne going to her head? Because her mind was swirling and she felt as if she were caught in a whirlpool that was pulling her helplessly toward him.

She feared the time was rapidly approaching when she couldn't turn back, that he had entered her heart forever and wouldn't leave without ripping it apart. She imagined her mind ringing alarm bells, like fire trucks racing down the street. She too was racing away. Away from a pleasant life, in which she was free to travel and entertain friends on a moment's notice, to a life as foreign to her as a life on the moon.

What did she have to lose? A simple but nearly perfect life. She tried to push those thoughts away; she could think all that through later. At that moment he leaned close and tentatively brushed his lips on hers. She held his face and drew him toward her. The car, the driver, the rushing trees and troubled world disappeared until there were only the two of them and one perfect moment.

That was the last stolen moment for what seemed like forever. During the third week in April, after nearly a week of not seeing Woodrow, Edith began to feel forgotten, just when she was longing for his companionship and feeling the stirrings of something stronger. Her marriage to Norman had not been a passionate one. The fact that she had managed to produce a son with him was somewhat of a miracle. In the intervening years, Edith had given up on romantic love, something found only in dusty books or on the silver screen.

It wasn't as if there weren't very pressing matters on the president's mind, she reassured herself. The papers were abuzz with reports of diplomats madly dashing across Europe, trying to find some way for the United

States to intervene in the terrible conflict that was tearing the continent apart. The Germans were beating back Russia; the Brits had suffered an embarrassing defeat by the German-backed Turks. Italy was dragging its feet, even while pledging to help the Allies. Mexico was in the midst of revolution, and every day it seemed the United States would be dragged into a conflagration like no other in history. She imagined Woodrow locked in intense negotiations and wondered how he could bear the strain.

But selfishly, she longed for the quiet times they had shared and believed him when he said her presence was the light that helped him endure. She pushed aside the fearful feelings, the doubts that nagged at her sleep. Altrude was a guilty party in that respect, encouraging Edith to spill all, begging for details and watching her tell them as if glued to a vaudeville show. How could a person, even a sensible person, long for the safe and stable if there was the possibility of a new love?

So Edith's heart leaped in her chest that day in late April, when the postman handed her a letter with a return address reading simply, "The White House."

April 28, 1915

My dear Mrs. Galt,

I have ordered a copy of Hamerton's 'Round My House' through the bookseller, but while we are waiting for it, I take the liberty of sending you a copy from the Congressional Library. I hope it will give you pleasure—you have given me so much!

If it rains this evening, would it be any pleasure for you to come around and have a little reading—and if it does not rain, are you game for another ride? If you are not in when this gets to you, perhaps you will be gracious enough to telephone Margaret.

Your sincere and grateful friend,

Woodrow Wilson

It was a sweet letter. An uncompromising letter. *Dear Mrs. Galt?* It could be read by anyone, and maybe it had been. Who knew how much privacy Woodrow could manage in that fishbowl? But the important thing was that he wanted to see her again. She would agree to that, of course. But not that very night. Despite her giddiness, she had to maintain some modicum of womanly wiles, lest she seem "common," as her mother would say.

Still, she'd see him as long as he'd have her. Not for a mere physical relationship, but she no longer thought that was his intent. If her role was to help him out of the grief and deep depression over losing his beloved wife, only to later be cast to the winds, then so be it.

She went to the mahogany desk by the front door, perfectly scaled for the small room. It had belonged to her father—not the large desk from his office but the small one from the study, where he would write letters as she read books on Roman and Greek mythology. She wanted what her parents had. A strong, loving relationship. The promise of that was worth whatever risk her heart might have to bear.

Father's fountain pen was still tucked into a drawer. She uncapped it, filled it with ink, and considered how to respond to Woodrow. She didn't want to dampen his spirit yet longed to put things on a slower pace without causing him any hurt.

My dear Mr. President,

How very good of you to remember my desire to read 'Round My House' and take the trouble to send it to gratify me.

Your wish to give me pleasure has been so abundantly fulfilled already that for you to take time to send a personal note is only generous good measure with which you fill my goblet of happiness—Thank you.

I am very tired tonight and can think of nothing more restful than to come and have you read to us—or—in case it clears, blow away the cobwebs in another way, by another life-giving ride. But (that word that so often destroys my pleasure) I have promised my dear mother to spend this evening with her. So I must not yield to the impulse to come.

Just a word more to tell you how deeply I value the assurance with which you send your note. Such a pledge of friendship blots out the shadows that have chased me today and makes April twenty-eight a red-letter day on my calendar.

Faithfully and proudly your friend,

Edith Bolling Galt

Altrude burst through the door just as Edith sealed the envelope. She was breathless and flung her hat at the coat-tree with uncharacteristic abandon. "It's all going to blow up. The Germans are threatening us. Cary says we can't remain neutral for much longer."

"What happened? And why do you look like you just ran the Greek marathon?"

"I decided to quick-walk from the White House to blow off steam. I'm afraid I can't tell you much more, but don't be expecting to see your beloved anytime soon."

"My beloved. Ha, you have the gift of exaggeration."

Altrude plucked the letter out of Edith's hand. "I think not." She gave it a sniff. "What, no essence of Jicky?"

"Stop it. That was one time, and it was Paris." Edith suppressed a smile as she remembered the perfume her French beau had decided he liked better on himself.

"Paris or not, love will find you again, dear Mrs. Galt."

"I've only known him a few short weeks."

"You're forty-two years old. He's what, near sixty?"

"Fifty-eight, but how does that matter?"

Altrude tapped her wristwatch and lowered her voice to a deadly whisper. "'Unknown is the length of life.'"

"Oh, clever girl. Did you just come up with that?"

"No, Buddha did. And he was right. But in all seriousness, you may not get an answer to that letter for what may seem like forever. But don't give up on him. And don't play those silly hard-to-get games. I overheard his secretary say, 'He's a goner,' when someone mentioned you." Altrude's tone turned more serious, like a teacher to an errant student. "If you care one whit about him, and about me, be honest and get out now if you need to."

Edith's spine tingled at the word *goner*, remembering Cary's words. But he meant she would save Woodrow from that fate, didn't he? She tapped the letter in her hand. Perhaps it was sending the completely wrong message. Maybe Woodrow was reaching out for the last time before history claimed his soul beyond her reach.

Her mother had taught her to trust her instincts and that usually a first instinct was the right one. A rushed meeting on the cusp of drastic change would do nothing to reveal her and Woodrow's true feelings for each other. Better to face whatever happened and see what, if anything, remained for them.

Two days later, the world was spinning out of control. The Germans had taken out advertisements in the paper warning Americans not to sail on British ships. The secretary of state, William Jennings Bryan, wanted to ban Americans from travel, and submarines were attacking merchant ships. But Altrude was wrong about Woodrow fading from Edith's life.

Even as the urgent demands stacked higher and higher in early May, the president sought Edith's attention every day, if not for visits, then with posted letters and hand-delivered messages.

Having tossed aside plans for travel, Edith turned to closely following the news in order to be a more interesting conversationalist for Woodrow. She read in the papers about the president's falling out with the secretary of state due to the very public disagreements within the department regarding maintaining neutrality, and Wilson's response to Germany's threats against American travelers through the war zone.

When a German submarine attacked an American oil tanker en route to Rouen, France, tensions heated even more. Former president Roosevelt demanded swift action, lest the Germans be even further emboldened. But there were extenuating circumstances, it was an accident, claimed others. War is rarely crystal clear. The tanker was accompanied by two British ships, who were of course not neutral. And the submarine captain claimed the tanker had no identifying flag, and they ceased fire upon learning of its neutrality.

"A direct torpedo hit is not an accident," Edith huffed to no one as she sat alone in her drawing room. She felt prepared to speak with Woodrow about all these pressing matters, even looked forward to it instead of reading the filtered news. But when she was with him, he seemed to crave solace from national and world events.

She didn't press him when they took drives up the Conduit Road. They cuddled in the back seat, growing bolder with every encounter. She still wondered if she was serving as a temporary distraction for him, to be tossed aside like a certain secretary of state when she was no longer useful.

A few weeks into their courtship, perhaps due to her increasing knowledge, or due to an increase in trust, Woodrow started to share more and more of the pressures he was under, sometimes asking her opinion on matters she knew little about.

On a rare date when she cooked dinner for him at her home, Secret Service men posted at her door, he flipped through a newspaper she had spread across her parlor table. "Ah, so the press has learned of the machine gun we ordered for the Wright brothers' aeroplane."

Edith was fascinated with the invention and saw a chance to show off a bit. "That's right. Some say the next war will be fought by air. Can you imagine that? I do think we need to stay ahead of the Huns."

"Quite right." Woodrow tapped the paper. "Congress just created the NACA, an advisory committee to study flight. Perhaps we need a heavier military representation on it. What do you think?"

"I think I haven't enough experience to offer advice on that." The aroma of roasted pork reminded her to check on dinner.

"You underestimate both your wisdom and your importance as a soothsayer, uncorrupted by the seeking of power and urge to form alliances."

"You speak like the professor you still are. I can hardly find the words to argue with you."

"Ha! Then don't." He gave her arm a squeeze as she headed to the kitchen.

That's just fine with me, she told herself. Just being with him was a tiny act that she could do for her country. And besides, she was enjoying his company, even as she longed for her former life of only a few months prior.

She wanted to be available if the president had a free moment to go on a drive or it was a good night to join him for dinner. Running off to the theater at a moment's notice, taking long walks in the park or city streets, even running errands in her electric car was put aside as she anticipated a phone call or letter.

Even when she waited, willingly and happily, part of her screamed in protest. She still served as an advisor to her late husband's jewelry business and enjoyed the excitement of new products and new customers. Was she losing her own hard-earned identity?

Edith was preparing to drop by Galt Brothers Jewelry, when a messenger showed up at her door. He handed her a plain envelope, then stopped her when she tried to shut the door after thanking him.

"Uh, ma'am, my instructions are to wait for a response."

A large black vehicle puttered in the street. Edith was keeping not one but two men occupied. She hoped the note was something she could answer quickly. She noticed a few neighbors peeking out their windows, some even standing in doorways, gawking. *Nosy Nellies,* she mouthed to them with an insincere smile and opened the envelope.

It was a handwritten note in Woodrow's elegant script:

Just back from Mass., so sorry to not bring you to the baptism, a mistake on my part most assuredly. I am desperate to see you; could you possibly free yourself for formal dinner this evening?

All thoughts of visiting the shop and dining in town left her. She had had no need to attend the ceremony for his first grandchild, but it was charming that Woodrow had thought of her. She told the messenger yes and tried to tip him but he refused. She then flew up the stairs to change her clothing as if borne on the wings of angels.

The president's car appeared at precisely five o'clock, thankfully without Secret Service escort. Altrude had arrived, and Edith scolded her, not for the first time, for keeping an apartment when she could very well, and often did, stay with Edith. Flower corsages had arrived earlier, and they fussed about pinning them on each other. Altrude's was a cluster of yellow roses, while Edith's was a huge spray of pale-violet-throated orchids, her favorite flower.

"Do you think my gown suitable?" Edith asked. She wore white satin, with a touch of creamy lace and a delicate green velvet border around the square neckline, with green velvet slippers to match.

Altrude inspected Edith as if gazing at a portrait in a museum, then unhooked Edith's pearl necklace. "These are sweet, but let the orchids have their moment." She grabbed her small purse. "Oh, I do hope Cary is in the car." Altrude ran out the door, her sweet perfume trailing like ribbons behind her.

Edith wanted the couple to have a moment to themselves, so she straightened up the front room a bit. As she adjusted the pile of newspapers on a side table, she viewed a headline she had formerly missed: "Germans Release Poison Gas at Ypres." She had to sit a moment. It was a punch in the gut, and she had to regain her breath.

She and Altrude had spent quite a bit of time in Belgium, and they had fallen in love with the country, with its neatly planted fields, wonderful cities, and the friendliest people she had found anywhere. She could still taste the rich chocolates and farm-fresh apples, smell the scent of sugar waffles wafting from the bakeries. Would Belgium be destroyed forever?

Sorrow tugged at her heart for the country and its lovely people. She wiped her eyes with a handkerchief and gathered herself to march out the door, a false smile planted on her face. The news from abroad was getting steadily worse, which would only intensify the pressure on Woodrow. Was he desperate to see her to tell her goodbye?

When Cary, Altrude, and Edith arrived at the White House, they were escorted to the oval room on the residential floor, where they were greeted by Helen and introduced to the president's sister and niece. Also present was his eldest daughter, Margaret.

Edith felt a bit like a show horse in the ring. While being ever polite, she would catch the other guests staring at her even while the attention should have been on someone else. Namely, the president, who was at his most charming, telling stories about being locked in a church in Scotland and other adventures he sorely missed. They expressed condolences for the loss of her late husband, followed by exclamations of how they loved Galt Brothers jewelry store.

In a rather awkward moment Margaret said, "You never had children?"

As Margaret had neither married nor had children, it seemed she was seeking a bit of solidarity. But Helen, knowing of Edith's loss, gave Margaret a stern look all the same.

"Only one. But my son was born too early, and we lost him."

The group murmured their regrets, but Edith assured them, "It was a long time ago."

But through it all, it seemed some kind of test. Edith searched Woodrow's eyes for some clue, but he carried on as if they were all at a family picnic.

They dined in the family dining room with only a smattering of conversation, the staff making more noise with the clattering of dishes. On previous occasions, the talk had been much livelier, and Edith wondered if it was the growing unrest in the world and nation or her presence that was causing such unease. The courses changed, and Edith tasted nothing. Feeling more and more uncomfortable, she wondered how soon she could politely ask to be taken home.

They had just finished dessert—ladyfingers with pudding? No, crème anglaise according to the menu card. She had hardly touched it. She thought about the sumptuous meals she had enjoyed in Paris and London. She would first feast her eyes on the presentation, notice the balance of colors and textures of the foods, and the delicate china it was served on. Then she would breathe the aromas and try to guess how the dish would taste. At the first bite, she would close her eyes in order to taste the layers of flavors. Her reverie was interrupted when Helen and the sister and niece (Edith tried mightily but failed to remember their names) rather suddenly excused themselves in order to take a walk on the grounds.

A moment later, Cary rose and pulled back Altrude's chair for her, saying something about catching a show that evening.

"Remember Buddha." Altrude tapped her watch.

Whatever was going on? This left Woodrow and Edith alone at the table, and he showed no indication of moving. In fact he chatted on about how she needed to visit Princeton, and said that he would love to be her guide.

As soon as he took a breath, Edith said, "It has been quite the lovely meeting, especially to meet more of your family. But I'm sure you've had a tiring day, and I should take my leave."

He waved her concern aside. "I've ordered coffee out on the South Portico. The others should be joining us. Won't you humor me for just a few more moments?"

They descended a grand staircase and passed through the wide center hall and into the Blue Room. The oval room was larger than Edith's whole rowhouse. True to its name, it was wallpapered in a stunning blue, gold, and white. Armchairs warmed the space, and a portrait of James Monroe hung over the marble fireplace. Woodrow opened the door leading to the balcony, and they stepped out into the spring air.

A semicircle of marble columns two stories high created frames for each segment of the expansive view of the grounds. The daylight was fading into the lavender streaks of a beautiful May sunset, and servants brought wraps for them to fend off the chilly air. Helen and the sister and niece made an appearance, then were off once again. Woodrow gave some instructions to the help and firmly closed the portico door. It seemed a rather awkwardly orchestrated show.

"I get the impression they don't approve of me," Edith said to Woodrow, her mouth curled in a smile to indicate her feelings weren't hurt.

"Not at all. They are simply giving me what I asked for, some time alone with you. It's not easy to arrange, after all."

"And yet, here we are." It was a stunning place, to be certain. Views of lights beginning to twinkle down the city streets, the magnificent grounds with their spring flowers lit by the warm glow of electric lamps.

Woodrow took her hand. "I need to confess something."

Here it comes, she thought. *Our last night together. Why did I spend it fussing over what others were thinking?*

His warm gray-blue eyes were sincere behind those little glasses perched on his nose. "I asked Margaret and Helen to give me an opportunity to tell you something tonight I have already shared with them."

She braced herself, holding her breath for the inevitable news. Visions of gassed soldiers and ships exploding forced their way into her consciousness, and she refused to feel sorry for herself.

He touched her cheek, made her look at him. "We've only been together a matter of weeks, but I know this as surely as the sun will rise. I'm in love with you, Edith."

It took a moment for her mind to catch up with what he said. She blinked, shook her head to clear it. With no thought to how it might hurt him, she blurted out, "Oh, you can't love me, for you don't really know me, and it is less than a year since your wife died."

"Yes, I know you feel that. But in this stage of our lives, time is not measured in weeks, or months or years, but by deep human experiences. Since Ellen's death, I have lived a lifetime of loneliness and heartache."

"I don't know what to say." Edith again felt the urge to flee. To go off alone and think about this impossible development.

"I was afraid I would shock you. But being a gentleman, it would be unseemly for me to go on seeing you while feeling this way and not let you know. I have told all those here tonight and my other daughters this."

She gasped. "They know?"

"For all we try to control the gossip, it will get out in any case. I can't see you openly, and they and Grayson have been most gracious in assisting in ways for us to be together. But this can't go on this way, nor do I want it to."

"Well, what then? Are you telling me we can't see each other anymore?"

"No, little girl. Oh dear, I am hopelessly mangling this." He leaned closer, taking both of her hands into his. "I want you to be my wife. Marry me, Edith, just as soon as humanly possible in this uncertain world. Let us spend the rest of our lives together. Happier times, for certain, once all this"—he waved toward the mansion—"is over, and we have done what we were called to do."

She felt as if there was no ground beneath her, nothing in existence except his hands on hers and his dear, earnest face waiting for an answer. But she had no answer. How could she? Her heart thumped with the thrill of the moment, but her more thoughtful self rang out an alarm. *Too soon, too soon.*

She had to say something. His eyes were growing distant as he prepared himself for rejection. But how not to hurt him while explaining how she felt? "If it has to be 'yes' or 'no' right now, I will have to decline your sweet offer." She spoke slowly, carefully, and with as much love and sincerity as she could. "It is a matter of grave importance, and I must have time to think. But I disagree that we must mind the gossips and not see each other in the meantime."

Woodrow reluctantly agreed to continue to meet as friends, and they shared a quiet ride back to her house. She sensed his disappointment in his stiffened countenance, felt it in all the words he didn't say. But she had to decide away from him, because his presence overwhelmed her and his eloquent ability to persuade was legendary.

That night, she wrote him, trying to explain her confused feelings.

What unspeakable pleasure and privilege I deem it to be allowed to share these tense, terrible days of responsibility, how I thrill to my very fingertips when I remember the tremendous thing you said to me tonight, and how pitifully poor I am to have nothing to offer you in return. Nothing—I mean—in proportion to your own great gift!

But, dear kindred spirit, can you not trust me and let me lead you from the thought that you have forfeited anything by your fearless honesty to the conviction that there is nothing to fear? We will help and hearten each other. You have been honest with me, and perhaps I was too frank with you—but if so, forgive me! And know that here on this white page I pledge you all that is best in me—to help, to sustain, to comfort—and that into the space that separates us I send you my spirit to seek yours.

Make it a welcome guest.

Helen rang up the next morning, wanting to have a walk in the park. Edith rankled a bit, sensing that Helen was being sent on a fact-finding mission for the president. But as they walked the familiar trails of Rock Creek Park, there was barely a mention of him. That was, until they sat upon some boulders for a rest, the temperature and humidity quickly rising.

"Looks like another wilting summer is on the way." Helen fanned herself. "Should have brought a parasol for protection."

Edith looked at her to nod in agreement and saw tears running down her face. "Oh my, it's certainly nothing to cry about."

Helen shook her head. "How do you protect a heart? I thought at long last that he would be happy."

Edith felt blood warm her face. "Woodrow told you."

"He was quite ill this morning. Wouldn't take breakfast, is rattling around the house like a horse with a wounded leg. He's been depressed since Ellen died, of course, but I've never seen him this desolate." She wiped her eyes with the back of her hand. "How could you? I thought you cared for him."

"I do. You must realize what a shock I've had. I thought we were friends; I barely dared to think he thought of me that way. And there's so much glamour around the man as president. I feel much admiration for him, but I must sift my feelings from the circumstance. You understand, don't you? I married once for the wrong reasons. I must have time to think this through. Surely you would agree it would be much more devastating to the president if I made the wrong decision."

Edith feared she could never separate her competing emotions. Logic was telling her not to upturn her happy and rather privileged life. Which she had earned on her own, she reminded herself. Although many assumed she was well off due to inheriting her husband's famous jewelry store, that was not entirely true. When Norman died, the store had a mountain of debt and was near bankruptcy. She lived on the smallest pension she could manage and returned all other profits back into the business. Her hard work had paid off. The debts were paid off and the store had regained its former glory.

But that was in the past. Now she faced a totally unexpected development. As the women turned toward Edith's car, they strode quietly on the familiar path running along a ravine. Now and again along its depth, the pretty creek would appear between the trees, like the truth that Edith was seeking.

Helen broke the silence, offering, "I'm sorry to push you. I have no right. I hope you will continue to be my friend."

"Of course," Edith responded. But in her heart, she knew there was only one path to that end.

❧

Another letter from Woodrow was waiting for her when she arrived home. From the time and date, he must have written it immediately after receiving her letter in reply to his proposal.

Dear, dear friend,

I am infinitely tired tonight—in brain and body and spirit—for it is still for me practically the same day on which I put my happiness to the test. There are some things I must try to say before the still watches come again in which the things unsaid hurt so and cry out in the heart to be uttered.

It was this morning—while I lay awake thinking of you in all your wonderful loveliness and of my pitiful inability to satisfy and win you, to show you the true heart of my need, and of my nature—that you wrote that wonderful note Helen brought to me today, with its fresh revelation of your wonderful gifts of heart and mind—the most moving and altogether beautiful note I ever read, whose possession makes me rich; and I must thank you for that before I sleep. Your words touch as if they knew every key to my heart...

Edith flipped through the additional pages where Woodrow went on in much the same vein. His outpouring of emotion was at the same time exhilarating and frightening. She, having had a marriage of respect but little emotion, didn't know how to respond. She came from a loving family, but romantic love was a foreign concept. She needed another woman's opinion. But Altrude was like a daughter; it didn't seem appropriate to speak of this with her.

Would it violate Woodrow's privacy to share his words with her mother? Sallie Bolling lived nearby, and while never intrusive, she was always eager to offer another point of view or bit of wisdom.

Altrude burst through the front door with no warning, a newspaper in her hand. "Have you heard the news from Europe?"

"I don't imagine it's good. Tea?" Edith was just about to have her evening meal, which she had taken to calling "tea" after her time in London.

"Might as well. Looks like I won't be seeing Cary for a few days." Altrude slumped into a chair at Edith's small dining table, setting the folded paper to the side.

Edith filled two plates with broiled chicken and fresh carrots she had gathered at the morning market and seasoned with cinnamon and mace. "You might as well spill the beans. You can't ruin my appetite."

Altrude splayed the front page. The huge, bold headline read: **OCEAN LINER *LUSITANIA* SUNK BY GERMAN SUBMARINE.**

"Oh my heavens. The Germans actually did it. They did warn us." Edith shook her head.

Altrude gave up on the meal and crossed her fork and knife over her plate. "All along, I thought we could poke along, helping out around the edges while all those countries worked things out. Turns out that I and the rest of the country have had our heads in the sand."

Edith perused the front page, then pushed the paper back toward Altrude. "I'm afraid we are already on a steady march toward war." She poked at her nicely browned chicken, noticed Altrude hadn't touched her meal either. "I guess there is something that can spoil my appetite."

Her thoughts turned to Woodrow. He had been sending a flurry of loving letters, each one more insistent in declaring his love and loneliness than the last.

He wrote: *What a terrible time to have to make the important decision regarding marriage.* That seemed a distant problem now, and Edith wondered if the letters would cease. So many hopes and dreams sank with that ocean liner. Why would theirs be any different?

FOUR

He wants sex, dear." Sallie, Edith's mother, had taken a quick reading of the letters on creamy White House stationery. She was perched on the floral settee that was a bit too large for Edith's narrow drawing room.

Edith picked up another letter. "Did you miss the part about 'You are by nature so radiant and full of the perfect light that shines in the heart of a completely gifted woman'? And here: 'I would rather see the light of joy and complete happiness in those eyes than anything I can think of for myself. I seem to have been put into the world to serve, not to take, and serve I will to the utmost and demand nothing in return.'"

"Well, he certainly has a lovely way of expressing himself." Sallie waved dismissively at the letters. "I stand by my assessment."

"As I recall, you had a wonderful and loving marriage to my beloved father. Is it really possible that Woodrow feels this deeply in love after a mere few weeks? Are there people who fall hard and fast in love, only for it to fade away when someone shiny new comes along?"

A demure smile crossed Sallie's face. "My dear child, there are no time-lines for these things. No guarantee that any love will last forever. All you can do is shut out the rest of the world, and plumb the depths of your feelings, and be brutally honest. Are you in love with him, or with the idea that the president is in love with you?"

That was a question for which Edith had no clear answer. Did she love Woodrow? Yes, so very much she couldn't explain to herself why she had not accepted his proposal. Was she also in love with the power and trappings of power? That was the harder question. It was thrilling to be sure, to be close to the heartbeat of the nation. How would she feel if Woodrow were a banker, or lawyer, or farmer? It would be wonderful, she told herself, to be able to live and love away from prying eyes. But the little devil on her shoulder told her that she couldn't really know. The presidency and Woodrow were forever linked in her consciousness.

Cataclysmic world events notwithstanding, the trip on the *Mayflower* was still on the schedule. Edith had found some pictures of the yacht at her library, but that didn't prepare her for the sight of the magnificent ship in her berth at the Navy Yard. She was narrow and sleek, with a single huge smokestack midship. Nests of rigging connected several masts, but to Edith's disappointment, the ship had no sails.

As they boarded in the late afternoon, navy seamen in their brilliant white uniforms stood at attention and saluted the president as he walked up the gangplank. Edith had seen many men in uniform, but there was something especially charming about the look of the navy enlisted. Each seaman wore a flat-topped Cracker Jack cap, nicknamed for the sailor on the box of popcorn treats, and a loose white jumper with blue cuffs and a collar that was wide across the back. The trousers had a slight flare below the knee, which with the black neckerchief gave the sailors a jaunty appearance.

A loud low-high-low whistle startled Edith, as the boatswain announced the president with the traditional call. The smell of the polish on the gleaming wooden deck, mixed with the slightly salty and fishy river water excited her, reminding her of ocean crossings in great steamships. The captain in blue dress uniform awaited them at the top of the gangplank in front of a banner with the presidential seal. He welcomed the president aboard with a salute, then greeted Edith as Woodrow introduced her.

The captain did something Edith thought might later be useful, should she decide to accept Woodrow's proposal. There were many others in the party lined up behind her. The captain welcomed her with a firm hand-shake, then moved his hand with hers, guiding her to the first mate standing next to him. He repeated her name to the first mate, who didn't shake her hand, but was now aware of her identity and passed it down to the executive officer next to him in the receiving line. In this way, the captain kept the guests moving, and the guests didn't have to reintroduce themselves.

After all were aboard, the first mate escorted the presidential party to a "smoking room" with richly paneled wooden walls and luxurious leather couches lining each long side. A marble fireplace held court in one end of the room, but no fire was necessary on the warm mid-May evening. The president's secretary, Joe Tumulty, and Dr. Grayson were aboard, as well as Altrude, who was to be Edith's cabinmate.

Champagne bottles popped, and they gathered around the small center table for toasts. Edith soon felt light-headed and wondered if it were due to the champagne or the thrill of being included to sail on the magnificent ship and perhaps share some uninterrupted time with Woodrow. Soon the others drifted off, leaving Woodrow and Edith alone.

They settled on the leather couch and he refilled her glass. "Well, little girl, you've been quiet. What do you think?"

His pet name for her gave her pause. It seemed strange, because he had three daughters for whom it seemed the endearment would be more fitting, and she could hardly be considered petite. Or young. But this was a happy moment, not one to spoil with something so petty.

She was more open to his question at hand. "It's rather overwhelming, all this." She glanced around the sumptuous space. "But I can't help feeling that when you invited me some weeks ago, you thought your proposal would have a different response. Is this awkward for you?"

"Not at all. I wish for you to enjoy it and, as you say, continue our friendship while you sort out—"

"Because I can disembark. It's not too late, and no one would bat an eye." Outside, the sky was rapidly changing from streaks of pink to a dusky purple-gray.

Woodrow looked at her with those intense but expressive eyes, and she felt her objections crumbling like oyster crackers into soup.

"Please stay. I have something important to discuss with you," he said, barely above a whisper as he pulled her close.

All thoughts of leaving floated from her mind as she lost herself in his warm embrace. Finally, he pulled away, just as she was contemplating somehow sneaking into his stateroom. He was much too proper for that of course, and there was no way it would go unnoticed.

He seemed to feel the same, as he said, "Well, this can't go on without havoc raining down on both of us." He looked out the window, which now showed night had fallen. "Shall we get some air?"

Somehow Edith hadn't been aware that they were underway, the ship sliding through the water with quiet grace. He led her to the top deck, where sailors tended to lines or were on lookout. The sky was inky black above the river, which the lights of the ship made silver in reflection. No moon shone, but a million stars twinkled in the heavens. The Milky Way spread across the cosmos, making her feel like a very "little girl" indeed.

They found a quiet corner in the fantail stern, far from any curious ears.

"We must be nearing the Chesapeake. Can you sense the change in the air?" Woodrow said, his hands on the rail as he leaned over, taking deep breaths.

"I do. Speaking of change, you said you had something important to discuss."

He sighed. "Indeed. I need your wise counsel. Today I received word from my secretary of state. In a nutshell, he says he can't support me in my warnings to the American people that we may have to take up arms against Germany. He says he is a pacifist, and therefore can no longer serve in the department, and has offered his resignation.

"Bryan has been a divisive force in the party forever. At one point, perhaps it was useful, as we tried not to take sides. But now, after the sinking of the *Lusitania*, everything has changed.

"But what will the effect be, to change someone in this critical position at a critical moment? It's not just a man and his predilections; it's an entire philosophy, which many of our people still hold. If I accept his resignation, it will be signaling that I am in favor of war, when I wish to avoid that end until and unless there is no other possible way for democracy to survive."

"Oh, my dear, you are wrapping your mind around things that no longer matter. This is a good thing. Now you can replace him with someone who is willing and able, someone who would command respect for the office, both home and abroad."

A foghorn bellowed in the distance, as if echoing her sentiments. But Woodrow still leaned on the railing, working his lips in and out as he did while in deep thought.

Edith continued, thinking a lighter perspective might help him see the sense in her words. "There is a line from a play that comes to mind. It's about a man who longs for a woman that he can't have. She offers him a kiss in condolence, but he isn't sure he should accept it. His friend tells him to 'Take it, sir, and thank God for the chance.' And that is my advice to you."

At last he turned toward her, a small smile on his face. "A most eloquent demand for a kiss?"

He kissed her, there in the shadows, secreted away from all the eyes eager to confirm the rumors. No longer did she touch the ground, the ship floating somewhere underneath her feet.

Woodrow, however, was still planted firmly on deck. He resumed his hand-on-the-rail stance. "Actually, I've been thinking of a suitable replacement. There is a counselor in the department, Robert Lansing. A little wet behind the ears, but I think that might be a good thing."

Startled that Woodrow seemed to be careening from romance to loyalty to status quo, and then boldly shaking that up, Edith struggled to catch up. "But he's rather low-level, isn't he? I would think you'd want someone with far more experience."

"I know his father-in-law, a man of great sense and experience, and he would act as a guide."

"Then why not appoint the father-in-law?"

"Because an older man may be rigid and follow precedent. But this is a new age in diplomacy, with rapid change. We must act quickly and decisively or be left behind to pick up the pieces."

"I like the idea of a team. You are brilliant, Mr. Wilson."

Altrude was already asleep in their shared stateroom when Edith retired for the night. Polished wooden paneling covered the walls, and a crisply sheeted bunk lined each of the cabin's long sides. A small brass-framed mirror hung over the tiny sink. She pulled the thick blue curtain over the porthole, now showing nothing but inky black night.

She lit the smallest lamp as she undressed for bed so as not to awaken her cabinmate. Tucked in her berth, Edith was lulled by the gentle rolling of the ship. She closed her eyes and imagined Woodrow's arms around her. Had she given him sound advice? She prayed for that and for him before drifting off to sleep.

A sudden lurch in the ship awakened her. Then an awful sound... Altrude retching in the little sink cubby, hands bracing herself on the wall.

"Oh my, are you all right, love?" Edith slid open the curtain for more light.

The answer was another violent retch. Gray morning light filtered through the porthole as rain pattered against the glass. The ship rolled much more severely than it had last night.

"Seems we're in open waters—the Atlantic, I should think. Bad timing for a storm to hit." Edith rose and made up her berth. "Can I get you something? Crackers or maybe I can fetch some ginger ale?"

Altrude's light complexion had taken on a ghastly hue. She pressed back damp tendrils of dark hair and leaned heavily against the oak-paneled bulkhead. "Some fresh air might help. And maybe a nip of brandy to settle things."

Edith hurried toward the kitchen, flattening her hands on hatchways and bulkheads to keep herself upright. She found a steward who guided her toward the liquor cabinet. He pulled out a bottle of brandy for her, apparently just in time, as his cheeks puffed out and he made a hasty retreat.

She took the bottle and headed back to the deck. The ship lurched even more severely, and so did Edith. And her stomach. She slapped one clammy palm on the hatchway to right herself, clutching the bottle in her other hand. Just as she passed through the hatch to the deck, her stomach heaved. She had to get outside quickly; watching the horizon was the key, she had been told.

She slipped out onto the deck, slick with rain. Thinking the brandy would help, she pulled the cork and gulped some right out of the bottle. But the ship slammed up and down with the waves, and she stumbled. There was nothing to do but lie on the deck, the bottom of the bottle of brandy safely clasped against her belly.

Woodrow, disgustingly hale and hearty, loomed over her. "Well, aren't you the sight. Are you ill?" He removed his special jacket with the presidential seal and tucked it under her head.

"For Altrude." She lifted the bottle in a toast to the gray sky. "It helps."

⌒✥

That afternoon, Joseph Tumulty tracked Edith down while she walked the deck, breathing the salt air and enjoying the now-calm seas.

"Ah, there you are, oh woman of my boss's desire."

Edith looked about to ensure no one else was in hearing range. "Now, hush with that. Do you need a scandal on your hands along with all your other duties?"

"Some things are out of my hands. The boss wants to see you in his stateroom, should you be so inclined."

"I am inclined." She spun on her heel and was starting to stomp off when Tumulty grabbed her arm.

"Listen, I don't give a tinker's damn about the president's personal *interests*, shall we say. Just remember, every minute he spends canoodling with you is a minute taken away from his vital work."

"Well, maybe I'm not just 'canoodling.' Maybe I'm helping with that vital work." Edith kept her voice level, not wanting to give away the umbrage she felt. "Just last night, I helped him with an important decision regarding the secretary of state."

As Tumulty stood, mouth gaping while working on some retort, Edith marched straight to Woodrow's stateroom, gossips be darned.

⌒✥

It was an expansive stateroom. Woodrow sat at his desk in the outer office, flanked by an American flag displayed on a stand on his right and the presidential and ship's seals on stands to his left.

Without any preamble, Woodrow tore a sheet of paper from his typewriter and held it out for her.

"My second letter to the Germans regarding the sinking of the *Lusitania*."

Edith took the letter. "What happened with the first one?"

"Never sent. Secretary Bryan of course raised objections, some of them even valid."

She read out loud, "'In view of recent acts of the German authorities in violation of American rights on the high seas which culminated in the torpedoing and sinking of the British steamship *Lusitania* on May 7, 1915, by which over 100 American citizens lost their lives, it is clearly wise and desirable that the Government of the United States and the Imperial German Government should come to a clear and full understanding as to the grave situation which has resulted.'"

The letter went on to outline other attacks that had resulted in the loss of American lives and emphasized the "enlightened attitude" the German government had shown previously, which made their current actions all the more surprising and distressing. The letter allowed for the extraordinary circumstances of the current war but underscored the serious risks to neutral countries from German hostilities.

"It's all very reasonable," Edith said. "But we're dealing with an unreasonable entity. I'm afraid their response, if they even bother to respond, will be more rants about blockades starving their people and so on."

"Thank you for the reminder, my love. It is for us to be the voice of reason, the responsible player. History will not look upon the Central Powers kindly, but we are measured by our every word and deed."

He needed none of her help with the writing of it. In fact, she marveled at his ability to rise eloquent, even under the intense pressure to convey a very difficult message. She watched as he carefully layered carbon paper between two fresh sheets of stationery, his mind focused on the task at hand. He could have stated his wishes to Tumulty, or Bryan or any number of staff, and gone off to enjoy the cruise while they wrote the letter.

But that was not him. The country, the presidency was what he existed for; she had no doubt he'd give anything, including his life, to preserve and protect them. She felt a warm glow throughout her body; she was witness to greatness. Resisting the urge to go around the desk and envelop him in a hug, she quietly said, "If there's nothing else…" then slipped away when he merely nodded and returned to his typing.

As she left the stateroom, she realized her love for him had grown above the simple physical attraction, beyond the thrill of his exuberant affection. She was falling for his precious ideals, his sense of duty, and his willingness to sacrifice whatever he could of himself and his reputation to do the right thing for the country and, indeed, the world.

The next morning, Woodrow gave a well-received speech in front of the New York Public Library. It gladdened Edith's heart to see the thousands who had turned up to cheer for him, the sun shining down on them all. A welcome parade followed, and Woodrow and she joined the mayor and other dignitaries in a grandstand festooned with red, white, and blue bunting. Woodrow saluted, and Edith held her right hand over her heart when the color guard marched by.

The next morning, back on the *Mayflower*, they sailed under the Brooklyn Bridge, jammed with waving spectators, then up the Hudson, the site for the presentation of the fleet. They passed cruisers and destroyers and other warships, each decked out with signal flags and firing gun salutes. A military band on the shore played the national anthem while thousands of sailors stood at attention on the decks, and hundreds of thousands of spectators lined both sides of the river. Edith bit her lips to hold back tears, witnessing the outpouring of strength and patriotism.

Woodrow saluted the troops and beamed with pride. He seemed so natural in this role, like a hand slipping into a well-worn glove. But would it be the same for her? For the first time, she imagined appearing in front of thousands as the wife of the president. Would it feel so different then? If all she had to do was smile and wave, it seemed like great fun. But what else would be expected of her? Other than her vague knowledge of Dolley Madison rescuing artwork from a White House fire and Mrs. Roosevelt installing bars on the windows to keep her children from escaping, Edith knew little of what First Ladies did. She'd have to add that to her studies.

Back home once again, Edith continued to struggle with a response to Woodrow's proposal. It wasn't just the suddenness of it all, and her fear of loss of privacy and freedom. It was her very real fear that she wouldn't be enough. Aside from the people's expectations for First Ladies, Woodrow seemed to rely on her for advice that she had no training or experience to give. His first wife had had far more education. What if Edith, in her naivete, made a terrible mistake? And was Woodrow so blinded by love (and Tumulty had said as much) that it could affect his judgment? She must be as selfless in her decision as Woodrow was in all of his.

It wasn't fair to keep him dangling; indeed, he had written:

...for God's sake, try to find out whether you love me or not. You owe it to yourself and you owe it to the great measure of love I have given without stint or measure. Do not be afraid of what I am thinking, but remember I need strength and certainty for the daily task and I cannot walk upon quicksand. I love you with all my heart.

Woodrow

Even though Edith had a telephone, communicating by letter when they couldn't physically be together became the daily norm, sometimes more than once a day. Since the phone line had to go through a switchboard, there was always the possibility that an operator would listen in. And who could have blamed one, as the gossip rags were abuzz with speculation regarding the president's love life.

So a messenger, usually Helen, arrived each morning at Edith's with a missive from Woodrow and returned with another from Edith. But one morning, it was the president's private secretary, Joseph Tumulty, who arrived with a letter.

Rebecca, Edith's longtime cook and maid, answered the door and let him in.

Edith shook his hand in greeting. "Oh, this is a surprise. To what do I owe the pleasure? I do hope Miss Bones is well."

The usually garrulous secretary curtly responded, "She's fine. Thought I'd come have a word."

Over coffee, he chatted a bit about his wife and children as he avoided eye contact and wrung his hands.

"Well, out with it, Mr. Tumulty. I'm not the lady of leisure you seem to think I am."

"Oh, not at all, Mrs. Galt. It's just that the president doesn't know I'm here, and I don't wish to speak out of turn. But I have this." He pulled an envelope with the familiar White House seal on it. "I convinced Helen to let me bring the president's letter this morning, saying I had an errand nearby."

"Let me guess. There was no errand."

"In my mind, there is."

Edith stirred her coffee, tilted her head, awaiting more.

"On the *Mayflower*, I mentioned a worry, my worry that is, that the president seems rather preoccupied. Now I don't know exactly what transpires between you, and it isn't my business, but the presidency *is* my business. And I think this preoccupation is not only impairing his usual judgment, but the time he spends doing this,"—he tapped the envelope lying on the table between them—"is time away from making timely decisions. You have no idea how I've had to save him from the sharp teeth of the press."

Edith picked up the envelope and examined its seal. It seemed to have been partially opened. She grabbed a letter opener from her desk and finished the job. "Do you want to know what it says, then?"

"No, no, you and he have a right to privacy. I try to only open non-personal correspondence. But...well, it seems he's waiting for some response from you. When he gets your letters, he paces, for hours sometimes. Then he spends the next few hours writing pages and pages. Many are crumpled and disposed of."

"And you wouldn't have happened to uncrumple them and have a glance, now would you?" Fury rose in her, the heat building in her face.

He lowered his eyes. "The point is, his schedule is quite demanding. I know, because I'm responsible for it. For example, yesterday he was to meet with a new senator from Ohio, Warren Harding. It was important for reasons I don't want to get into, but Mr. Wilson was so despondent after Miss Bones gave him your letter that he took to bed in the middle of the day. You must see that we can't have this?"

"Well, what am I to do? Not write to him? I hardly think that will help."

Tumulty ran his hand through his thinning hair. "There is a rather inelegant saying, which I will rephrase: 'Poo, or get off the pot.'"

She stared unblinking at him after the dreadful remark, but he had no more to add. Believing Tumulty had already read it, she pulled out Woodrow's letter and began reading it out loud. "'My sweet darling, a day when I neither see you nor get a message from you is blank on the calendar. I went to bed early feeling very lonely indeed. You have become indispensable to me, my sweet one, and it is so far from here to your home. My thoughts run back and forth across the distance every minute of the day and my heart knows nothing of it; it is always with you, never here while you are away.'"

She looked up at Tumulty. "I guess I see your point. Methinks our Mr. Wilson has read too many romance novels."

Tumulty's face and neck had reddened, and he mopped his sweaty brow with a handkerchief. "So you see my position?"

"I have no control over the president's thoughts or actions. I have been forthright in my feelings for him, and my ability to 'get off the pot' as you say will come in its own due time." She rose, and he followed her signal of his dismissal. "Do your job to the best of your ability. The president is a wise man. What may seem to you to be a dithering lovesickness may be his way of letting off pressure so that he may make good decisions, again in their own due time."

Tumulty forced a smile as he gathered his hat, then headed to the door. "This is all in confidence?"

"Of course." Edith closed the door behind him. Despite her dismissal of his concerns, her heart somersaulted in her chest. What was she to do?

❦

After Tumulty's visit, Edith composed a short letter, which she hoped would both assure Woodrow of her love for him and ease the agonizing wait for her decision regarding his marriage proposal.

My best Beloved,

This first June day has been so crowded with joy that my heart can have no more—and I must talk to you, and make you feel how splendidly I love you. Each time we are together, dearest, you seem more completely to fill my need and to stimulate and waken every emotion...

A very rare phone call from Woodrow followed. His voice sounded scratchy, and she thought she heard the clicking in of other parties. "Edith, my dear, there's been a development. Can you come this eve?"

Woodrow was not his usual charming self at dinner, with only Edith, Helen, and Margaret to entertain. Soon, he excused himself and requested that Edith accompany him to his study.

"I know there is no official status to our relationship, although I dearly wish there were. But still, I trust you with matters of the highest level and find your sane responses to be clearer than any of the hired brains about me."

"You'll have my opinions, dear, as long as you account for my level of experience."

"Experience, I'm afraid, is not the best teacher when you're up against an unprecedented threat. What is required is judgment, and I trust yours." He strode over to the large double-sided desk that dominated the room. A large center drawer faced the entrance of the room, opposite his chair. Woodrow unlocked and tugged at the drawer, brimming with folders. He picked up a few that had a square of heavy red paper clipped to them. "These are the most pressing matters of state. The most critical are these with the red indicators, requiring action within hours, if not minutes."

"Oh my, that drawer is packed full! How do you possibly get through all those in a few hours?" Her heart filled with guilt, remembering Tumulty's description of Woodrow's pacing and worry over her.

"Lucky for me, I don't require much sleep. I get up before dawn and attend to the overnights from abroad." He pulled out the top folder, one with a red tab. "This is what I wanted to share with you. We have a response from the Germans regarding my *Lusitania* letter."

She opened the folder and read the letter. The German response was, as

Edith expected, full of excuses and unjustified protests. The letter claimed the *Lusitania* was carrying Canadian troops, weapons, and ammunition, which itself had led to its sinking, and that the British were known to disguise their warships under neutral flags. While regretting the loss of lives the Germans claimed Americans had used as human shields, the imperial government believed it had been protecting its own citizens.

"Oh my, are their accusations valid? Was the *Lusitania* carrying troops and armaments?"

"Certainly not. I need to get exact numbers, but there is an allowable limit of ammunition and such. And if Canadian troops were aboard, they will have some explaining to do. All of this is top secret, of course, but if my presumptions are true and this is a bunch of rubbish, I want you to help me draft our response."

It seemed a weight was pressed upon her. But she could bear it, and if it lessened his burden, so much the better. "I'm happy to help in any way you deem best. But what about Bryan?" Despite his threats to the contrary, the secretary had yet to resign. "He is going to agree with the Germans and want us to call out the Brits for being naughty. What are you going to do about him?"

"I think his reaction to our letter will be telling. No need to do anything in haste in that regard."

"It's a terrible thing, this war. And every day it seems more and more likely that it will expand to swallow us whole."

"Believe me, darling, that is the last thing that I want to happen. You are too young, but I witnessed the Civil War as a child, and it's been a guiding principle of my life to use anything in my power to prevent such a thing. It's what has driven me to where I am today, the belief in negotiation, acceptance, and compromise to end hostilities before they erupt in battle."

"Did you see battles, then? Did you lose loved ones?"

"I think everyone lost somebody. Some lost many. No, I was kept clear of battles, but I smelled the smoke of Sherman's burning cities, saw the busted-up artillery and worse-off soldiers returning down the streets in ragtag formations. They went off bright, with buglers and drummers and cheers, and returned carrying stretchers of wounded, their faces raw, guns resting on tired shoulders, with only the sad beat of a single drum to set their pace."

Edith nodded sadly. "Slavery had to end. But was war the only way? My ancestors were plantation owners, but they once fed multitudes and grew enough cotton to clothe a city. They obeyed the law. If only there had been better leaders in the time leading up to it, the war might have been avoided. But everything was destroyed in the war and my parents had to move in with my grandparents, along with about twenty other homeless relations. I can't help but wonder if by education and leadership the needed changes would have happened peacefully."

"What's done is done. It's what we can learn from it that is critical. How to resist the human frailty that turns to violence to solve disagreements." He took the letter from Edith, slipped it back into the folder. "At the same time, we cannot stand by and allow our desire for peace to encourage others to take liberties." He tapped the folder. "We aren't the bully, but we must be strong enough to withstand them, and to protect our friends who are not as strong."

"Two rather opposing views you hold."

"And that, my dear, is why I need you so desperately."

Again, the huge burden of his expectations weighed upon her. As many times as he told her that she gave him good counsel, she feared she was not well-enough informed to do so. But he didn't seem to want a review of the background information; he had others for that. He seemed to want a voice of common sense, a voice from the people, not just the cloistered circle of a myopic government. That, she could do.

FIVE

With Congress out of session, the throngs of related hangers-on escaped the steamy Capital city for the summer. After church on a scorching afternoon, Woodrow and Edith climbed in the presidential limousine for a drive along the Potomac River toward Great Falls. The road twisted and turned amongst the rolling hills, and Edith turned her face toward the refreshing breeze. Helen was along as a chaperone, and the three of them chatted amiably, with Woodrow expounding upon the history of the area.

"Do you know why the Conduit Road is so named?"

Both Helen and Edith shrugged and laughed. Helen said, "Doesn't 'conduit' mean a path for something to get from one place to another? So all roads are conduits."

"One could look at it that way, but a conduit refers to a type of tunnel or tube that channels a fluid or electricity. In this case, it's water."

Edith looked at the passing thick forest. "I don't see any water."

"We're riding right on top of it. Below us is a tunnel of stone and concrete that is bringing water from above the falls of the Potomac to the thirsty city. That big lake by the park is actually a reservoir, where the water is treated and stored and the river silt is settled."

"All these things going on," Edith said, "so much work and planning, and we just open a tap and water magically appears. I should be more grateful."

"Civics lesson over, I do have a proposition for you ladies."

"Oooooh," they replied, with Helen giving Edith an elbow.

Woodrow ignored her teasing. "In a few weeks, I'll be heading up to Cornish, New Hampshire, and I'd like you both to accompany me."

"Oh, it's lovely." Helen turned to Edith. "We rent a charming estate when the president is there. They call it the Summer White House. I've been several times with Ellen and the girls. You'll love it."

Edith blinked at the mention of Woodrow's first wife. She wasn't spoken of a great deal, except by Margaret, but when she was, it was always in the most glowing terms.

Helen must have seen the stricken look on Edith's face as she fought back pangs of inadequacy. "Oh, sorry, Edith, I didn't mean..."

"I might have to rearrange a few meetings with my board of directors, but I'd love to join you. I can drive up, as I might visit some friends along the way." Edith liked the idea of having her own motor available, an easy means of escape if staying with Woodrow's family proved awkward.

"Drive up in a motorcar? By yourself?" Helen turned from watching the scenery go by.

"Of course. I'm quite skilled in my electric, and I've driven to New York City many times. I'll have you know I possess the first driver's license issued to a woman in Washington, DC."

"I'm sure you are, and I'm sure you can, dear, but I'm afraid that won't be possible for this trip," Woodrow said.

"Why not?" Edith's hackles were up. She couldn't vote, but that didn't present nearly as much inconvenience as not being able to drive.

"Well, I was hoping you'd accompany Helen, as she wants to arrive a few days before I can go. And of course, the Secret Service will need to be with her."

"All will fit in my electric." That wasn't true, but Edith was determined to hold her ground.

Woodrow and Helen laughed, making Edith feel like a silly outsider. She crossed her arms in protest.

"Oh now, don't pout," Helen said. "The Secret Service would never allow you to drive with me all that way, and I'm sure it would be against some protocol or other for them to drive your vehicle."

"But what about my visits to friends in New York? And I'd like to drop by Princeton that you've spoken so fondly of."

Woodrow sighed. "And yet failed to escort you there myself. But this is easily debated. The detail will go wherever you wish. Protecting you will be their only job."

After visits to Princeton and New York City, Helen and Edith arrived at Harlakenden House, where a letter from Woodrow was waiting:

My Beloved,

Here I sit at my desk; the hour is the same that finds me every morning pouring my heart out to you—but oh, the difference! The house is empty! The town is empty! My sweetheart, my darling is gone, and I sit here with a longing in my heart which I can hardly endure...

Helen tilted her head at the letter in Edith's hands. "What shall we do with that romantic old sod? You better hurry up and agree to marry him before he bursts into flame."

"Tut-tut, we have our own timetable. And if there's a conflagration in the meantime, let it brighten the corners of that sad old house." Edith tucked the letter into her embroidered carpet bag.

Helen retired early, exhausted from the long trip, but Edith wanted to explore the house. It was somehow cozy, even with formal sitting rooms with chintz sofas and a large dining room downstairs and several bedroom suites upstairs. She had her own room, lit by kerosene lamps, with a huge poster bed and a Queen Anne highboy. She found some lovely cream stationery emblazoned with a pen-and-ink drawing of Harlakenden House and sat at the desk to write to Woodrow.

Although she professed her love and admiration for him in her letters, she didn't wax as romantic as did he. She had contemplated telling him that perhaps he should be more circumspect, as whatever he put in writing would belong to history, if she didn't destroy it. But she could never bring herself to do either—not to destroy his letters or tell him how to write them. But she worried: how would he be judged a generation from now when the world would see him as a lover?

So be it, she decided. She could later destroy the letters, or release them and let the world see the extraordinary spirit of the man she loved.

The next day she walked the grounds, enjoying the view of the rounded peak of Mount Ascutney, and the wildflowers along the Connecticut River. Tiny blue and white anemones, toadflax, and buttercups waved in a colorful carpet. Butterflies flitted from one to the next in a happy dance. She picked a buttercup and held it under her chin. When they were children, her sister Bertha would do this and declare that the flower's reflection on her skin meant she liked butter. She must find time to go home and visit. But time in Wytheville meant time away from Woodrow.

When Helen appeared, she convinced Edith to cross a bridge over the river so they could explore a little village on the Vermont side. The sun was high in the sky on the brilliant day, spring just turning into summer. They meandered along a dirt path for a bit before they came to the paved road that led to the bridge.

Helen panted a bit to keep up with Edith while wearing a too-heavy dress. "You might want to save your energy, dear; the bridge is quite long."

Just then, the covered bridge came into sight. Edith spied two spans supported by a single stone pier in the middle of the placid river. "Oh my, that must be hundreds of feet long. Is it very dark inside?" She shuddered, imagining thousands of spiders and bats lurking in its depths. The thought of those creatures brought with them a memory of something she habitually put out of her mind.

"It has its secrets." Helen winked, which didn't help Edith's unease.

They followed a smoke-belching Model T onto the bridge, which was wide enough for opposing traffic. The interior was not dark as Edith had feared, as sunlight streamed in from small square openings. The truss work was visible, the crossed wooden beams much like a huge garden lattice.

Edith was surprised when they encountered a little booth, with a toll keeper inside.

"Oh dear, I forgot. Have you any coin?" Helen asked.

"None at all. I guess we shall have to turn back." Relieved, Edith did an about-face. She avoided looking up; there were sure to be bats clinging to the roof. Although with the moldy, damp wood and lingering exhaust from the Ford, maybe even bats wouldn't want to make their home there.

Helen turned to look behind them, where a Secret Service man followed. As he approached, she asked, "Could we borrow a nickel?"

"Of course, Miss Bones. But I only have a dollar."

Helen gave the dollar to the toll keeper, who Edith thought looked like a dried-up apple. She received ninety-five cents in change. "Is that for us two, or all three?" Helen asked.

The toll keeper coughed the raspy cough of someone who enjoyed his tobacco. "One way for the two of ya."

Edith raised her eyebrows. "Well, how much is it per person? Two and a half cents?"

"Two cents for one person. Five for the both of ya."

"Interesting." This amused Edith. "Now how much will it be when we return?"

"Ah now, that'll be three cents each."

"That's quite the inflation. How do you countenance that?"

The old woman shrugged. "Private bridge, they charge what they do. Ya can swim if ya like. Or have ya a boat?"

Helen piped in. "I would think the state wouldn't allow these capricious charges."

"Oh, it would take two states to agree. But I'm sure they'll get wind of it and buy it all up for a pretty penny. The owners will make out like bandits and the toll will be raised to a dime." The old woman laughed a hoarse laugh that descended into a cough. "And ya know why it costs more to cross to New Hampshire than the other way?"

The women shook their heads.

"Because all want to go to the Hampshire for a drink. No'uns wanting to go to dry ol' Vermont."

Helen and Edith laughed as they walked into the sunshine on the Vermont side.

"It does give me pause. About the public-private funding," Edith said.

"What about it?"

"On the one hand, being public, you have a reliable service with an equitable price. That woman could have charged you more for the wrong color dress or me for having wavy hair. But on the other hand, in the hands of government, the cost would inevitably be higher for all."

Helen stopped walking and grabbed Edith's elbow to stop her as well. "You know, in the years I've been coming here and crossing that bridge, my only thoughts were about it being called 'Lover's Bridge,' and imagining the dalliances that gave it that name."

Edith laughed. "Oh, if those creaky walls could talk."

"But you bring a higher level of thinking to this, as with everything. I admire you, Mrs. Galt and, I fervently hope, soon to be Mrs. Wilson."

"Well, thank you. You make me blush."

"I loved you from the moment I knew Woodrow loved you and I saw how happy you made him. But now I love you for the inquisitiveness of your mind, so much like his."

Edith felt her spirits lift and modestly suppressed a smile. "Come, Miss Bones. We shall buy lunch for the three of us. After the tolls, we'll have eighty-four cents left."

The next day Woodrow was to arrive by train. Edith talked the Secret Service man into allowing her to go in the big touring car to the station without a chaperone. It was warm and the top was down, so there was some risk of being seen, but it seemed New Englanders didn't stick their noses in other people's business like people did back home.

Woodrow's loving words in his letters, longing to be in her arms and expressing his pain at their separation, ran through her head as they drove. Always, in the back of her mind, she was afraid he would tire of her and wish to move on to someone who possessed his deeply intelligent sensibilities, someone more like Ellen. Woodrow didn't speak of his late wife often, probably understanding how that might make Edith feel an interloper.

When they arrived at the station, Edith's doubts faded when she saw him bounding up to the car, holding his silk top hat by the brim to keep it from flying off with a big smile lighting his face. She let herself out of the car and held out her arms to him.

"Thank you for inviting me. It's so lovely here, and Helen and I are having the most wonderful time."

"I'm so glad you like it. We'll have tonight to ourselves, and then my daughters and other family trickle in. I hope you don't mind. It's a rare treat for me."

She stepped back into the car, the driver holding the door for them. "Of course I don't mind." She lowered her voice to a whisper. "But I'm also hoping to have some time alone with you."

That night, they dined on fresh roast lamb and carrots and herbs straight from the garden. A maple glaze on the vegetables and on a sweet pastry dessert provided a local twist, and Edith savored every bite. After dinner, Edith and Woodrow retired to the smaller drawing room, cuddling on a soft couch in front of a roaring fire.

They watched the fire leaping, creating shadows that crossed the room like ghosts. They drank hot cocoa, and its warmth flowed through Edith as it did long ago when her grandmother had made it. He read from a book of poetry, and Edith thought there could be no more perfect moment.

As the fire hissed and crackled, Woodrow whispered into her ear, "I've missed you so. I'm hoping you're happy with me."

"Of course." She knew he was really asking something else. "And you've been so patient with me." She looked into those big, expressive eyes, always a mistake when she had to tell him something that wasn't quite what he wanted to hear. "I've made sort of a decision."

He stiffened away from her. "Sort of?"

She squeezed his hand. "No, I mean a real decision, and although I hope it will ease any doubts in your mind, it isn't exactly what you have requested."

He took a deep breath and looked down at their joined hands. Then he abruptly stood and strode across the room to the Victrola sitting under the window. He selected a record from the cabinet, set it on the turntable, and wound up the machine. When it came up to speed, he set the needle on the record. "Madame, will you dance with me?"

A bit bewildered, Edith followed him. The song he had chosen was familiar to Edith, but she couldn't quite place why.

He offered his hand, and she tentatively took it in hers. He wrapped an arm around her waist and led her in a slow sway to the music. Her body refused to relax into it, as she was frustrated with the abandoned conversation.

He leaned close. "Do you know why I call you 'little girl'?"

Edith shook her head. If she were to be honest, and she wouldn't for that would hurt his feelings, she wasn't fond of the nickname he used. She only hoped he hadn't used the same one for Ellen.

The record was a bit scratchy, but Edith made out the lyrics:

The nighttime, the nighttime is calling me,
It's dream-time, sweet dream-time, for you and me.
I'm longing, I'm longing to close my eyes, for there a sweet vision lies.

"It's because on the oh, so many lonely nights I have without you, I play this in my bedroom to help me to sleep." He sang along with the chorus:

My little dream girl,
You pretty dream girl,
Sometimes I seem, girl, to own your heart.
Each night you haunt me,
By day you taunt me,
I want you, I want you, I need you so.

Edith wanted to make a joke about putting him to sleep, but that would be avoiding the question hanging in the air, as naked and thorny as the antler chandelier over their heads.

"My darling, is December of next year soon enough?" she asked.

"For…?"

"I want to marry you, my dearest. But I think it's best we wait until after the election. Then we will be free to live as we choose, with nothing and no one having a say in our every waking moment."

He stopped dancing so abruptly that she stumbled. "While I'm happy to hear this, it seems you believe I won't win?"

Don't let me waken, learn I'm mistaken,
Find my faith shaken, in you, sweetheart.

"What are the chances, really? With the Republicans starting to unite? You can't fight those numbers. If it weren't for Teddy Roosevelt splitting..." She stopped. This was not something he needed to be reminded of, especially by her.

I'd sigh for, I'd cry for, sweet dreams forever,
My little dream girl good night.

He went to the Victrola and scratched the needle off of the record. The beautiful moment was lost.

"I see." He pressed his lips together. "You don't believe I'll earn another term and, in any case, don't desire to be married to someone in that position. This time you've needed...your reluctance... All along you just wanted to be sure—"

Regret ran through her in a cold shiver. "No, darling. I've said this all wrong. I think you are the best thing for this country. But whether that translates into votes in this crazy system is another matter and quite out of my control. Except for one thing. I think in light of the recent passing of Ellen, and the scuttlebutt Tumulty is constantly repeating to me, your chances are better if we have a longer engagement—if we marry after the election. It's not so long..."

His face relaxed some, his sad eyes brightening. "I don't think the wait is necessary. But if this progresses our situation from friendship to betrothal, then I will accept your proposal."

Edith smiled and pulled him to her and they danced without the music. Her heart eased its pounding and her breathing steadied as she finally relished the moment. Softly she began to sing. "Your little dream girl will be haunting your dreams tonight."

The next morning, still regretting her hurtful words, Edith felt the need to put her sentiments in writing. On Harlakenden House stationery she wrote a note to Woodrow:

A pledge:

I promise with all my heart absolutely to trust and accept my beloved, unite my life with his without doubts or misgivings.

She tucked the note into her skirt pocket and floated down the stairs in a happy mood. The dining room was buzzing with new guests: the Sayres—Woodrow's daughter Jessie and her husband and baby—and Margaret were eating breakfast. Of the three daughters, Jessie resembled her father the most, with her clear gray eyes, patrician nose, and handsome face. She was gentle and soft-spoken, which Edith imagined were traits inherited from her mother.

Edith tucked into some oatmeal with pecans and cranberries. "Does anyone know where our dear Mr. Wilson is?" she asked.

The ladies laughed. "We were going to ask you."

Edith blushed at the friendly insinuation. "I'm sure I don't know, but he must have a morning ritual?"

Margaret gave the ladies a cease-and-desist look. She was becoming Edith's strongest ally amongst the girls. "He'll no doubt be in the library, going over correspondence that has collected overnight."

Woodrow was indeed in the comfortable library, lined with tall bookcases and a marble fireplace. A tall window let in blue morning light and offered a view of Mount Ascutney across the river. He sat at an expansive desk; an extra chair had been pulled next to him.

"Good morning, my darling." Edith bent to give him a kiss.

"I trust you slept well?" Woodrow capped his pen.

"Yes, very well. I have put my promise in writing to you." She slipped the note to him.

"But don't read it just yet, with your mind on duty. In fact, I should leave you to your work, if there's nothing I can get you at the moment?"

"No, if you can spare the time, please stay." He patted the chair next to him. "I wish to share with you all that is going on."

She sat, a sense of worry arising. "Oh? Has there been an important development?"

"There are always important developments." He tucked her note into his suit coat pocket. "But now that we're engaged, I want you to know what I know, and this is a perfect opportunity, for there are many things I can't discuss over letters or telephone."

The fire spit and flared up, igniting a few sheaths of paper amongst the logs.

"These are state secrets then?" Edith felt at once thrilled to be trusted and apprehensive at the responsibility.

"I trust you're not a communist spy." He opened a folder full of yellow papers—Western Union telegrams. "This is from the German ambassador, and Lansing's recommended response. We must do something there very soon. And here is a full report on the manifest and cargo of the *Lusitania*. As predicted, all was within legal limits. Our next letter to the Germans must be more forceful. I would very much like your assistance to write it."

Edith had thought the *Lusitania* issue had been addressed after their discussion on the *Mayflower* and the recent resignation of Secretary Bryan. "I do understand we are still attempting a neutral position. But there is a reason you replaced Bryan with Lansing. He was too narrow in his focus and unable to see the problem in full." She tapped the folder with its red indicator. "Germany will only grow bolder and more dangerous with time if we show any loss of resolve or weakness. Are we going to allow her to control the waterways, our trade, and ultimately, our freedom?"

"I'm in agreement." Woodrow started stacking the folders into a drawer. "Lansing has his hands full with the rioting and revolution in Mexico. That old scoundrel Huerta hasn't given up and has asked Germany to come protect Mexico from us! Now that's just what we need. Oh, and Haiti is falling to pieces. At some point, we'll have to decide where to put our priorities: near us, or 'across the pond,' as the Brits say."

Taking his cue, she rose. "It's not either/or. It's about showing strength." Her own resolve surprised her. Remembering Helen's kind words on their

walk across the covered bridge and Woodrow's utter confidence in her opinions, she decided she should shed her self-doubt. Like a butterfly emerging
from its cocoon, she vowed to trust her renewed self.

"I agree. In any case, it's time to ramp up the military."

She stepped toward the door as Woodrow locked the desk drawer.
"But right now, how about we take a walk in the gardens? Now that we're
officially betrothed, there is something I need to share with you."

"That sounds ominous, but whatever is on your mind, I'm sure it is
better shared."

They headed out to the gardens, but Edith soon found herself drawn
to the path that led to the covered bridge. They stopped within sight of it,
in a place where wildflowers grew in perfusion. She picked a small bunch
of them and tucked some in the buttonhole on his jacket, and some in her
own. "The bridge reminded me of something. It was dark and spidery and
probably full of bats."

"Are these things you are afraid of? For I will defend you from them
with impunity."

"Yes and no. They make me...uncomfortable. You see, I lost my only child."

He wrinkled his brow in consternation. "Yes, born too early. I'm very
sorry. But what has that to do with..."

"That day, I was nearly eight months along, and I was helping out
at the jewelry store. Norman told me I didn't need to. That I should be
home resting with my feet up. But being the stubborn cuss that I am, I
insisted. I had gone to the basement storage area for a special tool. It was
dark and musty down there, very creepy. Something landed on me. I don't
know what."

She paused, the memories flying back and chilling her to the bone
despite the warm day. "I remember a sense that I couldn't breathe, then
screaming and running up the stairs and Norman trying to calm me. But
he didn't really know how. I fainted I guess, and when I woke up, he had
left me in a room to rest and then gone back to work. It should have been
nothing. I was frightened, but unharmed. But I felt so terribly alone. Then,
within hours, my waters broke. There was nothing the doctors could do; our
tiny little boy was on his way."

Edith felt Woodrow's calming hand on her shoulder. "I've always thought if I had just stayed at home, or if I loved and trusted Norman enough..." She fought back tears. "Well, it was long ago, but I thought you should know."

He took her in his arms. "I'm so sorry this happened to you. And I promise, from the bottom of my heart, to give you the love and protection you deserve."

As she thought back on it now, the feeling that had remained with her all those years was abandonment. Whether it was her incapability of sharing her needs, or Norman's failure to understand and meet them, she didn't know. She resolved that her second marriage would be different. She would take Woodrow's promise and return the same with all her heart.

But that love and protection would frequently have to be from a distance. Woodrow could only stay a couple of weeks, as duty soon called him back to Washington. He traveled back and forth, escaping Washington whenever possible to join Edith and his daughters in Cornish.

In August, Edith visited with some friends in upstate New York, then drove with them to see more friends in New Jersey. Although she missed Woodrow desperately, it was freeing to move about without a Secret Service detail, to blend in with the crowd at the Jersey shore. In Ocean City, she strolled along the boardwalk, enjoying the salt air and sound of the waves. She tried ice cream in one of the new waffle cones that had become popular. The thin waffle was still warm, which made the melting ice cream even more delicious. She wondered if she would have to give up such simple pleasures after she married Woodrow. Even if he were no longer president, surely they wouldn't be able to stroll about unrecognized.

But those reservations evaporated when she returned to her hotel and found a stack of letters from him.

My heart aches because you are not here, but it is full of joy and pride because you love me and have given me that supreme gift of love—your own dear wonderful delightful adorable self, the noblest, most satisfying, the most lovable woman in the world...

How could one resist such an outpouring? His love was so strong, almost overwhelmingly so, that Edith worried that she would eventually disappoint him when the fog of new attraction wore off and he saw her for the flawed mortal she was. He never compared her to Ellen, but surely Edith was in some way a substitute. A meager substitute for a wife who was by all accounts brilliant and completely devoted to him and their girls. But she also told herself, he had been wed to Ellen for over twenty years, apparently blissful years, with the one exception that Edith was aware of. Mary Peck.

The name was vaguely familiar to Edith, having something to do with an old friend of Ellen and Woodrow's. But it seemed there was a hush about it, Edith once overhearing Margaret saying to Woodrow as he sealed an envelope, "Another check for Mary Peck?" By Woodrow's grumble, Edith knew it was not an area to inquire about. If there was something she needed to know, surely Woodrow would share it with her in good time. In the meanwhile, she secretly relished the thought that his marriage to Ellen had been less than perfect.

The rest of the summer Edith spent in glorious visits all about New York State and New England. She and Woodrow wrote letters and sometimes telegrams to each other nearly every day, so Edith felt quite in touch. One letter in particular concerned her. Although she felt more confident in being his sounding board, she worried that he was a bit careless with his role in history.

He had sent her an envelope stuffed with correspondence from a friend, Walter Page, whom he had appointed ambassador to England. Woodrow asked her to tuck the letters away, if she liked, or send them back if they were in the way. He was still at the Summer White House in Cornish, but still, it seemed there should be a better way to handle this official correspondence.

Another sentence concerned her deeply.

It does not make me proud to think of myself as the (temporarily) beloved president of 100 million people of a great Nation, but it does make me proud to think of myself as the trusted lover of the sweet lady whom I adore.

Was this just part of his campaign to convince her to marry him sooner? His letters were filled with a thousand ways of saying he loved her. Edith secretly thought that if he had followed his truest ambition, he would be a writer of romance novels, and he would have been very successful. But alas, the great man had taken on great responsibilities. If she was to be the conduit for his literary needs, then she would accept it gratefully. Someday, history would need to see that a man consumed by responsibilities in a world being torn to bits by hatred and rivalry and lust for power still found the time to express love fully and deeply.

Once home, Edith had hardly unpacked her trunks when the phone jangled. She picked up the earpiece, and the operator connected her to Helen at the White House. The quiet crackle in the background reminded her that someone else was always listening.

"If you've had time to catch your breath, we are expecting you for dinner," Helen chirped cheerily.

Edith looked around her dusty home, sheets still covering the furniture and not a bit of food to be had in the kitchen. "Of course, but I would like to take out my electric after so much disuse. Would it be permissible for me to drive myself over?"

The crackle grew louder, and Edith would swear she heard a muffled giggle.

"What's that you say?" Helen's voice seemed farther than ten blocks away. "This is impossible. I'm going to ask Woodrow to put in a private line between us."

Good. She imagined Alexander Bell in New York heard Watson in San Francisco better than she could hear Helen.

"I'm going to drive over," Edith shouted into the mouthpiece. She hoped Altrude had charged the car as promised.

She arrived at the White House north gate at about 3:00 p.m., but no guard came out to greet her. Her quiet electric probably didn't alert them as did the foul-smelling gasoline engines. She climbed out of the car and yelled for attention, and just moments later Woodrow met her in the circular drive.

They immediately fell into each other's arms. The last few weeks having been much too long. She hadn't realized how much she had ached for him until he was once again with her in the flesh, not just a sweet letter from the post.

"My darling, I've missed you so." Woodrow still had a firm grip on her shoulders. "We were just about to send the car for you, and I was going to surprise you. But I'm happy you couldn't wait."

"That is true, but also my electric needed to stretch its legs."

"You realize electric automobiles aren't long for this world." He grinned. It had been a small point of contention between them. "Shall we walk the gardens? I should like to stretch my own legs."

They set out on a favorite path, where newly planted mums were just beginning to show their bright yellows and reds.

"My electric requires no cranking to start, is practically silent, and doesn't foul the air. All good points for a woman, or any driver."

"Ah, but you can't go above fourteen miles an hour and can barely leave the city before you run out of charge. Oh, and you're not keeping up. A fellow named Kettering has invented an electric starter for the internal combustion engine. You'll notice no crank on the new Pierce-Arrow."

"Your objections are highly exaggerated, but it's good to be back and arguing with you." She slipped her hand in his. Hopefully that wouldn't raise too many suspicions.

They had done a quick circle around the garden and were back at her car.

"We have some time before tea," Woodrow said. "Have you been to East Potomac Park? We can continue our argument, which I earnestly plan to win, there."

"I haven't. Is there something special there?"

"Hop back in your electric. It's a short drive to the streetcar, and if we're quick, we can dodge the Secret Service."

Edith climbed into the driver's seat after waiting a moment to see if Woodrow preferred to drive. Once he was aboard, she hit the throttle full-bore and laughed at his startled cry.

Having successfully escaped the grounds without alerting the security detail, she motored through the familiar streets. When she came to the intersection at South B Street, the traffic officer stopped all the other traffic to let them pass.

"Oh dear, I've been recognized," Woodrow said. Completely open, Edith's electric vehicle allowed no place to hide. He had already removed his eyeglasses and now pulled down his raggedy newsboy cap to further cover his face.

Edith laughed as she waved to the policeman standing on a wooden box, directing traffic from under a big sun umbrella. "No, you're safe. He knows me. Sweet man, always lets the lady driver through."

They drove around the Tidal Basin, where a few yellow leaves on the cherry trees announced the end of summer. They were known for their abundant pink blooms in the spring, but Edith enjoyed their colors and elegant forms at all times of the year. Past the trees, they reached a rather down-trodden neighborhood. They parked on a bumpy gravel street, then rode a streetcar over a small bridge to an island in the Potomac.

"It smells like river muck." Edith lifted her skirts to keep them from splashes of mud.

"Because that's what it is. The Army Corps of Engineers dredged the river and piled the silt here, creating this island." He spread his arms at the expanse of land. "Potomac Park, or Hains Point as some call it, is not nearly finished. But it has potential, lying as it does between the District and the Virginia side."

Edith sniffed the air. "Hmm, I detect something worse." She swatted a mosquito on her neck. "It's going to take quite a bit of time and money to make this habitable to human beings. Maybe it should be a nature preserve?"

"The city used the river for a sewer outlet for decades. That's all cleaned up now, but you're smelling the marsh we're steadily filling in. We need to dream of its best use. Take your mind off the bugs and stench, and imagine what it could be." He pointed across the river. "Just look at this view. The city is already planning for a park and envisions a neighborhood where children will play in the shade of elm trees, while their dads work just a quick streetcar ride away. Or a shopping village, where fishermen can unload their boats at the brand-new wharf, and fresh produce arrives over a bridge from Virginia or Maryland."

"The view and location are spectacular. And I suppose with enough vegetation the stench will dissipate, and the birds will come and take care of the bugs." She swatted another biting insect. Somehow, they didn't seem to bother Woodrow, who strolled along wide-eyed in his vision for the place.

"Let's go over to the other side." They crossed the streetcar tracks to the side facing Virginia where they could see workers in a field. "The city has been coordinating with the army, and they've been planting trees and flowers. Tens of thousands of them."

As they walked, and the landscape changed from stinky mud to a verdant paradise, Edith began to understand his point. "No, I don't think a neighborhood is the right thing. It would be enjoyed by too few. A sanctuary, yes, but not just for animals. I think the land should be preserved as a public park, for all to use. Both residents, and visitors to the Capital."

After another quick ride on the streetcar, they arrived back at her parked car.

"We're a good team," Edith said. "Your brains and my common sense."

"Indeed." He pulled her close for a quick kiss. "It's time to head back. The rest of the clan awaits you."

"Would you like to drive? You know I don't let just anybody..."

"Could I?" He sounded like a kid wanting a ride on a roller coaster. He jumped into the driver's seat and stared at the dashboard.

Emily got in the passenger side and pressed the starter button. He fiddled with the steering stick and throttle and stared at the floorboard. "Enlighten me."

Edith pointed out the brake and other equipment.

"What, no clutch?"

"This is why electrics are superior," Edith boasted.

He hit the throttle full on, then proceeded to whirl them around with no thought to the gravel road. Edith grabbed her hat with one hand and the door handle with the other.

After a few minutes of erratic driving, she yelled, "Who taught you how to drive?"

He laughed, "Why you did, just now!" He whooped and laughed, while Edith prayed for survival.

When they returned to the White House (with Edith driving, thankfully), Woodrow had to excuse himself to attend an important meeting with the secretary of war. Edith joined Helen, Margaret, and Altrude, who were having cocktails in the upstairs oval room.

They joyfully greeted her, but Edith sensed an undercurrent of worry in their sidelong glances. "Have I missed something?" she asked.

They looked at each other again, some mystery passing between them.

"You tell her," Helen said to Margaret. "You're his daughter and closest relation."

This made Edith's heart skip a beat. "What? Oh dear, is it Woodrow? He seems to be fine..."

The women raised their eyebrows and exchanged glances. Of course, no one knew about their little island escape.

"He's fine," Helen soothed. "It's just..."

"He's not fine," Margaret interrupted. "Do you know what he's been like since he came back from Harlakenden without you? A lost soul, that's what. He roams around here like a puppy who has lost his master. He barely eats and, by the look of him, can hardly afford to miss a meal."

It was Altrude's turn to pile on. "I'm afraid Margaret's right. His secretary told me that he spends so much time writing to you and mooning for you that he hardly gets a wink of work out of him."

"Well, surely that's an exaggeration on Tumulty's part." Margaret came to her father's defense. "But I firmly believe, and I know these ladies agree with me, that the fault lies squarely with you."

"Me?" Edith sat up straighter in protest. In doing so, she noted her low boots were quite soiled from her escape with Woodrow. Whisked quickly inside by the staff in order to keep on schedule, she hadn't had a chance to wipe them off. She tucked her feet back under the armchair as far as she could. "What have I done, except love him and try to make him happy whenever I am with him?"

Her attempt didn't fool Margaret. She pointed toward Edith's shoes. "If you were here with him, and not traipsing about Lord knows where, he wouldn't be so lonely and distracted. Really, it's becoming a matter of national importance. Don't you care about our country?"

Altrude chimed in, the gang of three united against Edith. "While I understand how consuming a new love can be, you do have to consider the one hundred million or so Americans he leads. Not to mention all of us who have to witness your dopey long faces."

Good God. As Edith considered how to answer such a charge, Woodrow stepped through the door. She popped up and rushed over to him, his arms outstretched for her. She could see that the meeting with the war secretary had not gone well, his eyes distant and clouded with concern.

She tried to ease his mood. "Are you not happy to see me, darling? You would make a terrible poker player, with that long face."

He acknowledged the other women with a nod and a curt "Ladies," then turned back to Edith. "Quite the contrary. Knowing you were here waiting for me helped immensely, as the bad news from abroad continues to mount. I'm sorry to say I now believe it inevitable that we will be drawn into the war in Europe. It's only a matter of how long we can put it off."

A butler in a white jacket entered to announce dinner.

"How long do you think we can? Put the war off, that is," Helen asked as Woodrow escorted them down the hall.

"I don't have an answer for that," Woodrow said. "But I can say that we must have a solid relationship with Mexico first. We can't have whatever faction gains control of a bordering nation to be on the side of the Central Powers."

Edith could see why the others were concerned. He was a different man than he had been even that afternoon on the island. His broad shoulders slumped, the weight of the world fully upon them.

She thought about what he had said, about them making a good team. At that moment, he squeezed her hand as they walked, as if he were reading her thoughts. It came to her then, in a blinding flash that nearly took her breath away. What was the point of waiting for an election, for after a "proper mourning time"? Why delay when she knew in her heart she most wanted to be at Woodrow's side always, not just his companion at dinner or guest during his travels. Every moment she could share with him was precious.

Suddenly, she felt lighter on her feet, and a smile crept across her face. She squeezed his hand back, just as the doors opened to the elegant dining room, candles blazing and a trio of string musicians playing soft music. He no longer had to wait for his *little dream girl*. She was already here.

SIX

After dinner, Helen, Woodrow, and Edith piled into the Pierce-Arrow for a drive, with Margaret begging off. They motored along one of their favorite routes, down Pennsylvania Avenue toward the park, then out Conduit Road to the Canal Road. Edith loved the drive along the Potomac, the mighty river sometimes hiding behind the shade trees, then coming around a bend providing a magnificent view.

A couple of young boys always seemed to be waiting for them at a certain corner. As the car approached, they would raise the nation's flag, stand at attention, and salute. This time, the Secret Service agent signaled the driver to slow down, and the passengers waved to the boys, who jumped with glee.

Edith wondered how to bring up her decision and hoped the sweet scene provided the right moment. She didn't mind that Helen was there, sitting in one of the chairs in the middle of the vehicle. She had been there all along in their relationship and would certainly be pleased. But the conversation swiftly returned to the torpedoing of the *Arabic*, another British liner with Americans on board, yet another step toward war.

"They will try to find excuses," Woodrow said. "But how much more can we tolerate? The ship was headed to New York, so obviously they can't claim we were sending arms to the belligerents."

"Oh, the papers have been full of stories about the German spies," Helen said. "Is it true they have been paying to influence our newspapers and motion pictures, infiltrating our factories, and trying to cause labor strikes?"

"I'm afraid so." Woodrow glumly looked out the window. "I wonder how soon the leaves will be falling?"

That seemed to end all conversation, with Edith lost in her own thoughts. They were passing through Rock Creek Park, nearly back to Edith's home, and she despaired at not having had the right time to tell him of her change of heart.

As if Woodrow were reading her mind, he suddenly grabbed her hand and said, "Little girl, I have no right to ask you to help me by sharing this load that is almost breaking my back, for I know your nature and you might do it out of sheer pity."

Edith, thrilled at the perfect opening, wrapped her arms around his neck. "Well, if you won't ask me, I will volunteer and be ready to be mustered in as soon as possible."

He pushed her away and looked straight into her eyes. "Do you mean, could you possibly mean...before the election?"

Edith nodded and Helen jumped from her chair and whooped, circling both of them in her arms. The driver, apparently hearing all the excitement, turned up a park road instead of heading toward Edith's street.

The next morning, Edith awoke with a sense of serenity like never before. The first thing she wanted to do was call Altrude with the news. She, as well as Helen, had been such an important part of Edith finding Woodrow that she deserved to be amongst the first to know.

Still in her nightgown, Edith hurried to the drawing room, where her telephone had been installed on its own little table, with its ring box hidden in a drawer. But a surprise awaited. Sitting next to her candlestick telephone, another rather bulky one sat, its earpiece and mouthpiece together in a horn shape, resting horizontal on a cradle.

Next to it was the familiar creamy envelope with her name written on it in Woodrow's elegant script.

My darling,

I hope you don't mind a bit of subterfuge. This line will connect you directly with the Residence. I am awaiting your call.

WW

Edith remembered Helen mentioning a private line but thought she had talked them out of it as too highfalutin for her sensibilities. Well, he could just wait, because she was determined to ring Altrude at that moment.

After the exciting call, something crashed into the big square window at the front of the room, thankfully without breaking it. The house was rather close to the street, and her first thought was that a tire had kicked up a stone. She opened the front door and saw a fist-sized rock on the ground, with a slip of paper tied around it.

Odd, she thought. She looked around, but no one was to be seen. She fetched it, despite her not being dressed for the day. Unwrapping the note, she read:

We know what you did.

Following that cryptic message was a crude drawing of a skull and crossbones.

Edith had no idea what the message referred to, or who sent it. Or even if it was truly meant for her. Her townhouse was one of many just like it along a busy street.

She had put off calling Woodrow, and now she wished she had called him before this discovery, for she was loath to tell him about it. For certain, it would speed up the inevitability of Secret Service intrusion into her life. She tossed the stone and tore up the note. There was no harm done to herself or the window. No one need know.

Wedding plans began in earnest, and Edith fought off all attempts for a showy White House wedding. She told Helen, "Only one president has married in the White House, so let's keep it that way. I want a simple affair, just my brothers and sisters, Woodrow's girls and their husbands and, of course, you and Cary and Altrude."

"What about Tumulty? And Colonel House and Marshall?" Helen replied, referring to the president's secretary, a longtime advisor, and the vice president.

"Tumulty if we must. But Marshall is a figurehead, not a friend. And not even a very good one at that. We have to draw the line somewhere, and it leaves him and Colonel House on the other side." House was an odd little man, who somehow made Edith uncomfortable with his mere presence.

Word got out quickly, even though they had yet to announce the engagement to the press. Edith heard through the grapevine of the grumbling of various members of Congress and their hangers-on. Ellen had been well beloved, and people didn't take too kindly to such an early remarriage. But Edith stood by her plan and so was not surprised she received a letter from Woodrow with an urgent request:

Dearest,

There is something personal to myself that I feel I must tell you about at once, and I am going to take the extraordinary liberty of asking if I may come to your house this evening…

She quickly wrote back saying that of course he could come see her but requested he come with Dr. Grayson for appearance's sake.

When Woodrow showed up at her door, he didn't greet her with his usual enthusiastic embrace.

Edith tried to make light of his scowl. "You look like someone stole your porridge."

Woodrow smiled weakly, which told her that at least no one had died. Grayson asked to be excused and hurried back out to the motor, which didn't ease Edith's mind. She invited Woodrow into the drawing room, where he hemmed and hawed and fidgeted, repeating how much he loved her, until she finally barked, "What is it already?"

He twirled the shot glass of bourbon she had given him. "I've had some dreadful news."

Her heart sunk. "Is it the war?" It would have to be very bad news indeed for Woodrow to be acting so strangely.

"No, this is of a personal nature. I want to tell you myself, before the whole embarrassing thing gets sprawled all over the papers."

Edith poured herself some bourbon to steady her nerves and sat next to him. "What is it then? But first, are you unwell?"

"Unwell? No, not physically. But something has come up. Something from my past has reared its ugly head, and I wish you to be fully informed." He stared into the fireplace, although no fire was burning.

"During my marriage to Ellen, I had a transgression. Blessedly brief, but utterly inappropriate. Ellen, who I must assure you was faultless in all this, was suffering from one of her prolonged dark periods. There was nothing I could do to help her find a ray of happiness, and I found myself sinking into despair and abject loneliness myself. At the same time, I had been humiliated in my attempts to reform Princeton into the tower of excellence that I knew it could be. So I proposed we take a holiday in Bermuda, but Ellen refused, and the girls would not leave her.

"So, in order to preserve my own sanity, I went to Bermuda alone. There I met a woman who delighted in my company. We had many, many long conversations, and my spirits began to lift. Once I had some perspective and energy, the demons of darkness left my brain."

"This woman was Mary Peck? I have heard Margaret mention her."

He nodded. "We came to be close friends, writing letters of encouragement, and more, for quite some time. I visited her in Bermuda several times and also met her in New York. Sometimes with Ellen, sometimes not."

"Tell me about the 'not.'"

He let out a groan and rubbed his face. Her maid, Rebecca, appeared to light the fire, but Edith shook her head and Rebecca tiptoed away. Edith lit the fire herself, more for something to do with her hands than the heat it might generate, while she waited for words she desperately did not want to hear.

The firelight flickered upon Woodrow's face, his eyes hollow and vacant. "Our actual times together were brief, and over the span of just a few months. But we wrote many letters over several years, expressing our mutual admiration. Letters that had no place, no moral excuse to be written by a man married to another. I'm afraid I led the poor woman to believe a fairy tale, and I've tried to make up for it by offering financial and other support."

"Did Ellen know about this?" Edith couldn't bear the hurt it would have caused the poor sad woman.

"Eventually, yes. When she was well enough, I told her everything. She forgave what she had no reason to forgive, and continued to love and support me until her dying day."

"And now? You decided I needed to know this because of our engagement?"

He coughed and cleared his throat. "In all honesty, no. It was put out of my mind years ago. I assumed you had heard a bit about it when the Republicans tried to make something of it in the campaign."

She shook her head. "I didn't pay that close attention."

"Well good, because it was just nasty gossip. Teddy Roosevelt himself quashed the rumors, asking how someone who looked like a drugstore clerk could possibly be that romantic." He gave a rueful laugh.

Edith saw through his attempt to make light of it. "What happened was ages ago, and I won't judge you now for it. But do tell, what has this got to do with me?"

He downed the last of his bourbon. "I've been advised by reliable sources that Mrs. Peck is incensed over our engagement. Although allow me to reassure you that I have not made her any promises. It seems she is threatening to release her collection of my letters to the press if we proceed with our marriage."

"Why, that's blackmail." Edith thought of her own concerns regarding Woodrow's florid love letters. "Are we going to allow her to do that?"

"I don't care one whit about it for myself. I will take the blame, the humiliation, all of it. And if it ruins my chances of reelection, if indeed I decide to run, then so be it. You should know me better than to think I would kowtow to such an act."

"I see." Edith's mind whirled. Was she engaged to an untrustworthy man?

"But I have no right to ask you to be dragged along in the mud with me.

As a gentleman, I cannot ask you to pay for my mistake." His voice broke. "Therefore, I release you of your promise to marry me."

That was a direct punch to her gut. She was dying to reassure him of her love and understanding, but at the same time she wanted to escape it all. It was already becoming overwhelming, and they weren't even publicly engaged yet.

Edith's eyes welled up and her vision narrowed as if all the air had been sucked out of the room. Woodrow didn't trust her love. Or he was seeking a way out. She searched her pocket for a handkerchief and, finding none, wiped her tears on her sleeve.

Woodrow offered his handkerchief, a dark-blue W monogram against the bright-white cloth. "I'm sorry to shock you with this news. If there was any way under the sun to undo the foolishness, I would. My only goal was to bring happiness into your life, and here I have cast a shadow on it instead. Tell me it is done, and I will not darken your door again."

How could he think that? He had brought only light and joy into her life. Still bewildered by it all, she feared saying anything impulsively. The worst part of it was not some improper relationship with Mary Peck. Indeed, she had already accepted that, and actually welcomed the evidence that he and Ellen were less than the perfect souls everyone pretended they were.

No, the worst was that he was so willing to give up on their own relationship, that he had pursued mightily for months, because of some gossip. Would marriage to him be a roller coaster of highs and lows, dictated by the whims of outsiders? She needed time to think. "It's late. Go, and I will write."

He nodded and stepped toward the door, then stopped. As if sensing her quandary, while doing little to abate it, he said, "Please understand. My feelings for you haven't changed. Only my worthiness in your own eyes."

Edith paced about her home like a tiger caged in a zoo. Several times she went to the telephone to call her mother or her sister Bertha, who had recently moved to town to live with their mother. Surely they would come by even at the late hour, nearly 10:00 p.m.

But she realized it wouldn't help her to sort things out by talking to them and would require revealing things that were better left unsaid. She tried to organize the thoughts running riot in her brain. Did she love Woodrow unconditionally? Yes.

Was his long-ago emotional affair a reason to call off their engagement? It seemed Ellen hadn't walked away, so why should Edith?

Was he less than the honorable man she thought he was? Again, yes, but flaws were human.

Did she trust him? This was the question that gave her the most pause. The leopard doesn't change its spots, her mother had often told her. Would he do it again? Was this something that was tolerated, perhaps even mutual in his previous marriage? Her gut told her no.

The rest she could work out with him before the wedding, if there was one. But what about the big ugly thing, the elephant in the room that he had hardly mentioned and too easily dismissed? She had the opportunity to end the blackmail now, before his reelection was threatened. Maybe she owed that to him. They could end the engagement and thwart the release of the letters and his resulting humiliation. His presidency hung in the balance, and, with it, the fate of the nation, and other nations as well.

Hours went by, and still there seemed to be no right answer. All energy drained from her, she flopped into her favorite armchair. A photograph of Woodrow in an oval frame sat on the small table next to her. She picked it up and studied his sweet face. "My darling, how like you to be more concerned with my sensibilities than your own future. But it's not just our future to consider."

Edith closed her eyes and let tears run down her cheeks. Should she give in to politics? Was the threat of scandal enough to send them scurrying into hiding like rats in a cellar? If it worked this time, what would prevent them from doing it again, using the power of gossip and opinion to sway elections? If she did not stand by him, what did that say about her?

No! she thought, a weight lifting from her chest. She wouldn't allow blackmail to succeed. Their love, their lives were more than a position, even if that position was the highest in the land. And that was all that mattered. Energized, she went to her desk, lit the lamp, and wrote what her heart had been screaming all along.

September 19, 1915

Dearest—

The dawn has come, and the hideous dark of the hour before the dawn has been lost in the gracious gift of light. I have been in the big chair by the window, where I have fought out so many problems, and all the hurt, selfish feeling has gone with the darkness and now I can see straight—straight into the heart of things and am ready to follow the road where love leads.

How many times I have told you I wanted to help, and now when the first test has come, I faltered. But the faltering was for love, not lack of love. I am not afraid of any gossip or threat, with your love as my shield. And even now this room echoes with your voice, as you plead, 'Stand by me!'

This is my pledge, dearest one. I will stand by you—not for duty, not for pity, not for honor—but for love—trusting, protecting, comprehending love. And no matter whether the wine be bitter or sweet we will share it together and find happiness in the comradeship.

I am so tired I could put my head down on the desk and sleep, but nothing could bring me rest until I had pledged my eternal love and allegiance.

Your own

Edith

She sent the letter by messenger so Woodrow would receive it that very morning. Unsure of how he would react—wondering if the truth was that he desired to end their engagement—she tried to go about her normal routine.

Helen and Margaret were both out of town, so the next day there were no visits from them to soothe her shaken nerves. Probably just as well, as they undoubtedly would have pulled away in embarrassment.

Edith took out her electric and motored to Rock Creek Park. She parked in her usual place and set out for a stroll. Happy couples walked their dogs; children splashed in the creek. The canopy of massive oak and elm trees cast a welcome shade over the trails, as if protecting her from the harsh world.

A jagged stone on the path reminded her of the rock thrown through her window. Was there more to that than she had thought? She had been happy and fulfilled before she ever laid eyes on Woodrow. She would be happy again.

SEVEN

A few days later, Edith had still not heard back from Woodrow. Although still not over the hurt and sorrow, she started making plans. She dragged out the travel maps and brochures and was listing places to visit when the doorbell rang.

Rebecca let in Dr. Grayson, appearing much as he had several nights before, his face drawn with worry.

Every muscle in Edith's body tensed, but she feigned serenity. "To what do I have the pleasure this morning?"

"Please come with me. The president is in a bad way. He looks like I imagine the martyrs looked when they were broken on the wheel."

She felt like someone had slapped her in the face. He was too ill to answer? Why hadn't she considered this? Did he not trust her love? Would seeing him make things worse? Her own words echoed in her ears: *I will stand by.*

"Of course." She stepped out, slamming the door behind her without so much as grabbing her hat. They climbed in the black staff motorcar. "What exactly is the problem? When did he take ill?"

"Some type of nervous exhaustion, I fear. Other than his usual high blood pressure, I find nothing physically wrong. But he is broken, just the same. He can't sleep, pacing the halls at all hours. He hasn't eaten for days, and we are truly worried." He patted Edith's hand. "I can only hope that a visit from you will give us some answers."

"But what if I am the problem?" She thought back upon the words in her letter of response. Could it have been misinterpreted?

"Mrs. Galt, I believe you are the problem, but not in the way you think."

At the White House, Grayson rushed to the elevator, with Edith making haste to keep up. He led her to a room on the second floor that she had never before entered.

The room was dark, the heavy drapes pulled across the windows. A lone candle flickered next to a four-poster bed, where Woodrow lay, pale and unmoving. She ran to his bedside, and he held out his hand to her. His fingers were icy cold in her grasp. She thought they felt like death.

"Oh my poor darling, whatever is wrong?" She nodded to the valet, who stepped out, leaving them alone in the room.

"You have come like an angel in the night."

It was midmorning. Was he being poetic, or was he confused?

"Did you receive my letter?"

"Yes, my love." His hand started to warm in hers, but he offered no cause for his distress. She sat silently by him, as he fell peacefully to sleep.

But as he slept, the warnings sounded by Cary, Margaret, Helen, Altrude, and Tumulty tumbled through her head. Who was this person, this dear but complicated person to whom she was engaged? So steady and strong on the outside, traits that drew him to her, yet possessing a strange fragility, a dependence on romantic love, that she found unattractive. It was far too late to back out of her promise to marry him. But perhaps not too late to postpone the wedding until after the election.

It was clear now that he had every intention of running, potential blackmail be damned. The passing remark he had made questioning whether he would or not now seemed a test of her support. In her mind—for many reasons—his chances of winning were somewhat less if he married her sooner. But was that a bad thing? The polls and pundits were saying his chances of winning were slim and getting slimmer. Selfishly speaking, it would be a relief to get back to some semblance of a normal life, and undoubtedly better for Woodrow's health.

There was one more thing. If they married, then he lost the campaign, his family and all those closest to him would blame her and their rushed marriage. Maybe even Woodrow would console himself that he chose love over his position. And offering herself as a scapegoat might be the best thing she could do for him.

He snorted in his slumber but didn't awaken. She kissed his cheek, then tiptoed out of the room. There would be no more dithering. It was time to marry the romantic old sod.

After several days of rest and rides in the fresh air, Woodrow returned to his usual duties, and they planned the official announcement of their upcoming nuptials.

"There is no going back at this point," he warned Edith. "Your private life will end."

"All the better," she responded. "At least we can see each other whenever and wherever we choose, instead of sneaking around like lovesick teeners."

Indeed, after the press was informed, unexpected visitors flocked to her home. The postman dumped canvas sacks full of correspondence at her door. She had no time to go through all of them, but a few were concerning. Several anonymous letters threatened to go to the press with evidence that she and Woodrow had plotted to kill Ellen. One contained the same ominous words as the note wrapped around the rock thrown at her window: "We know what you did."

She debated whether to tell Woodrow or Tumulty but decided that would be just what the miscreants wanted. Not to mention that they would insist on stationing Secret Service men at her residence. Let the troublemakers go to the press, she decided. There was nothing to the story, so nothing could come of it.

Her telephone rang incessantly, and people and gifts showed up at her home uninvited. A few days after the engagement had been announced in the press, a rather large gentleman appeared at her door, then barged in past Rebecca. He was someone Edith barely knew and didn't care for. He proceeded to envelop her in a bear hug and plant a slobbery kiss on her cheek. He told her how he always knew she'd do something big and expressed how very excited he and his wife would be to attend the wedding.

Shaken from that incident, Edith retired to her upstairs sitting room for some short-lived peace. Rebecca soon appeared, holding a tiny brown puppy in her hands. Much too young to be away from its mother, it mewled pitifully. A red, white, and blue ribbon around its neck proclaimed its name to be *America.*

"Please return it with my regrets," Edith told Rebecca with a sigh. She would have Tumulty plead with the public not to send gifts and to respect her privacy.

She was beginning to understand Woodrow's request to keep the engagement short. The White House was much better equipped to handle the public's need for contact. Dolley Madison might have fled the burning White House for safety, but to Edith it meant protection. And a shared life with her beloved at last.

EIGHT

E dith and Woodrow both loved baseball. They followed the season in the sports pages and argued over who was the best player. Edith favored Ty Cobb, who racked up the batting titles every year, while Woodrow liked Shoeless Joe Jackson, a perpetual runner-up.

"You have to consider the whole game, not just batting averages," he insisted. "Extra bases, outfield saves…"

"Oh, you just like Shoeless because he's a poor Southerner," Edith teased.

"Cobb's from Georgia, so your argument doesn't hold water. And Shoeless doesn't go around beating up defenseless fans like your boy Cobb."

The day their engagement was announced by the press, Woodrow had a surprise for her. Just after dinner, they retired to his study, where Edith expected he would check the Drawer. But instead, he motioned to the two leather wingback chairs for them to have a chat.

"I hope you don't have plans tomorrow, because we're off to Philadelphia for the World Series."

She clapped her hands and squealed like a little girl.

"That's not all. I get to throw out the first pitch! The first president to do so in a World Series game. I've already asked your mother, and she is keen to go, so what say you?"

"I say, 'Buy me some peanuts and Cracker Jack.'"

The whole trip was like a dream. Edith's mother seemed to thoroughly enjoy the adventure.

When Boston pulled ahead, the crowd bleated like sheep.

Edith asked, "What is that about?"

Woodrow laughed. "Baker, the owner, is so thrifty that he brings out sheep to mow the grass."

They could only watch a few innings before they had to head back to Washington, much to their chagrin. Woodrow stage-whispered to Sallie, "Best to slip out now. Not looking good for the home team."

Edith bit her tongue. Those were her exact feelings about the next year's election. But she smiled and waved to the crowd as they slipped down the rows of bleachers.

On a morning early in November, Edith heard her phone jangle while she was still upstairs. She could tell from the bells that it was the White House line. As she hurried downstairs to answer, Rebecca tried to stop her.

"Lord have mercy, Mrs. Galt, let me answer it before you tumble oxtail over apple cart."

Despite the warning, Edith reached the telephone first.

"Cheerio," Margaret fairly shouted in Edith's ear. "Can you come for dinner this eve?"

The telephone emphasized Margaret's patrician tone and the cadence of her speech, and indeed that of Woodrow and all the sisters. Although it was tempting to answer in kind, Edith replied in her soft Virginia drawl, "I'd be delighted, Miss Wilson."

That evening at the White House, Edith was surprised to find the study had been set up as a recording studio. Several technicians from Columbia Records had filled the room with many trunks of equipment— microphones, electrical cables, and other paraphernalia Edith had no hope of understanding.

She took a seat, and upon a hand signal from one of the men, Margaret sang "The Star-Spangled Banner." Woodrow quietly stepped in during the session and stood behind Edith's chair.

Once the song was done and the gentlemen had packed up, Margaret explained. "It's for the American Red Cross. I'm donating a portion of my royalty from every record sold. And there's more to come," she enthused. "Columbia wants to sign me for a whole series of patriotic tunes!"

"How exciting," Edith proclaimed. She looked at the president, who was beaming at his daughter. But the proposal troubled her. She set her lips, wondering if she should say something and risk upsetting her future stepdaughter. But her first duty was to her husband-to-be, she decided. And if there was even a remote possibility that something could hurt him, it was her duty to say her piece.

When the Columbia men left, it was just the three of them. This was the moment to say something.

"Shall we head into the dining room?" Woodrow offered his hand to Edith, still sitting on the chair.

"Please, if I can have a moment between just us." Edith fingered the strands of pearls at her neck. Their warm, smooth texture always calmed her nerves.

"Of course." Woodrow pulled up chairs for himself and Margaret, who seemed to be eyeing Edith with suspicion.

"Did you not enjoy my performance? Perhaps it was a little rushed and breathless? We recorded it in New York. This was just for backup…"

"It was perfect," Edith reassured her, even though she felt the high notes were a little thin. "It's just that, I wonder…" She looked at Woodrow, who was ever so slightly shaking his head. She decided on a different tack. "You see, my own father was a judge, so I'm not entirely without experience in public service. And there were certain things we couldn't do or couldn't say because of it."

"I'm not sure I follow you. What things?" Margaret pulled on the sleeves of her plain black dress. She had Woodrow's strong facial features, but without the attractive softening of them as did her sister Jessie.

"We treated all the servants kindly, of course. But should one fail at his job, we couldn't just replace him. We had to provide a large sum before sending him on his way. And should my brothers want to enroll in an exclusive school, my parents were careful to step away from any admission decision. Although my family lost its livelihood in farming in the war, we took in dozens of relations and cared for them their entire lives. I sewed my own clothes since I was a mere girl and took care of my grandmother instead of going to school. Indeed, I still support my mother and two sisters from my own earnings."

"Well, that's all admirable, but I fail to see what that has to do with me."

"It wasn't just a matter of giving to the less fortunate. My parents sacrificed their own well-being in order not to be seen as getting favors due to his position."

Margaret just blinked, while Woodrow steepled his fingers.

"Do you have some advice, dearest?" Woodrow said.

"I think selling your records for profit may appear to be taking advantage of your father's position." It was a relief to say it.

"But I'm donating to the American Red Cross!"

"One hundred percent?" Edith asked, knowing the answer.

Margaret popped out of her chair. "Of course not. This is my profession. I expect to be paid, as is my father. I have worked hard and trained all my life for this, and you expect me to give it all away?" Margaret's voice reached a shrillness that caused even Woodrow to cringe. "I'm a single woman, with no man to support me."

"Nonsense. You have a trust..." Woodrow started to defend the family honor, but his mouth snapped shut at Margaret's glare.

"We know that, dear. But the perception will be..." Edith kept her calm.

"The hell with perception. I have rights. But wait, no I don't." Margaret glared at Woodrow. "The two of you don't even support suffrage, so of course you don't think a woman should be able to earn a living. She should stay home and raise babies."

Woodrow finally chimed in. "Now that's not fair. You know very well my belief in the states' right to decide. Powers not expressly given to the federal government..."

Edith broke in, fearing she had pitted father against daughter. "And I fear the dissolution of the family, which is the essential human construct. Should women be drafted into war with the men? Who will raise the children when they are forced to hold jobs outside the home?"

"You're on the wrong side of this argument." Margaret paced back and forth in front of them like a caged tiger. "The Founding Fathers called for equality for all, meaning men and women, but we need an amendment to clarify this intention. Without the vote nationally, women will forever be second-class citizens."

She looked squarely at Edith. "The draft? The breakup of families and forced work outside the home? How does voting necessitate that? Right now, women could be drafted and wouldn't be able to say beans about it. This is about choice. This is about a voice. This is about being treated like equal human beings, not some belonging of a man. The ability to buy property in their own names. Good God, I can't believe I have to explain this to you."

Margaret stopped her pacing in front of them. "I have given up plenty due to my father's service. Why, he gave away my beloved grand piano because it doesn't fit in any of these rooms." She glared at Woodrow, who winced.

His expression didn't go unnoticed by Margaret. She lowered her voice. "But I guess I somewhat see your point. I was chosen to perform patriotic songs due to Father's position." She paused thoughtfully. "I will decline any funds for these performances and give them all to the Red Cross, under one condition."

Edith and Woodrow exchanged a glance and waited expectantly.

"That is, that you rethink your position on suffrage. The Democrats were on the wrong side of slavery, but the Republicans have derailed suffrage time and time again. It's time for Democrats to be on the right side of history, and it's up to you."

"Well said." Woodrow rose from his chair and again held out his hand to Edith. "I think we can agree to think it over, can't we, dear?"

Edith looked from father to daughter, who were all smiles now. As they headed toward the family dining room, Woodrow's arm slung across Margaret's shoulders, Edith marveled at how quickly any disagreeableness faded. They laughed and joked as if they had just returned from a vaudeville performance. If she had spoken to her own parents like that, there would have been months, if not years, of resentment for the umbrage, even if they finally agreed she was right.

Edith breathed more easily, relieved that voicing her concern seemed to have been accepted, if not exactly welcomed, by them. As she walked hand in hand with him, she was awash with certainty that everything she did, every decision she made from that moment forward, would be in his best interest.

❧

By mid-November, wedding planning began in earnest. No invitations were sent out, as Edith was determined to have only the closest family members and friends present and her home had only enough space for twenty or so guests.

Helen arrived and Edith began selling her on the idea of the wedding in her home. "Jessie and Nell were married at the White House, and that is how it should be. But somehow, for the president himself to be married there seems wrong. A big, glorious wedding is for first marriages of the young. And with Ellen still so recently departed, it seems a little disrespectful."

"No use being bothered about things like that now." Helen gave a wry smile. "You shouldn't be sneaking in under the cover of night. You will be the rightful First Lady, and the sooner all accept that, the better. Although I adore your home, darling, you don't have to get married in the East Room. The Blue Room is a more intimate space, or perhaps outdoors in the Rose Garden? Think of it, maybe in April when the world is beginning to bloom again."

"My biggest concern is there would be no end to the demand for invitations with the availability of such a grand space, and I want this moment to be shared with those we hold most dear."

There was no way Edith would be married in the garden the first Mrs. Wilson had designed. She'd never admit her pettiness, but growing up in a family of nine children, she had learned to rebel in tiny ways. "Hmm. About that. Your cousin and I will not be waiting until spring. You can be the first to know. We'll be marrying before Christmas."

Helen's eyes widened. "But that's less than a month away. No matter, I'm thrilled with any way and any place you choose, just as long as you marry that poor dear fellow." She circled the drawing room. "Yes, the preacher here, in front of the fireplace. The guests may have to stand. Oh, flowers here, and of course we can have a lovely dinner in the dining room."

"Rebecca can help, and I have another..."

"Nonsense. Please allow me to take all the decorating and entertaining off your hands."

"But—"

"Tut-tut, not another word. It is done." Helen plopped on the couch and patted the spot next to her for Edith to join her. "I've been meaning to tell you, I'm delighted to see Cousin Woodrow enjoying life again, and it's all due to you."

"Why, thank you. He means everything to me."

Helen lowered her eyes. "There are moments when I see the old Woodrow again."

"You mean how he was before Ellen passed? I do wish I had known them then."

"No, dear. I mean before his first episode. Back in Princeton." She looked up at Edith. "You know about this, don't you? I don't wish to speak out of turn."

Edith searched her mind for a clue of what she referred to, but Helen proceeded anyway.

"He wasn't the same after that. Oh, the physical problems, the blindness in one eye, the use of his right hand, those symptoms improved in a short while, but his personality changed. As might be expected with a scare like that."

"Changed how, exactly?" Edith breathed slowly and deeply, to disguise the panic her body wanted to betray. "What do you mean, 'first episode'? How many have there been?"

"He was always a pleasant fellow, and of course that hasn't changed. And prone to dark periods now and then. But sometime after his little stroke, I noticed he was more driven. He paid less attention to Ellen and the girls, and more with every mover and shaker he could find."

"Isn't that a normal progression for a career in academia?" Edith's muscles began to relax.

"I'm sure you're right. But still, there were more episodes, and each time he was a little different after. More stubborn. More talking, less listening. Quick to judge, and that whole Mary Peck thing..." Helen stopped and looked at Edith with something like fear in her eyes. "Oh, you mustn't tell a soul about this."

"Of course. Thank you for sharing, but you can stop worrying. Cousin Woodrow will be in my loving hands and Dr. Grayson's care." She would have to speak to Dr. Grayson about this. But how could she without betraying Helen's confidence? Her mind pictured Woodrow sleeping so peacefully, after she was so urgently summoned to his bedside. The roller coaster of highs and lows, of occasional irrationality that seemed so foreign to his personality, had some physical explanation. But what did Mary Peck have to do with this? She considered asking Helen, but that was such a sore topic that she didn't want to bring it up.

Even more reason to hope he'd reconsider running for reelection, or even lose. How did one have a "little stroke"? It had something to do with his blood pressure that Cary was always fussing over. "Exercise and rest" was his mantra. She had vowed to herself to protect Woodrow, and she would learn all she could from the doctor, or do her own research in the library if need be.

The opportunity came when Cary arrived at her home to administer a new vaccine for whooping cough. As he prepared the needle, she said, "Doctor, is this really necessary? With eight brothers and sisters, I'm sure I had it in childhood."

"Can you document that? It wasn't common in that part of Virginia then, and it is now."

"I can't. Mother doesn't know." She sighed and rolled up her sleeve.

"You will be around the president's grandchildren. You don't want to risk exposing them when a simple little shot could protect both you and them, do you?"

"Will the president be taking it as well?"

"Of course, he has already."

Within seconds, the shot was done. Edith pulled down her sleeve and tip-toed into another subject with a little white lie. "How is his blood pressure? He wants me to stay on top of these things. No more...um...episodes?"

Grayson looked at her curiously. "Fit as a fiddle."

"Is there anything I should be looking for, or doing, to keep him healthy?"

Grayson packed his vials and the syringe into his black leather bag. "I'll be on top of measuring his blood pressure, so don't worry about that.

If it starts to rise too high, we'll have to keep him as quiet as possible. Meanwhile, he needs his daily exercise. Perhaps you can become his golfing partner? The fresh air and walking are a tremendous help, and he's probably tired of seeing my old face out there."

"That's a splendid idea. I'll learn the game right away. Although he might become very impatient with such a beginner."

"Ha, not to worry; he's not that good. Rarely breaks a hundred. But don't tell him I said so." He winked.

"Not to worry yourself. I don't know what breaking a hundred means anyway." She laughed.

But Grayson didn't laugh. "Edith, there is something else that I wish to share with you, just between us."

She motioned for him to sit with her. "Of course."

"I exaggerated when I proclaimed the president to be 'fit as a fiddle.' He has a fairly serious condition known as hardening of the arteries. It can cause strokes and heart attacks."

"Yes, I'm aware that he has had several small strokes, from which he recovered."

Grayson nodded, but his shoulders slumped as he seemed lost in thought, which worried her all the more.

"Is there something else?"

"We don't have much in the way of treatment. All we can do is prescribe exercise and rest. During acute periods, we must severely limit any worry or excitement."

"Hard to do when someone carries the world's worries on his shoulders."

"Yes, that's it exactly." Grayson seemed strangely cheered by this, by someone understanding how difficult his job was, even if he had but one patient.

Her mantel clock chimed four times.

"Oh dear, I have an appointment. Thank you for all this information; this has been helpful. Is there anything else?" Edith rose, but he didn't follow her lead, fussing with the buckle on his bag.

"When Ellen was sick, I suspected Bright's disease. I thought I could handle it on my own. In any case, I didn't want to call in specialists unless it was absolutely necessary. I had him to think about, after all."

"What do you mean? I thought she had melancholia." She sat down again.

"Ah, not 'bright' as in cheerful. It's a type of kidney disease. I blame myself." He repeated, "I thought I could handle her treatment on my own."

His eyes pooled with sorrow, and Edith fought an urge to hug him and reassure him it couldn't be his fault.

"If I had called them in earlier—the specialists, that is—maybe she would have survived. But his headaches were fierce, and his blood pressure had soared, and it looked like the strain might kill him if he knew she was that sick. Nor was it entirely clear which symptoms were due to kidney disease and which stemmed from her melancholia. So I tried..." He trembled with the memory.

Edith gently laid her hand over his. "That's a terrible position to be in. I'm so sorry."

He nodded and regained his composure. "You see, by that time he had suffered small strokes that affected both his right and left sides. This increased his risk of permanent damage, not all of it physical." He tapped his finger to his temple. Glancing at Edith's worried face, he hastened to add, "But he's been stable for two years now." He gathered his bag and stood to leave. "I'm sorry for overstaying my welcome."

The poor man. How excruciating that must have been to go through, and to live with ever since. Despite his self-proclaimed failure to save Ellen, Edith had an even deeper respect for him. As she escorted him to the door, she told him, "If ever you have to choose between my well-being and Woodrow's, you are to choose him."

"And he would say the same about you." He put on his navy officer's cap. "Good day, Mrs. Galt."

Edith had corresponded with the Episcopal bishop who was to perform the wedding ceremony a number of times, arranging for his accommodations and advising him of the intimate ceremony they desired. She told him the invitation list was very limited, and therefore he shouldn't bring a guest, even his wife, or they would be sure to hear the objections of the multitudes of others who were not invited.

But when the bishop arrived in town, he sent a note saying that his wife was very excited to attend, as she would shortly be visiting with royalty in Europe, and they would want to hear all about the wedding. Furious, Edith picked up a pen to scratch out her exact thoughts on the matter. But before sending the note, she decided to consult Woodrow, remembering he was much more of a diplomat for these types of things. But Woodrow waffled, asking her to think it over.

"I have thought it over, and we must stand our ground," Edith huffed.

"As you wish." He threw up his arms with a chuckle. "I just feel sorry for the poor fellow, being married to such a woman."

So the bishop was out, and clergymen from the local churches were invited, a Presbyterian for Woodrow, and an Episcopalian for Edith.

Sallie met Edith for the final fitting of her wedding gown. "It's simple, yet stunning. But since you've chosen black velvet, I believe I will wear blue lace, to match my beautiful daughter's eyes."

Sallie seemed distracted, barely looking at the low-heeled pumps Edith was proposing to wear, offering a succinct "Yes, very nice," which was out of character for someone who had once said not having one's purse exactly match one's shoes was a venial sin. She wasn't even Catholic, which had amused Edith all the more.

"Something on your mind, Mother?"

Sallie balanced her purse on her knees. "I'm not sure I should bring this up. It's just a silly joke after all, so I shouldn't bother you with it."

"Then stop worrying about it. Shall we go have some lunch?"

Edith had too much on her mind to be troubled with silly jokes, but her mother didn't move, aside from rocking slightly to and fro.

"But it's making the rounds of the Washington party set, and it rather defames you."

Edith sighed. Why did all the problems have to leak out when she was in a hurry? "Fine. Out with it then."

"It seems there is a British naval officer, here on official business as assistant to their ambassador. His name is Craufurd-Stuart. He's a rather dashing bachelor. Have you met him?"

Edith shook her head and checked her watch.

"He's said nasty things about the president. And his favorite joke is that Edith Galt was so surprised when President Wilson proposed that she fell out of bed."

Anger rose in Edith, but her first instinct was to soothe her mother. "Oh, people will say anything for a laugh. I'm afraid we shall have to get used to being targets."

Later that night, she confided in Woodrow, who annoyed her by laughing at the joke.

"Is there anything we can do about this man? Isn't he here as a guest of the government? Can he be quietly asked to leave?"

But Woodrow waved it off. "Better to grow a thicker skin. And we do allow free speech, even for our guests."

NINE

The December 18th wedding was splendid, small and intimate, just as Edith wanted. Relieved of the duties of setting up, decorating, and supervising, she was free to fully enjoy the moment. Ike Hoover, the head White House usher, had done all the planning with Helen, even obtaining their marriage license.

The people of California had gifted them with a gold nugget, with a request that the wedding rings be created from it. A simple gold band was fashioned in time for the wedding for Edith, but she ordered something more special for Woodrow. After the brief ceremony, they enjoyed a special dinner in her dining room. Then they were whisked to the train station, bound for their honeymoon.

Their destination had been kept secret from the public for their security and privacy. Special railcars were added to a train at the Alexandria station. They had a fine car with a double sleeping berth, offering them time alone at last. By the time the midnight train departed, an exhausted Woodrow and Edith fell asleep in each other's arms.

When they woke up the next morning and drew the curtains, the world had changed to a winter wonderland. The tracks ran up a valley between mountain ridges, and a thin blanket of snow brightened the bare trees.

"It looks like home. Wytheville, I mean." Edith remembered the joy of sledding down hills with her brothers and sisters, followed by hot cocoa in front of the fireplace. "I do miss its mountains and small-town charm."

"Isn't it fitting we're smack in between our birthplaces? We must go back and visit both." He looked out the window and frowned. "It doesn't look like we'll be doing much golfing, anyway."

"Golf? I rather had other activities in mind." Edith slipped a hand under his pajama top.

Edith had dozed off but woke to Woodrow singing:

Oh, you beautiful doll! You great, big, beautiful doll!
If you ever leave me, how my heart would ache.
I want to hug you but I fear you'd break.
Oh, you beautiful doll!

As he sang, he danced down the narrow space, even jumping up and clicking his heels.

Oh, to have that energy so early in the morning, Edith thought, as she slumped back in the berth.

Woodrow answered a knock on the cabin door but protected their privacy. "I'll take it from here." Then he pushed in a white linen-covered cart, laden with dishes under silver domes and an arrangement of pink silk orchids. He positioned the two dining chairs in front of it and poured coffee for both of them, all the while singing:

Hug me just as if you were a grizzly bear.
This is how I'll go through life,
No care or strife, when you're my wife.

Lured by the aroma of bacon and eggs, Edith grabbed her robe and joined him. "You're a hopeless romantic, but I love you for it."

Soon after they finished breakfast, they hurriedly bathed and dressed as the train chugged to a stop. Peering out the window, Edith saw the sign at the station read *Hot Springs*. She had been entranced by photographs and artwork featuring the beautiful brick hotel, set in the mountains, with flowers and trails and spas. She looked out at the heavily wooded area, with just a few shops and tumbledown shacks in view. "This doesn't look like the brochure."

"This is as far as the train takes us. We have a bit more to go to get to the Homestead, but it's just over the next pass."

Sure enough, a horse-drawn cabriolet appeared, with a driver and a footman suited in black with brass buttons. Edith shivered, thinking about the ride through the mountains in the open cab.

Wrapped in her hat and fur coat, and with Woodrow in his favorite kangaroo leather coat, she stepped with him into the carriage fit for a prince and princess with its shiny black paint and gold trim. But she needn't have worried about the cold, for the footman provided a thick wool blanket and flasks of hot tea as they nestled into the leather seat. The driver snapped the reins, and the horse trotted off, its bells jingling in the fresh mountain air.

"This will be the best Christmas," she said.

Woodrow's smile warmed her heart, erasing any lingering doubt regarding the hastiness of their marriage.

Their spacious suite was beautifully appointed. A fire blazed in a fireplace in the sitting room, a lovely porch overlooked the mountains, and the two bedroom suites each boasted a bathroom with a huge claw-foot bathtub. Edith requested limited newspapers and messages so Woodrow might finally get a reprieve from his responsibilities. Instead, they had been provided with the latest society magazines. They rarely left their suite, except to play golf each morning.

The snow had melted, but the grass was crunchy underfoot. This did not deter Woodrow, who had woken Edith at daybreak. "Let's get ready and out there before anyone else appears."

They played nine holes before the weak sun crested the mountains, and Edith was grateful to get back inside to a warm fire. They cuddled on a sofa, sipping warm milk, a habit of Woodrow's that Edith had also taken up.

Woodrow said, "I have a confession to make."

"Whatever it is, I'm sure I will absolve you." She smiled, sure he was about to reveal something akin to preferring his milk be cold.

He patted the chest pocket of his afternoon coat. "I keep something here, next to my heart." He produced a worn-looking envelope. "I only read the first paragraph, fearing what the rest would say."

She took the envelope from him. In it was the letter she had written after he had told her about Mary Peck.

"I don't understand. If you didn't read all of it, how did you know my response?"

"You pledged your love, then came to me, an angel in the night. That's all I needed to know. Will you read it to me now?"

Edith did as he asked. She rarely, if ever, had seen him shed a tear. But his eyes filled, and he kissed her so tenderly she thought she too would weep. How awful it must have been for him to tell her about his failings, even afraid to read her letter. How very lovely and odd was this man, so bravely leading a country, yet so tender in his heart.

"Promise me you'll never destroy it," he said.

She gave the letter back to him. "Like me, it is yours to have and hold until my dying day."

They were greeted each morning with a breakfast cart piled high with sweet, flaky pastries and fragrant coffee. The croissants and homemade jam alone could raise her out of a deep slumber. Unlike Woodrow, who seemed to require little sleep or food, Edith needed an appropriate amount of both. She hadn't been in favor of the separate bedrooms that Woodrow expected, but she was beginning to see their value, given his chronic insomnia and propensity to get up and work in the middle of the night.

On the third night, Edith awoke to the tap-tapping of his typewriter. Curious as to what could be so important at 3:00 a.m., she stumbled out to the sitting room.

He was quite the sight, hair askew and striped pajamas framed by the bold floral wallpaper and chintz sofa featuring even more flowers. He tore a sheet from the machine and was rolling in a new page when he noticed her.

"I'm sorry; is the noise bothering you, my dear? There are just a few more things I need to take care of, but I can move to my room."

"What bothers me is that you don't get enough rest. Is there no one else to do these things for a few days? What about Marshall?"

He laughed scornfully. "That's not what vice presidents are for."

"Well, what then?"

"So there's someone in position, at least in the interim, should I suddenly kick the bucket."

"Couldn't you change that? You like to say that you 'have not only the brains you own, but all those you can borrow.'"

"I suppose I could, had I any confidence in him."

He resumed typing, and hearing the clackety-clack of marching orders, she returned to bed.

One morning, feeling a little out of sorts with Woodrow taking phone calls and tapping away at the typewriter, she headed to the front desk in the sunlit and expansive lobby. Other guests smiled, perhaps recognizing her from pictures in the newspapers. Christmas was a few days away, so why not host a little reception so the other guests could meet the president?

"Good morning, Mrs. Wilson. How may I serve you today?" The young hotel concierge appeared freshly scrubbed, his slick dark hair neatly parted down the middle.

She told him of her idea of a Christmas reception, and he enthusiastically offered to arrange it. Belatedly, she realized she hadn't consulted Woodrow with the idea, but she couldn't imagine him objecting.

"One other thing. Can you recommend a short day trip? It's lovely here, of course, but if there's something we shouldn't miss?"

The concierge reached under the desk and produced a brochure of the Greenbrier Resort. "It's less than fifty miles away, so no need to stay overnight, but the drive is scenic with waterfalls and streams, and of course the mountains. The Greenbrier itself is much like the Homestead, but I think you and the president would enjoy the trip."

The next morning, they had the Pierce-Arrow loaded up with picnic baskets and headed out with the Secret Service. Edith had worried about taking Woodrow away from his duties for an entire day, so she was pleased to see him looking happy and relaxed.

"Did I do the right thing, getting you away for a day?" she asked.

He patted her leg. "Indeed, just what I needed."

The road was winding but not especially hilly as they followed a valley south to the West Virginia border. Edith had been lulled into a light sleep but awoke when the car stopped suddenly.

"Uh-oh," the driver said. He clambered out of the vehicle, with the Secret Service agent and Woodrow quickly following.

A burst of cold air hit Edith through the open door, and she pulled up the wool blanket to warm herself. Outside, the problem was evident. The road had reached a stream that had escaped its banks. The bridge had either been washed out or was under ice-crusted water. The men were engaged in a spirited conversation, with arms waving and fingers pointing in different directions.

Woodrow climbed back in next to her. "We can turn back or try to cross. How badly do you want to see this resort?"

"How deep is the water? Can the motorcar make it through?"

"The driver thinks so, if we get out."

"And then how do we get to the other side?" Edith looked at the water rushing down the open center part of the stream. "A little nippy for a swim."

"Come, I'll show you."

They climbed out of the car and joined the men at the bank.

"I vote we turn around," said one of the Secret Service men.

"The president wants us to try," said another.

"We can see if the car can go through." Woodrow pointed to a large log that had fallen across the water, just upstream. "If it does, we can walk across that. If it gets stuck, we'll head back in the staff car and send help."

Edith laughed, but then saw that he was serious.

"I'm sure you've crossed a few logs in your day, dear. Are you up to it?" He was already rolling up the legs of his trousers.

Luckily, she was wearing a simple but fashionable skirt that reached just past her calves and sturdy boots. Not wanting to be seen as a coward, she said, "If that big pile of metal can get over, I'm game."

So the driver inched the Pierce-Arrow into the water, its weight keeping it steady, even as the water came over the floorboards. It stalled midstream, and everyone gasped, but soon it was started again and climbed up out of the stream.

Cheers went up, and then it was time for them to cross. They created a human chain, holding hands with the Secret Service agents leading and following Woodrow and Edith. Her foot slipped on the icy log, and rotten chunks splintered into the water. It creaked ominously and she feared it would give way under all the weight. But they all safely crept across, much to her relief.

By the time they reached White Sulphur Springs, they only had time for a brief tour of the Greenbrier, as it was nearly time to head back, taking a different route. But Woodrow was cheered, laughing and joking, years of tension and worry fading from his face.

The next night Woodrow dressed in black tie and Edith wore one of her gowns from Worth to host their reception for the other guests of the hotel. They held the soiree in the Jefferson Parlor, a lovely round room with presidential portraits and murals depicting the history of the resort. Hors d'oeuvres were offered, and waiters in cutaway coats served champagne from silver trays. There were no speeches, not even a formal toast. Woodrow and Edith simply milled about the room, greeting the guests.

Edith noticed that for all his eloquent speaking skills, Woodrow was fairly awkward at chitchat. He remained beside her at all times and relied on her or the others to begin a conversation. Where was the man who reveled in telling stories at family gatherings, who never failed to offer a prayer, a toast, a joke? Maybe he was wisely reticent. Edith would tell stories about her personal foibles to someone she had just met. Perhaps that was something she needed to change. It seemed Woodrow needed to get to know a person before being so comfortable, whether by nature or due to his position.

Then again, was this a role she could play for her new husband? She couldn't quote the greatest literary minds at the drop of a hat like his first wife, or engage in deep political analysis as he did with Colonel House or Tumulty. But she could cover for his tendency to shrink from purely social engagements and perhaps coach him to be more friendly to the press.

❧

Even though Edith was enjoying their getaway to the Homestead, the distance and delay of communications were hampering Woodrow's work.

He never complained as his middle-of-the-night working hours steadily increased, but she suspected he'd be happier at home. Especially since the torpedoing of the *Persia*, another passenger ship, had occupied his mind while the State Department sorted out whether more American lives had been lost at the hands of the Germans. The country's neutrality was rapidly fading.

So just after New Year, she said to Woodrow, "There is so much for me to do, moving into the White House, so would you mind terribly going back a few days early?"

The relief on his face when she asked to go home confirmed her suspicions, and they soon departed.

TEN

1916

On a morning soon after their early return from their honeymoon, Edith kept Woodrow company in his study adjacent to the family quarters. He preferred it to the Oval Office in the West Wing, because it was much quieter, with fewer interruptions from staff. Compared to the rest of the Residence, his study was simply furnished, with bookcases, two wingback chairs, and a small table. An exception to the simplicity was an immense flat-topped desk. Exquisitely carved, the oak desk was the centerpiece of the study.

Seeing her admire the desk, Woodrow called her attention to a brass plaque. "See here, the story of a British ship, the *Resolute*. It was lost on an arctic expedition and was found by American whalers. The U.S. government purchased it from them, had it restored to its former glory, and sailed it back as a gift to Queen Victoria. Years later, when the ship was taken out of service, Queen Victoria had its timbers made into this magnificent desk, as a gift to the American people."

"Quite an honor to work at that desk," Edith said.

"Indeed. And this is my own." He pointed to a rather ordinary green-glass shaded lamp. "I've had it since my college days. It keeps me humble."

He resumed his work, and she perused the bookshelves, gently nudging the already neatly arranged books into perfect order.

"Have you read all of these?" she asked when he looked up from his papers.

He adjusted the pince-nez spectacles that sat on the bridge of his nose. "Some of them all, and all of them some."

He came around his desk and joined her in the section for classics. "Ellen and I enjoyed reading to each other every evening."

He pulled out Homer's *The Odyssey*.

"What a lovely tradition," Edith said. "I should like to continue it, if it doesn't cause you sad regrets."

He smiled. "You've brought the light back into my world, Edith. Far from regrets, sharing my passion for books could only deepen my love for you."

He looked at his pocket watch, and she thought she was about to be dismissed. "Do you need me to leave so you can get back to work?"

"I do have quite the pile of papers to sign, but if you can spare a moment, you can be of assistance." He moved back to his desk. "These piles are military commissions I must sign. Nothing to decide upon, just sign and move on quickly. So quickly that the ink hasn't time to dry, so I spread them out on the console table, then gather them up again in batches. Which all takes time of course."

"How can I help? Should I lay them out and gather them for you?"

He opened a desk drawer and pulled out several sheets of thick paper. "You can blot them after I sign; then they can go right into the completed folder, saving me two steps." He ran his hand affectionately along her arm. "I know it's completely mindless, and you are welcome to decline."

"I don't mind, but I don't want to step on the toes of an aide or secretary. Surely you have staff to do this?"

"I find their presence distracting, so I dismissed them from this duty." He gave her arm a squeeze. "I would much more enjoy you to be here."

So the routine began, first blotting signatures on routine things, then on to matters of more importance, when he would ask her to read a document, and then they would discuss the matter.

Woodrow asked Edith's opinion of his latest letter to the German ambassador.

"I can't imagine your message being any clearer," she said. "At the same time, I have scant hope of it making any difference."

"I quite agree," Woodrow said. He picked up his fountain pen and tested it on a scrap of paper before laying the letter in front of him.

Edith held a piece of blotting paper at the ready.

"Oh no, not that one. I have something much more special for this occasion." He opened his top left drawer and pulled out another blotter.

"Feast your eyes on this."

The thick paper, about seven inches by four, had photographs or likenesses of all the U.S. presidents.

"There's yours truly, front and center." He pointed to a handsome picture of himself.

"Oh what a wonderful idea."

"It was one of the last things dear Ellen did before she took ill." He rubbed the blotter, as if it would conjure her memory.

Edith had become accustomed to living with the ghost of a woman who seemed perfect in her husband's mind. She could never fill the gaping wound of her passing, nor did she want to. But she fought against the pangs of jealousy anyway, not because of fears she couldn't live up to the memory of the woman but because of the time Ellen had had with Woodrow that Edith had missed.

Woodrow took off his pince-nez and wiped his eyes.

"Did she do this for you?" She held up the blotting paper. "Is that why you can't allow your staff to do it?"

"Why yes, but that's not..."

"I'm not sure how I feel about this." Edith bit her lower lip. Was he trying to replace someone irreplaceable? Would she cease to be her own woman in his eyes?

"Please, I don't want you to do anything that makes you feel uncomfortable. I do enjoy having you"—he paused until she looked him in the eye—"you, and only you, here with me."

"Of course, but I'm afraid I have another engagement at the moment." Which was only partially true, as she was due to meet with a Red Cross director much later that afternoon. She scurried away, needing time to gather her thoughts and chart a path in the tricky world of being a second wife to the president.

Soon the campaign interceded to remove any cares or wonders about Edith's role. Despite the initial threats and rude gossip, she was now cast as the president's devoted wife. They were constantly on the go, with a whistle-stop tour of all the battleground states. Even though he varied his speeches for each location, she had heard them so many times that she could recite them from memory.

They had their own personal car on the train, and the last cars were reserved for campaign staff. If time didn't allow for them to enter the town, Woodrow spoke from a small balcony at the end of the caboose. Edith would frequently join him there, and the sight of the crowds yelling their support gladdened her heart and seemed to energize her husband. Each time he emphasized how he had kept the country out of the war, with his slogan, "Peace with Honor," her breath would catch. He had told her it was only a matter of time before he would have to ask Congress to declare war. But she smiled and waved, accepted bouquets of flowers, and looked at him in adoration.

They also attended many of their favorite events, like throwing the first pitch at the opening of the baseball season and speaking at town halls. But now the tenor of the events was different, afflicted with the need for self-promotion and the constant criticism of the press, and even some from the crowds, with Republicans always among them.

Security was tightened. Three U.S. presidents had been assassinated. Two of those, Garfield and McKinley, Edith remembered. Although Woodrow seemed unafraid as he delved into crowds, shaking hands and being slapped on the back.

He scoffed when she asked if it would be prudent to limit his exposure. "I understand your concern, but I believe God is looking after me. If God sees fit to allow me to serve, then I must, undaunted by fear and visible to those who support me, as well as to those who don't."

Edith prayed and kept a watchful eye. If he wasn't going to be cautious and fearful, she would have to be enough for the both of them.

When not traveling for the campaign, Edith and Woodrow soon developed a rhythm to their days. First, they shared breakfast in the sitting room between their bedrooms. Then, they went off on their separate ways, Woodrow to meet with senators or congressmen, and Edith to consult with the housekeeper and social secretaries to review menus and entertaining schedules.

At noon, they would have a quiet lunch in the family dining room if no dignitaries were visiting. In the afternoon, Edith would join him in the study, where he would update her on developments in the country and the war in Europe. Edith delighted in planning and attending grand dinners with heads of state. Three thousand people attended the first event they hosted together.

Grand affairs, such as the one put on by the Pan American Council in her honor, were an exciting new part of her life. Her favorite flowers were orchids, and the council filled the entire ballroom with them in every imaginable size and color. They had even built a small pool in the center of the room to reflect their beauty.

But Edith most looked forward to weekend getaways on the *Mayflower*. Every few months, they would meet the ship at the Navy Yard and embark on a relaxing cruise. Of course Woodrow would have to work some and always had his trusty typewriter aboard.

They explored all the navigable tributaries that emptied into the Potomac, enjoying the sight of great blue herons and flocks of ducks. On one trip, Woodrow noticed a tiny island they had yet to explore. He asked about visiting it, and the Secret Service brought back a report while she and Woodrow were still having breakfast.

"It's Tangier Island, the home of a small fishing village. The water is too shallow to land, but we can take you over in a rowboat. I'm afraid there isn't much to see..."

"What do you think, Edith?" Woodrow poured more coffee for her in the special blue-and-white china cup, *The Mayflower* emblazoned on it in gold.

"I love an adventure."

Later that afternoon, they donned the life jackets that the crew insisted they wear and made their way down a narrow gangplank to the waiting rowboat. Shell-encrusted rocks formed the shore. There was no sand to land on; they'd have to tie up to a rickety dock with a single plank leading from it to the island. They held hands, forming a human chain across the plank, reminding Edith of their West Virginia adventure.

After a short walk, they entered the village, with rows of neat cottages, each with a garden with a few vegetables and white picket fence. It seemed like a scene from a fairy tale, except for the white stone grave markers in most of the yards. No people bustled about; no children played in the streets.

Edith shuddered at the eeriness of the abandoned place. "It looks like a village of the dead."

They meandered up and down the quiet streets, with just the cry of seagulls breaking the silence. They stepped around bicycles seemingly abandoned midride and peeked through the windows of some closed-up shops. With no one to see, they soon headed back to the dock.

They had once again put on their life jackets and were ready to cross the plank when Woodrow said, "Just a moment. I'd like to take one more look."

He rushed back to the village, with Edith behind him trying to keep up with his long strides. When they arrived at the first street, she was amazed to see women and children, as well as a few men, out in their yards or riding bikes in the street. When the people looked up and saw them, they scurried back into the nearest homes and slammed the doors.

Edith looked at Woodrow. "What on earth?"

"Come on." He took her hand and they wandered down the street, calling out and waving at no one there.

Reaching a corner, they came upon an elderly fellow, who widened his eyes and started to flee.

"Wait!" Woodrow called.

The gentleman stopped, and his eyes grew even wider. "Isn't this the president?"

"Yes, I have that honor, sir." Woodrow tipped his newsboy hat and nodded.

The villager laughed. "I'd like to shake your hand. People around here think a lot of you."

The man explained that earlier that morning, they had seen a large ship approach, followed by uniformed men pulling up in small boats. "We thought the Germans were landing! Being defenseless, we decided the best thing to do was to hide in our houses and lock the doors. We were relieved when they left. But then, this afternoon, they were back again, this time patrolling our island." The man took off and wiped his smudged eyeglasses. "I peeked out the window and saw your lady with you, and figured she wouldn't be with the Germans. So I stayed put, figuring she wouldn't allow any harm to come to me."

"I'm sorry to give you such a scare. But good thinking for all. Believe it or not, we've been traveling the country, trying to inform our countrymen of the growing threat to us. But they seem to think our oceans will protect us."

"We're a village of fishermen. We know the seas. Oceans can be crossed and the Germans will. Please, Mr. President and Mrs. Wilson, come with me. Everyone would love to meet you."

The man knocked on doors and passed the word, and soon the villagers surrounded them. Woodrow and Edith shook every hand and admired every child. A young man led them to a small market, where fresh fish and blue crab shone on top of blocks of ice.

As they headed back to the boat, with a basket full of purchased seafood, their entourage followed them to see them off.

"We must come back," Edith said, her spirits high. She had been mentally preparing herself to help Woodrow through a bruising, unsuccessful campaign and then create a new life together afterward. But the warm reception they received on Tangier Island, as well as whenever they appeared in public, gave her hope that the people saw what a good man he was. Maybe their love of country and admiration of Woodrow would overcome party affiliation.

She was startled to realize that she was actually hoping for a win. Woodrow seemed to thrive on being loved by the people, going on jaunts on the *Mayflower*, throwing opening pitches from be-ribboned boxes, and shaking hands with a sea of midshipmen. Dr. Grayson never complained about Woodrow's blood pressure when he returned from public events; quite the contrary. Perhaps that is what his health most needed—not a rest away from the world but a reason, a passion, a mission to be in it.

That is, if he even got to run. First, he needed to win the nomination at the Democratic National Convention in June. And neither of them needed to be reminded that the hugely popular former president Theodore Roosevelt had not been renominated by his own party, setting up their loss in 1912.

But all the delegates to the convention, save one, voted Woodrow Wilson to be their candidate for the 1916 election. Although his formal acceptance wouldn't come until the official notification in September, the campaign would begin in full swing. His Republican opponent would be Charles Hughes, an associate justice of the Supreme Court.

In between grand events, such as the graduation ceremonies at West Point and Annapolis, party officials demanded more and more of Woodrow's time. In order to spend more time together, Woodrow and Edith started having breakfast at 5:00 a.m.

Edith refused to ask the staff to prepare the meal at that early hour. She asked the head housekeeper to leave ingredients for the next morning in the small icebox in their suite. She had a hot plate installed and looked forward to cooking a few eggs herself. The few times she had cooked for Woodrow, he had eaten every scrap.

But it was not to be. Each morning, instead of raw eggs and bacon, linen-lined trays of fully prepared breakfasts appeared at the appointed hour.

Their habit of meeting in the late afternoon in the study to sign papers became an even more important ritual. She had swiftly moved from blotting wet ink to reading and advising. After lunch, Edith would empty the Drawer and have the most critical files ready for Woodrow. When he arrived, they would discuss the important issues of the day. Again and again, he thanked her for making what would have been a lonely, tedious task the highlight of his day.

Assisting Woodrow with paperwork led to a rather embarrassing event, which taught Edith something about the ugliness of political gamesmanship. After a particularly long session of signing military commissions and prisoner pardons (or refusals of the same), Edith had to rush to dress for a state dinner that evening. Rebecca had laid out her gown, a lovely cream silk overlaid with sheer lace embroidery, along with matching shoes and fresh undergarments.

"Your bath is drawn." Rebecca stood at the ready with a fluffy towel in hand.

Edith looked at her watch. Their guests would already be filing into the dining room downstairs. "Took a quick one this morning, thank you. No time now."

Rebecca laced Edith into her corset, slipped the ivory lace gown over her upraised arms, and quickly managed the multitude of buttons up the back and sleeves. With a touch of face powder, rouge to cheeks and lips, and hair brushed into a low pompadour, she pronounced Edith ready to go.

Edith raced down the stairs, carrying her shoes. She slipped them and her gloves on and tried to calm her breath before she emerged into the hallway of the State floor. She pictured Woodrow waiting impatiently in the Blue Room. But when she arrived, he was all smiles, bearing a huge corsage of orchids in both hands. How he managed to change into a tuxedo and arrive on time as cool as you please mystified her.

She offered her cheek for a kiss. "I'm so sorry. I hope I haven't kept you waiting too long."

He pinned the corsage under her left shoulder. The cluster of lilac-throated, creamy blooms complemented her gown perfectly. "Don't apologize. It was me who unfairly kept you too long, and despite that, you are a vision of loveliness." He offered his arm. "Shall we?"

Members of Congress and the Cabinet and their wives stood behind their chairs in the dining room, awaiting Woodrow and Edith. Three long tables were set up, each with a cream-colored tablecloth and tall silver candlesticks dressed with English ivy. Ike Hoover, dressed nattily in white tie and tails, guided them to their seats. Next to Edith's chair stood Senator Henry Cabot Lodge.

He was a proper-looking fellow, with curly gray hair and a carefully trimmed full beard. He smelled oddly like foot powder, but it was probably his hair tonic, or possibly the excessive starch in his shirt. Edith remembered that Woodrow rather despised the pompous Massachusetts senator, saying that he would oppose anything, no matter the justification or importance, just because a Democrat was for it.

There were a number of toasts to the country, the servicemen in uniform, and lastly "to the president." Then Woodrow said, "Gentlemen, please seat your ladies."

She took her seat, and Lodge gracefully helped push in her chair. She removed her gloves and placed her napkin on her lap, which all the women took as a signal to do the same. Then Woodrow, standing to her right, held his glass out toward her, then toward the rest of the room. "A toast to the ladies, whose grace brightens our days and this room."

"To the ladies," all the men toasted.

The men then took their seats, and Senator Lodge greeted her with a nod and "Good evening, Mrs. Wilson." He then took in her ensemble, raking his eyes from her hair and probably imperfect cosmetics to the large corsage and finally to her hands as she reached for a sip of water. The sense of his gaze made her self-conscious. Steadying her jiggling glass, she saw to her great mortification that her fingernails were blackened. It must have been ink from her afternoon of blotting Woodrow's papers.

She quickly put the glass down and hid her hands in her lap. Hoping to distract the senator, she tried to engage him in conversation. "I'm sorry for your loss of Nannie. Having been widowed myself, I know how devastating it is."

But his remark did little to comfort her. "She enjoyed gardening as well."

She hoped he said that in sympathy, and that it was just an embarrassing moment, certainly not her first or last. But she was stunned some days later when the senator described her dirty nails at the formal dinner to the press.

Once again, she felt the need to apologize to Woodrow. The subject came up on a day they had lunch alone together, a rare occurrence. She enjoyed her meals, always having a healthy appetite. But the way he picked around his slice of chicken and green beans, while glancing at the newspaper, worried her.

"Your cheekbones tell me you need to eat more."

"Really? I have no control over the speech of my body parts. Nor do you, I see. Perhaps your hands have been chatting about your love of gardening?" He laughed, which did little to assuage her.

"That awful man. I'm sorry about that. It was the ink..."

"Oh, don't be. I'm sorry he was so uncouth; you don't deserve that. But if this were the worst thing the old man said, I'd be whistling happy tunes. There is something you need to realize about Lodge, and actually a good number of people in Congress. They are not our kind."

"Oh? How so?"

"They have no class, no couth. Like it or not, our society is stratified, just like the British. We just don't admit it like they do."

"I'm pretty sure no one would consider Lodge to be lower class."

"It isn't a mere matter of income. It's a higher sensibility. A refusal to be distracted by pleasures of the moment or feel rewarded by the attentions of others."

Edith wasn't fond of his line of thinking and wasn't quite sure she understood his point. It all sounded rather elite to her. So she changed the subject. "Speaking of which, the Greatest Show on Earth will be coming to town. Wouldn't that be fun?"

He didn't look away from his paper. "The Barnum and Bailey Circus? I'd rather go to this minstrel show." He showed her an advertisement for a vaudeville show, with actors in black face.

"Probably not a good idea. Minstrel shows are happily disappearing." Edith, mindful of the time, folded her napkin and placed it on the table.

"They are? Why?"

"It's seen as disrespectful toward Negroes."

"Hmm. White actors pretending to be colored. But there are plenty of shows with singers and actors of all colors."

"The point is, everyone should be given equal say in things. Colored roles should be played by colored people."

"I'm not sure that's the issue."

"Of course it's an issue. Just one of many that we'll be resolving for generations, and not just for Negroes. For women, and for those who can't speak for themselves. Not to mention we fought a war..."

"And most accept its outcome, even if the rights of states had to be compromised for the greater good. But we can't just force societies that have for hundreds of years been separate to suddenly merge into one. It has been a generation, if not two, and still old feelings persist."

"What are you saying?" Edith felt heat raise in her face. She had certainly lived through deep changes in the South, but she had been raised to see all humans as equal in nature.

"In good time, I think these divisions will blur, as people get used to things like sharing swimming pools and offices and such. But it needs to happen naturally, not by force, which will lead to violence and more mistrust."

"Is that why you allowed the Cabinet to segregate its offices?"

"I don't condone it, but I don't interfere with the process. It is not my job to force integration, and as I've mentioned, I think that does more harm than good."

"Permit me to disagree. This is not the intent of the Founding Fathers. You can choose your Cabinet members so that you don't wind up on the wrong side of history."

"Let's agree to disagree. History is a process, and we must choose our battles. I'm trying to keep us out of a war, end child labor, stave off a strike of railroad workers that could paralyze the country. We are sorting through policy for the Federal Reserve we created to ensure our national financial stability, and need I go on? I've chosen the best men for those jobs, and they in turn find the most suitable people to carry out the work. It's not the chief executive's place to inspect the racial makeup of every government official."

Edith didn't know what to make of his comments, but it clearly wasn't a subject they would agree upon. She knew instinctually that he was wrong about his theory of a naturally occurring solution through time, but she didn't know what the answer was.

Her general mistrust of the federal government led her to believe the changes needed to come from elsewhere, but where? She could start with herself. After all, she was now a public figure. But what would the people think if she admitted views that opposed those of her husband? The right to free speech didn't seem to apply to the wife of the president.

She could start with her choices of entertainment. "I'm not going to a minstrel show."

ELEVEN

An acquaintance of Woodrow's offered his mansion and estate, Shadow Lawn, near Asbury Park, New Jersey, for the Summer White House. Although they had thoroughly enjoyed Harlakenden House in Cornish, the isolation and distance had become an issue. Edith foresaw her husband having to make so many trips back to Washington that he would get no rest.

In New Jersey, they would be closer, and she thought the girls would enjoy coming and being close to the seaside. Both Nell and Jessie had small children and were quite anxious to move them away from the city. Infantile paralysis was raging, and the gated grounds seemed a perfect place to keep them safe.

But that summer was frantic with events, and Woodrow and Edith didn't have time to go to Shadow Lawn. In addition to trips to the military academies, they went to New York for Cary Grayson and Altrude's wedding, to Connecticut to see Woodrow's ill sister, and then, sadly, to South Carolina for her funeral. Woodrow gave speeches at events in Kentucky and Chicago as well as all the ordinary business.

He began having severe headaches, a sure sign he desperately needed rest. So in early September, Edith insisted they go to Shadow Lawn. Named for the tall trees that surrounded the forty-acre property, creating the feeling of an oasis protected by a forest, the estate was much more elaborate than Harlakenden House.

Upon arrival, Edith gasped at the size of the three-story mansion. Massive columns and a wraparound porch dominated the first-floor facade, with balconies on the upper levels.

Once they were inside, the ornate rooms and furnishings made it hard to imagine being comfortable living in such a space. Huge, rather dark chandeliers hung from coffered ceilings. A wide marble staircase with carved balusters and newel posts led to a landing with a grand piano. From there, two staircases ascended to the next level. The effect was elaborate and showy, not warm and comfortable.

Edith didn't express any of this to Woodrow, or the girls or the Graysons, of course. That would be ungracious. But for everyone's comfort, she arranged to have some of the gaudier paintings and statuary draped from view and had some furniture moved into cozier conversational arrangements.

Woodrow's nemesis, Theodore Roosevelt, used the elaborate estate to poke fun at him. He wrote a piece haranguing Woodrow for keeping the United States out of the war:

> *Mr. Wilson now dwells at Shadow Lawn. There should be shadows enough at Shadow Lawn: the shadows of men, women, and children who have risen from the ooze of the ocean bottom and from graves in foreign lands; the shadows of the helpless whom Mr. Wilson did not dare protect lest he might have to face danger; the shadows of babies gasping pitifully as they sank under the waves...*

Reading the unjustly critical treatise, Edith boiled with indignation. She wanted Woodrow to answer the attacks in the press but already knew what his answer would be. His main goal was peace, and nothing would be gained from engaging with the likes of Teddy Roosevelt.

Aside from Joseph Tumulty, Woodrow's trusted secretary, he had another close friend and consultant in Colonel Edward House. Edith had met the diminutive man on several occasions, always at Woodrow's request. Her husband wanted her to trust and admire the man as much as he did, but Edith's intuition advised her otherwise.

It seemed he held much ambition but knew he didn't have the personal charisma or forcefulness necessary to be a leader of men, so he had attached his star to Woodrow Wilson. In addition, he hadn't earned the military rank of colonel. That was an honorific bestowed upon him by grateful patrons, and he clung to it.

Colonel House was gracious, if not fawning, in Edith's presence and was one of the first to offer his congratulations upon the engagement. He showed up at Shadow Lawn in full-battle mode for the campaign, lining up speeches in town after town.

Edith came in from a refreshing walk about the grounds to find the two men with papers and maps spread across a table in one of the grand sitting rooms. After listening to a litany of proposed stops on the train tour across the country, she left them to their work.

The grueling pace of the planned campaign worried her. How would Woodrow be able to get the exercise and rest he needed to stay healthy, as well as stay on top of all the vital things he needed to do during a most challenging time? Sixteen years his junior, Edith had a bit more physical stamina. But even the thought of the constant travel and jam-packed schedule made her weary. At least it would be for only a couple of months. Then they could go back to their merely hectic schedule.

After a rousing speech at Shadow Lawn, where Woodrow formally accepted the Democratic Party nomination, Edith immediately set to work preparing for the campaign train trip. Many trunks were packed, as she would need to attend parades and receptions and rallies of all sorts in the mountain states, deep in the heart of the country, and up and down the West Coast. It was both exhilarating and exhausting to think about.

The events started to run together in her mind, with Woodrow's speeches only slightly altered for each cheering audience. But one stood out from the rest. They were in Omaha, Nebraska, where there was a large Indian reservation. It was thrilling to see some tribal elders, who turned up in their ceremonial dress. Then, the mayor introduced Edith first, proudly declaring her a direct descendant of Pocahontas.

The crowd roared, and Edith beamed. Although she had been received warmly everywhere she went, this was the first time she felt her heritage might be an asset to Woodrow's campaign. In this tight race, that could make a difference.

She felt even more sure of this later that day. After a quick change of clothes at their hotel, they motored to the fairgrounds, where they were treated to a swine show and contests for every sort of farm and home project imaginable.

Edith was drawn to a pen thickly surrounded with laughing and cheering people. She made her way through the crowd to view the attraction. There, in all its white-and-pink glory, was the most immense hog she'd ever seen. "One thousand, one hundred and fifteen pounds!" the judge shouted, and bestowed a big blue ribbon on the hog's considerable shoulder. Afterward, at a large dinner, she spoke with several members of the press, who had also admired the big pig. They all laughed, and Edith told stories about her father, a circuit court judge, being asked to judge similar contests. "He knew nothing about animals but always said yes, and we had a grand time."

That night on the train, Edith and Woodrow were relaxing after the long day, when they were interrupted by a knock. Woodrow grumbled something about the late hour, but Edith, still spun up from the excitement of the day, answered it.

Three of the reporters she had talked to at dinner, plus another, who introduced himself as Louis Seibold, a senior reporter at a major New York newspaper.

"I'm sorry to have missed the swine fair," Louis said, to the whiskey-fueled jeering of the others. "But I'm hoping you can settle a bet."

Edith crossed her arms. "I don't know. Someone who misses the best part of the day to take a nap..."

The reporters laughed, but Louis continued. "It seems my colleagues claim to have seen a thousand-pound pig. Can you verify this information?" He held his spiral pad and pen at the ready.

"Eleven hundred fifteen."

The reporters cheered and profusely thanked her. The scent of cigars and whiskey trailed them, even as she shut the door. Maybe she had presented a lighter side, but wasn't that important too? She returned to her dear husband, beloved by her but truly understood by few others.

The next morning, a gift from Louis Seibold arrived—a sweet toy pig, adorned with a blue ribbon and necklace of tiny silk flowers. When she squeezed it, it squealed. From then on, the pig had a place of honor on her mantel, always reminding her never to underestimate the value of small, fun things in life.

After another campaign stop and speech in Chicago, Edith and Woodrow had some private time and headed to Grant Park. Here they walked along new trails, with views of both Lake Michigan and downtown. The scent of freshly mowed grass invigorated Edith, and she breathed of it deeply while they strolled.

"It reminds me of Hains Point," Edith said.

"Indeed. This park also sits on landfill, debris from the great fire, and silt from dredging the shipping lanes." But he didn't seem to be in the mood to discuss land development. He stopped walking to admire the view of the city, electric lights twinkling on as dusk approached. "We have to sort out what to do, should we lose." He used his walking stick to clear some stones on the path.

"Aside from living happily ever after?" she mused.

He placed a warm hand on her back. "In addition to. But these things don't come without planning. I had a long conversation with Colonel House about it. My concern, as always, is for the country. The Constitution clearly outlines the orderly transfer of power. Something our friends in Mexico should take note of."

"If only they had the genius of our forefathers."

"But here lies the question. The Constitutional procedure doesn't take into consideration the extenuating situation we find ourselves in. A nation on the brink of war. A prolonged transfer of power at a critical time when the future of not just our nation but of entire continents is at stake. And a lame-duck president is worse than no president, as he, in Lincoln's words, just 'needs to be cared for.'"

The hairs on the back of her neck prickled. "What are you saying? You can't be thinking of attempting to hold on to power past March, should you lose."

He gave her a sharp look. "Good gracious no. I was thinking that the months from the election until the inauguration in March might better be served by Justice Hughes, should he win."

"Oh." The idea did make sense. "You would step down early? How would that work?"

"This is where House's plan comes in. I would need agreement from the vice president and Lansing, and of course Hughes, and we wouldn't proceed unless that was in place. First, Lansing would resign, and I would appoint Hughes as secretary of state. Once he is confirmed, Marshall and I would resign, bringing Justice Hughes into the White House."

Edith blinked as she considered his plan. She looked at him to see if he was just pulling her leg, but the stern set of his features told her he was indeed serious. Worry crept in, as she feared the backlash if this idea were to become public too soon. It could be the death knell of Woodrow's campaign. "Who else knows of this?"

"No one. Just you, me, and House." He glanced back at the Secret Service agent, who was keeping a respectable distance. "And not to be discussed any further, for obvious reasons."

She felt some relief, until he added, "I have drafted a letter to Lansing, as that would be the first step, but mum's the word."

During the last days before the election, stress was evident in Woodrow's weakened voice, his usual passion waning with fatigue at the huge rallies in New York City. But it seemed only Edith noticed. The crowds cheered and sang "Hail to the Chief" as the band played the lively tune. Woodrow's plan to resign early if he lost the election underscored for Edith how critical the transition was. Theodore Roosevelt had a vastly different approach to the war, wanting to get involved much earlier. What would happen to the delicate agreements Woodrow had fostered? They had been able to tamp down Germany's submarine threats, but what would happen if he lost the election?

Edith spent endless hours worrying over such details, while Woodrow seemed to take it all in stride. Instead he focused on the good news, such as Roosevelt's declining influence. The former president had thrown his support to Hughes, but his followers in his Progressive Party didn't necessarily follow suit. Edith was happy to read stories in the newspapers of labor unions siding with Woodrow, as the Republicans fought against the eight-hour workday rule.

And there was one more bit of good news. Hughes had failed to meet with California's influential Republican governor, who then refused to back him. With its thirteen electoral votes, California might decide the election.

❧

Woodrow and House's plan of early succession didn't feel quite right to Edith. Woodrow could accomplish so much more in those four months that to rush that transition of power made little sense. But it was pointless to discuss it with him now. After the election, should it not go their way, there would be plenty of time.

Woodrow and Edith took a road trip from Shadow Lawn to Princeton in order for him to vote. Edith waited in the motorcar as he went into the fire station of his appointed polling place, as neither the District nor New Jersey allowed women to vote.

She mulled the suffrage movement, but despite the many letters from women, and some men, to join their cause, she hadn't changed her mind. The suffragettes who insisted on staging protests at the gates of the White House, frequently getting arrested for their efforts, infuriated her. She couldn't understand how breaking laws helped their cause.

Woodrow was softening his position, however, leaning ever more toward an amendment to force all states to allow women to vote. A change most encouraged by Margaret, of course. Publicly, Edith would align herself with whatever position the president took, but she hoped he would find a way that also supported states' rights.

"The states will have a say," Woodrow had assured her one night as they read newspapers over breakfast. "Passing the amendment doesn't make it law. It has to be ratified by at least thirty-six states before that happens."

"And what about the others?" she asked, doing some quick mental calculations. "Up to thirteen states could object, and still it's forced upon them? What happened to your position that it is better for these things to resolve naturally? That it causes nothing but strife to force something on the people that they're not ready for?"

"There's been over fifty years of strife over this issue and it's getting worse by the day. Besides, as Margaret points out, it's just the right thing to do." He folded his newspaper and set it aside, signaling the conversation was over.

Edith bit her lips; Margaret was the ace in his pocket. He knew Edith tiptoed around anything to do with her, not wanting to be seen as an evil stepmother to a Cinderella Margaret.

Edith and Woodrow gathered with Helen and the girls and their husbands in the grand parlor at Shadow Lawn, while messengers brought in news of election results. The early returns showed a race even tighter than expected. First Charles Hughes was ahead, and then the vote swung toward Woodrow. To pass the time and settle her nerves, Edith knit and chatted with Helen and the girls.

That evening the family gathered in the Great Hall, which Edith liked to call the lounge, and played charades and twenty questions. Contrary to the usual exuberant play, all were subdued, anxiously awaiting the phone to ring. Except for Woodrow, who laughed and chatted as if nothing could deter him from a good game.

Around ten o'clock, just when Edith was about to excuse herself for the night, the phone rang. A jittery Margaret jumped to answer it. She held her hand over the mouthpiece as she told everyone that it was a friend of hers in New York. "Condolences? What for? But he's not defeated. What are you talking about?"

At this, everyone circled around her and she reported her friend's response. "He says Hughes is winning the entire Northeast and Midwest." Her eyes reddened and she took on the demeanor of a caged badger. "Impossible. They are still at the polls… Oh, I see…"

Woodrow waved at the telephone in dismissal. "It's still too early to tell. The entire West Coast has not come in."

Margaret rang off and was speechless for a moment. "He said it's over. The *New York Times* flashed the light from their building. Red for Republican."

They telephoned the Executive offices in Washington but received the same sad update.

"We'll not concede yet," Woodrow said. "Let's see what the morning brings."

But there was nothing new the next morning. Woodrow seemed neither worried nor excited. After breakfast, he folded his napkin from his lap and set it aside. "While this is sorted out, what do you say we head over to Spring Lake and play a round of golf?"

Woodrow's daughter Nell and her husband, William McAdoo, completed their foursome. As the house staff loaded their clubs into the Pierce-Arrow, William fussed at them, telling them to mind the club heads and shaking his finger at them as if they were naughty children. With his deeply set eyes, angular cheekbones, and high-strung temperament, he reminded Edith of a painting she had seen in Kristiania, Norway: *The Scream*.

William wasn't Edith's favorite, but since he was both Woodrow's son-in-law and secretary of the treasury, she hesitated to point out his faults. He was vain and ambitious, not a good combination. Nell was much more fun and tended not to take him as seriously as he did himself.

Edith rolled her eyes at William's nitpicking of the staff, and Nell responded by nudging her husband. "Hey there, big shot, give them a break. You put your trousers on one leg at a time, just like everyone else."

William ignored her. "A bit chilly, wouldn't you say?" He tugged on his cable-knit sweater.

Edith followed her mother's advice: *If you don't have anything nice to say, say nothing at all.*

Arriving unannounced at the golf club, the president's party had the staff scrambling to find caddies. The Secret Service men offered, but the manager wouldn't hear of it. After a bit of a wait, four rather elderly gentlemen were rounded up. There was some testy bickering regarding competing as two teams using the best shot of each player. "This way, the men can go full out on their drive, having their partner to simply plop it on the green, should he miss it completely," argued William.

"Let's just play," retorted Woodrow. Edith heartily agreed.

Of course, all wanted to carry the clubs of the president, so they drew straws. The caddy with the shorter straw was assigned to Edith, not without a bit of grumbling on the caddy's part.

The grumbles and bickering vanished due to a surprise awaiting them at the eighth tee, a far distance from the club house, when Dr. Grayson came running up. As he stopped to catch his breath, the foursome left the caddies to meet him.

"Just had a call from campaign headquarters. California is coming in for us. It's still very close, but right now it's going our way."

Everyone cheered, but Edith felt her heart was being yanked one way, then another. The news lightened the spirits of the foursome and caddies alike. A cart appeared with chilled champagne, and they sipped as they laughed at winding up in yet another sand trap or malevolently placed pond.

Although Nell and William were fairly good players, Woodrow was well known to have beautiful drives, only to three-putt away his good score.

Edith leaned on her club as she watched his painful series of putts. "I think I'd like the game much better if we didn't keep score. Wouldn't it be more fun for everyone just to be out here, enjoying fresh air and exercise and each other's company?"

Her companions exchanged wide-eyed, incredulous looks. William broke out laughing and the others joined him. Even the Secret Service. And the caddies. Especially the caddies. Apparently Edith was the only one who would consider such blasphemy.

By the eighteenth hole, Edith was determined to show she could do well if she put her mind to it. She carefully lined up her next drive, taking the time to stand precisely and hold her club exactly as she had been taught by Grayson. But the ball refused to cooperate, and it took two more swings to reach the fairway.

Her caddy looked at his timepiece, a pained look on his face.

She felt compelled to seek his good graces by requesting his advice. "Do you think if I used a midiron that I could reach the green from here?"

"Yes," he said. "If you hit it enough times."

⁓

Visitors continued to pour into Shadow Lawn. An emissary from Poland joined them for dinner, then requested time alone with Woodrow. Edith didn't want to intrude, but since the man had been so effusive with praise for her husband at dinner, she lingered in the hallway above the lounge, where if she kneeled by the balcony, she could hear everything they said through the pillars of the balustrade. And what he said pleased her, as he poured on more praise and beseeched the president to help the suffering people of Poland.

Another tense evening followed as they waited for the California vote count to be completed. Finally on the morning of Friday, November 10, while Edith and Woodrow were enjoying breakfast on the sunny porch, the butler came to them, a telegram in his hand. It was from Joseph Tumulty in DC.

CALIFORNIA PUT US OVER STOP FINAL 277 WILSON 254 HUGHES STOP CONGRATULATIONS MR. PRESIDENT

Overwhelming relief flooded Edith, followed by a sense of dread. She had convinced herself that Woodrow wouldn't win and had been envisioning their life together, free of the overwhelming responsibilities. She had watched as he suffered terrible headaches, often taking to his bed in the middle of the day when he didn't get the proper rest and exercise he needed.

But mainly that had been during the frantic pace of the campaign. She consoled herself with the memories of the pure joy he gained from so many of his duties—using his oratorical skills to convince his opponents to see his side, the many events where he was cheered and, sometimes, the simple act of signing a military commission or a farmer's homesteaded deed. It was the life he had chosen, that he felt called to do. She had to respect his decision, while vowing to do all in her power to protect him.

TWELVE

The world had not stopped its convulsions just because the United States needed to decide who would be its next president. Returning from Shadow Lawn, Edith and Woodrow found that the air in the White House seemed to have shifted in their absence. The staff had seemed to be holding their collective breaths throughout the campaign, and now, with the election over, the impossible ugliness of a world at war came tumbling out.

Edith's desk was buried under a teetering tower of newspapers, each one with headlines grimmer than the next. Germany's menacing attacks on shipping, unrest in Mexico and Russia, the domestic economy suffering from rising prices, and threatened railroad and other strikes at home were all pressing matters.

Rebecca came by late one afternoon, just as the long shadows of deep autumn painted Edith's office in a golden hue. Edith thought she had come to turn on the electric lights, but instead Rebecca presented herself stiffly in front of Edith's desk.

"What have I done or not done now?" Edith pulled her calendar toward her. By Rebecca's expression she had definitely missed something.

"Excuse my interruption, but have you seen this morning's paper? Section C?"

"News from the Western Front? Ypres? Verdun? I don't know; enlighten me." It wasn't like Rebecca to play games, and Edith didn't have the patience for them now.

Rebecca just happened to have a copy under her arm. She snapped it out with a flourish and read out loud, "The rate of inflation has more than tripled so far in 1916, and 1917 looks to be even worse."

"I'm afraid you're speaking to the wrong Wilson for a discussion on the national economy."

"I think I do a good job. At least you haven't complained, ma'am."

"True. Would you like me to start?" Edith stole a glance at the mantel clock. Her calendar had shown she had invited Altrude for tea. Realizing she was being snippy, she softened. "Why don't you have a seat and tell me what's bothering you."

Rebecca remained standing. Her brown hair, perhaps now leaning more toward salt and pepper, was neatly coiled on the top of her head, her pressed cotton work dress showing some crinkles and marks from a long day. "I appreciate the generous room and board. But I still require a salary. A fair salary. And it was fair, in 1914 when you last gave me a raise and when my duties were considerably fewer."

It was a slap in the face. One that Edith deserved, and needed. She had become detached from the headlines. She had to, or risk crumbling in a heap at the tremendous problems in the world, all of which seemed to land on the White House steps each morning. But that was no excuse to be blind to the needs of others who worked so hard to serve her and asked so little in return. Inflation wasn't just a small headline in the boring financial section. It deeply affected the lives of the people, their ability to feed and clothe their children. And it seemed 1917 promised to be an even more difficult year on many fronts.

"I'm so sorry, Rebecca. It will be taken care of."

For a week, Woodrow failed to meet Edith for their customary breakfast. Even though she had much correspondence and other business to take care of, she feared falling into a pattern of seeing each other only when exhausted at the end of the day.

In order to decrease the burden on her husband and spend more time with him, Edith learned to code and decode encrypted messages. They developed a routine: while he held morning meetings, she would go to the Drawer in his study and gather the flagged folders. She decoded as necessary, then piled them on his desk. He wrote his responses, which she would then encode. Woodrow would then type the numbers himself to complete the message and dispose of their drafts.

In this way, she learned all the most important issues of the day. Sometimes, he would ask her opinion before writing his response, particularly if it had to do with someone she knew.

One of those was William McAdoo. But as much as she disliked the man, she couldn't bring herself to say anything negative, even as he seemed to be grooming himself to be the next Democratic presidential candidate, giving speeches that barely concealed this. One person Edith did not withhold feelings about was Henry Cabot Lodge. Not a day went by that the newspapers didn't quote him saying something negative regarding the president or his administration.

"He's abominable. He's anti-American," she complained, slamming down the morning newspaper. Seeing Woodrow merely shrug his shoulders, she asked, "How is he allowed to say these things?"

Woodrow lowered his own paper, sipped his coffee. "It's very American, dear. The ability to voice contrary opinions is the heart of what makes us great. He and his friend Teddy Roosevelt have been banging the drums of war for some time. Although I have, and will continue to try any means to keep us out of it, I'm afraid we are quickly running out of options."

"So it's inevitable?"

"I'm afraid so. The German answers to our objections have been met with utter disregard. There is to be no changing their agenda, which is control of the entirety of Europe, and beyond. Not only Germany is the aggressor, but Austria-Hungary, Bulgaria, and Turkey as well. All with a history of warring with each other for centuries."

"Britain, France, and Russia have long histories of war as well."

"Quite so. But in choosing sides, we must determine which side proposes sovereignty of each nation, and ultimately peace. I think it's clear who are belligerent to democracy, and who are just trying to protect themselves."

The longcase clock in the hall chimed seven times, echoed by the muffled bells from clocks in other parts of the Residence. They always reminded Edith of the Sunday morning church bells in Paris. What would happen to that beautiful city if the Germans got to it?

Woodrow rose and neatly tucked in his chair. "This is the time to raise preparedness. And our friends Roosevelt and Lodge, for all their premature bluster, may be useful in this."

By late November, the news from abroad was no better. The Allies and the Central Powers were locked in a war of attrition, with battles fought and ground gained, only to be lost in the next campaign. The Wilsons maintained their hectic schedule and resumed state dinners at the White House. They also managed to sneak in a little shopping trip in the District. Edith wanted to buy Woodrow a handsome leather portfolio, due to his habit of carrying important papers everywhere. The clerk at the store was clearly nervous, fumbling with the case, unable to open its latches. Then he couldn't pronounce *wristwatch*. Feeling sorry for the fellow, Edith purchased both the wristwatch and the portfolio, and she and Woodrow neatly made their escape.

They stopped for lunch at the Occidental, very close to the White House. Edith loved to look at the many portraits of presidents and cabinet members and members of Congress. But they had hardly sat down when a photographer came by, requesting permission to take Woodrow's portrait. Of course, Woodrow smiled widely and agreed, but she could tell he was irritated and more preoccupied than normal. He didn't notice a waiter offering him a menu.

"What's bothering you, dear?" Edith accepted the menus, and Woodrow waited until the waiter left before answering.

"I'm thinking I need to make a great effort, a last-ditch effort, to convince the Powers to declare a truce. A letter to all to end the fighting, and let's all broker a peace. It has to be carefully done." The deep lines in his face belied the hope his words expressed.

Edith reached across the table to take his hand. "This has already been done, so many times. But I understand you must keep trying as long as there's even a whisper of a chance for peace."

"I'm to meet with Colonel House tomorrow. He's not in favor, but he's coming to help me write the letters nonetheless."

In early December, an exciting event gave reprieve from all the exhausting stress and work. The Statue of Liberty in New York Harbor was to be illuminated, and Woodrow was invited to give the signal for the spectacular event. At the Waldorf Astoria hotel in Manhattan, he gave a moving speech on peace, which he said only comes with liberty and that liberty can never exist when small groups controlled the destinies of the people of a country.

Afterward, they boarded the *Mayflower* and headed into the harbor, with numerous boats and tall ships already there.

"Have you climbed her?" Edith asked Margaret, when the statue came into view.

"Yes, I have. The view from the crown is spectacular. Even more so is the view from the balcony of the torch. Although it was frightening to be up there, so I stayed only a moment."

"Sadly, the torch is closed. I may never get the chance to see that view again," Edith said.

Some six months before, German spies had blown up an ammunition supply in nearby Black Tom Island. Edith peered into the waters, wondering what might be hidden in its inky depths. The huge explosion damaged the statue's upstretched arm and torch. But this was a day of celebration, and Edith pushed the disturbing thoughts from her mind.

Rockets were shot off the *Mayflower*, and fireworks lit the sky. Then Woodrow gave a signal, and powerful spotlights lit Lady Liberty in all her glory. Nearby boats played "The Star-Spangled Banner" over loudspeakers, and they all cheered with glasses of champagne. It soothed Edith's frayed nerves to see such an outpouring of love for their country. She could feel the strength of freedom. Nothing could ever take that away.

A few days later, back at the Residence, Edith joined Woodrow in his study, finding him writing a letter to the nations in the European conflict.

"Would you like me to read the newest draft?" she asked.

"Yes, but I will have to translate it first."

Edith screwed up her face in confusion. "From what language? You don't know German."

He chuckled. "No, it's my own invented shorthand. Look."

She peered at the pad. The page was covered with lines and lines of squiggles, dashes and dots, little curlicues, and other strange symbols. It looked like the phonetic shorthand she had learned from her brief formal schooling, only there were shapes and symbols she didn't recognize.

"I've never known a man who knew shorthand. They only taught it to the girls."

"I taught myself because I had such a difficult time reading and writing. I couldn't read until I was about twelve years old."

Edith gasped in surprise. "But you went to school for years before that." How could such a brilliant man not read? Her father and grandfather had taught her before she was six.

He shrugged. "Guess I was just too busy with my chores. But listen, I will read this to you."

He read the letters, one for the countries of the Central Powers, the other for the Allies. They struck an even but stern tone, requesting an immediate cease-fire, and offered assistance in peace negotiations.

"If only they will listen." Edith knew the chances of that were slim.

Tumulty entered the office, his face grim. "Mr. President, we have a message from our embassy in Berlin. The Germans have sent an offer of armistice, and we have received a copy."

"From the look on your face, it's not an acceptable offer." Woodrow barely looked up from his letters.

Tumulty shook his head. "They have the advantage now, having gained ground in recent weeks, and having looted coal and other resources from newly occupied areas. The offer concedes nothing and threatens all-out submarine warfare if it is not accepted."

Woodrow twiddled the pen between his fingers. "I understand. Thank you, Joseph."

As the secretary left, Edith moved behind her husband's chair and wrapped her arms around his shoulders. "I'm so sorry, dear. It seems every last hope is gone. Will you still send the letters?"

Woodrow tore out the pages he had been working on. "I will rewrite yet again, although it is pointless." He took off his eyeglasses and rubbed his face. "I keep seeing those lines of broken soldiers, straggling back to Augusta. Hearing the weeping of the mothers and sisters and children of the fallen at the cemeteries. Seeing the burned cities..." He pulled her around to see her face. "War is so awful, Edith. I'd do anything in my power to end it."

"I know, my darling. I know."

⁓❧⁓

A few days later, Edith woke to see snow falling gently on the lawn. The trees already wore a dusting of white, and the serene scene brought her comfort. It was December 18, their first wedding anniversary. She dressed quickly in order to meet Woodrow in his room, but he was quicker. He swooped into her room, planted a big kiss, and presented a small black velvet box. She flipped it open to reveal a necklace with an opal and diamond pendant.

"My birthstone. It's beautiful, dear. But I have nothing to give you just yet. I've arranged for a special showing at an art gallery, and I want you to pick out a piece that calls to you."

After breakfast, they tried to play golf, but the snow was so deep, even the specially colored bright balls kept getting lost. Edith couldn't stop shivering, so she wasn't disappointed when Woodrow decided they'd had enough golf for the day.

At the art gallery, they wandered about, looking for just the right piece to add to their collection. Edith sensed his heart wasn't in it, even though he greatly admired some of the featured artists. It seemed he was only pretending to look at an oil of a ship in a stormy sea, staring too long at the same spot.

Concerned she was asking for too much on their special day, she slipped her hand in his. "You don't have to decide on something right now, my dear. Why don't we come back another day?"

He turned to her, his face relaxing with relief. "I'm sorry, my darling. You've put so much thought into arranging this, but my letters to the belligerents are being sent today. It's hard to think of anything else. At the same time, I learned something distressing that I need to share with you."

"Oh no, what?" His words didn't match his behavior. He wasn't looking Edith in the eye; he was scanning the room as if suspecting they were being spied on. "Is it about the letters? Or the girls? Or the grandbabies?"

"No, don't worry; they're all fine. But let's talk in the motorcar, shall we?"

They bundled up and headed back to the waiting car. He drew the velvet curtain between them and the driver, as if that offered any true privacy.

"Okay, out with it, before I spin myself into a frenzy," Edith said.

"I'm sorry; I shouldn't have brought it up at a moment when we couldn't discuss. But as this is our anniversary, I realized I shouldn't be keeping something from you."

Edith glared and rapped her fingernails against the purse in her lap. The purse that still held the special wedding ring she'd had her favorite jeweler make for him from the California nugget.

"You may recall a little incident during our engagement, when we were advised that an old acquaintance of mine was threatening to release some old letters."

"Mary Peck. Oh no, is she making more threats? Honestly, you need to ignore these kinds of people, or more opportunists will pop out of every dark corner."

He winced. "Well no. As it turns out, Mrs. Peck never did as she was accused. Colonel House admitted as such."

"What? Explain." Edith thought back to that terrible night, when they had nearly given up on each other. "What does House have to do with this? And Grayson? Did he…"

"Grayson was there at your request, so don't blame him. House and William McAdoo cooked up the scheme out of true concern for us. House knew about the letters and truly believed they would come out at an even worse moment."

"Good God, they lied to try to end our engagement? Falsely accusing an innocent woman in the process? That's monstrous." The motorcar had started down the street, but Edith had an urge to insist they stop so she could get out and pace and scream. But that, of course, was not possible. "And why are you so blasé about this? Your closest advisor and son-in-law plotted against us, against our marriage. House should be fired, and William…"

"I don't actually pay House, and William…" Seeing the fury on her face, he snapped his mouth shut. He reached for her hand and softened his tone. "They were doing what they thought they needed to do to delay the marriage for our own good. There was an even bigger, more sinister plan—something about spreading rumors that you and I had plotted to…" He shook his head. "Oh, never mind about that."

"Tell me, right now. I want to hear the whole gory truth."

"Something about leaking to the press that the two of us plotted Ellen's death. Thankfully, wiser minds prevailed. But not before a little intimidation was started, with a rock thrown at your window." He rubbed his face in anguish. "I'm grateful you never knew of this and only tell you now because you insist."

She wouldn't tell him that the rock had met its mark. His own anguish was enough; she had no need to add to it. "And William?"

"William had only a small part in it. It was done out of love, Edith. We must forgive them as the good Lord has taught us."

Edith couldn't be quite that gracious. She fumed in silence as she stared at the buildings flying by outside her window. Didn't the good Lord also say something about what the road to hell was paved with?

Outside the White House, a group of suffragettes lined up along the fence. Edith groaned as she saw the women marching, holding signs and banners saying Votes for Women and a few with disparaging comments on the president, calling him Kaiser Wilson. Edith caught a whiff of smoke. Woodrow pointed to protestors huddling around a ball of flames. It wasn't just paper they were burning. She couldn't be sure, but it seemed human-shaped. She realized they were burning someone in effigy. Probably her dear husband.

"It's so cold, should we invite them in for tea?" Edith asked. She had planned a small celebration with his favorite cake after she presented him with his monogrammed wedding ring. That could wait for a better day.

Woodrow looked at her with eyebrows raised. "I thought you didn't approve of these protests."

"I don't. But it seems the human thing to do." She gritted her teeth, wondering how cordial she could be to people who so disparaged her husband. Especially in her dark mood.

As the butler hurried to invite the suffragettes, Edith contemplated whether or not she should join them. On one hand, she didn't want to set a precedent she couldn't possibly maintain, but on the other, what could it hurt to hear their arguments and offer her own opinions. There were two sides to every story, and she feared the suffragettes hadn't thought through all the consequences of the changes they so earnestly sought. But just as she was about to change her clothes in order to properly greet them, the butler returned with the news that they had declined the offer.

Despite her lack of enthusiasm for the visit, she felt rather like she had been slapped in the face. It only decreased her desire to support their cause.

A few days before Christmas, Nell, Jessie, and Margaret and the three grandchildren joined Edith to trim the family tree in the oval sitting room. As the babies toddled around, taking ornaments off as fast as they were put on, Woodrow came in. He picked up little Francis and helped him place a tiny toy rocking horse on the tree.

"Well what is this?" Woodrow reached for a gold ring, hung just at his eye level.

The women laughed. Margaret said, "I told you he'd find it straight away."

Edith took the ring from Woodrow and placed it on his finger. "I'm sorry it wasn't ready for our wedding, but look how special. It has your initials in your own script."

Although he smiled as he kissed her, his daughters, and the babies, Edith could tell by the way he glanced at her that something had happened. She took his arm and pulled him away. "Something up?"

He kept his voice low. "That darn Lansing. He spoke to reporters about my letters to the Central Powers and concluded that it looked like we'd be forced into the war." He shook his head. "Good God, I'm tiptoeing in between the belligerents, trying desperately to make peace, while the State Department and press give up."

"Can he retract it?"

"It's rather late now, but yes, I can ask him to clarify. I expect the letters to be soundly rejected by both sides anyway. I've been working on this." He handed her a folded note. "What do you think?"

It was written half in his lovely cursive and half in his shorthand, which she had learned to decipher. It was yet another plea to the combatants, but this time the key phrase was "peace without victory." Woodrow argued that when wars end after one side has taken all, it merely sets the stage for future uprisings to settle the score. He proposed a cease-fire and creation of a formal means of negotiating.

"If I get the tiniest inkling of acceptance, this will be the next step."

But that inkling didn't come. A few days later, the family gathered in the sitting room for a showing of some animated short films of Krazy Kat and Ignatz Mouse. The children laughed at the crudely drawn antics of the characters. In one, Krazy Kat tried to save a bee by covering it with his top hat.

Margaret laughed. "That's you, Papa."

Krazy Kat goaded Ignatz to scare someone, and the mouse quickly did by running up a woman's leg, saying, "Anyone could scare a mere woman."

Woodrow guffawed and Edith playfully jabbed him with her elbow. "Mere woman?" How glorious it was to be doing something so ordinary, watching cartoons with family, laughing and joking and teasing each other like she had done with her siblings.

Of course, his mind was never far from his duties. "Sorry, but I needed that." He told her that both sides of the conflict had rejected his proposals for peace. "We have little time left. A month, maybe two."

They watched another cartoon. This time Krazy Kat was unsuccessfully trying to court Ignatz Mouse. Woodrow, apparently having had enough, got up, offered his hand to the still-seated Edith, and repeated a line: "I'm waiting, Ignatz."

Ignatz was waiting as well. Waiting for a time when pressing matters didn't creep into every peaceful moment like a bad-news telegram at a birthday party. Waiting for a time when they could eat waffle cones on a New Jersey boardwalk or enter their home without passing through protestors. When Krazy Kat and Ignatz could love and laugh and play like anyone else.

THIRTEEN

1917

After the holidays, the official ceremonies, speeches, and events resumed. One of the most important was the president's late January peace message to the Senate. Edith read his notes to him, adding bits here and there to clarify, but his words were both strong and eloquent. As she read, he typed as fast as he could with his two-finger method.

Finally, he had all the words typed. Edith poured them tea while he spread out the papers and scratched out lines and added more.

"You're no doubt sick to death of this by now, but would you mind listening to it from the horse's mouth?"

"Mind? How could I mind a front-row seat to watching history unfold?"

He smiled and patted her shoulder, then paced a bit while clearing his throat. Then, barely reading from his notes, with the words already committed to memory, his voice, sharp and clear, filled the room with authority and the confidence of a man who understood exactly what he was saying, and what he was asking of the country and its leaders.

"Gentlemen of the Senate:

"On the eighteenth of December last I addressed a note to the governments of the nations now at war requesting them to state, more definitely than they had yet been stated by either group of belligerents, the terms upon which they would deem it possible to make peace. I spoke on behalf of humanity and of the rights of all neutral nations like our own, many of whose most vital interests the war puts in constant jeopardy.

"We are that much nearer a definite discussion of the peace which shall end the present war. We are that much nearer the discussion of the international concert which must thereafter hold the world at peace." He paused, making notes on his pages. "So that's the opening."

"I like that your address will focus on peace. I think everyone is expecting it to be about the reasons we may be pulled into the war."

"That too. But the main thrust of it is to determine what this peace should look like. I'm going to propose a solution that's never been tried before."

He read on in his moderated tone, sounding like a very reasonable and intelligent college professor. "In every discussion of the peace that must end this war it is taken for granted that that peace must be followed by some definite concert of power which will make it virtually impossible that any such catastrophe should ever overwhelm us again." He paused, looked about the empty room, as if scanning the audience. Then his voice rose, and it kept rising until there was no doubt that every ear in the room would be reached. "Every lover of mankind, every sane and thoughtful man must take that for granted. The treaties and agreements which bring war to an end must embody terms which will create a peace that is worth guaranteeing and preserving, a peace that will win the approval of mankind, not merely a peace that will serve the several interests and immediate aims of the nations engaged."

Woodrow looked at Edith, seeming pleased with himself. "Well, how do you like it so far?" After his strong and eloquent start, he now seemed a nervous schoolboy, awaiting her approval.

"Nice setup, but I'm waiting for the never-been-tried-before part."

"Ah, you're paying attention. I'm still working on the wording." He flipped to a new sheaf of paper and read. "Mere agreements may not make peace secure. It will be absolutely necessary that a force be created as a guarantor of the permanency of the settlement so much greater than the force of any nation now engaged or any alliance hitherto formed or projected that no nation, no probable combination of nations could face or withstand it."

Edith tried to imagine what this "force" would look like. "It seems you are suggesting some sort of outside power to swoop in and control the countries." Alarm sounded in her common-sense mind. "Who and what would establish such a force, and how do you contain that?" She got up and paced about the room. "And you're still working this out in your mind? Perhaps the idea isn't quite ready to bring to the Senate. Is this one of House's brilliant ideas?" She shuddered as she mentioned the advisor's name, still smarting from his duplicity.

"We've discussed it, yes of course. But I don't think you're fully understanding. This isn't to be some omnipotent outside force. It will be a coalition of countries…"

"Then what would prevent a country with grievances from disregarding the opinion of the coalition and attacking another?

"This is all to be part of a treaty. If we are to get into this war, which is inevitable now, we must know what the end goal is. And in my mind, that is enforceable agreements in place to ensure this is truly a war to end all wars."

"So you want to establish strict rules upon the defeated. For example, make Germany give up all invaded lands and spoils of war. They need to pay for the destruction. Perhaps they could sell off their immense war-making assets, as they can't be allowed to keep them anyway."

Woodrow tapped his pen against his teeth. "I think we have to be very careful about the sanctions we impose. To create a desperate and destitute nation would set the stage for revolt. We need reasonable sanctions, spread over time."

"Reasonable? What about the Central Powers has been reasonable? Invading sovereign nations, death and destruction as have never been seen before?" Edith thought back to punishment she had suffered in her child-hood. She once had a dear friend sent away forever when the adventurous duo had broken some rules. She learned her lesson and never attempted the stunt again. "If the Germans aren't soundly punished, they will do it again. There must be a strong deterrence in the treaty, not some stretched-out slap on the wrist."

But it seemed she was talking to the walls. Woodrow merely nodded; his eyes focused on the imaginary Senate in front of him.

On the frosty January night of the president's speech, Edith sat in her usual place in the balcony of the Senate chamber, watching her husband deliver his address with even more passion than he had shown in the previous night in his study. It seemed the vast chamber with its rows and rows of desks attended by a sea of sometimes disdainful men in dark suits didn't intimidate him; it brought out his inner tiger.

Most of the men were paying rapt attention. Even Woodrow's nemesis, Henry Cabot Lodge, seemed to be nodding in agreement, despite his incessant calling for war, rather than peace.

Woodrow pounded his fist on the lectern as he expressed his belief that the only way to end wars was to create a coalition that would include our country: "Is the present war a struggle for a just and secure peace, or only for a new balance of power? If it be only a struggle for a new balance of power, who can guarantee the stable equilibrium of the new arrangement?

"Victory would mean peace forced upon the loser, a victor's terms imposed upon the vanquished. It would be accepted in humiliation, under duress, at an intolerable sacrifice, and would leave a sting, a resentment, a bitter memory upon which terms of peace would rest, not permanently, but only as upon quicksand."

Edith was still bewildered by this notion. Dismissing her concerns, he seemed to be proposing some overarching world government authority. The audience seemed similarly perplexed. Several side conversations erupted, until Woodrow's voice rang out with force:

"Only a peace between equals can last. Only a peace the very principle of which is equality and a common participation in a common benefit. The right state of mind, the right feeling between nations, is as necessary for a lasting peace as is the just settlement of vexed questions of territory or of racial and national allegiance.

"And there is a deeper thing involved than even equality of right among organized nations. No peace can last, or ought to last, which does not recognize and accept the principle that governments derive all their just powers from the consent of the governed, and that no right anywhere exists to hand peoples about from sovereignty to sovereignty as if they were property."

A wave of pride ran through Edith. Woodrow had added that last bit after their discussion. If he could catch her eye now, she was sure he'd give her a wink. She had accused him of being too thoroughly American in his opinions. "You seem to believe these countries have the same love of democracy as we do. I don't think you can expect them to ignore their own histories and beliefs."

To which he had replied, "Democracy should be the goal of every society. Lincoln insisted on a 'government by the people, for the people' for good reason. It is the only acceptable way humans can live together without hostility."

Edith and Woodrow had discussed a dramatic ending. That, she reminded him, was what people remembered best. But there was only so much even his powerful words could convey. He needed to ensure they were felt in the pits of their stomachs, that his audience would feel his passion and adopt it as his own.

She watched carefully as her beloved built up some steam for his critical moment. He paused, the room thick with anticipation, his intense gaze roving across the chamber, from the Democrats seated to his right to the Republicans on his left, ensuring he had the attention of all. The preacher's son studying his flock.

"These are American principles, American policies. We could stand for no others. And they are also the principles and policies of forward-looking men and women everywhere, of every modern nation, of every enlightened community. They are the principles of mankind and must prevail."

The men on his right rose first, clapping and cheering. Slowly the men on the first row on the left rose, followed by the men behind them. Woodrow climbed down from the dais and made his way down the center aisle, shaking hands and receiving many hearty pats on his burdened shoulders. Edith sat quietly for a moment, dabbing the tears in her eyes. Pats and squeezes on her own shoulders reassured her that his speech was well received. But an uncomfortable thought irritated her like a stone in her shoe. She remained unconvinced that his diplomatic approach to dealing with the aggressors was the right one.

Eloquent speeches in Washington, DC, with lofty goals of peace and cooperation did not sway the opinion of the warring nations. Nine days later, the Germans announced they were proceeding with unrestricted submarine warfare.

The cold, gray days of February brought no relief from the dreary news. Edith decided to bundle up and take a walk on the grounds. The brown grass crunched under her feet, and the sun seemed to be making little effort to melt the frost.

A newsboy, who couldn't have been more than eight years old, walked just outside the iron fence. "War is coming! German ambassador sent packing!"

On Inauguration Day, a day Edith had been anticipating for months, her heart was heavy with worry about the burdens facing the country. Of course it was thrilling to ride in an open carriage, to see the waving flags and buildings covered in bunting and the exuberance of throngs of well-wishers lining the way. She forced the worries from her mind and urged herself to revel in the moment.

It was time to think about what she wanted to accomplish in the next four years. The presidents' wives before her had a mixed record of achievements, from the amazing artistry of Caroline Harrison to the social and political savvy of Dolley Madison to the troubled mind and sacrifice of Mary Lincoln, but all had left their mark.

Inevitably, she was to be a wartime First Lady. Although the title felt awkward, she needed to accept it and make it meaningful. As she waved to the crowd, she wondered what she might do for them. What would be her legacy?

Immense crowds gathered outside the Capitol building, with people packed shoulder to shoulder as far as she could see. She tingled with pride as her husband took the oath, his hand on his family Bible.

She stood tall, feeling warm and confident in her stylish coat and hat. She thought of her Grandmother Bolling, who had constantly reminded her to stand straight and behave and dress like a lady. As an impatient child, she had tried to resist, escaping her invalid grandmother only to run into her mother, or her other grandmother, who were just as demanding. How important those lessons turned out to be. Except for the need to look up protocol for rare situations, she didn't need to think about manners or good posture or ways to address a person in a high position. It came as naturally to her as taking a breath of air.

How amazed her grandmothers would have been to see Edith now. Her mother was standing next to her at the ceremony. Edith took Sallie's gloved hand in her own and gave it a squeeze. "Thank you, Mother."

Sallie raised her eyebrows in question.

"For preparing me for this."

Sallie beamed. It mattered not to Edith whether or not her mother knew what she was talking about. When she had arrived in Washington all those years ago, she was barely out of her teens and worried what the people of the big city would think of the girl from a small mountain town. For a long time, she didn't feel as if she really belonged. Even now, she felt she could act the part, but was she really one of them?

From the carriage on the way back to the White House, Edith noticed Capital police stationed all along the route, both on the road and atop the buildings. She had never seen so many men with rifles. It looked to her like a battle scene, despite the cheering crowds. She tapped Woodrow's leg to get his attention as he was busy waving to his well-wishers. "Why so many?" She pointed at the guards on the rooftops.

His smile faded, and he leaned close so that she could hear him above the cacophony. "It seems there's been a threat of a bomb being thrown from one of the buildings along the route." He quickly resumed his smiling and waving, as if he had just declared it to be a sunny day.

Edith struggled with it a bit, looking at the rooftops for anything suspicious. But she decided there was no use worrying about it. After all, they had hundreds, if not thousands, of protectors all around them. She had no sooner put it out of her mind and started smiling and waving herself, when something fell into her lap. For a moment, she was afraid to move a hair, terrified of setting off a bomb. She slowly looked down and was relieved to see a big bundle of flowers.

Back in the Residence, Woodrow promptly went to work.

Edith brought him some milk and crackers as he toiled late into the evening. "Can I tempt you to retire by the fire in my room?"

He sighed and put down his pen. "The darn Senate. Filibustering the bill to arm defenseless merchant ships. Can you imagine?"

"I imagine that as the Commander in Chief you can order them armed yourself." She wasn't trying to be flippant; she just wanted her husband to come to bed.

His eyes lit up. "Splendid idea. I'll run it by the attorney general."

Edith got her way. Woodrow grabbed a cracker from the tray and followed her.

FOURTEEN

The in-house phone jangled as Edith was reviewing her daily calendar. Rebecca having run off on an errand, she answered it herself. It was Woodrow. Unusual for him to call; he preferred to pop in whatever room she occupied, not trusting the many workers who had access to the telephone system.

"Good morning, Ignatz. I want to share some wonderful news."

"My big mouse ears are listening, Krazy Kat."

He chuckled. "It seems you were right. The attorney general has agreed, and I quote: 'The president has the power to arm the merchant ships,' and I have so ordered. So thank you, from a country and a president that loves and needs you."

"I'm glad for you, dear." She sighed, remembering the Germans' hostility toward arms on the *Lusitania*. "It's yet another step toward war. But they have made it inevitable, so we must protect Europe from starvation and help them defend themselves until..."

She didn't need to complete the thought. Woodrow was quiet for a moment. She pictured him at his desk, the piles of paperwork representing thousands of important decisions awaiting him, yet he was taking the time to thank her for a small suggestion.

"Yes. It's another step in a march I never wanted to take. It is important to be cognizant of the greater picture, not just react to the situation at hand, no matter how grave."

The Germans kept to their word and accelerated their submarine attacks. Tons of vital food and supplies were sent to the bottom of the sea as the people of Europe grew more desperate. Three American ships were sunk by German submarines. The long shadow of war had reached across the ocean.

In mid-March, the Russian people overthrew their government, raising hopes that Russia would turn its attention to defeating the Central Powers. Edith read over Woodrow's message to Lansing regarding recognizing the new government. There was nothing in the expression of the sentiment that she could disapprove, but she did wonder if it were too soon. How were they to know that the czar or some others wouldn't claw themselves back into power?

All through this, Edith kept up with the comings and goings of various family members, playing the piano and having sing-alongs or games of charades. Another popular distraction was a Ouija board, a fad racing across the nation with as many tongue-in-cheek supporters as it had bitter spoilsports.

One evening Margaret, Nell, and Helen joined them for the parlor game, and they summoned Abraham Lincoln and Lord Nelson. Woodrow refused to play, citing the game's lack of respect for the dead.

On a sunny Sunday at the end of March, Edith and Woodrow took a drive down to Mount Vernon. George Washington was Woodrow's hero and most important role model, and he wanted to consult with his spirit.

"You have your Ouija board; I have this." He opened his arms to encompass the wide view of the Potomac. They had toured the mansion and the burial crypt, but it was the sloping back lawn above the river that entranced Woodrow. "I feel him looking out there, determined to fight for freedom. I feel him envisioning how a peaceful nation will be formed from small states and large ones, all having a voice in the whole." He sat on the grass, still stiff in its winter brown, and patted the spot next to him for her to join him.

She sat, the ground hard and cold under her bottom. "As you want for Europe."

"It's a good model for them, don't you think?" He pulled up his long legs, tenting his knees, and tilted his head back to look into the sky. "I have to write the speech I had hoped would never be given."

She knew the date had been set for an address to a joint session of Congress. He would ask them to declare war.

"I know. How can I help?"

"As you always do."

"What do you think George would say?"

"If it was happening in his time, he would say to stay out of it. They wanted to be free of the rule of Europe, and to become entangled in their thousands of years of squabbles would only lead to great loss. But these are different times. The great oceans no longer provide a shield; the interdependence of trade now includes Asia, Europe, and the Americas." He stood up and stretched. "I think he'd say the time has come to defend the very country we once fought against, along with countries that once fought for us."

She waited a moment too long, gazing at the river and thinking about the speech to be written. Another step, another turn in the gears that seemed impossible to stop.

He held out his hand and said, "I'm waiting, Ignatz."

On the evening of April 2, they rode to the Capitol Building. The streets were thick with crowds, almost as many as on Inauguration Day. But this time they rode in the sturdy Pierce-Arrow instead of an open carriage, which along with the still and quiet crowd emphasized the somber occasion.

"Ah, it is lit," Woodrow said. "I didn't know if it would be done in time."

Edith looked ahead and saw the Capitol shining brilliant white amid the darkness. The sight took her breath away, the magnificent dome crowned by the Statue of Freedom declaring to the world the strength and power of the nation. She thought of Lady Freedom's Roman helmet, adorned with an eagle and feathers to represent the Indian tribes, from which Edith was proudly descended. Lady Freedom also held a sword, to symbolize the strength to defend. And now the country was being called on to defend not only itself but the world.

Woodrow made a tremendous speech. As Edith knew it word for word, she spent the time watching the somber faces of the assembled congressmen, as the decision to declare war fell upon them. After such a long period of building up to this moment, Congress and the nation took the decision with steely resolve and barely a whimper of protest.

⁂

Edith thought about her role as First Lady, a title she despised but didn't seem able to change. She should use it to be the first to do things to help the war effort. Europe had its victory gardens; maybe she could lead an effort for communities to dedicate space for growing crops. Maybe she could host fundraisers or sew warm pajamas. Unsure of what exactly she would do, she did want to be a role model for American women.

One of Edith's favorite activities had been regular lunches with the wives of members of the Cabinet. She thoroughly enjoyed getting to know them and learning their perspectives on the many activities of the federal government. But the meetings had served their purpose, as the ladies found kindred spirits to support each other, and with the increasing demands on all of their times, Edith feared the meetings were becoming less valuable.

Woodrow's daughter Nell, a Cabinet wife herself, had told her as much. Edith was glad Nell was comfortable enough to share how the ladies felt. It was awkward, but Edith knew what she must do.

She planned an especially healthy lunch menu of cucumber sandwiches and soups with hardy parsnips and carrots as well as the first tender vegetables of spring—asparagus and early peas. This would serve to launch her topic: forming a national food program. For several days, she worked with the kitchen staff and her private maid, Rebecca, to decorate the oval Diplomatic Reception Room on the ground floor for the occasion.

A gentleman named Charles Pack had organized a group he called the National War Garden Commission. He had sent Edith several letters, pamphlets, and rolled-up posters of what he envisioned. Edith had the posters mounted and set on easels about the room. She arranged pamphlets at each place setting. Down the center of the long table, Rebecca and Edith artfully arranged the most colorful assortment of fresh fruits and vegetables they could find, along with jarred preserves.

The early spring produce didn't quite give the bountiful effect Edith desired, so she roamed the White House, finding bowls of waxed fruit to add. The addition of greenery cut from the gardens completed the look.

When the ladies gathered, Edith told them of her idea. "As we've been hearing, there's a severe food shortage in Europe, with so many farmers having to leave their fields in order to fight, and money and resources directed toward that effort. Not only do we need to help them, but we will be faced with similar challenges. Over there, households are encouraged to have war gardens. Even people who never grew so much as a daisy are urged to plant an edible garden. In the tiniest plot of earth, or pots on the windowsill, if that's all they have. The point is, the men will be gone, by the millions, eventually. Manufacturing of tractors will be replaced by building trucks and tanks, and it will be up to the women to keep things going, to feed their families from their own resources."

Some of the women nodded, especially the older women, who had probably lived through the difficult Reconstruction period.

One held up a pamphlet. "This is informative, but so plain. Couldn't we make it more colorful, more captivating to the eye?"

There were murmurs of agreement.

Another piped in, "So these posters and pamphlets, that's how you propose to get the word out?"

"That's what Mr. Pack is proposing, yes. Do you have more ideas?"

"Newspapers," several said in unison, then laughed.

"I have a friend who has a friend who knows Frank Lloyd Wright," Nell, Edith's daughter-in-law, chimed in.

This started a buzz of laughter and good-natured kidding.

Edith interrupted. "How could this friend help?"

"What I was going to say," Nell said with mock indignation, "is that Mr. Wright introduced this friend to his sister, Maginel Wright Enright, who is a very talented artist. She has illustrated lots of children's books and magazine covers."

Visions of beautiful, colorful artwork spun in Edith's mind. She would have to check the collection of children's books upstairs. Maybe they had one. "Do you think you could ask your friend to see if she would do something for us? For the country, that is? Having the Wright name on them could only help with publicity."

Nell wrote a note for herself. "Maybe we should come up with some general ideas for her? Make a nice presentation?"

"Ooh, I can see women with shovels and dirty faces, with beautiful vegetables like this in the foreground." The speaker pointed to the extravagant centerpiece.

"Can you make a sketch of that?" Nell seemed to be taking charge of the project, which warmed Edith's heart.

The ladies chatted in several side conversations, ideas being hatched, new working groups formed. Edith beamed. The excitement in the room was palpable. They had come in somber, as everyone was for the past few days, but hopefulness and duty had raised their spirits.

After several minutes, Edith called for their attention. "Ladies, I know several of you are already involved with other organizations that can help with the war effort, such as the American Red Cross. I would urge you to join, be as active as you can, with whatever talents and time you have. If not the Red Cross, then the Girl Scouts, or a knitting circle, or your church. Find some way to give of yourself, to use your position for the good of our people.

"I wrote this pledge and take it myself. I hope you ladies will consider doing the same. 'I pledge to reduce living to its simplest form and to deny myself luxuries in order to free those who produce them for the cultivation of necessities.'"

The ladies clapped, and Edith looked around at each of their faces. Next was the hard part. "With all of your demands, some of which I myself have imposed on you, there is less time for other things. Time with your family is paramount; that cannot suffer. So it is other things that will have to be put aside for now. Sadly, I've decided this very meeting, although it is very dear to me, is too much to ask. From now on, we will meet as a full group only for very special purposes. Likewise, the regular entertaining at the White House will be postponed."

There were "noooo"s voiced and groans from some.

"When the war is over and our side is victorious, we shall have a celebration for the ages!" Edith lifted her glass, and the others followed suit. "To victory!"

❧

A journalist, Abby Baker, had worked with Mrs. Theodore Roosevelt in preserving the china collection from previous administrations. Mrs. Baker had pleaded in a letter to Edith for a dedicated space for the historic collection. Edith had been so consumed with the election, and helping Woodrow in any way she could, that she feared she had neglected her own role in history.

How would she be remembered? How could she leave something tangible from her time in the Residence? Abby Baker's request seemed to offer something that would last for the ages. So after unpacking and reviewing the many sets of china, mostly kept in a ground-floor storeroom, Edith decided to take on the challenge as a nice break from thinking only of war. She met with Ike Hoover, the head usher, and the head housekeeper, and together they toured the various spaces that could serve to both display and store the china.

They settled on a room on the ground floor next to the Diplomatic Reception Room. It was a nice size, and the location made sense. Edith imagined the walls lined with lighted cabinets with elegant molding, with lots of glass fronts so that the collections could be displayed yet protected.

Dr. Grayson, whose office was just on the other side of the Reception Room, popped in.

"Ah, I was told you're on a campaign to update this grand old place."

The housekeeper and usher wordlessly stepped out, and Edith briefed Grayson on the plan.

"I don't know much about china, but I'm all for preserving history," he said. "Have you time for our regular meeting on the president's health?"

A wave of embarrassment ran through her. In these hectic days since the declaration of war, she'd forgotten a meeting so regular and important to her that she'd never entered it on her official calendar. "I'm so sorry…"

He held up his hand, "No need to apologize. There's not much to report. The president's health remains stable, despite the intense pressures of the past few months. However, I think we need to vary his exercise routine a bit. He seems to be getting bored with golf, and it leaves him vulnerable to passersby, or messengers who continually interrupt."

"Do you have a suggestion?"

"I was thinking of riding horses. Nothing above a trot. It would be fairly easy to plan out some different routes..."

"This wouldn't have anything to do with your love of the sport?" she teased.

Grayson cracked a smile. "I am planning to accompany him, of course. And I understand you were quite the equestrienne?"

She laughed. "That's a grave overstatement. I can ride acceptably well, like most Southern girls."

"Well, then I'm hoping you'll join me in a little subterfuge. If you happen to mention that you'd enjoy riding, I'm betting Mr. Wilson will be eager to accompany you."

The plan worked. Soon they were riding several times a week. Edith adored getting out in the fresh air. She borrowed riding breeches from Margaret and boots from Altrude, as shopping for these items would have clued in the public.

Most of the White House stables had been changed into a garage by President Taft, but Grayson had friends with stables. When they were on horseback and dressed in riding gear, no one seemed to recognize them as they rode down city streets and parks, with unmarked Secret Service cars discreetly following.

Altrude joined them on a ride through Rock Creek Park on a spring day, when the pink and white azaleas were peeking through the woods. She and Cary were still newlyweds, yet he spent so much time with Woodrow, it hardly left them much time together.

Altrude seemed a bit terrified of the activity, holding the reins with white-knuckled fists.

"Perhaps you and Dr. Grayson would rather do something else during our rides? I love your company, but..." Edith said.

Relief passed over Altrude's face. "Oh, that's sweet of you, but no, Cary adores these rides. It's brightened his mood, getting to do it on official time."

"And you?"

"Well, as you can probably tell, I wasn't born in a saddle like he was. But I did want to ask you what I could be doing for the war effort."

Edith thought back to all the women she had spoken to—the Cabinet wives, her entire staff, the press. But with regret, she realized she had not discussed this with Altrude. "You remember the sewing machine you teased me about bringing to the White House?"

"Yeeesssss," Altrude said suspiciously.

They pulled the horses up to a water station and dismounted.

"I've ordered lots of flannel, and Mother, my sister, and I are going to start making pajamas for soldiers, nurses, and others overseas. You could join us, cutting out patterns, if you're not comfortable with a sewing machine, or organizing fabric and thread, posting the packages…"

"I'll do it! And it will give me an excuse to be near Cary. Maybe we can have lunch occasionally."

Edith looked at her curiously. "You don't need an excuse to come to our home." But then she realized with sadness that of course she did. Edith didn't live on Twentieth Street any more.

In fact, she now knew she would never live there again. In a time of financial stress, her late husband, Norman, had sought investors to help him buy the rowhouse. With DC real estate becoming much more valuable, developers had persuaded her investor partners to sell, and Edith had no choice but to allow it.

She took one last trip by it on her way to sign the papers. Much to her chagrin, there already was a sign pronouncing a new modern apartment building was coming.

Silly to be attached to a house, she chastised herself. But she imagined herself and Altrude inside, chatting over tea, making plans for their next adventure. Gone was the savvy businesswoman, a company board member, owner and driver of her own car. All the things she had done on her own now faded away, replaced with being an important man's wife.

She had made the choice and didn't regret it. But it seemed there should be some sort of ceremony for a lost life. *Perhaps I'll write a book*, she thought. "Go on, please," she told the driver. It was a memory she needed to tuck away in her mental scrapbook.

The War Gardens project captivated Edith's interest. She brought it up to Woodrow one evening as she hand-stitched a hem on some pajama pants. He was poking at logs in the fireplace and expressing his relief that the unions had called off a planned strike. "We need those trains to transport troops and war materials. I may have to nationalize the rail system."

"Have you heard of the War Gardens Commission? Like the victory gardens in Europe. The idea is for each family to have a garden, to increase the supply to send overseas, and also to relieve the transportation system of having to move food."

Woodrow left the fire and sat next to her. "Sounds like a splendid idea. We should start one right here, as an example."

"Of course, we can easily add to the White House gardens, but I'm thinking something of a bigger scale for the city."

They both thought for a bit, and then the idea occurred to them at the same time. "Hains Point!"

"I knew that land would be critical for something. And now we have the answer." Woodrow took a card out of his chest pocket and wrote himself a reminder.

The Cabinet ladies had arranged for a meeting with some officials in the District regarding space for war garden plots. Edith and Altrude joined them near Hains Point on a drizzly gray morning, in an area as gloomy as the day.

A stench like rotting fish floating in a sewer hit Edith as she climbed out of the motorcar.

Altrude held a handkerchief to her nose to stem the smell. "Well, isn't this a lovely spot for a picnic? I suppose you're going to tell me about how fish guts made good fertilizer back home."

Edith ignored Altrude's disparaging remarks as she took in the scene. The area east of the river was run-down, with dilapidated huts that seemed inhabitable by humans, even though they were less than three miles from the White House. They crossed the small inlet that led to the Tidal Basin and met carriages waiting for them on the island. From there, they drove down Riverside Drive, retracing the route Edith had taken with Woodrow the year before.

At the southern tip, where the Anacostia River met the Potomac, fences marked a sprinkling of garden plots and neglected fruit trees struggling to survive.

The DC official met them and spoke about how they could clear a long run of land along the road, all the way back to the train tracks. Construction of a golf course had started but had been halted due to the war. The official described how the city could till the land, divide it into plots, and lease them out, first come, first served.

Some of the ladies seemed skeptical, particularly Altrude. "This is city land. Already the Corps of Engineers has been involved, obviously, but isn't it time for the federal government to step back? It's easy to cede control but difficult to gain it back."

Edith and Altrude had had many such discussions, both being of a mind that services should be performed at the most local level possible. What families could do themselves, they should. Then communities could step in when necessary with schools, parks, policing done at a local level, and so on.

"Normally, I would agree," Edith said. "But when the federal government ceded control a couple of years ago, they handed the improvement of it to the Corps of Engineers, as the city isn't equipped for such a large project. Here we have the potential for the park to serve as an example for the country, which is about to be at war, and it will be created and managed locally. The river will provide water for irrigation, and the location is easy to get to by streetcar. Once cleaned up, it would be nice to have gardens in this underused area, and the publicity will help the idea spread."

A glance at Altrude's skeptical face told Edith what she was thinking. One of her favorite phrases was "It's a slippery slope." She added, "But you do make an important point that I will keep in mind. Why don't you get in touch with some local groups—maybe the Boy Scouts—who might like to participate?"

Edith pulled one of her calling cards, which said simply *Mrs. Woodrow Wilson*, from her bag. She wrote her secretary's phone number on it and gave it to the city official. "Please keep me informed of your progress."

FIFTEEN

May 1917

A flurry of visitors from heads of state from the Allied nations came, but after that the official social calendar was vastly reduced.

The first official visit from the newly allied nations was from Britain. Headed by Arthur Balfour, a former prime minister and current foreign secretary, the mission was eager to speak with their American counterparts.

The morning of the official dinner, Edith checked on the setting up of the State Dining Room. White linen tablecloths covered the rows of long tables, with sharply folded black napkins in contrast. Workers were setting red tulips into crystal vases. She was surprised they hadn't chosen red, white, and blue to reflect both of the countries' colors. The black napkins, although striking, were not quite right. In a flash, she realized why. White, red, and black were the colors of the flag of the German Empire. This would not do. She grabbed as many of the napkins as she could and, upon closer look, saw they were actually a midnight blue. Nevertheless she took them to the staff member in charge, with a request to replace every one of them with a true blue.

Before the reception, Edith took Mr. Balfour on a tour of the State floor of the White House. He looked about the rooms, but the dignified-looking man with a thick gray mustache and hair neatly parted in the middle seemed to take little interest, just nodding politely as they entered each room so filled with history. Finally Edith asked, "Is there anything in particular you'd like to see?"

"The gardens," he said, surprising Edith.

She took him to the South Portico, from which they had a wonderful view. In the distance, the Washington Monument could be seen, glowing in the sinking sun. On the grounds, early spring daffodils and tulips were giving way to colorful coleus and begonias. The streetlights were twinkling on, making the tender new green leaves of the trees glow.

"After the dreary dark of London, this does my heart good."

Indeed, it seemed his face was relaxing, the color returning to his cheeks in the fresh, cool air.

Edith thought about the tremendous pressure the man was under to secure the critical support of the entire country. And she knew how packed the schedule was with receptions and a parade of people eager to meet him and the rest of the mission. He was an experienced diplomat, of course, but not necessarily aware of who truly held power and who would simply waste his time. He might, for example, fall into an extended conversation with the congenial but powerless vice president.

"What is the most important thing you wish to accomplish here tonight? What do you need most from us?"

He answered without hesitation. "We need doctors and nurses. After three long years of war, the hospital staffs are worn out. And unfortunately, many have been sent into battle, as our units are desperate for soldiers."

Edith reviewed the guest list for that night's reception in her head. "There's an influential doctor on the president's advisory committee here tonight. His name is Franklin Martin. Tell him exactly what you need. Give him numbers so that we can go to the president right away and gain support before too many other concerns get in the way. Then follow up with a letter. Encrypted, of course."

Mr. Balfour looked at her with a gaping mouth, blinking back his surprise. "Yes, ma'am. Thank you for your advice."

Later, she was delighted to see Dr. Franklin Martin cornering Woodrow. The two of them were glancing at the foreign secretary, now engaged in conversation in another cluster of men.

Helen, the only other woman at the reception, sidled up to her. "And so it begins."

Edith replied, "Yes indeed. We are witnesses to history."

☙

Some days later, after her morning work of answering correspondence and meeting with the head housekeeper, she went to Woodrow's study after lunch. There waiting for him was someone she had only met briefly before, Newton Baker, the secretary of war.

He was a slight and serious man; his face and manner rather resembled Woodrow's. He certainly could also have been a pastor's son.

Woodrow strode in and the men got right to the work at hand. "We've had tens of thousands of men sign up for military service. And I have a pile of pleas from former officers and others wishing to lead a brigade or such." He tapped the pile of papers on his desk. "Teddy Roosevelt's experience notwithstanding, I don't think that's how we want to do this."

Saying nothing, Baker looked back and forth between Woodrow and Edith as if he expected her to leave. When she merely crossed her ankles and remained in her chair, he finally relented. "First the numbers. We will need upward of a million or two in uniform. A few tens of thousands will not be sufficient. Therefore I propose we restart the draft."

"Agreed," Woodrow said. "How soon can we begin?"

"I want to do some things differently than were done previously. A system of local boards with the power to draft, assign to specialties, oversee the various excuses and objections…"

Edith broke in. "I read about riots over draft board decisions during the War between the States. I believe they had to do with the fairness of the system. Can we do things differently to avoid them?"

"Indeed." Woodrow again tapped the pile of papers with volunteers for leadership positions. "I've not approved any of these, because I don't believe it's the best and fairest way."

"Other than the very top commanders, the services need to choose their unit leaders." Newton steepled his fingers. "As for fairness in the rank and file, I think we need to question the policy of allowing conscriptees to buy their way out of service or hire someone in their stead. In this way, the wealthy avoid service."

Edith brightened. "Yes, exactly. No more of that."

The men talked on, about details such as assigning serial numbers and a sort of lottery to pick who was to be drafted in each round. There would be screening for physical and medical fitness, as well as exemptions for those who provided critical skills at home.

"But what about the farmers? Many of these men work the farms and provide the food. If you can't draft them, how will you ever reach the numbers you need? And the doctors and druggists and factory workers?" Edith said.

Baker looked her square in the eye. "You know, I had to pass through a line of women trying mightily to prevent me from passing through the gates. They were carrying signs imploring the vote and equality for women. It seems this is what they want, and it is an answer to the dilemma."

What Baker apparently didn't know was that Edith was not in favor of suffrage and deplored the women making nuisances of themselves in the streets. But she knew her opinion was becoming a relic of times long gone. A new order was coming into place whether she liked it or not. She feared for the survival of children when mothers were caught up in the draft or forced to work in fields or factories.

With the sudden loss of the rounds of entertaining and events she had become used to and for the most part enjoyed, Edith cast about, seeking more to do for the war effort.

She was already spending several hours a day patterning, cutting, and sewing pajamas and other articles of clothing, but she wanted to get out into the community. So without previous announcement, she appeared at the local American Red Cross office.

The tiny space bustled with activity. Edith's spirits lifted as she saw the colorful posters aligning the walls, supporting the war gardens and the draft, and seeking donations. Workers huddled in several small groups, all intent on their tasks.

A young woman led her to the office director who outlined the various areas for which to volunteer. He didn't seem to recognize her until she slipped him her calling card.

"My apologies, Mrs. Wilson. Of course, we're eager for you to do whatever suits you."

Edith wasn't concerned with being known; she just wanted to avoid embarrassment such as his. "Please, I want to do whatever is most needed, or work where I can be most helpful."

The director thought for a moment. "You know, trainloads of troops go through Union Station on their way to basic camp and eventually to the ships for overseas. How would you like to see them off? We'll have coffee and sandwiches for them and..."

"I'd love to." At last, she'd be able to connect with the people doing the hardest work. It would be a nice change from the politicians and diplomats who were her steady company.

Her first train station assignment came just a few weeks later. Unfortunately, it was a hot, muggy day, and the blue-and-white-striped uniform she was issued clung to her like a mop of seaweed. She had envisioned pouring coffee for the troops, so she went to the big black tank truck, where she saw girls with Red Cross armbands filling large steel pitchers. They looked like they could hold three gallons each. But the young girl at the distribution table took one look at Edith and advised her to get a sandwich basket instead. Edith wasn't sure if it was due to her advancing middle age or the fact that the girl had recognized her, but she was relieved not to have to lug the hot and heavy pitcher.

Her once crisp uniform had become a droopy mess, and she only hoped her blue cap was containing her hair, no doubt exploding in a frizzle from the humidity. She took a basket of sandwiches to the platform and put a smile on her face. She saw that many of the girls had tied gauzy scarves around their hats, keeping the sun from their faces and necks. She wished she had one, if only to hide her hair and dripping face.

A long, crowded train came huffing into the station, and the soldiers in crisp new khaki uniforms tumbled out of the railcars, quickly encircling Edith and the other volunteers. They wolfed down the sandwiches and quickly grabbed cups of coffee, as they had only a brief stop at the station.

After only a couple of minutes, the conductor was already yelling "All aboard!" Only a couple of half-sandwiches remained in Edith's basket. As the crowd thinned, a fresh-faced soldier rushed up and grabbed both of them.

"I heard a rumor, but I don't think it's true," he said, his brown eyes squinting at her.

"What's that?"

"That you are Mrs. Woodrow Wilson."

"I have that honor."

He shook his head, looking her up and down. "Well, you don't look like a First Lady to me."

She laughed, tried to smooth her crumpled uniform. "I agree I don't look the part now, but come back and visit me when you're back, and I'll give you a warm welcome to convince you." She waved as he scurried to the train. He held up his sandwich in thanks as the whistle blew and the doors closed. Edith hugged her empty basket, wondering how many of those boys wouldn't come back and hoping the brown-eyed one would take her up on her offer.

The Sunday drives were the hardest to give up, especially for Woodrow. No one would have blamed him if he took a drive, but Edith insisted they needed to do what they were asking of the country: no unnecessary travel on Sunday. Instead they rode horseback or in a carriage.

Soon she came to enjoy the quieter streets. It was a little eerie to drive down Pennsylvania Avenue and not see a single moving motorized vehicle, the *clip-clop* of the horses once again being the loudest sound.

Free of the constant whirl of entertaining and social duties, Edith enjoyed sewing with the ladies, volunteering for the Red Cross, and decoding and encrypting correspondence for Woodrow. Inspired by the new war gardens taking shape on Hains Point, and in cities and towns all across the nation, Edith decided to ask Woodrow about forming some sort of official commission, an idea Nell had brought to her, along with sample art posters done by Maginel Wright. She found the time on one of their Sunday carriage rides.

"Rebecca is helping the Boy Scouts in the new war garden," she began. "I make sure she leaves early enough to tend her plot."

"That's wonderful. Please give her my thanks," Woodrow replied.

As he was always so thin, Edith worried about bringing up food conservation with him, fearing he would cut back on his already meager portions. So she approached it from the aspect of preventing hunger.

"Along with the war gardens, I was wondering if we could create a national program to coordinate efforts to grow more food and educate the people on healthy alternatives if some foods become scarce. We've a lot of soldiers to feed, the shortages in Europe, and now the draft taking farmers away from their fields. And Nell has been working with an artist—the sister of Frank Lloyd Wright—on publicity posters."

"I like the idea."

Edith grew more excited, sensing his support. "The Food Administration, or something like that."

"It's a timely idea. And something positive to present amongst all the bad news. I'll have Colonel House look into setting something up, get Congress on board." He took a card from his pocket and began jotting a reminder for himself.

The mention of House sent a cold shiver down Edith's spine. She still struggled with forgiving him for the Mary Peck debacle. "As much as you admire and trust House, I had someone else in mind. I've heard great things about Herbert Hoover, who nearly single-handedly has saved Belgium and France from starvation."

"Yes, he's quite a noble fellow and good organizer."

"Maybe Mr. Hoover could head it up."

Woodrow looked out the window, where the Potomac had come into view. "I don't know the fellow well, but it seems a good fit for his interests. House will be busy as my emissary in Europe in any case."

Edith wasn't any happier with that idea, but at least she wouldn't have to coordinate her own project with that weasel of a man.

❧

Leading by example, Edith instituted meatless Mondays and wheatless Wednesdays at the White House. Like the rest of the nation, they ate more fish and local produce, and the chefs became creative with using preserved fruits rather than sugar for desserts.

Although much formal entertaining was off the calendar, there were still some officials invited for smaller, private dinners. One of them was William McAdoo, giving Woodrow extra time with his daughter Nell. After a simple Monday meal of an omelet and wonderful whole-wheat bread, the men started talking about financing the war. William, never too shy to boast about his successes, was proclaiming that his four-month shutdown of the stock market had saved the U.S. economy from certain collapse.

Nell's eyes started to glaze over, and Edith suggested they retire to the Oval Sitting Room for coffee. She was hoping to get some inside scuttlebutt on the progress the Cabinet wives were making on their various projects. She hadn't realized how much she would miss their lunches.

"If you don't mind, I'd like to use your telephone to check on the children." In addition to Nell's baby girl, William had several children from his previous marriage living with them. Nell excused herself, leaving Edith with the men and a prospect of a dull conversation involving tax structures and new fees for luxuries like yachts.

But just as she placed her napkin on the table and prepared to make an excuse to leave, William said something interesting. "We need to involve everyone in this, not just the rich. We all must be willing to give up something of personal convenience, something we treasure—and if necessary, our lives in the bargain, to support our noble sons who go out to die for us."

"I like that. You should use it in your speech when we roll this out," Woodrow said.

"I'm sorry, roll out what?" Edith's curiosity outweighed her embarrassment for not having been listening.

Woodrow seemed pleased to offer a review. "What the secretary is saying is that he sees three ways to raise money for the war effort. One, we simply print more money. We don't want to do that as it will devalue our currency and cause rapid inflation. Two, we can increase taxes, especially on the wealthy. But there's a limit to how far you can go with that until the money starts leaving the country and we destroy incentive to do things like build factories and invent better weapons. And third"—he nodded toward William—"I'll let you explain it."

"The other alternative is to borrow money. I'm proposing that the government sell war bonds. The advantages are we can involve more of the population; we frame it as the patriotic thing to do. It encourages saving and investing, not only for themselves, but for the country. And it would change spending habits, causing people to cut back on other purchases, leaving more goods available for the war effort."

"I see. So a woman might decide to buy a war bond, instead of a new dress, leaving the fabric and thread and the labor to create it free for the manufacture of uniforms," Edith said. "I like the idea of connecting it with patriotism. We could have an advertising campaign like we're developing for the war gardens. Have librarians give out flyers with each book. Posters in train stations."

"Yes," said both Woodrow and William.

Ideas swirled in her head. "Even schoolchildren can get involved. Girl Scouts and sports teams can hand out flyers, maybe come up with their own incentives and competitions."

Woodrow caught her enthusiasm. "People love competition. Maybe encourage towns to have contests—who can raise the most? Companies, baseball teams, service clubs. There are so many possibilities." Then his more contemplative side emerged. "But we must be careful in its administration. We don't want to create a government bureaucracy that winds up costing the bulk of funds coming in."

"The campaigns can be run by volunteers," William assured him. "We'll need to hire some professionals, an advertising agency perhaps, but the feet on the ground will be unpaid. The bonds can be sold in banks. Since I head the Federal Reserve Bank system, I can make that happen."

Edith tried to think of any downsides. "What if it's a big bust—people don't buy them?"

William stirred his coffee. "I think we need to have several campaigns. Put a time limit on them to create a feeling of urgency. Right now, it seems like the war might go on forever, and people crave a sense of finality. It motivates them. So, we say the first campaign goes until a certain date. Then we re-evaluate and make adjustments for the next campaign."

That seemed reasonable to Edith. "But that first campaign, it needs to be splashy. I'm wondering, do we have to call them war bonds?"

Woodrow asked, "Do you have another idea?"

Edith ran some names through her head. Peace Bonds? Service Bonds? Patriot, American, Great War Bonds? She thought of the statue atop the Capitol Building. "Maybe Freedom Bonds?" But then she remembered the magnificent lighting of the Statue of Liberty, a gift from France that was at the heart of the war. "No, I've got it. Liberty Bonds."

"Brilliant." Woodrow enthused. "Liberty Bonds it is." He held up his glass to toast the new name. "May they be a great success, furthering our causes of peace and liberty worldwide."

"Hear, hear." William raised his coffee cup. "And I'd like to suggest that for the launch of each phase, the two of you travel to different cities."

"Marvelous idea. A whistle-stop tour, like the campaign," Woodrow agreed.

Edith looked askance at him, thinking of how the presidential campaign had thoroughly worn him down. "There would hardly be time for that."

Woodrow was undeterred. "Maybe we can even get Edith to make a speech."

But Edith knew where her strengths lay and where they decidedly did not. "I'll start spreading the word as soon as we have the pieces in place. But I'll leave the speeches up to you, my dear."

As the Liberty Bonds program was being built, the Food Administration was also created. Woodrow asked Herbert Hoover to lead it, and he accepted. Public campaigns were begun encouraging meatless days and cutting back on sugar and wheat. Recipes were circulating in magazines for making bread with rice or potato flour.

Edith was asked to sign a pledge as a charter member of the Food Administration, which she happily did. Soon after, she received a card with the new logo: a shield with the stars and stripes of the flag, surrounded by spears of wheat. At the top, the card read "Member of the United States Food Administration." Edith proudly hung it in a window on the second floor of the Residence. She telephoned Mr. Hoover to thank him for the card and offer any services she could provide.

"No, thank you, Mrs. Wilson. I understand you and Mrs. McAdoo were the inspiration. I hope to make you and our country proud. Your enthusiastic support is all we need at the moment."

"You have it, of course. I do have a question. Why so much emphasis on eating potatoes rather than wheat. Is it cost, or nutrition, or...?"

Hoover laughed. "There's a simple answer. We need to conserve wheat to send overseas. It's less perishable and lighter and easier to ship than potatoes. And you know how the French love their bread."

How refreshing was this selfless man. Edith enjoyed a moment of self-congratulation at convincing Woodrow to choose him over House for this quiet but important role.

SIXTEEN

June 1917

O ne morning, Edith was delighted to read in the newspaper that American doctors and nurses were headed overseas to relieve the exhausted staffs of the British and French. Troops were still being recruited and trained. She was amazed at how quickly civilian medical personnel were able to organize and move out, another wonderful group to add to her nightly prayer list.

Rebecca quietly handed her a slip of paper. "From the carpenter working on the China Room."

The note, written in a strange-looking cursive, requested that Edith come see the progress. So Rebecca and Edith headed to the ground floor. The three oval rooms in the White House were stacked in the center of the south side. The ground floor held the Diplomat Reception Room; the State Floor had the elegant Blue Room, which led to the South Portico; and above that was the oval sitting room used by the family. All had marble fireplaces, and the upper two had lovely views looking toward the Potomac.

The Diplomatic Reception Room was being prepared for a meeting. Edith nodded to the workers and asked them to carry on, as she passed by into the China Room, which had been vastly transformed. Once a dark storage room, it now was lined with beautiful wooden cabinets with glass cases on the top. Electricians on ladders in the center of the room were working on a huge gold-and-crystal chandelier, and other workers were laying drop cloths in preparation for painting.

The carpenter was fitting the last of the glass doors on the upper cabinets. "What do you think, ma'am?" He spoke with a strong accent, maybe Russian, Edith thought.

She peered into a cabinet and admired the careful handiwork, with small bumpers set on the shelves to keep plates upright. "I think this will be a most worthy place to exhibit the china collections. In fact, we should name this the Presidential Collections Room." She walked the length of the room, admiring how the new cabinets fit in with the existing crown molding, as if they had always been there. "Can you make some nice signs for each section, indicating which presidents first used the china and the dates? And can we line the shelves with felt to protect the verge?"

The carpenter pulled a measuring tape and pencil from his pocket. "Yes, ma'am." The handsome man had light-brown skin and curly black hair; his faded coveralls failed to conceal muscles built from hard work. He chomped on an unlit cigar. Since the president didn't smoke, it had become a sort of unofficial policy that no one did while in the Residence.

The room was warming up as the sun poured in, the window now drapeless due to the construction. "Shall we open the window?" Edith headed toward it, but workers beat her to it.

As soon as it was opened, Edith regretted it. Sounds of a protest outside the gates assaulted her ears. "Ugh. You would think the suffragettes would have some respect. We're at war, for God's sake."

"You would not have women to vote?" The carpenter approached the small gathering of workers at the window. "Even in my poor country that has suffered under the rule of many different empires, and mass killings by the Turks, will find that progress."

"Where are you from, Mr..."

"Dimidjian. I am from Yerevan."

Edith winced, remembering the genocide Armenia had recently suffered. "How long have you been here, Mr. Dimidjian?"

"About two years. I escaped the purge. They attacked the young men first—the ones who might be able to defend our country. We are very thankful to your husband and to the United States. You came to our aid and saved a great many of us, and helped many others like me to escape."

The shouts from the suffragettes grew louder.

"And yet you criticize our rule of law. Are you aware, Mr. Dimidjian, that the states each have the power to offer women the vote? And that our Constitution limits the federal government to specific powers, with the remaining powers left to the states?"

"Yes, ma'am. You had a war about that. And now we know some things, like individual freedom, are too important to leave up to the states."

"So you know your United States history."

"Yes, ma'am. I study to become citizen." He folded his arms across his chest, a look of pride on his face.

"That's wonderful. Please let me know if you need help." Edith needed to be careful. It was unwise to make promises to one that she couldn't make for all. "And you say that Armenian women can vote?"

"Not yet. But my part of Armenia is now under Russian rule. And of course, with the revolution, things are changing. But the new regime says women are to have a say in the new government."

Edith felt that Mr. Dimidjian, like so many others, missed the point: the rights of states to have their own laws, except as outlined in the Constitution. But after all, the United States was a unique country. One shouldn't expect a citizen of a country with a strong national government to understand. "We have great hopes for the new Russia. With them as our allies, the war will end in victory."

But her enthusiasm didn't have the cheerful effect on him she had hoped. His face fell with despair. "I am afraid I have spoken out of turn. It is not my place to judge this country's laws, nor predict what the Bolsheviks will do. Please accept my apologies."

"Nonsense. Free speech is one of our founding principles."

His face brightened. "I have idea. I have friend who is very talented artist. He too emigrated from Armenia. I shall speak to him about painting something very nice for you and Mr. Wilson. In gratitude from our people."

Woodrow was spending more and more of his working hours in the West Wing. His oval-shaped office reflected the rooms stacked in three levels on the south side of the Residence. He wasn't happy with the arrangement of the rooms in the wing, as he couldn't get to and from his office and the Residence without passing by a number of staff. He was unable to make the trip without being stopped for questions, or just in greeting, and it took up far too much of his precious time.

But on some days, when there were meetings with the Cabinet, senators and congressmen and staffs, it made sense to work there. Edith sometimes joined him, as otherwise she might not see him the entire day.

She tiptoed in the open door one hot day, hearing him shouting into the telephone. "We've appealed to their every last civic duty, and they're still threatening to strike. It's time. You know what to do." He hung up with a slam.

"That didn't sound promising." Edith placed a tray of cheese sandwiches on his desk. "You missed lunch."

He grunted and grabbed a sandwich as he motioned for her to sit on a chair opposite his desk. "Do we have any open nights on the calendar this week?"

Edith consulted the notebook with the calendar. Although he always had a copy of it on his desk, he rarely consulted it, relying on others to remind him where and when he needed to be. "Nothing tomorrow evening. Why?"

"Do you think you could invite the McAdoos for dinner?"

"Of course. Just William and Nell? Any special reason?"

He nodded at the telephone. "That was about the railroads. The combination of strikes and sudden increase in the need to move people and goods has them on the brink. We're going to nationalize them."

"Like the National Guard?"

"More like the draft. But the workers will remain civilians. They'll just work for the government."

He said it so calmly, Edith wondered if he realized the significance of such a move. "That sounds like something Karl Marx would do."

Woodrow leaned back in his chair, gazed at the ceiling. "I know. But we have tried everything, and we're backed into a corner. They've been given plenty of warning and resources to work things out. But they can't get it together, and we can't conduct a war overseas without them. It will be temporary." He pointed a finger at her. "I will ensure that with a firm end date."

"I see. And how does this involve the McAdoos?"

"I need someone I know well and trust to be in charge. And William, if he accepts the position, would be perfect. He was president of a major railroad sometime back and is a financial and legal wiz."

"But he's the secretary of the treasury. Can he do both?"

Woodrow paused. "No. The appointment would be conditional on giving that up."

Edith imagined a very awkward dinner to come. "He will see that as a demotion from a Cabinet-level position. Are you sure you want to do that to your son-in-law?"

He snapped back upright in his chair. "He wasn't my son-in-law when I nominated him. I don't give out political favors to friends and family. And this is an important position. He wouldn't turn it down."

"Okay, don't get hot under the collar." She didn't say what she was thinking, that Woodrow certainly did appoint men into positions due to his trusting relationships with them. Maybe he didn't consider them "friends," but supporters like Colonel House and Joseph Tumulty hadn't earned their way through a meritocracy. Not that it bothered her; she felt most would do the same. But why did he claim to be innocent of such personal decisions? Wasn't it just human to rely on those close to you, whom you would trust with your very life? She'd love to get Woodrow to admit this, but it was an argument she didn't have the psychological energy for, and besides, what would be the point?

As for William, he might not turn the position down, but he wouldn't be happy with it either. She'd seen him gleefully showing his children his name on dollar bills.

It turned out they were both wrong. McAdoo politely but firmly turned down the railroad position with the condition of resigning from the Treasury. "It would be irresponsible for me to turn over both the Federal Reserve and the Treasury at this critical moment. I ask for the opportunity to do both. And Mr. President, if you are unhappy with my performance, we can reconsider my resignation."

Woodrow begrudgingly respected William's decision, even though he complained it made him look weak. Edith realized she had held back in her advice, not wanting to anger Woodrow. But if she was to be the "soothsayer" he had said he needed, she would have to risk his wrath in the process.

Some months later, a group of Armenians came to the White House to present the most beautiful portrait Edith had ever seen. Mr. Dimidjian's friend, the artist Hovsep Pushman, had sent his work, titled *L'Esperance*. It was a portrait of the artist's niece, Dora, a girl with big brown eyes and a wistful face, holding a flower. With rich colors, the artist had painted the girl dressed in an elegant green dress from their culture.

The artist's wife presented the portrait. A translator interpreted her remarks. "The title means 'Hope.' The sadness on Dora's face represents the suffering of the Armenian people and the thousands of little children who perished as a result of the genocide. Dora holds a mountain snowdrop. In Armenia, this flower brings good luck and protection from evil. Its appearance is a sign that winter is ending and that spring is on its way—a sign of hope for better times. Dora and the flower symbolize the hope for the future of Armenia, helped by Americans."

The carpenter, Mr. Dimidjian, now dressed in a handsome brown suit, had tears running down his cheeks. Even Woodrow had removed his pince-nez glasses and was wiping his eyes.

Hope indeed, Edith thought. How gracious were these people who had suffered so much. With all the fighting amongst nations, the eternal hope and perseverance of the people would put the world right again.

After the ceremony, Edith and Woodrow admired the painting in private.

"I shall miss it when we become private citizens once again," Edith said.

"You won't have to, Ignatz. The Armenians love the French and have taken a page from their book." Woodrow tapped his foot on the elegant rug at their feet.

"How's that?" But then Edith remembered. The beautiful and very large rug, with images of cherubs and angels looking over a wedding couple, had been a wedding gift from the French people. When Edith mentioned they hadn't decided which room in the Residence would be its final home, the French emissary had been indignant.

"No," he had huffed. "This is our personal gift to you and the president. It is a wedding rug. You must keep it, or we will have to move it back to France at great expense."

It had made both Woodrow and Edith uncomfortable, as they did not want to be seen as profiting unduly from his position. But legal counsel advised them on how to keep it.

They sat in the velvet settee in their customary way, with Edith's legs on Woodrow's lap.

"I love the painting, and the meaning behind it. But I know whenever I look into those girl's eyes, I will wonder if we've been wrongheaded about something. Dora is fourteen years old and lives in a conquered country. Yet some would say that she will be voting before some American women are."

Woodrow raised his eyebrows, questioning. She hadn't told him of the conversation with the carpenter, so she explained that to him.

"To my dying day, I will believe it is a decision best left up to the states. But the political pressures for a constitutional amendment are growing," Woodrow said.

"But those hideous protestors, disturbing the peace and insulting you at every turn. Should that be rewarded? Do we want more of that every time someone is unhappy with their state of affairs?"

"Yes, little girl, that is their right as Americans. When they have done something illegal, they've been thrown in jail."

"Hmph."

"And there's something else. Your friend the carpenter was right. The Russians are giving women the vote. How much that means in a country prone to government power by coup remains to be seen. But if we want them to come into the war on our side, then coming to terms with this issue and agreeing with their position may help. And even more important, we need to be united as a country."

"But there are still many opposed to suffrage. How would it help to force it through on a national level before the various states are ready?"

"We'll let the Congress battle that out, shall we? In the meanwhile, I will remove my objection."

Edith felt at once relieved and concerned. There were still so many questions to be ironed out. The military conscription was now underway. Would this mean that women would be drafted as well? What would be the effect on families? What fiscal responsibilities would fall on women? Would having and raising children no longer be seen as women's work? There were suffragettes in many states working for things like the right to own property, hold jobs if they wanted them, and manage their own children and affairs. A prominent suffragette from Kentucky, Laura Clay, was against a women's vote amendment for these reasons. What would happen to all these efforts if a sweeping new federal law superseded their efforts?

Woodrow nodded off to sleep, his mind made up. Edith needed to find a way to support him while voicing her reservations.

While uncrating the pieces of presidential china, Edith marveled at the history and design of each. The earliest pieces from the Monroe and Jackson administrations had indistinct eagles in the center, while those of Polk and Grant depicted lovely flowers. Though she much admired the Lincolns, the purplish hue, clumsy eagle, and busy format of their pattern was not her favorite. The Hayeses' collection featured lifelike nature scenes but seemed less than presidential. Her favorite china pattern, if not her favorite administration, was that of the Roosevelts—a delicate geometric pattern with the presidential seal at the top bordering a field of pure white.

With constant entertaining and state dinners, the china was much used, and as even the most careful of servants would drop and shatter the delicate pieces, she was advised more needed to be ordered. Edith sometimes longed for an ordinary life. What could be more normal than a new bride choosing a china pattern? Of course, it wouldn't be theirs to keep, but somehow it helped satisfy the yearning to do something traditional.

Turning each piece over to read its make and place of manufacture, Edith realized with a start that none of the china was made in the United States. This led her to research the reason, only to find that strong porcelain china was not something perfected by any of the country's factories. The Roosevelts had tried to order from an American company, but they couldn't manage the large order.

So when she received a letter from the head of the Lenox Company in Trenton, New Jersey, it piqued her interest. He had heard of her effort to preserve White House china and said the company had invented a new way to make very strong yet delicate-appearing porcelain. But their ration of coal to fire their kilns was running out, and they risked losing a year's worth of production.

Letter in hand, she went to Woodrow's study. Luckily, he was in a jovial mood, bantering with Joseph Tumulty, who quickly excused himself.

Edith reviewed the situation of the Lenox Company. "This is not only important for them but for the U.S. industry as well. Did you know that the entire White House collection was made overseas? Can't we spare a couple of carloads of coal?"

"I see." Woodrow looked over the letter. "It's not a vital industry for the war, so their ration would have been severely curtailed."

"That bit of coal isn't going to hamper our war effort. Can't we make this effort to save this company and their lives' work?" She was prepared for him to object on the grounds of not wanting to request special treatment with a whole list of reasons why it made good sense. But Woodrow surprised her.

"I'll see to it." Woodrow wrote a note on the letter and added it to a stack on his desk. "I hope by next year we're dining on fine American-made china."

SEVENTEEN

September 1917

A heat wave struck the city in early September. Edith encouraged the head housekeeper to allow as many of the staff as possible to flee the city with the rest of its residents. Electric fans were placed in every conceivable place and windows opened to allow cross-breezes, but still Edith had to mop herself with wet rags to maintain any sense of comfort. She invited her mother and sister to stay in the Residence, as the rooms in their hotel were stifling.

Altrude also joined them as they gathered in the family dining room, waiting for lunch to be served. Sallie, sitting stick-straight, seemed cool in her gauzy white dress.

"Ugh, I'm sweating like a pig." Edith fanned herself with her napkin. "How are you not?"

"First, dear girl, a lady doesn't sweat," her mother said. "She glows. And second, you have been away from the countryside too long. Pigs can't sweat to cool themselves, so they wallow."

Just then, Woodrow popped in, seeming to be in a better mood than Edith. His only concession to the heat was not wearing his suit jacket.

He kissed, or rather came close to kissing, Edith's sweat-beaded forehead. "Ladies, I hope I haven't kept you waiting."

Bertha assured him that he had not. She glanced toward Edith. "Can you believe she's a Southern lady? What ever will she do if it really warms up?"

Woodrow seated himself next to Sallie and held up a finger to beckon a waiter. "We shall fill a bathtub with gin and ice and place her in it."

Altrude and Sallie laughed, but Edith was too hot to be amused.

"No? Well, how about this?" He took a card out of his shirt pocket. "President and Mrs. Wilson's schedule, September 7. Depart by train to New York City. Motor to Twenty-Third Street wharf. Board the *Mayflower* and immediately set sail..."

Edith whooped. "Do you mean it? Can you actually get away?"

"That's what they tell me. I will have several meetings along the way, most importantly with Colonel House."

"So we're going to Massachusetts? Thank you, Lord; it will be cooler there." She saw Sallie's and Bertha's expectant faces. "Oh, they can come, can't they? And of course Cary and Altrude will be joining us."

"Of course." Woodrow beamed.

"Oh, I don't know about me. I became dreadfully ill last time," Altrude said.

Edith waved away her concern. "We'll be in protected waters this time. No ocean waves to worry about."

"Still..." Altrude hesitated, staring into her lap.

"Wait a minute." Edith had noticed that Altrude had put on a few pounds but dismissed it to her more settled life as a married woman. "Do you have some news to share?"

"I wanted to tell you when Cary was with me, but yes. We are expecting a baby in late January."

Edith shrieked and jumped up to embrace Altrude. "Oh, it will be like having another grandchild!"

"I was hoping you'd feel that way." Altrude beamed.

Having just moved into the Residence, Edith's mother and sister declined the voyage so it was just Woodrow, Edith, their valet and maid, and the Secret Service detail who caught the midnight train to New York. The next morning, the captain met them at the wharf in a skiff, and they buzzed out to the *Mayflower*, anchored nearby. The ship's profile had changed since

Edith had last seen it. The beautiful yacht now bristled with armament. She was a navy vessel who had seen war before, but it still saddened Edith to see her so transformed.

Pouring rain kept them inside their cabins as they left the harbor. Edith hoped they wouldn't see rough seas. But by the time they arrived at their first stop in New London, the skies had cleared. There Margaret and Jessie came on board, and they all had a lively dinner. Margaret bubbled with excitement about the sales of her records, now raising money for the Red Cross. Jessie, as usual, smiled and said little.

As they set out again, the rays of the sinking sun turned the water into liquid gold. Woodrow had taken to his office, so Edith enjoyed the view from the fantail by herself. As they sailed down Long Island Sound, she relished the cool wind in her face as she watched the lights on the shoreline dwindle until all was dark, except for the star-studded sky.

The next day, they passed through the Cape Cod Canal, then sailed north toward Boston. Edith had a few precious hours to catch up on correspondence while Woodrow tapped away at his typewriter.

"What are you doing, rewriting *War and Peace*?" she asked after a long spell of constant tapping.

Woodrow looked up long enough to reply. "In a way. But just the peace part."

Curious, she came around behind him to take a peek, but he waved her off. "You'll see it soon enough. But if you must know, I'm going to ask Colonel House to do something unprecedented—head up a team of experts to map out the plan for peace. And I mean literally. We need to create the physical and political boundaries for countries for the new world order. So we need geographers, historians, cultural experts, businessmen, industrialists, economists..."

"I get the idea. Brilliant, as usual, if perhaps a bit too soon." She consulted her watch. "But world order aside, it's time to dress for dinner."

He was ready before she was and came to her cabin in a nicely fitted black suit and crisp white shirt. "Can you help me with these?" He handed her his gold cuff links with the presidential seal.

As she put them on, she noticed that he had some trouble lifting his left hand. But he shook it off, saying he had done too much typing.

Edith straightened his tie, really an excuse to study his face. Sometimes, when he was fatigued or his blood pressure was acting up, his mouth drooped a bit. She was relieved that didn't seem to be the case. "So, we will meet with both Mr. and Mrs. House. How much secret information is she privy to?"

"That's *Colonel* and Mrs. And I don't know. Good point; I'll make sure to meet with him separately."

Edith rolled her eyes at the honorific "Colonel." It had been given to him by some politician in Texas, and she thought it presumptuous for him to use it. "Hmm. I see. So I have to entertain Loulie all by myself." She was teasing. The few times she had met the woman, she had found her delightful. "But I guess I still don't understand why you need House to do this. Isn't that the job of the secretary of state? Isn't there an entire diplomatic corps who are paid professionals?"

He sighed. "They have their place, but their hands are full implementing policy and running their agencies. I need a full-time advisor, one I can trust implicitly. Not someone interested in his own political gain. House and I are of a mind. But he's not an echo chamber, which too often appointed officials are." He softened. "I'm sorry, dear; I don't mean to say that your advice isn't important as well."

She forced a smile to hide the disappointment he must have read on her face. "He is much more experienced in these things." She thought Woodrow was wrong in at least one aspect of the man, however. He seemed very much to be an echo chamber, rarely disagreeing with Woodrow.

She was still seething about McAdoo and House's plot to upend her and Woodrow's engagement and couldn't fathom how Woodrow could dismiss it as well intentioned but misguided. But politics was a strange beast, and men's relationships even stranger. Edith did her best to accept what had happened, even as she kept a close eye on House and his advice.

The Houses met them at the pier in Gloucester, and they all went for a long motor ride. Edith and Loulie sat together, teasing the men and each other.

"I hear there's no more grits to be had on the White House menu," Loulie said. "Or is that just on Wednesdays?"

"Grits are made from corn, not wheat, and are most acceptable. And what do you do for the war effort?" She looked around at the luxurious motorcar. "I guess gasless Sundays aren't observed here? Does meatless Monday mean no filet mignon for breakfast at the club?"

"Yes, because we're fresh out of possum."

Woodrow joined the ladies' laughter. But House, ever the serious one, looked from one to the other as if they were mad, his gray mustache twitching. "We don't normally drive on Sunday..."

As it turned out, dinner was not at their home but at the Houses' country club, causing House more embarrassment and profuse apologies.

Edith gleefully noted the things not on the menu. "No muskrat, possum, or armadillo. Whatever am I to eat?" But even as she made fun of her small rural town upbringing, she felt a note of discomfort. She meant to poke fun at a stereotype, but what did these sophisticated Bostonians really believe? Did they really think the people of the South were as backward as they had teased?

The way the men hurried through dinner, it was clear they were anxious to get to the business at hand. House returned to the *Mayflower* with them, while Loulie returned home. She couldn't resist a last dig at Edith, pretending to wave off the driver of her limousine. "That's okay; I'll walk. It's only twenty miles."

Back on the yacht, Edith, Woodrow, and House gathered in the library. Woodrow outlined his plan for creating a study group in order to draft a peace agreement.

Edith voiced her concern regarding the timing. "We've only been in the war for five months, and it doesn't seem anywhere close to being over. Isn't it rather soon to be divvying up the spoils?"

"Fair point," House said. He was not a large man, and he seemed swallowed up by the large leather banquette. "But we are getting pressured by numerous sources to make a peace offering. Our people know the Germans have made several peace proposals, as they've been most public about that. What Americans and our allies don't seem to understand is that the Kaiser's proposals are entirely in their favor, giving them the 'spoils of war' as you say. We could never agree to them, nor should our allies."

Edith hated to admit House made sense. "I guess it's never too soon to study the idea. Then when the time comes for an agreement, we won't waste time. And we can back up whatever terms we ask from a scholarly viewpoint. We don't say we want this port, or these coal mines, or this side of a mountain range without proving why, through history, it makes sense."

"Precisely." Woodrow beamed and tousled her hair. "There's a lot of deep thinking inside that pretty head." He turned back to House. "Here is the crux of it. If the agreements make as much sense as possible to both sides in all those much-contested places, then there will be less probability of unrest in the future."

"And then there's Russia," House chimed in. "A massive nation with critical resources. But frankly, they're a mess. They need the leadership we bring to the table."

House pulled some folders from his briefcase and Edith rose, taking that as her signal to leave. Woodrow's slight nod both thanked and dismissed her. She would have much preferred that House be the one dismissed. Maybe she didn't have all the geopolitical background that he professed, but she was a trusted sounding board for Woodrow.

The next morning dawned bright and clear. A touch of coolness in the air gave promise that fall would soon be upon them. The ship headed into Massachusetts Bay and followed the coastline into Cape Cod Bay. Edith enjoyed seeing the lighthouses dotting the pebbled shores and the mansions here and there. What wonderful views they would have. She imagined spending retirement years with Woodrow, sitting on ladder-back rockers on a porch overlooking the ocean. But then she remembered how frigid she was playing golf in two inches of snow in Virginia. How would she manage a New England winter?

Woodrow found her. "We've been invited to join the captain on the bridge."

They climbed the stairs and arrived on the narrow outside passageway just as the ship approached the Cape Cod Canal. This time there were people lined up elbow to elbow waving and cheering. Edith and Woodrow smiled and waved back.

But Edith's stomach tightened. Something wasn't right. "How did they know we'd be here?" she asked the captain. Their whole trip had been kept a secret due to security concerns. Even the girls and the Houses hadn't known they were coming until a crewman went ashore and made telephone calls.

"I'm afraid it's hard to hide a thousand-ton ship." The captain explained. "Once it was reported we sailed through the canal, everyone knew we'd be coming back."

As they neared the south end of the canal, Edith grew more concerned when several navy ships were there to greet them. A sailor, brilliant in his white uniform, waved a signal flag atop the crow's nest of the nearest vessel.

The captain put binoculars to his eyes. Edith couldn't read wigwag, but it was apparent the sailor was repeating the same short message.

The captain lowered his binoculars. "They're requesting permission for an officer to come aboard with an important message." He looked at Woodrow, who nodded his permission.

Edith started to follow the captain as he hurried down the stairs, but Woodrow held her back. "Whatever it is, they will sort it out. Let's just enjoy the sea air, shall we?"

They watched as an officer in dress uniform boarded a skiff that then motored toward the *Mayflower*, whose steady engine noise had reduced to a faint rumble. By the time the skiff arrived, the *Mayflower* had slowed to a halt. Woodrow made small talk, but Edith could hardly focus on anything other than the conversation happening below. She thought of Rebecca, who was alone in her cabin and probably frightened. She had had misgivings about coming on the trip, but Edith had blithely dismissed them.

After several tense minutes, the captain came up the stairs, huffing, his face ruddy. He was not a young man. "Mr. President, a German submarine has been spotted off Nantucket. The whereabouts of the *Mayflower* are clearly known. The Department of the Navy has ordered the *Mayflower* to reverse course and take shelter in the canal, which can be guarded on both ends."

Woodrow crossed his arms and looked out at the navy escort ships. "How many knots can a U-boat do?"

"Fifteen knots at the most on the surface, sir. Nine submerged under battery power, with a range of about eighty miles."

"And how far away are we from Nantucket, or however much closer could they be since last sighted?"

The captain rolled his eyes up, calculating. "I'd say around forty miles."

"So still within submerged range. If we were to stay on our current course, how far is it to the next safe port?"

"Oh, there's New Bedford, Newport, Narragansett. We would be in New London by about five…"

"And remind me, Captain, how many knots can the *Mayflower* do?"

"Fourteen in fair weather."

"So we can simply outrun the sub and duck into a harbor that is on our way if need be."

"Yes, sir. But the navy says to go back into the canal, and I agree that's the safest thing to do."

"And for how long? Is the U-boat captain going to telegraph *auf wiedersehen* when he decides to slink back to the fatherland? While we cower in fear on our own well-protected coast?"

"I take your point, sir. Are your orders to proceed on course?"

"Those are my orders. Please inform the officer, and thank him for his message."

The captain saluted and headed back down the stairs.

Edith was trying to track the speeds of the ship against the fuzzy map in her head. It seemed to make sense, that they had speed and time on their side, not to mention an escort of anti-torpedo boats. But the prospect of being chased by an armed submarine made her light-headed. She grasped the handrail to steady herself. Woodrow seemed not at all concerned, probably because he was much braver and his brain told him the risk was low. She needed to check on the less-brave Rebecca.

By the time Edith got Rebecca calmed down, for indeed she was wide-eyed with trepidation, they were halfway to Newport. There were no more submarine sightings, and their navy escort departed when they reached New London.

After more stops to visit friends in Connecticut, they received a message from Woodrow's daughter Jessie.

Woodrow handed the note to Emily. "She wants us to visit them at a cottage in Siasconset."

"Where is that?" Edith asked. She was knitting a hat for the Red Cross and tugged at the tangled yarn.

"Nantucket. On the coast."

"Is there anything that's not coast in Nantucket?" she mused. "It's out of the question, of course."

"What do you mean? We have no more visits scheduled until we head back to New York."

Edith looked up from her knitting, incredulous. "We narrowly escaped with our lives. We can't take that risk."

"Oh, you exaggerate. These waters are well patrolled, and nothing's been seen of that sub in a week."

"It's not only us to consider but our crew and the crews of the escort ships, should they be necessary. Jessie can jolly well come back to New London."

"Oh, Edith." Woodrow moved a completed hat and sat beside her. "What would it say to people if we hid ourselves away? What would it say to the navy... That we don't trust them to protect us? If we are not safe two miles from our own shoreline, then we ought to be preparing for a very different war."

"It would say that we are responsible human beings. That we realize that this ship has a big target painted on it."

"That's what we signed up for. It isn't different in the streets of Washington, nor anywhere else for that matter." He returned the knit hat and stood. "Try not to worry so much. Because we're going."

᪔

Rebecca was having none of it. She paced her room, twisting the ties of her apron. "I'd do anything for you, Miss Edith. You know that. But I haven't slept more than an hour straight since the whole scare. Every time I drift off, the engine makes a funny noise, and I'm sure we're hit."

"Why don't you take a few days off? Then return to the Residence a few days before we do. There'll be plenty to do."

So Rebecca disembarked while they were in port to replenish supplies before setting sail for Nantucket. Edith expected their navy escort ships to reappear, but they never did. They arrived in Nantucket harbor on a day so clear and crisp it seemed the air could shatter into a million pieces. The water had nary a ripple. Edith felt comforted that the sailor up in the crow's nest would be able to see for a long way through his scope. It occurred to her that maybe part of Woodrow's objective was to lure any subs out of hiding. If they were lurking, that was something the navy and the country needed to know. She shuddered, pushing the idea out of her mind.

They had a spectacular time in Siasconset. Woodrow built a huge sandcastle for the children and romped with them, laughing and playing tag until they all collapsed in a heap.

He needed this, Edith admitted. She still didn't agree with his decision, but she understood. He had evaluated the risk and determined the reward was worth it. There would be no point in a life you were too afraid to enjoy.

EIGHTEEN

After two glorious days on Nantucket, they sped all the way back to New York. There were more dinners and entertainment, and Woodrow met House again. In the week's time, he already had a list of prominent experts to serve on the team they now called "the Inquiry." Plans were made for the team to go overseas by early November.

In mid-October, Woodrow invited Secretary of State Lansing, Secretary of War Baker, and Colonel House to the Residence for an emergency meeting. Edith attended the informal meeting in Woodrow's study as well.

Woodrow got right to the point. "As Colonel House knows, as he received the cable from the British foreign minister, they and the French beseech us to send an envoy to Paris to participate in a war council. The object is to form a plan for how together we will win the war. We are here today to determine who shall represent us."

Lansing grumbled. "Remind me once again, why is the foreign minister communicating outside our diplomatic channels?"

Edith wasn't impressed with Lansing. He didn't seem to have enough experience to manage the huge State Department, not to mention develop critical relationships overseas. He seemed more interested in being seen as in charge than actually doing the work. She knew that Woodrow would want House to go, as he had already developed a strong relationship with the allied leaders. However, she didn't fully trust House either. She eyed Baker.

Baker, like House, was a slight, slender man of about Edith's age, which made him the youngest member of the Cabinet. Unlike House, he was clean-shaven, dark-haired, and wore small thick eyeglasses. He had been a student of Woodrow's back in his undergraduate days and had followed him like a puppy dog ever since. He was a strong supporter during Woodrow's campaigns and had earned Woodrow's trust, if not full confidence. Baker himself, upon his nomination to the Cabinet, had told reporters that he knew nothing about the job.

House cleared his throat, interrupting side conversations that had erupted. "I think we should send either of the fine secretaries here with us tonight. I must proceed with the critical work of the Inquiry. Baker is a lawyer, and I think that will be most useful. That the secretary of state is a logical choice goes without saying."

Baker looked like a scared squirrel. "I'm not sure..."

House continued, "Another gentleman to consider is Secretary William McAdoo. He has excellent diplomatic skills."

Edith sensed Lansing's umbrage; his words were clipped but modest. "Of course, I am ready to go at your word, Mr. President. But perhaps Mr. House is the better choice, knowing the other parties as he does, and not having a large and critical agency to run."

"Thank you, gentlemen. I'll let you know my decision tomorrow."

After they left, Woodrow and Edith remained in the study. Surrounded by packed bookcases and seated in his leather desk chair, Woodrow always seemed most comfortable in this room. Edith cracked the window open to let the scent of overly talced men out of the room.

Woodrow was working through documents that Edith had placed in a stack for him to sign. Some were mindless things, such as certificates of land rights for homesteaders. Another pile held tasks that took more thought, such as requests to name navy ships. Edith had been coming up with names for months and was running out of ideas. She liked the idea of naming them after Native Americans, but with spellings and pronunciations unfamiliar to most Americans, the supply of realistic possibilities had dwindled.

"Well, dear, did you want to chime in with an opinion of whom to send to Paris?" He didn't take his eyes off his task, scribbling his signature, then moving on to the next.

"Actually I don't. For I would decide on completely different grounds than would you."

"How is that?"

"You're going to send House. You trust him the most, because he's not a politician, and won't even consider taking an official government position. Baker is clearly out of the question. You've asked William to lead the railroads, which also would keep him home and keep peace in the family. That leaves Lansing."

"That's who you would send?"

"It's his job. I don't think it's right to go around someone you've appointed to a position. If he can't or won't do the job, or you don't have full trust in him, then replace him."

Woodrow continued flipping through his stack. "Duly noted."

She turned to go, knowing without a doubt that he would choose House. "Don't forget to close the window before you leave."

As she predicted, House and a small team formed a mission that quietly sailed to France to meet with the war council. But by the time they got there, so much had changed that they could hardly do the work for which they had come. Russia was once again in upheaval. Kerensky, the revolutionist in power who had promised to secure the Eastern Front for the Allies, had barely escaped with his life as Lenin and the Bolsheviks took over. Italy had lost another brutal battle, and it was apparent they were too weak to protect themselves, never mind try to push Germany back. Fierce fighting had led to devastating losses, and the weather had already turned sharply colder, further weakening the troops.

Edith imagined the Allies barely holding on as fall darkened into winter. She feared American troops could not arrive soon enough. Would Henry Cabot Lodge and Teddy Roosevelt be proved right?

❧

Late in fall, Edith watched from the portico as gardeners raked and raked, cleaning up the fallen leaves from the expansive White House lawn. She always enjoyed the earthy smell of them, as well as that of freshly mown grass. But it occurred to her that a lot of labor was involved. Labor that perhaps could better serve in the war effort. In addition, small noisy and smelly tractors were used at least once a week to keep the lawn tidy.

Edith remembered the World Series game at the Baker Bowl in Philadelphia. Woodrow had laughed at the idea of the owner using sheep to trim the field. But back in her hometown of Wytheville, the few people who had a grassy lawn also engaged sheep or goats to keep them trimmed. Why not do that at the White House? It was already fully fenced, and what fun they would be for people to watch. It would also be a much more visible sign of the First Family's personal dedication to the war effort. After all, the public couldn't see their bean dinners and pajama sewing.

With Woodrow's wary approval ("But what about the flowers?" was his main concern), Edith sought out Dr. Grayson. He knew so much about horses; wouldn't he know where to get sheep?

It turned out he did. "I have a friend in Maryland who raises sheep. I think mostly for lamb..." Grayson hesitated.

"It's okay; I'm a country girl and not squeamish. But of course our little lambs will not be so sacrificed. In fact, I think we could sell the wool. To raise money for the war effort."

"Hmm. I like that. Maybe auction it off. White House wool wouldn't be ordinary wool after all."

On the exciting day, a wagon carrying a flock of sheep and several adorable lambs pulled onto the grounds. People had somehow gotten word and lined the fence watching the sheep as they tentatively nosed about the grounds. Parents lifted children for a better view, and Edith wondered if they should allow families to come pet the sheep occasionally.

She asked Grayson's friend, who had delivered the sheep himself, about the idea.

"Well now, that's not such a good idea. At least not yet. It'll be quite the adjustment for them from a quiet ranch to all this." He nodded toward the busy streets that encircled the grounds.

"Oh I didn't think of that." As far as she knew, sheep were pretty adaptable, but she would heed his advice.

Woodrow and Colonel House used a special code in their communications, and Edith was the only other person to know it. She spent hours decoding cables from France. In the first few messages, House went on about how he was enthusiastically welcomed and thanked for arriving in Europe's darkest hour. Edith rolled her eyes at his self-aggrandizement but said nothing.

After decoding a particularly long message in mid-December, she dreaded showing it to Woodrow. Its content was that just as she had feared, Britain and France's plans were to desperately hang on until the Americans came in full force in the spring.

Meanwhile, Woodrow had to make rounds of speeches to keep up Americans' spirits, support for the draft, and all the other sacrifices they had to make. It wouldn't do for them to believe the situation was as bleak as House had reported.

Feeling defeated, Edith checked the Drawer one evening after dinner. She hoped for some encouraging letters. Sometimes Tumulty would place hopeful missives from ordinary citizens amongst all the urgent messages, as he understood this is what gave Woodrow the strength to carry on.

But that evening, she found instead several letters that threatened their lives. One was addressed to Edith herself.

Woodrow had told her many times to pay no attention to these missives. "If someone was going to blow us up, they wouldn't write to us beforehand. That's just one less person you have to worry about."

"I wish I could be as calm about it as you," she said.

"You believe in God, don't you?"

"Of course."

"As long as we are doing the work for which He has put us on earth, then we shall survive."

Edith pushed away her anxieties, trusting her fate in God as well. But her faith was sorely shaken on a train trip to Baltimore. They had been invited to fly there in an airplane but declined, not believing it was safer or even quicker for that short a distance. But to prove a point, a young man in the administration had taken the airplane on the same route, leaving at the same time as the Wilsons. But he barely escaped with his life, as the wheels collapsed on landing. Edith wondered if the plane had been sabotaged.

From the Baltimore train station they headed downtown, where a grandstand had been erected for speeches. Edith sat next to the mayor, who leaned over and whispered to her, "I need to apologize for the absence of my wife. I have received anonymous letters that this stand will be blown up today, so I would not let her come."

Edith looked at him, incredulous. "And yet, here we are."

"Of course, I had to come."

She looked up at her husband, who was grasping hands and waving his top hat at the crowd. She had to trust in God, and the Secret Service, or they could not do what he felt they were put on earth to do.

⁓

As the months marched on, the country transformed into a well-oiled war machine. Draft boards filled their quotas, units were manned and trained. Automobile manufacturers transitioned to making artillery and tanks and airplanes.

The border skirmish in Mexico had proved the value of motorized vehicles over horses and mules, and there was no turning back. American manufacturers such as Dodge, Studebaker, Packard, and Cadillac had been producing ambulances for the French Army. The Ford Model T, already widely adapted for many purposes in the United States, was sent overseas partially disassembled in crates. Once in the country, the vehicle was put together, and the wooden crate used as the body.

More food was produced and sent overseas, strengthening the Allies. Edith continued to do her part, knitting and sewing and greeting trainloads of soldiers. She had been advised the soldiers needed a warm cap to wear in the trenches, something that would fit under a helmet. Many church and community groups had taken up the task, as well as making socks and blankets. After several failed efforts, her mother helped Edith figure out a suitable pattern for a helmet liner. When Woodrow's own cousin, Captain Woodrow Woodbridge, was ordered to France, she gave him her first one.

Even her sheep contributed. The flock was expanding with new lambs and was keeping the lawns clipped nicely. Fences had to be erected to keep them out of the flower gardens, but their wool was in high demand. Edith had the fleece divvied up amongst the states to auction off or use how they saw fit. Edith was pleased when Rebecca informed her that over one hundred thousand dollars had been raised for the American Red Cross.

As fresh troops and weapons arrived at the front, the Allies gained back land. Edith often visited the map room in the West Wing and was pleased to see the red squiggly lines representing the fronts moving back toward Germany.

From her dressing room, Edith could see the State, War, and Navy building. Even late at night, there were workers in the various offices, typing, transcribing, and talking on the telephone. She was comforted watching these hardworking men working around the clock to win the war. She had an idea whether the news would be good or bad from their demeanor. One evening, she could almost hear the cheers as the workers gathered, clapping and waving. She couldn't wait to find out what had happened.

The next morning, Woodrow was late to breakfast. Concerned, she went to his room. She had recently recovered from a bad case of the grippe and was fearful he had caught it. But he was in his bathroom shaving and singing to himself.

She rapped lightly on the door, not wanting to startle him with a razor on his throat. "Running late, dear?"

He opened the door for her, wiped his face with a towel, and slapped on some pleasantly scented powder. "Up late with the boys last night."

"Boys?"

"The War Department."

She brightened, remembering the celebration she witnessed. "Some good news, I hope?"

"News? Nothing out of the ordinary. We were trading stories. I told them about the time I got locked in a church pew."

She blinked, not remembering this particular story. "Tell me."

He laughed. "I was cycling around Europe, back in my salad days. Oh, how beautiful the countryside. In Scotland, I heard the church bells, and it being Sunday I decided to join the service. But I was greeted with little enthusiasm. You see, I was wearing my cycling knickerbockers, not proper church attire. So the pastor led me to a separate pew with a door. After

I entered, he locked the door behind me and didn't let me out until the service was over and the church cleared." He laughed again. "Didn't I ever tell you this story?"

She shook her head. "I do know you enjoy cycling. Why don't you take that up again? It would be easier for all concerned than dragging out the horses."

"Splendid idea! I shall have Grayson round up bikes for all of us."

"Oh no, I can't go; I never learned." She rubbed her elbow. "I tend to fall off things."

"What? How is that possible? It was my main method of transportation for years."

"I was a hell of a carriage driver." She turned to leave. "I'll see you at breakfast then."

"Wait a minute. I've an idea. I'll teach you to ride. It's not as hard as it looks, and you will love it. Someday, we'll bike around Europe together. What do you say?"

He looked so earnest and hopeful; how could she turn him down? "That would be lovely."

The next few days were hectic, with Woodrow tied up in meetings and visits from several ambassadors and heads of state. They hadn't had time for their usual lunches, and Edith was feeling a little forlorn when Rebecca brought her a short note.

Meet me in the basement at 1:00—W

The cavernous basement was familiar to Edith, as she had frequently gone down there to find furniture for special events or decorations. But things had been rearranged, with an area cleared straight down the center of the long hallway. At the far end, Woodrow stood next to a shiny new bicycle, a big grin on his face.

"Your new wheels, madame."

She managed a weak smile, having hoped he had forgotten this idea. Perhaps, as he'd said, it wouldn't be as hard as it looked. "Oh, you shouldn't have. You're far too busy... I'll get Rebecca or Altrude to teach me."

"It will give me much pleasure. You wouldn't deny me that, would you? Once we are pedaling through vast fields of tulips in Holland or along the green countryside of Belgium, you will be grateful we shared this moment."

Edith pushed visions of farmers getting blown up when their plows hit artillery shells straight out of her mind. This was about a dream about going back to a world set right again. Of Woodrow going back to the little kirk and volunteering to be locked in only to be cheered wildly and treated like the conquering hero. She could do this.

So she tried after lunch, day after day. He would steady her on the bicycle, and she would pedal a few feet before crashing each time. She didn't complain; she just tried it over and over, the bumps and bruises making her hips and elbows ache. They asked Altrude and Grayson, who were both experienced riders, to help, and Edith followed all their guidance as well.

They all laughed at first, enjoying the camaraderie and time away from more pressing duties. Once, they all dressed in knickerbockers and had a picnic lunch on a blanket on the basement floor before gathering on each side of her bike and running alongside her.

"Look, if I can do this with my big belly, you can too." Altrude effortlessly demonstrated moving a pedal to the high position before engaging her foot and taking off.

But then came a day when all were too busy for the lesson, and then another and another. Edith didn't ask about it, and no one else mentioned it. She just let her failure fade into the dark corners of the basement, along with her dreams of cycling Europe with Woodrow.

Right after Thanksgiving, Woodrow requested that Edith help him write his annual address to Congress. First, he took her to the Oval Sitting Room, where the portrait of the Armenian girl now hung over the fireplace. "We are in perhaps the darkest days of the war. But my main theme is hope. Like the white flower Dora is holding, I want my speech to signal that despite how hopeless things may seem, liberty and justice will prevail, and a lasting peace shall come. So if my words stray from this theme, I want you to so advise."

Edith met with him in his study each night for a week. He would tap madly, rip each sheaf of paper out, and hand it to Edith. She crossed out more than she added and pointed out the lines with the most weight. He would recite those lines in several different ways until she felt they had the right emphasis.

Sitting up in the gallery the afternoon of December 4 and looking upon the assembled Congress, the vice president, and the justices of the Supreme Court, she beamed with pride. He was announced to great applause, and she was pleased to see it coming equally from both sides. Woodrow raised his hand to quiet them and immediately began his speech.

He skillfully translated her suggestions into his own style, knowing exactly when to slow down—for example, when he recommended a declaration of war against Austria-Hungary—and when to speak lightly to ensure all were listening carefully. At his conclusion, he gave full voice to his words: "With victory an accomplished fact, peace will be evolved, based upon mercy and justice—to friend and foe."

Colonel House's cables praised Woodrow's speeches and reported they had an encouraging effect on the Allies. But the war council for which he had gone over had been postponed due to the instability of the players. Nevertheless, he seemed to be enjoying himself, meeting the king and queen in London, many ambassadors and emissaries and military leaders.

Woodrow called him home, and they met almost immediately after his arrival. The need to address the railroad situation was the most pressing domestic concern. William McAdoo had agreed to head up the federal takeover, but Congress still needed to be convinced. Woodrow had carefully scripted a message for them and asked House's opinion.

They were to have dinner together, but House appeared in the open doorway of Edith's private suite late that afternoon. "I was hoping to meet with the president before dinner, so he can have his rest afterward. But I'm afraid he's tied up."

Edith invited him in and ordered tea for the both of them, and they chatted a bit about his trip to Europe.

He took some papers out of his briefcase. "But moving on, I have read the president's message regarding the railroads and have made some suggestions." He nervously cleared his throat. "Would you be so kind as to read them? I do value your opinion."

"Of course." His obsequiousness was like an odor that flowed from him like the stench of the river at Hains Point. But she managed a smile as she held out her hand for the papers. She scanned both Woodrow's original words and the notes House had added. To her surprise, she agreed with all his proposed changes. "You have some valid points here. I'm sure he'll be open to your suggestions. It will be an interesting session tonight." She handed the papers back, then looked at her watch. It was time to dress for dinner.

House stuffed the papers back into his briefcase and stood to go. "Suppose you mention my reservations to him and give him some time to think about it."

She agreed, if only to get him moving along. Shortly after, Woodrow appeared. Glancing at the table still laden with a teapot and cups, he said, "I heard House had tea with you. Did he say anything about my message?"

"He did. I'm afraid he wasn't in favor of about half of it." She reviewed, point by point, his reservations. "And I have to agree with him."

"Hmm. I worked hard on that, but I'm eager to hear more from him before I change anything."

After dinner, the three of them met in the study. Woodrow sat at his desk, lit his green-glassed desk lamp, and pulled the railroad folder toward him. "Edith tells me you are not in favor of my message. That's disappointing because I've weighed every word of it. But I'm not all-knowing, so let's hear it."

House pulled at his shirt cuffs, wriggled his mouth so that his mustache twitched. "Yes, Mr. President. I did tell Mrs. Wilson that. But after hearing what she had to say, she convinced me that you are right on all counts."

Edith sucked in her breath. "What? That's not... You said..."

"Yes, but I have changed my mind."

"Very good." Woodrow closed the folder.

Clearly Woodrow was done with the conversation, but Edith was boiling. She wanted to grab House by the scruff of his scrawny neck and make him confess his true opinion. Why did her husband trust this man so? He couldn't be a true advisor when he merely echoed what he thought his boss wanted to hear. She clenched and unclenched her fists, holding back the words that would tumble out if she didn't maintain control. The still raw wound of his subterfuge before their wedding would always color her feelings toward him, despite his apologies. She wished Woodrow could see the weak, obsequious man as she did. Surely then he would fall out of favor.

It occurred to her that House might acquiesce to Woodrow's opinions too easily because he feared angering him, just as she formerly did. His role was to bring information to light, not to argue with Woodrow's decisions. Edith was Woodrow's wife. He couldn't just dismiss her if he didn't like her advice, but House had no such protection. Perhaps he wasn't quite the spineless jellyfish she imagined but had learned when to step back. Realizing this didn't help Edith like House any better. In fact, she added self-preserving to the list of his undesirable traits.

NINETEEN

January 1918

E dith collected local newspapers from across the country. She enjoyed reading about local boys being honored for their service and Liberty Bond drives. The program was exceeding its goals, with celebrities such as Douglas Fairbanks and Charlie Chaplin leading efforts, and Boy and Girl Scouts selling so many bonds, they had to increase the number of them available.

Altrude gave birth to a baby boy, James Gordon Grayson, eclipsing all other news for Edith that month. She insisted Altrude and Cary move into his old quarters in the Residence during her recuperation. "Completely selfish on my part," Edith explained. "I don't want to miss a moment of these precious first days."

Although little Gordon, as they called him, was not her flesh-and-blood grandchild, she felt every bit the proud grandmother as she inspected his tiny fingers and swaddled him after his feedings. An empty space in her heart felt filled for the first time.

❧

Through the winter, the Allies held on as they waited for American troop units to increase. Secretary Baker had appointed General Pershing, fresh from the conflict at the Mexican border, to lead the American Expeditionary

Forces. One of Pershing's first decisions was that the Americans would remain under his command, not used to reinforce British or French units.

Woodrow spent many hours crafting and revising not only how the Americans would fight but his ideas for what a just peace would look like. He had come up with fourteen major issues that needed to be agreed on. He called them his Fourteen Points.

On a much-needed drive through the Virginia countryside, Woodrow reviewed the points that he wanted to share with Congress, ticking them off on his fingers. "The basic tenet is that countries must not act only in self-interest but in a moral and just manner."

Edith wondered how these warring nations might suddenly behave in such a way, but she held her tongue.

"The Inquiry has looked deeply into the contested lands," Woodrow continued, "researching the histories and cultures. But in the end, we must leave the drawing of borders up to the countries in question, but demand that the determination be based on sound reasoning."

"I don't see how..." It seemed to Edith that if the borders could have been determined in a fair way agreeable to all parties, they would have done so already. But not wanting to interfere with Woodrow's vision, she backed off.

"Germany must vacate all occupied lands and return them to their sovereign states. In addition they must finally make restitution for the Prussian invasion of Alsace Lorraine in 1871. At the same time, it's critical that we don't demand crippling penalties from the defeated countries. That will only foster bitterness and desperate attempts to save themselves." He paused, seeming to finally invite her opinion.

Edith thought her most important role was as devil's advocate. "But there are bound to be disputes. Perhaps later on, as the memories of the defeat and the devastating losses fade, they'll remember how that part of Italy or Belgium or France used to be theirs. What will stop them from encroaching on these boundaries, which will seem arbitrary to some?"

"That, my dear, is the most important part. I'm going to propose—no, insist upon—an association of nations. A permanent body with representatives from each of the signed nations dedicated to resolving disputes diplomatically. This must be a part of the peace treaty, or we will just be kicking the ball down the field."

The way Woodrow's eyes glistened and his voice rose, Edith knew this was his new vital cause. He had found the reason this preacher's son was put on earth. She thought about telling him this but decided to cuddle closer on the leather seat instead.

On a chilly evening in late March, a fire roared in the sitting room fireplace, so hot Edith worried about the priceless painting hung above it. As if on cue, the valet came in and knocked some logs down, then silently padded out again.

"I should have done that," Woodrow lamented, but soon he was on another topic. "How about a little field trip?" He waved a pamphlet in front of Edith as she ripped out an errant line of knitting.

"Where to?" She took the dull-appearing pamphlet. "The National Bureau of Standards?" She screwed up her face. "My goodness, darling, you are such a romantic."

"We've been invited to tour the new aero science building. I think it will prove quite interesting."

"What do they do at this place?"

"It's quite sophisticated. They develop standards for everything you can imagine. How much electricity can a utility line carry? How thick should the steel be on a building girder? When you buy a gallon of milk, these are the people who make sure you get every drop. They've got the most accurate instruments and testing equipment in their labs. I'd like to see the new wind tunnels, but if you're not interested..."

Edith imagined a cross between Thomas Edison's and Frankenstein's laboratories. "I have no idea what a wind tunnel is, but I guess I'll find out."

The next day, they traveled up to the northwest corner of the District, a hilly and somewhat rural part of the city. They were admitted through the iron gates of what resembled a large university campus, with many stately redbrick buildings and neatly tended grounds. The campus wasn't well marked and the driver seemed a bit lost, motoring up and down the curving streets.

After consulting with a passerby, they arrived at the four-story aeronautical building, where they were met by the secretary of commerce, William Redfield. He was a rather ordinary-looking fellow, with a graying mustache that swept into muttonchop sideburns and small oval spectacles framing watery gray eyes.

Redfield gave Woodrow a hearty handshake but seemed too preoccupied to greet Edith, so she introduced herself as the two men started walking away.

Woodrow was so excited at the prospect of learning all about the place that he'd forgotten his manners. "So sorry. I've forgotten you haven't yet met my lovely wife, Edith."

"Mrs. Wilson, forgive me. I'm delighted to make your acquaintance. But there seems to be a problem. No one is here to let us in."

His New York accent hurt her ears, dropping R's like the Southerners did, but without the pleasing lilt. But she had to forgive his momentary rudeness, as he was clearly distressed.

They walked up to the entrance and tried the door, which was locked.

"I don't understand." Redfield peeked through the sidelight windows, then looked at the watch attached to his vest. "This is terribly embarrassing."

"Some sort of holiday?" Edith offered.

"Come on; let's go around the back." Woodrow was already taking long strides across the lawn. "I think I saw a wind tunnel."

The giant metal tube was next to an old wooden building that was barely more than a shed. How much more impressive were the new buildings. Woodrow explained the tunnel was used to test how an airplane would act in flight. It reminded Edith of a giant tuba.

They turned back to the main brick building. "I really wanted to see the experimental airplane," Woodrow groused. "Especially the landing gear. Did you know we barely escaped traveling in one that suffered a landing-gear collapse? I want to see how they will prevent that in the future." Woodrow knocked on a window, but no one seemed to be in the building. The double-hung window was open a crack at the bottom. Woodrow braced his hands on the window frame. "Redfield, come help me."

"Sir, I don't think..." Redfield called out, "Hello, anyone here?"

"Mr. Secretary," Woodrow snapped. "What are they going to do, arrest us for trespassing? I'll cover your bail. Now get over here."

Redfield looked at Edith, his mouth agape and alarm in his eyes.

She shrugged her shoulders. "He's not kidding, and it's not the first time he's done this. Go ahead; it'll be fine," she reassured him. "Just don't tell anybody."

Soon the men had the window wide enough to climb through. Redfield went first; then Woodrow helped Edith before hopping through himself.

Inside the building they found a single-engine airplane made entirely of metal; a Ford truck connected to many wires and gauges; and more cables, pulleys, and instruments than Edith had ever seen. Unattended workstations with engine parts and paper-covered rotating drums filled the room, but were completely unattended. Edith wondered what was on the other floors and inside all the other buildings. It was a tremendous amount of space.

As the men climbed into the airplane cockpit, Edith wandered around, trying not to trip on something important. She wondered how many laws they were breaking, or if they were breaking any at all. She had not had the opportunity to study much science but was awed by the evidence of the intellectual strength and engineering feats and brainpower of their great nation. Even in the absence of the workers, she felt their dedication, their ingenuity. This important work would keep Americans and their allies safe and ensure progress for generations to come.

By spring, troops were arriving in Europe by the hundreds of thousands per week. The Germans were retreating. Day after day, the red lines on the maps moved east. The country had vastly changed to a wartime economy, and patriotic posters supporting the troops or promoting liberty bonds or war gardens were everywhere. Along with the good news, Edith followed the more appalling news: the lists of the fallen that started appearing in newspapers from coast to coast. It was hard to look at those long lists, knowing that each name represented a son, a brother, a father who would never return. But she forced herself to read them, out loud if she was alone. She never wanted to lose sight of the true cost of war.

When time allowed, Woodrow liked to get out in public to say a few words of encouragement, or just to be seen. One of those occasions was a short parade and display of a new British tank. Said to be more reliable than its frequently out-of-action predecessors, it was touted as the weapon that could finally match Germany's tanks.

Edith and Woodrow circled around the beastly hunk of metal, which smelled of greasy oil and smoke. They waved at the tank commander, who stood halfway out of the top hatch.

"Can I come up?" Woodrow shouted over the idling engine. Receiving a wave from the commander, he entered the lower hatch and disappeared into the tank.

Edith shook hands in the crowd, until she heard a frightening yell coming from the tank. Her heart jumped; it sounded like Woodrow. The tank commander disappeared from the hatch. Edith flew to the lower entry but found it closed. Tense moments passed, until Woodrow finally appeared, his right hand wrapped in a wet cloth.

They were quickly whisked away in the motorcar. Edith held her breath as Woodrow slowly loosened the cloth, gritting his teeth in agony. His palm was badly burned, with strips of skin hanging from it.

"What happened?" Edith had to look away as the world started to swirl and she feared she would faint.

"I was climbing up and grabbed the wrong pipe."

"That's horrifying. Wasn't it marked?"

"Soldiers know their weapons inside and out. It's not a playground."

Anger welled in her nonetheless.

Several weeks later, Edith's anger returned when they received a letter from their insurance company denying their claim for compensation due to Woodrow's ability to continue to work using his left hand. "This is an outrage. We must appeal."

"Forget it," Woodrow advised. He held up his still heavily bandaged hand. "It won't make this get better any more quickly. And besides, I don't want to get any special favors due to my position."

"Then why have insurance at all? You refuse to take any money or favors that could be seen as taking advantage of your position. Have you looked at your finances? Your salary doesn't even cover..."

He held up his good hand. "Stop."

"If I had run my jewelry store like this..."

He glared at her, and she swallowed her words. But she made a promise to herself that once he was out of office, she would turn around their finances as she had with Galt Brothers.

TWENTY

B y July, over half a million American troops were overseas, and it was clear the tide of the war had changed in the Allies' favor. Colonel House came to Washington at least once a week as he and Woodrow made plans for another war commission to craft a peace agreement.

But even as the outcome became evident, the Central Powers did not give up. They were throwing everything they had at the Allies in a last desperate attempt at victory, or at least peace on their own terms.

The strain clearly showed in Woodrow. His chronic indigestion grew worse, and he lost weight he couldn't afford. Edith noticed more lines on his face and sometimes twitching about his eyes or mouth. His headaches returned, and Edith frequently went to the Oval Office late in the evening to find him slumped at his desk, fast asleep. When she spoke to Cary Grayson about it, he encouraged her to insist Woodrow get more exercise. If only he had more time.

By mid-August, it was clear to Edith that she needed to get Woodrow out of Washington. The long workdays extended into the night, when his sleep was frequently interrupted by news from Europe, six hours ahead. She feared his thinking was becoming muddied and his health suffering. So she implored Colonel House to find a suitable place to rest. He came through and produced an invitation from the wife of Jefferson Coolidge, a descendant of Thomas Jefferson and industrialist who owned a summer mansion near House's in Manchester, Massachusetts.

Their trip was announced as a retreat for the purpose of outlining the rules for the proposed League of Nations. But this work had largely already been done. Woodrow and House had pieced together recommendations from the Inquiry and, along with similar proposals from British and French scholars, had developed what Woodrow referred to as the Covenant.

Woodrow and Edith had a long weekend in the "Marble Palace," as the Coolidge property was locally known. The three-story brown brick mansion was named for its white marble trim, including four Ionic pillars supporting the front portico, reminiscent of Monticello. The great lawn offered an expansive view of Massachusetts Bay, and when the fog lifted over the water, they could glimpse the Boston skyline on the horizon.

When Woodrow had objected to the mansion's extravagance, House quickly advised him that the home had previously hosted Presidents Taft and Roosevelt, as well as many others, so neither special influence nor political cronyism was to be suspected.

Edith asked Rebecca to wake her early each morning so she could be sure to catch Woodrow before he disappeared into his work. Whatever pressing news there was could wait until after their morning walk.

They strode along the warm sand, searching for seashells and enjoying the lap of the small waves against their bare feet. Oh, how normal it seemed to enjoy those simple pleasures and how Edith missed ordinary life. Soon enough, Colonel House and the world would claim Woodrow back, but she reveled in the moment of having him to herself. Selfish, she knew, as his work was so important and at the cusp of a momentous achievement. But as the sun rose to the east, waking the crying gulls, and the wind carried sweet and salty air to her lips, she could feel it in her bones; there would be peace.

Through September, the battles raged, but soon Turkey and Bulgaria were no longer able to fight, agreeing along with Austria-Hungary to a ceasefire. Germany fought on, but they'd been cut off from their supplies and were suffering devastating losses. Invasion seemed imminent, and the end appeared to be in sight.

On October 6, Woodrow came to Edith's dressing room, his eyes clearer and face having more color than she had seen since Manchester.

"Great news! Germany has offered an armistice."

Sitting at her vanity, Edith blotted her lipstick, preparing for dinner. "That is great news, but they've offered before. How is this different?"

"They've agreed to our general terms. Specific details will have to be worked out, but it's over."

She jumped from her chair and hugged him. "Is the fighting done then?"

He pulled away. "I'm afraid not yet. Not until the armistice is signed. So I must get back to my office, for we must put together a team to go over it immediately."

Of course that team would include Colonel House, as Woodrow's most trusted emissary. Edith insisted that the secretary of state be included, as well as representatives from the Republican Party. She and House had met separately with the president, joining forces on these points, as Woodrow was becoming more and more stubborn.

Before dinner some days later, House came to Edith with obvious concern on his face. "You've got to talk to him. He wants to release a statement pleading with the voters to vote Democratic in the midterm election. He says we need a united front to establish the League of Nations."

Edith thought of the pressures Woodrow was under and her precarious efforts to sway him, mindful of his moods. She had to choose her battles carefully, and this didn't seem to be one of them. "That seems reasonable."

House paced. "It's the timing of it. Just now, we need to unite the nation, not the party. Any treaties that are made have to be approved by the Senate. The Republicans will be incensed by this message. As it is, the president is refusing to let Henry Cabot Lodge represent us in Paris. The Republicans will take revenge and refuse to sign. We simply can't have this. It's his legacy, and we can't let it go up in smoke."

"I'll talk to him." Edith understood House's concern, but her efforts to change Woodrow's mind were for naught. He released the offending statement, and the Republican backlash was worse than House had predicted.

Worse still was the pick for a Republican on the armistice team. Woodrow chose Henry White, an experienced diplomat whom he trusted, but though White had been appointed ambassador to Italy and France by Roosevelt, he wasn't popular among the Republican party leaders. With the secretary of state humiliated to not be the head of the group, they left for Paris late in October a disjointed, unhappy team.

The first days of November were filled with anxious meetings and the waiting for cables with news. The Germans' leadership and military were swiftly crumbling, with sailors revolting against orders for a suicidal mission in Kiel on November 3, triggering revolution across the empire.

It angered Edith to see a long list of wounded and killed in newspapers. As Woodrow had said, the fighting would go on until the armistice was signed. But the fact that the end was so near made these deaths seem even more senseless. And a new threat had emerged: the Spanish flu. Even the young soldiers who managed to escape death from the guns couldn't be sure of their fates.

Late in the morning of the seventh of November, Edith heard sirens and whistles. She looked out a window to see people pouring into the streets. She opened the window to hear someone shout from a bullhorn: "The armistice is signed!" Newspapers floated about like in a ticker-tape parade.

She rushed to find Woodrow, who was quietly reading in his study.

"Is it over? They say it's over!"

"Who says this?"

She led him to a window. "Come; let's go out on the portico."

"No, I can't. It's not true. It will be soon, but we have just learned the Germans were on their way to sign the agreement."

Disappointed but still feeling there was reason to celebrate, Edith decided to pick up her mother and sister and ride in the streets. They didn't get far in the open car, as throngs of cheering people encircled them. By then the news was out that the celebration was premature, but still people were celebrating, and Edith felt a heavy weight lift from her chest.

The next two days were a blur of decoding messages and bringing them to Woodrow. One cable made her stop everything and weep with a mix of relief and sorrow for all that had been lost. Kaiser Wilhelm II had abdicated, signaling the end of Imperial Germany.

Edith checked the Drawer every hour and still could not keep up with the cables. Finally she asked permission for her brother to help. Woodrow agreed, and they worked long into the night.

November 10 was a Sunday, and Woodrow and Edith went to church as usual. Woodrow held the worn, khaki-covered Bible given to him by a soldier early in the war. The soldier's unit had visited the White House before their departure, and Woodrow had sent them off with advice to keep their faith. This soldier handed him the dog-eared Bible and asked if the president would read a chapter every day, no matter what. Woodrow had agreed, although sometimes Edith had read it to him late at night, when his own eyes were too tired.

"I think it will be tomorrow at eleven." He tapped the Bible. "The eleventh day of the eleventh month. The eleventh hour is in the Bible. It has come to mean the last possible moment, but Jesus told a parable about men who complained about being paid the same as their fellow workers, even though they had worked more hours. The lesson was it didn't matter if His followers found Him at eight in the morning or eleven at night, they would be rewarded the same, that is, let into the Kingdom of Heaven. This eleventh-hour armistice will represent the hope that as nations lay down their arms, they will all be equal and all forgiven in the eyes of the Lord."

"I hope you're right, and that they choose eleven in the morning, not night. Twelve more hours without an armistice will cost lives."

They did choose morning. At 3:00 a.m. Washington time, they received word. The armistice had been signed, to take effect at 11:00 a.m. Paris time. The war was over.

TWENTY-ONE

For a moment, Woodrow and Edith stood silently in his study, the telephone receiver still in his hand, as if uttering one word might shatter the fragile new peace. It was a moment so long awaited, but when it came, it felt surreal. It was as if they were afraid to move or say something, or it might slip away. It was the moment that she realized the war had been felt in every fiber of her being, and now her body was afraid to let go. Then he wrapped his arms around her and she bawled uncontrollably.

"The eleventh hour of the eleventh day of the eleventh month. You were right," she said when she finally found her voice. She wiped her eyes. "What's next?"

Woodrow checked his calendar as if it were any other day. "Nothing here that can't be put off. I suggest we get some sleep; then I'll make the official announcement to Congress. After that, let's see what the day brings."

After returning from delivering the short speech to Congress, they watched the celebrations in the streets, increasing throughout the afternoon as word spread. Impromptu parades marched down Pennsylvania Avenue, and revelers set off firecrackers and danced to music played on all sorts of instruments. Someone even had wheeled out a piano and was banging away on patriotic songs, with the crowds joining in. But watching from the

Residence seemed too removed from it all. Edith begged Woodrow to join her for a drive, and he agreed.

It was both harrowing and exhilarating as they slowly made their way through the crowds in the Pierce-Arrow. When the Secret Service could no longer keep the people from climbing aboard, the city police stepped in. When even that wasn't enough, National Guard troops intervened, clearing a path and forming a ring around the vehicle.

All the while, Edith and Woodrow stood and waved and smiled and laughed at street entertainers. Her heart was so full she thought it might burst.

That evening, they were still too wound up to stay home. Edith tried to read the newspapers, but her mind wouldn't take it in. One exception was an announcement of a ball at the Italian embassy to celebrate the birthday of their king. An idea hatched in her head, something bold and unexpected, just right for the high emotions of the day.

Woodrow watched fireworks from the window. She told him of the birthday and ball and asked, "What do you say we drop in?"

He laughed, but she didn't. "Are you serious? Presidents are not customarily invited to foreign embassies. It's some sort of diplomatic protocol."

"We won't climb in through a window. Do you think they'd turn us away? Of course not," she said, answering her own question. "Let's get dressed up and surprise them. We needn't stay long."

She was a bit surprised when he agreed to go. "What the heck; this is a new world," he said.

It was after the second eleventh hour of that day when they arrived, he in a crisp tuxedo and she in a simple but elegant ball gown. They did indeed surprise the king and queen, who greeted them with an exuberant welcome. Thousands of white candles lit the grand ballroom. The men dressed in colorful uniforms with medals and ribbons and gleaming brass buttons, while the women swirled in flowing silks.

Woodrow offered a toast to the king, and the cheering went on for many minutes. When the music started up again, Woodrow and Edith bid their hosts farewell and quietly slipped into the night.

Although the armistice had been signed, the treaty that would outline the national borders and international law still had to be negotiated. The many competing interests, as well as the overarching goal of preventing another war, promised tense and delicate negotiations. Of course, Woodrow fervently hoped his Fourteen Points would be included and, most importantly, the League of Nations formed.

The War Council had decided on holding the negotiations in and around Paris, and the leaders of the allied nations were invited. So on December 4, Edith and Woodrow set out for France on the steamship *George Washington*. Accompanying them were the ambassadors and their wives to all the nations, Secretary and Mrs. Lansing, Dr. Grayson, representatives of the press, some fresh troops coming over to help keep the peace, and many others.

Edith hated to leave Altrude, as little Gordon was not quite a year old, and Altrude was expecting another baby in March. But Altrude had told her, "You must go. We'll be fine here, and this is a critical moment in your husband's presidency and our country's history. And besides, I'd rather remember Paris as it was when we were single ladies before the war."

As they steamed out of the port of Hoboken, New Jersey, they waved at the crowds who lined the streets and piers. American flags waved everywhere, and music could be heard from all along the riverbank. Edith relished the joy of the moment, for she knew once they arrived in France, the pressures on her husband would mount. Nine million dead soldiers, more than twice that number wounded, and countless civilian casualties all deserved to be honored with a lasting peace.

The seas were calm, and the ten-day voyage was spent resting and spending time with other passengers, learning about their war experiences and hopes for the future. This caused some consternation for the crew, who had taken pains to isolate and protect the president and his wife, with meals with the captain and a staged private show. But instead, each night Woodrow and Edith requested to dine with a variety of guests, then afterward made their way down several decks to watch movies with the troops, shunning the special theater set up for them and the diplomats.

In the small gatherings, Edith felt free to ask questions that she would never have dared to at public events. She learned much about how families had managed through food rationing and the loss of their wage earners as many husbands went off to war. She heard from leaders of churches about how they banded together with schools and hospitals to help families thrive while women went to work.

These were the real stories, she thought. The important ones. It seems government, in all its power to do good, sometimes forgot who it was really serving.

They arrived in Brest, France, on December 13, escorted by a fleet of French destroyers. French officials came aboard to greet them, and Woodrow was overjoyed to see his daughter Margaret, who had arrived shortly prior to them.

The townspeople turned out to greet them in native costume: The men dressed in velvet trousers and short embroidered jackets; the women wore fluffy black or red skirts and white peasant blouses beneath laced bodices. The women and girls all wore huge, stiff lace bows on their heads. They performed lively traditional dances and played pleasant tunes unfamiliar to Edith.

The Americans piled into motorcars and ascended switchbacks, each turn taking them higher above the colorful town set against glistening water. All along the route red, white, and blue banners stretched across the streets, and the people cried, "*Vive Vilson*." Edith's heart pounded with their chants, even more than it had during the celebrations back home. These people had suffered so very much more—their homeland invaded, families torn apart, their hearts and country forever scarred.

Arriving at the train station, their party boarded the train normally reserved for the president of France. It took quite a while to get the official party on board, along with an even larger number of French officials. But the French had been prepared and had previously requested the names and relationships of everyone in the delegation.

As Woodrow and Edith made their way down the cars, they stepped around the luggage and trunks set outside each cabin door. The procession stopped after the second car, and Edith heard some arguing in French and English up ahead. Presently they moved along, only to be stopped again, with more raised voices and some laughter. Finally, she could make out what was being said. Apparently, the French had some creative ideas on who should share cabins, with a senator paired with an unmarried woman, Margaret with Mrs. Lansing. When the cabinmates objected, the sharply uniformed stewards pointed at their names on their lists, and said, "*Oui, oui. Mais voilà.*"

The French did see fit to allow President and Mrs. Wilson to share a car. They each had their own private suite with a shared bathroom. They rested overnight, sure that it would be their last quiet moment for some time to come.

The next morning, the train pulled into Paris. The president of France and Mrs. Poincaré and representatives from both embassies greeted them. The entourage filed into open carriages, pulled by gleaming horses. They passed through wide avenues lined with cheering crowds and uniformed soldiers. Edith heard shouting from above and waved to multitudes of children and young men and women who filled the branches of the horse chestnut trees like flocks of birds.

The grand Arc de Triomphe took Edith's breath away. She had seen it before, but never with such crowds and flags flying all around. They passed under its arch and made their way down the Champs Élysées. Flower petals fell from crowded rooftops and balconies like snow. Soon Edith and her seatmate, Mrs. Poincaré, were buried up to their elbows in fragrant blooms.

The French president's wife did not have the delicate bone structure and fine facial features Edith had come to associate with the French. With her dark, soulful eyes and dark curls, she appeared more Italian or Greek.

"How wonderful that Paris was spared." Edith tried to speak to Mrs. Poincaré, but it was useless amongst the noise. Instead, she enjoyed the wondrous buildings and reflected on the very different time of visits before her marriage. This was certainly an exciting lifetime experience, but it was overwhelming. She would enjoy a quiet café in a bistro even more than the adulations of the crowds.

Led by French troops in shining brass helmets and mounted on horse-back, the procession of carriages soon arrived at the Palace of Prince Murat, which Edith was astonished to learn would serve as their lodging. She had expected nothing more than a nice suite of hotel rooms, so the palace stunned her.

The Poincarés soon departed, after advising the Wilsons to return for dinner at the Élysée Palace. "Sorry to drop you off and run," said Mrs. Poincaré. "But we have much to prepare."

"Will it be a large affair?" The staff would have received a list of the invitees, but Edith had not yet seen it.

"Oh, let's see. There are thirty-two countries represented. The Big Four each will have an entourage of twenty or so, the lesser states maybe ten. Marshal Foch will be there, and Joffre and of course General Pershing. So that makes somewhat more than three hundred, I think."

Edith blinked. She had an hour to find her room, change into a gown, and be ready for a large international dinner. She said, *"Au revoir,"* and hurried into the palace. It seemed more museum than home, with marble statuary and ornate everything. Every possible surface was coated with gilt and carvings, with crystal chandeliers casting a soft glow. She had little time to take it in, however, and barely acknowledged the multitude of servants and guards lining each hallway as she was escorted to her suite. Woodrow had been taken to another suite across the hall, so she felt relieved to have him close.

Happily, her trunks had arrived and were partially unpacked, with her gown laid out for her. It had already been a very long day, and she wanted nothing more than to lie on the big bed with its enticing blue-and-white toile spread, but there was no time. She desperately needed to freshen up, so she did what she could in the huge marble-and-brass bathroom. On a leather-tooled table that looked like it could have belonged to Napoléon I, she found a beautiful glass decanter filled with orange-scented water. She wasn't sure if it was to drink or apply as a scent, so she did a little of both. It was refreshing both ways.

Another parade of carriages and troops on horseback took them to the Élysée Palace. Edith had been advised that their custom of gentlemen escorting the ladies was a strictly held ritual, and she must not become detached from her escort, who was to be President Poincaré, until she reached her seat. Sure enough, after a brief reception in a grand salon, the Poincarés greeted them again. Woodrow was to escort the Misses, and President Poincaré held out his arm for Edith. She had a horrifying moment when she couldn't remember whether she was to lay her hand on top of his offered arm or curl it underneath. He was a good bit shorter than her, and the over position would have been more comfortable. A quick glance around told her that was not the custom. He quickly crunched his arm to his side, with her arm attached. She definitely wasn't going to get lost.

They threaded through a maze of rooms, each becoming more ornate than the last. Being steered through it all by her diminutive host, she felt rather like a steamship being pushed by a tugboat. Finally they arrived in what appeared to be a ballroom. Enormous crystal chandeliers warmly lit the space, and the hardwood floor gleamed as if they had been polishing it for days. In the center of the ballroom were tables set into an open square. Around the perimeter of the room, servants in black-and-white livery stood at attention like a formation of troops.

There wasn't quite enough space for two people to pass between the chairs and the troops. But tradition was tradition, and Edith and the French president pushed through, sometimes stepping on toes or rearranging the formerly perfectly aligned chairs. Finally, at the very far end of the room, they found their seats. All others stood as they waited for the hosts to arrive.

Edith took in the magnificent decorations. It was good to get fresh ideas for future state dinners, which would restart as soon as they returned home. There were tall tapered candles in silver candelabras, lovely porcelain figurines, and a vase of flowers at each setting, and more down the table center.

Toasts to the troops, countries, and their leaders were given in several different languages with much cheering and camaraderie. Edith tried to memorize every detail. How different from the state dinners they had given at the White House before the war. This was more festive, due to the occasion, but somehow the political rivalries and judgments seemed to have been left outside the palace doors.

After Woodrow and Edith returned to the Murat Palace, they were called on by an emissary from Greece and dozens of others. The reception room became a blur of blue and red and gold uniforms, of bushy mustaches and difficult-to-understand English. Edith's hand was grasped and kissed so many times she feared it would be rubbed raw right through her thin silk glove. Although she had never been fond of the tradition to wear gloves indoors, she now found them useful.

Finally, she and Woodrow were left alone, and they gathered in her sitting room.

"Good Lord, it's freezing in here," he said. "Have you called for more heat?"

"There doesn't seem to be heating in this room, except for the fireplace."

Only a few embers glowed amongst the blackened logs, but Woodrow added more and soon a roaring fire warmed them.

They settled on a low sofa with glasses of brandy, and Woodrow pulled her close to him. "Are you enjoying all the folderol?"

She sipped her brandy, letting the warmth soothe her throat and relax her muscles. "Everyone has been so kind, but it is rather much, don't you think?"

"And no end in sight." He pulled a typed schedule from his pocket. "Four more days of receptions, embassy visits, a hospital tour. They want to keep us busy, hoping that we don't notice that they aren't actually ready to commence the negotiations."

"Oh no, is there anything you can do to hurry it along?"

He groaned and made strange faces, stretching his face and contracting it. "Afraid not. I've just learned that the Brits want to wait until after their elections. Understandable, I guess, but frustrating for me."

She watched him scrunch up his nose and wiggle his ears. "What on earth are you doing?"

"What? Oh this?" He twisted his mouth and stretched up his eyebrows. "My face gets tired after a day of talking and smiling so much. Like an athlete's legs, facial muscles need to be stretched and relaxed."

As usual, he made much sense. He was adept at taking lessons from the past and applying them to the present, something at which she wasn't nearly as skilled. "So we're to entertain and be entertained while the days tick away, when so much is to be done?" She tried to stretch her face as well but didn't feel any benefit. Maybe she hadn't smiled enough. "Paris is wonderful, of course, and I'm not complaining, but..."

"Oh, not to worry. We won't be staying in Paris. After I meet with

Premier Clemenceau, we are requested to go to London, then Rome before the talks are to begin."

"Forgive my confusion, but Poincaré is the president. Is that a figurehead position, or is he in charge?"

"Yes, it's a bit confusing. The president is head of state and does wield power. He chooses the prime minister, who runs the nuts and bolts of government. So it will be Clemenceau doing the negotiations, at the pleasure of the president." He carefully folded up his schedule and returned it to his pocket.

"Oh." Edith wished she had spent more time studying European history, now that she was thrown into the middle of it. But there was little time for that now. She mentally reviewed the contents of her trunks. Surely the weather and fashions weren't too different in London, but Rome was another story. And Christmas was rapidly approaching. "Do you think we can block out time to go shopping?"

He took her empty brandy glass and set it aside. "I would love to. But right now, I think we have six and a half hours completely to ourselves."

TWENTY-TWO

After a few more days of receiving visits from and then making return visits to various heads of state, royalty, and diplomats, one morning they were rushed through breakfast and then motored out to the train station before Edith had had a chance to review the schedule of planned activities. She knew only that they were heading to Tours, about 120 miles southwest of Paris.

After settling into a sumptuous deep-blue velvet seat on the special railcar, she watched as the city she had hardly had a chance to visit rapidly faded into farmland.

Woodrow had already fallen asleep, still sitting straight up in his seat. She opened the binder containing the daily plans and nibbled on some warm salted nuts someone had thoughtfully provided.

Date: December 19
Schedule for Mrs. Wilson

Noon: Arrive Tours, disembark. To be greeted by City Leaders. Exact names/titles to be delivered.
1:00 p.m.: Tour of Tours Base Hospital and Infirmary for War Wounded.

Followed by lunch with Hospital staff.

3:00 p.m.: Tour of Rehabilitation Center.

...

Edith read no further, as her stomach was roiling and she became quite light-headed.

Why hadn't she been consulted? Of course, Woodrow would have been briefed, but he should have known she would want no part of it. Not that she didn't feel the visit was worthwhile and appropriate. But she was afraid she would embarrass herself with her reaction.

Edith's family had had a comfortable home in Wytheville. Her father was a judge, and everyone in town tipped their hat to him when he passed by. But even with a good and stable income, there were few extravagances like new clothes or store-bought toys. In addition to her many siblings, the household included grandparents, cousins, and an assortment of relations who came and went as their needs changed.

Also living with them was a family of servants who were descendants of her grandparents' slaves. The family had a little girl her age, Annie, and she and Edith were thick as thieves.

Little girls in petticoats were not supposed to be climbing trees. They were to be inside, reading a book or learning how to sew. But restless and cramped in the crowded home, Edith and Annie escaped to a little park just down the street. Edith knew the household was too busy for anyone to notice they were gone.

White and pink flowers bloomed in the shrubbery circling the park, and a big, old oak tree dominated the center. They brought a plank of wood and some lengths of rope, from which they hoped to fashion a swing.

"We can hang from it, or sit and swing higher and higher, then jump off into that pile of leaves!" Annie said.

They scrambled up the tree, which had fine limbs for climbing. "Here, this is high enough," Annie said when they were about twelve feet off the ground.

They balanced on a limb, wrapping ends of rope round and round. Edith was at the far end, and she needed to edge just a little farther out when... *crack*, the limb started to give way.

"Get off!" Annie cried, and she scurried backward. Edith grabbed for another branch, but soon they both came crashing down.

A sharp pain like a knife tearing through her arm caused Edith to shriek. Her head throbbed in the back, and she frantically tried to push away the branches, twigs, and leaves that poked her face.

"I'm coming," Annie cried.

But Annie didn't come. Edith blacked out for a while, and when she woke, her father was standing over her, breaking apart the tree to get to her. She took one look at the blood smeared across her homespun dress and fainted again.

But the real horror was what happened to poor Annie. Grandma Bolling insisted that this was what happened when you made friends out of servants. There were arguments about slaves and servants, with the words all mixed up, and her mother and father screaming about war and freedom. It all ended with the grandma crying and offering lots of apologies, but somehow nothing was the same again.

Annie's family moved out, and she never saw her again.

Now, Edith rubbed her left elbow, tracing the jagged scar that ran across it. She had avoided injuries and the injured ever since. She refused to ride a bike when they could finally afford one, and for a long time wouldn't climb upon a horse. But the sight of blood always made her woozy.

Maybe, she mused, if it had just been the fall, she wouldn't have developed such a phobia. But it was the generations-old family's anger from so much loss, and guilt over slavery, running like the stream under the trees through their psyche, that forever scarred her mind.

"Woodrow." She gently elbowed her dozing husband, who snorted, then resumed his snooze. But she didn't want her husband to have to fight this battle for her; it would put him in an awkward position. Better to find Tumulty and get this changed straightaway. She gathered the binder and worked her way through three railcars to find him.

"I'm sorry; it's much too late to be changed now." The usually caring Tumulty now dug in his heels. "I'm sure you can manage a brief visit. No one will be asking you to change a dressing, for goodness' sakes."

"You don't understand. The smell alone will send me plummeting to the ground. I don't want to cause embarrassment for the president."

"We'll put a mask on you. Maybe pour some smelling salts on it. Not a bad idea anyway, with the terrible influenza going around. You'll be on my arm the whole time, and you just say the word and I'll get you out of there."

She remained unconvinced, her hands shaking and clammy just thinking about it. Not to mention the deadly Spanish flu.

"You can do this, and it's important to try, for God's sake. To refuse… Now that would be an embarrassment." Tumulty snapped closed the offending binder and handed it back to her.

Against her better judgment, she put a smile on her face and agreed.

They arrived on time and, after a quick freshen-up, headed to the base hospital. Unlike the tent hospitals Edith had read about, this was a sturdy brick building with not a pockmark of war damage to be found.

As promised, Tumulty had provided a face mask of soft white cotton, permeated with the unpleasant smell of ammonia. Her eyes watered, but no other smells seeped in.

She took his arm as Woodrow walked ahead with the head of the hospital. They were introduced to several walking patients and some who were confined to bed. It was hard to make small talk through the mask so Edith mostly listened to their stories and concentrated on remaining standing. For the most part, the injured doughboys thanked them for ending the war and counted out on their fingers, if they had them, how many days until they would be shipped home.

Edith and Tumulty caught up with Woodrow and the hospital chief, who escorted them to a ward filled with men who had injured faces. They made their way down the long rows, greeting soldiers with missing noses and jaws and eyes. The men were remarkably cheerful and greeted the president with enthusiasm. One introduced himself as Thomas Wilson. Thomas being his given first name, Woodrow said, "I'm proud to be the namesake of such a brave man."

The chief doctor moved them along. "We put these men together in this facial ward, so they will be less sensitive to seeing their own injuries. They help each other by letting them know they're not alone."

Edith blinked back tears. "When will all of our boys be home again?"

"Ah, we're getting many of them out regularly now, many on the *George Washington*, the very ship you arrived on."

"And the rest? Are we lacking for ship capacity?"

Woodrow cleared his throat, his signal that she was straying into difficult territory.

"I think it might be helpful, Mrs. Wilson, for you to visit the post-op ortho ward."

"Splendid idea." Woodrow guided her in the wake of the good doctor. "If you would be so kind as to explain what that is?"

"Oh, sorry. Post-op, or operative, is where we place the patients recovering from surgery, and in this case orthopedic surgery to mend broken arms and legs or, in some cases, amputate if we can't save them."

Woodrow's hand squeezed hers. Its reassurance and dogged determination kept her walking. In a mental battle to overcome the thoughts of surgery and amputations, as well as the ammonia stench of her mask, she thought of an advertisement she had seen on the streets. She too would like to be sipping a sidecar in a quaint little Paris bistro. The imaginary taste of brandy, orange liqueur, and lemon juice slid past her lips and tickled her tongue.

But her pleasant fantasy ended abruptly when they pushed through double metal doors into the post-op ward, with four long rows of beds. Most of the beds had wooden contraptions strung over them, each resembling the framework of a small boat.

"Welcome to the carpentry workshop."

Edith was startled by the sudden appearance of a very imposing woman with a booming voice. If a hospital typically required hushed conversation, this woman was having none of it.

"I beg your pardon?" Edith wasn't sure whether to be amused or perplexed. She chose amused.

The chief made an introduction. "President and Mrs. Wilson, this is the chief nurse of the American Expeditionary Forces, Miss Julia Stimson."

Miss Stimson shook hands all around. It was not the limp-wristed dainty finger-squeeze of most women but a full-on hearty grasp. Edith, never accused of being dainty, matched her grip, resulting in an amused look in a pair of intense blue eyes.

The chief nurse explained, "It does resemble a workshop, doesn't it? So much wooden infrastructure. Its purpose is to hold the bones in place as they heal with weights and pulleys and such."

"Goodness, it's as though each of them is attached to their very own roller coaster," Edith said, quickly regretting the comparison. These poor soldiers were far from such frivolities.

But Miss Stimson merely raised an eyebrow with an amused smile. "As you can imagine, Mrs. Wilson, these patients are not easily moved. Even if we could roll them out—lock, stock, and barrel—imagine putting them on a tossing ship for ten days if we're lucky, more if we're not."

"Well then, how will we get them home?" Edith knew the likely answer but was trying valiantly to make up for her untoward earlier remark and to keep her mind off the sight and smells of the hospital. She felt she was seeing it all through a tunnel. Voices started echoing, and she knew she was in danger of dropping to the floor.

Miss Stimson came to her rescue. "If the gentlemen don't mind, I'd like to escort Mrs. Wilson to my office for a ladies' chat."

Once seated in the small but neatly organized office, Edith took off her mask and began to breathe easier. Miss Stimson brought them both cups of tea, piling several spoonsful of sugar into Edith's cup without asking.

"You looked rather green about the gills," the chief nurse said.

"Thank you for rescuing me, Miss Stimson. I'm terribly sorry and ashamed to have a rather weak stomach for the suffering of others."

"Please call me Julia. No apology necessary; it's quite the normal reaction. Sometimes we medical professionals are numb to it, but your reaction is very human."

They made small talk about Julia's adventures and the heavy weight of her responsibilities. Then, after a bit of a silence, Julia said, "I understand you oppose women's suffrage. I just wonder... If you had watched my nurses, tens of thousands of them now, working beside the men, doing amazing things, and not asking for much other than the right to vote like the men, wouldn't you change your mind?"

Edith took a breath. So this was the nurse's true motive in bringing her here. She no longer had any illusion that Miss Stimson wasn't the force behind the invitation she had fought against.

"Your assessment of my opinion on the matter is not quite accurate." She stirred the overly sweet tea, then poured herself a little more from the pot in order to dilute the sugar.

"As you may know, I was raised in the South, and believe me, the hurt and divisions of the Civil War were and are still rumbling under the surface. Not the end of slavery, of course, which was always wrong, and though it was certainly the most critical and emotional issue, it wasn't the root cause of the problem."

"Which was?" Julia asked. "In your mind?"

Edith felt blood rush to her face and realized that she had had a headache for some time. Though Julia's tone and words sounded a bit inflammatory, the look in her piercing blue eyes was of intellectual interest. It wouldn't do to get emotional, even over this most emotional of issues.

"States' rights versus federal control, of course. Every time we force decisions on the states, we take away more of their autonomy. And the Constitution says that the powers not specifically granted to the federal government belong to the states and the people.

"The president and I have been researching and reviewing this very thing. It's important that we follow the rule of law. If the rule of law is wrong or outdated, then Congress has means to amend. And that work is indeed in progress. Even so, we need to ensure the new law will be accepted and correctly implemented. So we need to take this argument to each and every state. As a resident of New Jersey, Mr. Wilson can vote for the president, while I couldn't vote for my own husband. But if I want that to change, I should be marching on Trenton, not Washington."

"Well, my girls weren't sent here by Trenton. Or Atlanta or Austin or Richmond. They were sent by the federal government to a war entered into by the federal government. To tell them they need to go home and fight in forty-eight different states is an outrage." She abruptly stood. "Sorry, but I've got to make rounds. Stay here as long as you like." With that, Miss Stimson walked out, seeming to take all the air in the room with her.

Too late, Edith thought to tell her about the recent progress, news of which might not have reached there. And it was progress, she told herself. She thought about all the women who had risked their lives to come here and all who toiled at home. Though she despised the methods of the suffragettes—their burning Woodrow in effigy came to mind—their message had value. There wasn't the time to wait for every state to come around, and who knew what demands they might legislate in retaliation.

They returned to Paris, only to be sent off again to visit General Pershing in Chaumont, about halfway to the German border from Paris. Edith thought of begging off. She would like nothing better than to have a few days to shop for Christmas, read something wonderful, and take hot baths. She had felt a chill in her bones since stepping off the ship. She feared the constant travel and chill would give her the grippe. But she knew staying back would disappoint Woodrow, who with the giddiness of a child announced they would have the whole afternoon of Christmas Eve to shop.

That night they again boarded the French president's train. But something had gone wrong with the heat. Even with snow swirling all around, it seemed colder inside the train. The Wilsons and Dr. Grayson, along with several generals and escorts, wandered from car to car, trying to find the warmest. They wound up in the saloon car, where whiskey warmed their souls and raised their humor.

They retired by 3:00 a.m. but were awakened at six by a rap on their cabin door. Another full day lay ahead of them, and they ate and dressed quickly before loading into motorcars. The sun filtered weakly through the fog as they passed through a landscape of rolling fields, with snow following the plowed ridges. They rode along the Marne River, and it was evident where battles had taken place, with entire fields burned away and forests reduced to ghostly timber.

They made several stops along the road at army encampments. They met soldiers and heard their stories. Every time a soldier thanked Woodrow, he winced and shook his hand and said, "No, thank you for your brave service."

General Pershing had joined them, and Edith was most impressed. He was tall, with a thick, dark-gray mustache and silver hair. His bearing was regal, but his eyes had a kindness, or perhaps weariness, about them.

They visited the billets of the enlisted men, some in tents, some in wooden huts, and a few in farmhouses or cellars of homes. The villagers rushed out when they saw the parade of motorcars with American flags, many of them carrying American flags as well. Edith's French wasn't adequate to fully understand, but the enthusiasm needed no translation.

Their last stop along the river was outside of the village of Humes. Here there was a great field, with lines and lines of uniformed soldiers as far as the eye could see. The ground was so muddy, wooden planks laid a path toward the grandstand, from which they were to view a parade of troops.

A band played the French national anthem and "The Star-Spangled Banner." Edith stood with her hand over her heart, thinking there could hardly be a day to be prouder. The troops filed past, their rows straight and steps even, despite the thick mud. Then mules pulled carts of artillery, with somewhat less order, the mules seeming to prefer firmer ground. Then the roar of tanks filled her ears as the clanking, camouflaged vehicles lumbered past.

And to think she nearly missed the sight for want of a rest and a hot bath, she scolded herself. It had been a long day, and she was suffering from lack of sleep, but she would not have wanted to miss a minute of it.

They had a traditional American Christmas dinner, turkey and stuffing and all the trimmings, with an army unit. Pumpkin pie had been made in great sheets and was cut into big square servings. Edith could hardly eat a bite, her stomach already full. She was seated next to a French general, who must have been equally sated, as he stared at the pie in consternation.

"I have heard of this delight but have never tasted it."

Edith cut herself a forkful. It was just creamy enough, with a nice balance of spices. "Oh do try it. We have a saying, 'as American as apple pie,' but I think pumpkin is more uniquely ours. But don't worry about finishing the whole thing. These servings are more suited to the ravenous eighteen-year-old soldiers."

He took a bite and declared it *magnifique*, but the way he delicately rested his fork on his plate made her doubt he was sincere.

A visit to the home occupied by General Pershing concluded the visit. There was a roaring fire in each room, and Edith made polite conversation with war heroes while thawing her bones near one. There was still a long train ride back to Paris, and she felt she needed to store up some warmth in preparation. General Pershing greeted them and shook Edith's hand. Next to him was a much younger woman, a daughter, she thought. But Pershing introduced her as Micheline, his artist friend.

As their host stepped away, Woodrow whispered in Edith's ear. "Pershing lost his wife and three daughters in a fire a few years ago. The army is his life."

"That's heartbreaking." Edith wondered how a person could endure that tragedy and yet be strong enough to lead millions in war. She thought of President Roosevelt, who had lost his beloved mother and wife on the same day. Somehow, he managed to not only move on, but to excel as a leader as well. Strength from adversity, she concluded, and felt a warm glow of respect for the man now commanding the room.

The guests were herded into the modest drawing room. It was too small to accommodate everyone, so some stood on the furniture or squeezed into the doorframes. Edith was crushed on all sides by men in rough wool uniforms. Small white candles were passed to each person.

Pershing stood on a small table and made a short speech, extolling their victory and remembering the fallen. His eyes seemed full of a deep sorrow, even on this happy occasion. Edith's heart tugged for him and all he had done and lost.

The candles were lit from one person to the next. "And now, let us sing with our hearts full. Full of hope for a lasting peace, full of gratefulness for our nation and our allies, full of love for God who watched over us." Then he began singing, "Silent night, holy night."

The crowd raised their candles and joined him in the Christmas hymn. Edith's heart was indeed full and her eyes watered as she sang along. Woodrow stood next to her, his arm draped gently across her shoulders. Next to him was his ever-faithful physician, Cary Grayson. Edith imagined he would have rather been with his pregnant wife and son on this most holy night, but he would never put himself before duty.

They spent Christmas night at Prince Murat palace, which was beginning to feel like home, despite the spotty heat. Woodrow eagerly inquired whether the treaty talks had been scheduled but was advised only that the king and queen of the United Kingdom were awaiting their arrival the next day. So they headed up to Calais on Boxing Day, where a British hospital ship awaited.

Edith had a delightful time on the ship, chatting with British and American admirals and enlisted sailors alike. They seemed pleased to have someone new to share their war stories with, and she enjoyed them all, especially the humorous ones. She found the British humor to be rather different than the American, seeming to favor embarrassing moments and bodily functions.

All too soon, the coast of England came into view. A steward came to fetch her to see the white cliffs of Dover. He explained their symbolic importance as the last thing sailors saw when they left home and their first welcome back. Then he quoted Shakespeare: "There is a cliff, whose high and bending head looks fearfully in the confined deep: Bring me but to the very brim of it." The late-morning sun shone on them, and indeed the cliffs were a powerful sight.

As they passed closer to the chalky cliffs on their way to the port, the steward pointed to the grassy top. "I understand you like orchids. Do you know of the rare spider orchid? It can be found up there, along with rare butterflies and plant species that thrive in the chalky soil."

Edith said, "Oh I would love to go up there." But she knew her time would be scheduled to the last second. She would have to come back another time.

They were met by the lord mayor in his red velvet robe with an ermine collar and a gold chain with a large medallion, fit for a king. He gave Woodrow the key to the city in a small celebration. Then they boarded the king's train, which thankfully was fully heated, to London. Edith watched the countryside go by. It was a blue-sky day, but the weak sun and dreary gray-brown of winter dampened the spirits.

The king and queen consort met them at the Charing Cross Station, with their coaches just steps away. They were stunning coaches, each pulled by a team of four black horses that had been brushed to high shine. Two coachmen sat on the driver's box in front, dressed in crimson livery, with powdered wigs under black top hats. Two more coachmen rode on an elevated platform on the back. Gold coats of arms were emblazoned on the doors. When they were opened, steps seemed to magically fold down from them.

Edith felt like a princess herself as she was helped into the carriage. King George V and Woodrow went in the first coach, and Edith in the second, along with Queen Mary and Princess Mary. She wanted to make a joke about the boys and girls being separated for their own good, but she had just met these royals. Although they were impeccably courteous, she found them stiff and proper. The royals sat in the carriage as if perched on a horse, their backs barely grazing the seat back. She needed to be careful of every word she uttered, which was not easy for someone who loved to tell humorous stories.

As in Paris, the streets were lined with throngs of people, some atop buildings and perched in trees. Each sidewalk was crammed elbow to elbow with well-wishers, waving Union Jacks and the American flag. Edith took mental photographs and let the happiness flow through her. The war was over, and the world was thanking her dear husband for his part in ending it. She felt as if she were floating in a hot-air balloon. Only the crisp air against her face reminded her there was still so much to do. It would be up to Woodrow and the other leaders to hammer out a lasting peace. She vowed to do whatever she could to help, even if it was merely to listen.

They were given enormous and elaborate suites in Buckingham Palace. Edith had a view of the gardens. Although there wasn't anything blooming, the maze of evergreen hedgerows was pleasant against the trees behind it. Princess Mary escorted her around the suite and, as they gazed at the gardens, pointed out a spot where she had seen an orangutan a few years back. It had apparently escaped from a zoo or private collection, she wasn't sure.

But there were no exotic animals to be seen at the moment, and the princess advised Edith that the first order of business, after a moment to freshen up, was an appearance on the second-floor balcony. Edith had seen pictures of the king and queen waving to their subjects from it. Apparently, it was a tradition for the people to assemble outside the gates in great numbers for special occasions, and the royal family never wanted to disappoint them.

True to the princess's word, ten minutes later, there was a knock on Edith's door. She hurried to keep up as she followed the trail of royals through wide halls and smaller passageways. Then, she saw sunshine at the end of a hallway, and she stepped out onto the small iron-balustered balcony with Woodrow, the king and queen, and Princess Mary.

The crowd filled the plaza in front of the palace, as well as all the streets leading to it. They cheered loudly at the royals' appearance but were otherwise still and orderly. Edith and Woodrow had done something similar on the portico at the White House, but the gates were much farther away. Edith thought this was a more intimate celebration with the people and a lovely tradition.

Another whirl of visits to various members of the royal family, who seemed to be related to every royal family across Europe, followed. The king was related to the kaiser in Germany, had a sister who was queen consort of Norway, and had an uncle who was king of Greece. In her reading before the trip, Edith had learned that the British royal family had changed their surname to Windsor from the German Saxe-Coburg due to the anti-German sentiment during the war.

On their second day in London, Edith had lunch with Lady Reading, the wife of the ambassador to the United States, while Woodrow dined with the prime minister, David Lloyd George. Then they all met at 10 Downing Street for tea. The news had just come out that it seemed the prime minister would win reelection, and the men huddled around a telephone in a cloud of cigar smoke. Edith managed to exchange a glance with Woodrow across the room, knowing just what he would be thinking, that at last the treaty negotiations could begin.

They returned to the palace just in time, where they received two visitors who wanted to clarify the dress for the big event that evening, a dinner hosted by the king and queen in the Throne Room for nearly one hundred guests. The woman remarked how excited the ladies were to finally wear their tiaras, after having stored them away during the war. Edith advised that she would not be wearing a tiara, as she didn't own one, but would love to see the other ladies in theirs. Meanwhile, Woodrow informed the gentlemen that American presidents did not wear uniforms.

This caused some consternation for the messenger. "Oh, but all the men, even the king, have worn nothing but uniforms for the past four years."

Woodrow assured him there was no need to change their custom on his account.

At the appointed hour, two elderly lords appeared outside their suites in order to escort the Wilsons upstairs to the throne room. This they did by walking backward a few steps ahead of them with a baton between their hands, stopping to perform a low bow every few feet. Edith winced each time, especially as they ascended the broad staircase, backward the whole way. She was afraid they would put their backs out at any moment.

Thankfully, they all made it upstairs and to the huge hall set for dinner. Edith noticed with some disappointment that none of the elegantly dressed ladies were wearing a tiara. She hoped it wasn't in deference to the Americans. As they made their way past an endless receiving line, there was a distinct odor of mothballs. Edith realized it was coming from the men's wool suits, which also had tiny holes here and there. With horror, she realized that each of them had hurriedly pulled them out of storage. She was then sure all the tiaras were put away for the same reason. The white wigs, however, were still very much in evidence. At least they hadn't given up their most cherished tradition.

The room was more spectacular than she had even imagined. There were gold plates and serving utensils, mountains of flowers, and sparkling crystal everywhere, from the chandeliers down to the wine goblets. All around the room stood men with long, pointed gray beards in elaborate red-and-gold uniforms. Edith recognized their distinctive look as the Beefeater guards from the Tower of London, specially chosen military pensioners who took great pride in their role. There was an odd little ceremony, whereby another elderly gentleman in a pink coat and white breeches walked up to each of the elderly guards in turn, like an inspection. He would then tap the boot of each one with a long, polished baton.

The king explained, "This ceremony is a tradition hundreds of years old. It started when at a similar formal affair, the head Beefeater was inspecting the guards. He noticed that one of them had his foot slightly out of alignment, so he tapped it with his staff. This caused the guard much shame, and his face turned redder than his uniform. To save his humiliation, the head guard then tapped the foot of each of the rest of the guards. It is a memorial to a kind heart."

"And it's a wonderful tradition," Edith replied. She didn't always understand the fuss with lords and dukes and the seemingly endless and senseless rules and traditions, such as the backward-walking escorts. But this one touched her heart. Maybe if she learned more about the others, she would appreciate them more. But in the back of her mind, she could hear her mother's voice, saying, "Oh my, such a fuss."

It was a sumptuous meal, but still being rather full from a large lunch and then tea, Edith ate little. There was the seemingly required roast beef with Yorkshire pudding, which wasn't dessert pudding at all but a rather gooey popover. A pang of guilt rang through her as she thought of how thin the people were after four years of rationing for the war effort. They had their victory gardens of course, but certainly there wasn't much roast beef on their tables. But then again, this was a very special celebration, and the portions were modest. She decided to enjoy the graciousness of their hosts and hope that peace would bring bounty to all.

It was in Manchester that Edith got to see a clearer picture of the English people. They were to stay at the Town Hall, which also served as the home for the lord mayor and his wife. They were greeted by the mayor and two of his assistants, wearing rather comical and ill-fitting wigs. This would never have passed muster in London, but the assistants were very official in performing their duties. One of them remarked that the lord mayor had only recently earned the title, having previously been a lowly farmer.

Upon arriving in her clean but simply furnished room, Edith found a woman who appeared to be a housekeeper assisting Rebecca in laying out Edith's belongings. It turned out the woman was the mayor's wife. She seemed rather uncomfortable in the role and to be hosting such important guests. She laced and unlaced her fingers, apologizing profusely for the humble accommodations.

Over tea, Edith tried to set her at ease as they discussed the similarities in their lives, the sudden change from a happily ordinary life to one of end-less ceremony and expectations and little privacy. When Edith asked if she should put on a gown for dinner, or just a nice dress, her ladyship had the look of a frightened cat. They decided on dresses, and later Edith regretted asking the question, as the mayor's wife was still wearing the same simple skirt. Reddened with embarrassment, the mayor's wife apologized, saying the dress she had ordered for the occasion had not yet arrived.

It lifted Edith's heart to see that ordinary people did rise to important positions, and it wasn't just about the luck of birth or marriage. As courteous and interesting as the higher classes and royalty were, she wished she could spend more time with people like she had met in Carlisle and Manchester.

Upon returning to London, it was time to pack for the trip back to Paris. It was Woodrow's birthday, and the king and queen consort presented him with a lovely set of books on Windsor Castle before seeing them to the train station.

As Edith waved goodbye, she was filled with warm feelings, knowing she would have wonderful memories for the rest of her life. Wanting to share the happy moment with Woodrow, she said, "I shall miss them, and London."

Woodrow, apparently in a sulking mood, replied, "The conference has been set to open on January 18. Three more weeks wasted."

"I'm sorry for the delay, but try to enjoy this time. It's all about interna-tional relations, and that is the heart of your peace plan, is it not?"

He grumbled. "We're off to Italy next. I imagine it will be more pag-eantry and pleasantries, and little real progress."

The weather seemed to echo his mood, with leaden skies and continual rain from London, across the Channel and on the train to Paris. There, they transferred to yet another royal train, that of King Emmanuel of Italy. It was sumptuous, with ornate brass and shining wooden paneling everywhere, with liveried attendants at every turn. In the several days it took to travel to Rome, there were elegant formal dinners and receptions, as if they were staying in a palace.

Edith wished she could spread out all these events over the rest of her life, when she could enjoy each one thoroughly. But she tried her best, making pleasant conversation, sometimes answering the same questions over and over to a parade of dignitaries, royalties and others, while her feet ached and she longed for a quiet evening alone with Woodrow in front of a fire. That would come soon enough, she consoled herself.

Arriving in Rome renewed her spirit. The sun shone brilliantly in the bluest sky Edith had ever seen, and the balmy air warmed her bones. They met with the king and queen and rode to the palace in coaches even more elaborate than those in London. Part of the palace had been turned over as a hospital during the war, and there were still recovering soldiers there.

The king, who spoke perfect English, requested that President and Mrs. Wilson visit the wards. "It would mean so very much to them, and they have been dressed up and waiting for hours."

Of course, they could not turn down such an honor, and Edith tried to ignore the rising bile of her stomach. But the wards were spotlessly clean and there was only the faint odor of rubbing alcohol. Edith walked with the queen, who was greeting patients who seemed to know her personally, and she was very gracious with them, even hugging some who came running up to her. This Edith had never seen with the royalty of France or Great Britain. It seemed more American in some way.

The queen, who spoke in French, explained that many of them were "her patients." An interpreter translated that she had worked in the X-ray department all through the war. The queen pushed up one of her sleeves, revealing reddened, scaly skin. "Radiation exposure. The doctors tell me it will get better with time."

Edith thought of her own work with the Red Cross. It paled in comparison.

Departing Rome, they stopped in several cities en route to Paris. In Milan, the crowd that greeted them numbered in the tens of thousands. Her heart soared as she listened to the Italian and American national anthems, with the flags of both countries on every building and waved by thousands.

But again, Woodrow seemed out of sorts. "If they ask me to speak, I shall have to keep it very brief. I don't want the government to shoo away the crowds as they did in Rome."

"Whatever do you mean?" Edith remembered that the huge crowds had dissipated after his Vatican visit and her ladies' tea, but she hadn't thought it unusual.

"The ambassador has informed me that the Italian government has no intention of supporting my Fourteen Points in the treaty, even though they previously agreed to them. They didn't want me making a speech about it and swaying the people."

"So they made thousands of people leave the streets."

"Exactly." He worked his jaw, a sure sign he was irritated.

"Well, that doesn't seem to be the case here."

Thunderous applause and chants for "Presidente Wilson" grew louder and louder, while their carriage became completely surrounded until Woodrow stood up in the carriage and waved to the mass of humanity. Only then did the crowds part for the carriage to pass.

Once again, they were guests in a palace. This one smaller, but no less elegant. When Edith entered her room, it felt welcoming and warm. Perhaps too warm. She noted a faint smell of smoke. As Rebecca helped her unpack her things and lay out an outfit for the next event, the smell became stronger.

Rebecca said, "Shall I open a window? I was told these rooms hadn't been used since before the war. Maybe the old pipes are burning up some dust."

Edith advised her to check with the head housekeeper, then hurried to dress for the event that evening. She checked her schedule of events, printed on thick vellum. "Oh dear, isn't today Sunday?"

"It is," Rebecca said.

"We are to attend an opera. Woodrow doesn't believe in going to the theater on Sunday. It goes against his upbringing as a pastor's son."

"Maybe he'll make an exception. He also speaks of honoring the traditions of the host countries. Or maybe he'll forget." Rebecca ran her hands over the radiator, which was making a steady *tink-tink-tink* sound.

But Woodrow didn't forget. He met Edith in the hallway, his face a dark cloud. He didn't offer his usual compliment on her attire. "Did you see this?" He waved his copy of the schedule. "Special performance of *Aida* at the Scala Theater. I'm sorry to disappoint you, but of course we can't go."

"Oh, but we can't insult our hosts; I'm sure they went through much trouble, and there will be so many there eager to see you."

He waved aside her concern. "I've already sent our regrets." He stormed off, leaving Edith overdressed for a glass of champagne in the bathtub, which is what she decided was the only amusement she required.

But that was not to be. The king's emissary soon appeared at her door. "The king requests your honorable presence for an evening of sacred music."

"And my husband has accepted?"

"Yes." The emissary eyed her dress, now lacking the short jacket and jeweled necklace she had already removed, down to her bare feet. "We must leave immediately. Don't worry, your present attire is most suitable."

The "sacred music" was the national anthems, and then some lovely solo performances, before a gorgeous presentation of *Aida*. Sheltered in their private box, Edith glanced at Woodrow to see if he was angered by the Italians' duplicity, but he seemed relaxed and to be enjoying the show. Relief flowed through her, as his stubborn streak seemed to be growing each day.

After the show, Edith motored back with the queen while her husband was with the king and their entourage. All thoughts about the strange evening evaporated, when she found Rebecca outside her room, nearly in tears.

"It's my fault. I should have listened to you and told the housekeeper."

Just then several men in working clothes exited the room, carrying buckets half full of water. "It's safe to go in now."

Edith rushed in to find the entire window wall blackened with soot. "Oh my heavens! Are you all right?" She quickly checked over Rebecca, who seemed fine, then the rest of the room and her belongings. The only damage seemed to be the wall itself.

"I'm so sorry..." Rebecca broke down in tears. "The radiator caught fire, from the years of dust I guess, and spread to the wall before I saw it. I called for help right away..."

"Now we'll have none of that," Edith reassured her. "These things happen in these old buildings, especially after having been abandoned for so long. No one and nothing were hurt." She hoped no one would tell Woodrow. He didn't need another reason to be angry with the Italians.

They were back in Paris on January 7, with eleven days still to go before the peace conference was to begin. That evening Woodrow and Edith finally had a quiet evening to themselves.

Woodrow stoked the fire in his sitting room, and they assumed their positions on the green velvet sofa as they had at the White House. Edith let her mind wander over their many adventures since their arrival nearly a month prior.

But Woodrow was focused on the future. "I think, if you agree, I will request a moratorium on the social visits and entertaining. There is much to do to prepare for the conference, and it will go much more smoothly if things are already in order and agreed to."

"You don't need my agreement, but you have it." Edith thought of all the things she'd like to do while the men held their meetings. She had friends in Paris whom she had not yet seen, and there were museums and cafés and art galleries, enough to keep her quite busy.

Lying on a table in front of the sofa was a strange suitcase. It was narrow, about five feet long, and three-sided. "I can't imagine what you have in there. Golf clubs?"

He chuckled. "Let me show you." He unclasped the case and pulled out several large rolled-up maps. He then spread them out on the floor, nearly covering it. The maps represented all of Europe, the Balkans, and northern Africa in great detail.

"The future of world peace depends on how we divide this up," he said.

"I'm afraid there is no solution that will make everyone happy."

"There will be compromises made. We just have to make sure they are ones they can live with and a way to address grievances that is fair to all. Now, part of the repercussion for Germany's aggression is they will have to give up territory and colonies. Our idea is to either transfer those to our allies as compensation for their losses or to begin the process of moving colonies toward independence."

Edith considered the prospect of a former colony suddenly on its own. "But what would happen, if someplace, like German South West Africa, was suddenly left on its own? Wouldn't that just encourage some sort of dictatorship to take over?"

Woodrow rejoined her on the sofa. "Ah, you are a good student of international affairs. That is another good purpose of the League of Nations. The League will have temporary control, while the governments are formed. Not in all cases, as we don't want to burden the League with too much. So there will be cases where countries are simply recognized as sovereign, like Poland, and others that will become protectorates of another country. Germany's position in China will go to Japan, for example."

The maps sprawled across the floor had many color-coded markers. "Is that what those markers mean?"

"That's today's plan. Every day, things move about a bit, as France fights for more reparations, Britain tries to keep France from gaining too much power, Italy tries to forget who kept them afloat, while the United States tries to find a solution to bring a lasting peace."

TWENTY-THREE

The next day, Edith studied texts on European history she found in the library. Most of them were in French and proved too complex for her conversation-level fluency, but there were a few in English as well. There were also several books on the great scientist Louis Pasteur. She was surprised to learn that much of his life-saving work had been accomplished after he had a paralyzing stroke.

Rebecca rapped on the open door. "Sorry to disturb you, ma'am, but you have an unannounced visitor, Mr. Henry White."

Henry White was a former ambassador to France and had lived in and had strong relationships with Britain and Germany as well. Due to his diplomatic skills, he was chosen by Woodrow as one of the U.S. representatives to the conference. The appointment also served a political purpose of bipartisanship, as White was a Republican.

"Show him in, please." Edith liked the affable, gentlemanly diplomat and had had many pleasant conversations with him. She secretly wished Woodrow would replace Colonel House with him but knew Woodrow would never trust him enough for that role.

White looked weary as he entered, his silver hair neatly combed, perfectly matching the thick mustache on his lined face. "Good morning, Mrs. Wilson. Thank you for seeing me on such short notice."

Edith asked Rebecca to bring them tea, then led Mr. White to a small sitting area. Having spent many years living there, he invited her on a personally guided tour of Paris to visit places she would otherwise never see. Of course, this excited her greatly, and she quickly accepted.

"But I feel that is not why you came here today." She poured tea for both of them.

"Ah yes." He quickly came to his point. "Outside of the negotiations for the major issues of the conference being held by the heads of state, there are separate meetings at the Hotel de Crillon amongst the foreign secretaries working out the myriad other details. It seems there are festering resentments on the part of Secretary of State Lansing regarding the location and leadership of these meetings, which are being held by Colonel House in his hotel suite.

"It has become a sore spot to which, with a word to the president, you can bring balm. I have to agree with the secretary. It is an insult. Furthermore, the press naturally go to House for the daily updates, making Lansing feel even more insignificant."

"I'm sure my husband is not aware of such a small thing. Lansing is like a schoolboy whining about someone taking his rubber ball."

"Yes, they are small things, and Lansing is a small man. But personal vanity can sometimes make or mar the success of large affairs."

The urge to disparage Colonel House rose in her like an overfilled toy balloon. Oh, how she would love to share her experiences with him. But she held her tongue, for idle gossip about Woodrow's trusted emissary would only come back to bite both of them. Instead, she assured White that she would speak to Woodrow about it, and they made a plan for their Paris tour before he left.

She wondered why Lansing or White didn't simply address her husband directly with their concern. Of course, their time with him was exceedingly limited, and there would be others around; to make such complaints might be embarrassing to them. But she thought there might be something else. If they won her favor, they knew the president would not say no to her request to help him. It was a power she realized she must use with great discretion, for her own time with her husband was precious, and she did not want it occupied with a stream of personal requests from others.

But she had made a promise and believed the issue was something Woodrow would want to know about. So that Sunday, on their customary drive through the countryside after church, she brought up White's concerns. It was a cold, rainy day, the sort of day when winter seemed to seep into her bones. She pulled the woolen car blanket up to her chin, even as Woodrow tossed it off.

"Henry and Lansing are right. I didn't know about this and will get it changed." He shook his head. "It does bother me that Lansing doesn't have the guts to simply take charge. As for the press, there's a plan I've been meaning to implement. I will assign a press officer to come to me each evening. I'll brief him on the decisions of the day and what is fit to be released."

Edith saw an opportunity. "Would you mind if I attend those meetings? Then you won't have to waste time repeating things for me."

"Time with you is never wasted." He gave her a peck on the cheek. "And yes, you are most welcome to attend."

Sundays were a precious day of rest for both of them, and Edith was loath to discuss any official business with Woodrow. They would speak of family or their future plans, reminisce on their childhoods, friends, and dreams. But there was another request, coming from many angles, that threatened to usurp their Sunday.

Ever since they had arrived in France, Woodrow had been pressured to visit the vast landscape of war destruction. As he felt he was quite aware of it, and that his primary mission was peace, the president had not seen fit to schedule it. He worked eighteen-hour days, six days a week to that end. But having seen many pleas in letters and in person, Edith knew that if they didn't take the time to do this, they would forever be remembered as not caring enough. So she convinced Woodrow to spend a weekend visiting the battlefields.

It was an enlightening trip, even considering how much they already knew, the photographs and films they had seen. But staring at fields pockmarked by thousands of bombs, forests reduced to burned stumps and twigs, newly homeless people taking shelter in caves, and feeling snowflakes melt on her face as they drifted through the roof of a ruined cathedral were experiences she would never forget.

Woodrow was advocating for reasonable sanctions placed on Germany, in order not to destroy the country that was the industrial and economic heart of Europe. But standing in a destroyed village, Edith understood the deep anger of the French and the urge to finally destroy a hideous enemy.

She shuddered. How could a treaty possibly make amends for all that had happened? How could they create new frontiers over land that had been occupied by many different cultures over centuries? There was no clean slate, no reclaiming of time where all lived in peace. She grasped her husband's hand as they climbed the rubble of steps to a factory that no longer existed. What a terrible burden lay on his shoulders.

The plan had been to agree on the tenets of the treaty and return to the States before the close of Congress in March to present the terms. This would give Congress time to formulate any objections to be renegotiated before the final signing by all parties.

A critical meeting of the initial Paris Peace Conference was scheduled for February 14, at which they were to vote to accept the terms of the treaty to be presented to each of the involved nations.

Edith was keen to attend the momentous event, mostly to hear her beloved make his plea to accept the League of Nations Covenant in the treaty, as he believed it was the best hope for achieving a lasting peace. But she had been informed that only conference members and the press had been invited.

She thought of the glorious reception they had had from the French people, and the graciousness of the many kings and queens and heads of state she had met. Surely, they wouldn't object if she quietly slipped in?

Knowing Woodrow abhorred requesting special favors, she went to Dr. Grayson. He was also eager to attend and agreed to ask the head of the conference, Clemenceau, for permission, if Woodrow did not object.

Edith chose a Sunday evening, Woodrow's most relaxed time. He had just had a warm bath and was enjoying a detective novel when she slid next to him on the sofa. A fire was crackling in the fireplace, and she thought how she would miss the lovely Murat Palace.

"If I can interrupt…"

He put his book down. "Please do."

"It's a little favor. Something important to me."

"Anything, my dear."

"All I ask is for you not to forbid it. You needn't lift a finger, call in any favors…"

"Now I'm suspicious." He pulled away to look into her eyes. "Not forbidding is the same as approval, and I have a feeling you know I won't. What is it?"

"I will be a fly on the wall. That's all. No one will know we're there."

"The days of you being unnoticed are long gone." He picked up his book.

"I want to hear you speak at the conference. Is that such a crime? Dr. Grayson will ask Clemenceau for both of us to attend. It will be his decision." She watched him pretend to read. "So, you won't object?"

He sighed. "Edith, Clemenceau can hardly object. It would be considered a command, not a request. And Colonel House would surely recommend against it."

"In that case, we shall definitely make the request."

"Willful woman, your sins shall be on your own head if the Tiger shows his claws."

Tiger was Clemenceau's nickname.

"Ah, but he never takes off his gloves."

It was arranged for Grayson and Edith to watch the proceedings, provided they arrived before the delegation and left after they had departed. When he gave Edith the exciting news, Grayson said, "Clemenceau made me promise not to breathe a word of it to anyone. He said he'd have every wife of every delegate pestering the soul out of him."

That just made it all the sweeter for Edith. A little taste of forbidden fruit appealed to her slightly rebellious nature.

At the appointed hour, Grayson and Edith arrived at the Ministry of Foreign Affairs and were escorted through the great hall set up with long tables and chairs in the center for the principals, surrounded by desks and chairs for the delegates from smaller countries and the press. It was known as the Salon d'Horloge (Room of the Clock), and indeed there was a timepiece big enough to rival Big Ben at one end of the room. At the opposite end, their escort parted thick, burgundy-colored curtains to reveal two straight-back chairs in a space barely large enough to contain them. At least they would have a fine view of the speakers, Edith thought.

They took their seats and listened as the room filled, with many languages echoing off the muraled walls. Every once in a while, Edith peeked through the curtains to see if Woodrow had arrived. Soon, the meeting was called to order, with Mr. Clemenceau giving a fine welcome and thanks to all. Grayson and Edith took turns looking through a crack in the curtains until evening fell and they felt comfortable in the darkness to leave a small opening they could both see through.

Even with that, the tiny space was stuffy, and Edith was much too warm. She removed her suit jacket and hat and was contemplating rolling up her shirtwaist sleeves when she heard her husband introduced. In a flash she stood up, and she and Grayson were head-to-head as they listened.

He could have been a Shakespearean actor on a magnificent stage, with his tall and strong presence and his heartfelt but forceful words. Edith felt as if her insides were melting to see this man she cherished doing what he was born to do. In the briefest words, he outlined his position. He spoke about ending the practice of powerful nations annexing smaller ones. If they were poor and helpless, the strong needed to consider their needs first and not step in out of their own selfish interests.

He acknowledged that the treaty was the result of much hard work and deep thought but that the resentments and injustices of the war were too poignant, the wounds too fresh. There needed to be time for healing, and they would find some things they hadn't quite gotten right. Thus, the League of Nations was to be established so that all the countries, great and small, could be heard and adjustments made. "Wrong has been defeated… The miasma of distrust, or intrigue, is cleared away. Men are looking eye to eye and saying, 'We are brothers and have a common purpose… This is our covenant of fraternity and of friendship.'"

A great applause went up, and soon ballots were distributed. As the room fell silent when the votes were counted, Edith saw her husband looking about the perimeter of the room. She knew he was looking for her.

She parted the curtain a little more and held a single finger to her lips. He found her, held her gaze, and gave a small nod.

He did it, she thought. They would win the vote.

There was hardly time to celebrate. As soon as they returned to the palace, they needed to prepare for a last round of goodbyes before they headed for the train station. They thanked all the staff at the Murat, then stopped at the Élysée Palace to bid farewell to the Poincarés. When they arrived at the train station, a red carpet had been rolled out, and thousands of well-wishers had turned out, singing and cheering to the sound of a band. Edith let their voices imprint in her mind so that she might call it up again whenever difficult times or doubts arose. They waved from the train door as long as they could, then had a quiet, contemplative ride to Brest and the waiting *George Washington*.

Aboard the ship, Edith and Woodrow split their time between visiting with returning wounded servicemen and various dignitaries. Edith especially enjoyed chatting with Mrs. Franklin Roosevelt, the wife of the assistant secretary of the navy, whom she found bright and witty. In private hours, Woodrow worked on his speech to the Senate Foreign Relations Committee, while Edith wrote many long-overdue letters.

After ten days at sea, they landed in Boston. Edith wondered if their reception would be as warm as their farewell in France, as this was Henry Cabot Lodge territory. In addition, Governor Calvin Coolidge was a Republican. Woodrow waved off her concern, saying, "If local politics makes them turn a cold shoulder to us, then so be it."

But to their surprise, a massive crowd gathered to greet them. The governor welcomed them with a warm and heartfelt address. Edith was thrilled to see her husband honored as the hero he was. After the grand reception, they boarded the train to Washington. Edith took advantage of a rare quiet moment to acknowledge how welcoming the people of Boston had been and that Woodrow was indeed a hero. But he didn't acknowledge it personally; he saw it through the lens of his next important step. "It seems a good indication that the people have accepted the terms of the treaty. That bodes well for the Foreign Relations Committee," he said.

TWENTY-FOUR

Washington, DC

I
t was an odd time, a transition from war to peace, with the details of that
peace still up in the air. Edith didn't want to jump back into the social
whirl too soon, despite the many calls to join in celebrations. Just as the
country needed to find its way again, she wanted to move cautiously, out of
respect for the fallen and for the great amount of work still to be done.

The White House staff was eager to show the progress on renovations
and repairs, especially the new China Room. Collections from many former
presidents were now safely displayed and stored here, and the room would
make a fine entertaining space.

Chef Oliver issued a special request to meet him in the China Room.
The formerly rotund chef seemed to have lost some heft and had aged much
in the past year.

"It seems you need a new white jacket," Edith said mildly.

"We took wartime rations seriously here, but I'm happy to be adding
meat to the menus once again. But that is not why I've asked you here." He
bent to open a large leather trunk and brought out something flat and round
wrapped in deep-blue velvet.

Oh joy! It had to be the new Lenox china. Edith had seen the design
she had advised on and a photo; here finally was the real thing. The chef
slowly and carefully unwrapped a dinner plate and handed it to her. It was

beyond anything she could have imagined, thin and delicate-appearing but somehow strong and solid at the same time. It had a creamy white center, with the president's seal in the middle. Then a small band of pure gold, a wider band of deep blue, with a final gold verge of gold. Stars and bars representing the flag were embossed in the verge. It was simple, elegant, and stunning.

"There is also this, for less formal occasions." The chef unwrapped a slightly smaller plate, which lacked the blue band but otherwise featured the same cream and gold design.

Edith wiped a tear. Perhaps it was silly to be over the moon about china, but this was more than a pretty plate. Woodrow had saved the company that might have gone bankrupt for a lack of coal. And how many thousands would dine from these pieces and enjoy the elegance of an American creation?

"Thank you, Chef. May I place the first piece in the cabinet?"

The head groundskeeper implored Edith to view the gardens with him. As it was late February, she didn't expect to see much in bloom, but she bundled up and met him at the flower beds lining the South Lawn. Except there were no flower beds. Where there were once azalea shrubs and overwintering greenery, there was bare earth. The lawn itself had bare patches and many small holes, reminding Edith of the pockmarked fields in France.

"What on earth has happened? It looks like a herd of elephants has been living here."

"Not elephants. Sheep." The groundskeeper pointed to a huddle of thirty or so sheep, which she had found adorable just a few months ago.

"Oh no! There are so many more now. Are they getting enough to eat?"

"Of course, but they seem to prefer the lawn and flowers. There's close to fifty of them now."

"Can we move them to the North Lawn? Fewer flowers there and fresh grass. And perhaps it's time to thin the herd." She petted a lamb that nuzzled her knee. "They've done their job, but I'm afraid some must go."

"Only some? We would still need to move them, put up more fencing, repair the damage they do on the North Lawn..."

"They're not just a few pesky animals. The children love them, and so do the people. And did you know we raised over a hundred thousand dollars for the war effort with their fleece?"

The groundskeeper shoved his hands in his pockets and brought out a few tattered receipts. "Yes, ma'am. And are you aware of the costs to the government—the people—to raise those funds? Fencing. New plants. Two truckloads of fill dirt. Feed. Veterinary bills. Shearing fees. And you'd be surprised how much costs for everything go up when the customer is the White House."

"All that couldn't possibly cost hundreds of thousands..."

"No? How much did it cost to ship the wool all over the country? To pay people to clean up the droppings? I know your heart is in the right place, but it isn't honest to go around saying you're raising money for the cause."

"I get your point." She should have known better. Where had her common sense and general mistrust of government spending gone? But even if it wasn't a financially sound project, it was a morale booster during the darkest of days, bringing people together at the auctions with a more tangible product than Liberty Bonds. "Well, let's thin the herd, keep a more manageable number for the people who love to come see them. Do you think you can find a good home for the rest of them?"

"Yes, ma'am." But the way he looked at her darling sheep, she knew he was thinking a good number to thin to was zero and that lamb chops might be one way to accomplish that.

Just two days after their return, the Wilsons hosted a dinner for the Foreign Relations Committee. Woodrow had asked the committee not to discuss the League of Nations Covenant until he had had the opportunity to speak to them directly.

During the sailing from France, Edith had listened as he went over the crucial points again and again, until she could recite them from memory. "Why, of all the speeches you've made, are you so concerned over this? By all accounts, the reception we had here and in Boston, the positive press, it seems everyone is ready to ratify the treaty and finally move on."

He grimaced. "Pure politics. The Republicans gained control over the Senate in the midterm elections. They're not going to bless what we've done without wanting to make changes, even if just to have their own fingerprints in there somewhere."

"What's wrong with that?"

"Do you remember the two agonizing months of negotiating to get to where we are? The Italians are already squirrelly about supporting the League, and Britain and France are still at odds regarding reparations demanded of Germany. Personally, I think France is being too harsh and Britain too lenient, but we drew the line at a place we could all live with. Anything other than changing 'happy' to 'glad' could set off another round of disagreements, so I need to keep this thing as intact as possible."

At the dinner, once again, she was seated next to the newly proclaimed leader of the Senate, Henry Cabot Lodge. This made her rather nervous, due to his power over Woodrow's political opposition and his barely hidden disdain for her. She had not forgiven him for tattling to the press about her dirty fingernails.

She had painted them a bright-red color this evening to match her dress. When Lodge complimented her on its color as he pushed in her chair, she couldn't resist a little dig. "I considered wearing my gloves even during dinner to hide my ink-stained hands. Just like Clemenceau does."

"Does he? I wasn't aware."

"Yes, but he wears them due to eczema. Although no one would see fit to release something so personal to the press."

Edith was the only woman in attendance, and suddenly she felt every eye on her. Realizing she had probably misstepped with Woodrow's political opponent, she tried to make amends. "I must compliment you on your wonderful city. The people there could not have been warmer and more welcoming. It was quite the honor to return from abroad to a place so important to our nation's birth."

Lodge looked at her, his face pinched and his teeth set. "It was not at my invitation but the mayor's. So I shall not take credit."

She was chilled with a sense of foreboding. The viper had not withdrawn its fangs.

For two wondrous days, they enjoyed being home. Edith had a joyful reunion with a very pregnant Altrude and little Gordon. They had Woodrow's girls and their husbands, and Edith's mother, brother, and sister over for dinner. There was so much to talk about, so much to celebrate. Edith didn't know how fleeting the moment was.

Woodrow was quiet throughout the dinner, unusual when he was around his girls. Afterward, Margaret suggested playing parlor games, but by the way Woodrow glanced at her, Edith could tell he was looking for an excuse to get out of them.

"If you don't mind, Woodrow and I have to catch up on a number of things. We've been gone so long."

They made their exit and settled into Woodrow's study. He didn't go straight to his desk, as she expected, but perused his bookshelves in the poetry area. After selecting one, he sat on the sofa near the fire.

"Come sit with me." He laid the book in his lap but didn't open it. It was *Rewards and Fairies* by Rudyard Kipling. She had seen him page through it in a bookshop in London and later purchased it for him.

"You seemed preoccupied at dinner."

He sighed. "It's about Lodge. We've got some thinking to do."

"Oh dear. I was trying to make small talk with him at the state dinner, and I'm afraid I only made matters worse. He really seems to dislike me."

"My darling, that cannot be true. You just happen to be one of the many he can't bully onto his side."

"Perhaps so. But what has changed? Why are you worried about him now?"

He opened the book of poetry and found the page he wanted. He read out loud,

"If you can keep your head when all about you
Are losing theirs and blaming it on you;
If you can trust yourself when all men doubt you,
But make allowance for their doubting too:
...If you can bear to hear the truth you've spoken
Twisted by knaves to make a trap for fools,
Or watch the things you gave your life to, broken,
And stoop and build 'em up with worn-out tools."

He paused. "It's as if Kipling wrote this specifically for me, for this very situation we find ourselves in. Here—read the last stanza for me."

She took the book.

"If you can talk with crowds and keep your virtue,
Or walk with Kings—nor lose the common touch,
If neither foes nor loving friends can hurt you,
If all men count with you, but none too much:
Yours is the Earth and everything that's in it,
...And—which is more—you'll be a Man, my son!"

It was a beautiful poem and did reflect so much that made him who he was. The last line bothered her. "I think there's one word missing. Being a man is not of one's own doing. It should say 'you'll be a *great* man.'"

"I think that's understood."

"What are you stooping to build with worn-out tools?"

He gazed at her, his eyes clouding in sorrow. "I thought this would be the easy part. A difficult treaty hashed out, the belligerents waiting, willing to accept and move on. An agreement of historic proportions. And it seems our work is just starting here. If I don't convince the Foreign Relations Committee to support ratification, it will all come crumbling down. And I'm tired. So very tired."

He took her hand. The defeat in his voice seemed out of character.

"You are the great man in the poem. This *is* the easy part. The committee will not jeopardize..."

"In normal circumstances, no. But there is one thing of which you are unaware."

She felt her heart sinking.

"Whom do you think the Republicans have appointed as chairman of the Foreign Relations Committee? I'll give you a hint. It is the same man who once said he never expected to hate anyone in politics with the hatred he felt toward me. It's the man who has fourteen objections to my Fourteen Points, the man who believes the treaty needs to crush the German people once and for all. You should be pleased to note he's come out against women's suffrage, but I think that's mainly because I've taken the opposing side." He looked at her with a wry smile. "I get your point about Kipling's missing word."

Edith didn't need to hear him say the man's name. Henry Cabot Lodge.

From the tight-lipped look on Grayson's face, Edith knew he wasn't about to present good news. They were in his office, at their weekly meeting regarding the president's health. She scanned the posters depicting the various body systems, especially the one of the brain and nervous system that Grayson had so often pointed to.

"What is it? His blood pressure again?"

"No, no, nothing like that. It's the sheep. My friend will be coming for them today."

"Oh." Edith felt like she had been slapped. Instead of relief that her husband was fine, she felt the loss. Of course she knew and approved of them being moved back to the countryside, but it felt like another loss at a time when there had been so much.

"They'll be happy there. Away from the traffic noise that is making them skittish..."

"I know." Edith reached for her handkerchief. "It's still sad."

"Maybe you're not quite the city girl that you think you are."

At the arranged time, she went out to the North Lawn to meet the shepherd. The sheep had been moved there to keep them from the flower beds. Her request to move only some of the herd had not met with much enthusiasm from Woodrow. Once he heard about the damage they had caused, and that some had gotten sick from the stress of traffic noise, he agreed with the groundskeeper. "Just consider it one more step back to peace and normalcy," he had said.

And she had given in. Not a single sweet lamb would remain.

She approached the animals, still fat in their winter coats. They came to her, nuzzling for a treat. "Goodbye, my little friends. Thank you for your service."

She thought about all the doughboys returning home. Were they receiving warm welcomes? Would they find their girlfriends had moved on, or that their mother was terribly sick and no one had had the heart to tell them? Would the brown-eyed boy at Union Station return? She said a prayer for a safe and joyful return home for sheep and soldiers alike.

❧

There was some encouraging news. Henry Cabot Lodge promised Woodrow that if the Foreign Relations Committee approved, he saw no reason that the Senate wouldn't also approve the terms of the Treaty.

Edith was overjoyed. Perhaps her attempts at smoothing over their differences at the dinner had helped after all.

But whether Lodge kept his word to the president depended on the interpretation of those words. To Woodrow and Edith, surely he meant he would support the treaty. But two days after his promise, he gave an address that was quite the contrary. He outlined every detail of the agreement that gave him pause, especially disagreeing with promises made in the Covenant of the League of Nations. He implored the people not to agree with the stipulation of supporting the other nations, feeling the country could be drawn into another war.

When he heard of it, Woodrow was deadly calm at first. Edith thought he was too calm, as for sure he was holding in all his anger and frustration. She thought she should summon Dr. Grayson to check his blood pressure but didn't want to interrupt their own family time, especially with a baby due any day.

So she watched, as her husband moved from silent introspection to fits of writing and typing, his jaw clenched and her company dismissed.

And so the great battle over accepting the terms of the treaty began. Lodge made impassioned speeches, urging further review, and was espe- cially opposed to language that would drag the United States into any war that erupted amongst the fourteen signing nations and beyond. Edith felt torn, as her loyalty to her husband and knowledge of the difficulties of reaching an agreement collided with the points Lodge was making.

She read in the papers of another of Lodge's concerns, one that she had heard little about from Woodrow. He feared that the Peace Committee was focusing on hammering out borders and ensuring the interests of the victors were met, and not enough attention was being paid to the control of Germany. Lodge claimed Germany had not been disarmed. Her factories and fields were intact. No decisions had been made for reducing her military or annexing Austria, and the people were hungry and already building resentment.

She also had to agree with Lodge's disapproval of leaving Colonel House in charge in Paris during Woodrow's absence. Lodge stated that treaties should only be negotiated by persons in positions approved by Congress. But she feared that her own mistrust of House might be swaying her opinion. She wished now, months too late, that she had been more outspoken when Woodrow announced the members of his Peace Commission. She had thought at the time that it would be wise to include Lodge, or at least another strong Republican, both to have two viewpoints and to ensure acceptance of the treaty.

When she'd tried to discuss these concerns with her husband, he reacted with anger and defensiveness. "Not you too. I can bear the criticism from the small minds who were not there and yet presume to have all the answers. But I won't tolerate it from my own family, whose love and trust I can't live without."

So she stopped asking questions and stopped reading the papers. She held her tongue as she read a draft of a speech he had prepared for the Democratic National Committee. It was extremely harsh against the Republicans. As they had won the majority in the midterm elections, it seemed he should be more conciliatory. She didn't attend the speech but was chagrined to hear quotes from it, which were even worse than his planned remarks. He called his political opponents little and contemptible. Edith hardly believed he said it, but there in print was this: that they "reminded him of a man with a head that is not a head but is just a knot providentially put there to keep him from raveling out."

She was reminded of Woodrow's opinion that Lodge and many members of Congress, not to mention most of the people, were "not of their kind." Usually he kept these opinions to himself, but it seemed without her constant attention to his speeches, his inner thoughts leaked out like ink from a fountain pen.

The press was excoriating her husband; it was clearly not the time for her to confront him. As he had told the conference, there were wounds that needed time to heal. And now, those wounds included those inflicted on leaders of their own country.

TWENTY-FIVE

After the triumphant return home had rapidly descended into division and turmoil, Edith was relieved to be returning to Paris. It seemed there they were loved and appreciated and not picked apart for every unwise comment.

Following an address in New York City, they drove over to Hoboken, where they once again boarded the *George Washington*. Ten days later, they arrived in Brest late in the evening, so it was a much quieter reception than the one previous, which Edith was thankful for. After dinner, they boarded a train for Paris. Colonel House and his wife, Loulie, met them on the train, and the two men soon excused themselves to discuss the latest developments.

It was nearly midnight when Woodrow finally appeared in Edith's stateroom, looking haggard and fretful.

"You look spent, dear. Why don't you head to bed?" Edith asked.

But Woodrow paced. "I can't believe it. We lost it all. All my hard work, gone."

Panic rose in her throat. "Whatever do you mean?"

"House has given it all away. Agreed to separating the League from the treaty. Given France everything she's asked for. It's a disaster!" He was visibly shaking.

Edith tried to calm him. She hated to defend House, but something seemed off. "That can't be true. I saw the cables he sent. Even as we were crossing, he was saying there were issues, but he put them off until you arrived. He said..."

"Don't tell me what he said," Woodrow thundered. "You weren't there!"

Edith knew what she saw; she had an excellent memory. Either House was lying in those cables, or now, or Woodrow had misunderstood. She thought back on the warnings from Cousin Helen, and times when he had forgotten odd things, like whether he had eaten lunch. Normal, she thought, for someone so under pressure. And he was clearly exhausted from the months of overwork. He was too driven to be capable of protecting himself from this vulnerability. She would need to be strong and draw the line for him. With rest, he would surely become his passionate yet reasonable self again.

And the next morning, that's what happened. He groused about the opposition back in the States along with the need to address the demilitarization of Germany and find a reasonable solution to France's demand for German coal mines. If he was still furious with House, he didn't mention it.

There was little pageantry when they arrived in Paris at the train station, or on the ride to their new quarters, a wonderful hotel on Place des États-Unis. Edith was grateful there should be no delay in resuming the work of the Peace Commission this time.

Again, the meetings went on long into the night. Woodrow said sometimes the work of the previous day was undone by noon the next. Edith could feel his frustration and felt powerless to help him. Instead, she would have tea ready for him in his suite at bedtime, and they would share a calm conversation, trying to focus on the good parts of the day.

By the end of March, it seemed his patience was growing thin. She heard reports of a nearly physical brawl between her husband and Clemenceau. Ridiculous, she thought, as the French premier was nearly eighty years old and hardly a scrapper, but he certainly was determined. As a leader of the country most damaged by the war and having the longest boundary with Germany, he was understandably most anxious for the demilitarization and weakening of their adversary. By the next day, the commission had worked out their disagreement, with Clemenceau happy with a plan to control Germany's Rhine River military and industrial corridor for fifteen years. The cities of Cologne, Mainz, and Coblenz were to remain under Allied control. She couldn't help but wonder what would happen once those fifteen years were up.

That night, she and Woodrow gathered in his suite as usual. But he was irritable and reticent before falling asleep sitting in his chair. Helping him to bed, Edith noticed how frail he seemed, his arms lost in his shirtsleeves, his hair graying to white.

On May 7, the allied nations were to present the treaty to the Germans. Edith very much wanted to attend the ceremony, but this time Woodrow would not concede to letting her sneak in. "You got away with it one time, but let's not chance it again. The tensions are too high," he said.

The German delegation was to have fifteen days to review the treaty and respond with objections, which would be considered and then responded to. After some back-and-forth disagreements, which led to the threat of allied invasion of Germany on June 29 if the treaty was not signed, the Germans capitulated.

The date for all parties to sign was set for June 28, the fifth anniversary of the beginning of the hostilities. The Wilsons were to depart for the States immediately after to begin the process of gaining ratification by the Senate.

During these anxious weeks of waiting in Europe, a big change was occurring back in the States. Edith still had mixed emotions regarding a national women's right to vote amendment, but it seemed the movement was finally coming to a resolution, and the Nineteenth Amendment would soon be passed by Congress and turned over to the states for ratification. At least the war was over, and Edith's most feared consequence, of women being drafted into service, would not be an issue.

Dawn comes early in late June in northern France, and the deep-blue sky followed by red streaks reminded Edith of the flags of France and the United States. Even the sun was heralding the 28th, a momentous day. Edith's emotions were a mix of joy, relief, and apprehension as they rode in the open car to the Palace of Versailles.

Woodrow's face was serene, and he even nodded off during the ride, while her stomach tumbled and she fanned her sweating face. What if the Germans bolted at the last minute? What would happen if the Senate failed to ratify? Woodrow had warned the French and British that the agreed-to terms were too harsh. The required reparation amounts were far too great, especially considering how hampered the Germans were by other restrictions.

Even as she entered the great Hall of Mirrors, filled with members of the other delegations, the press, photographers, and others, doubts plagued Edith. She found comfort in chatting with Margaret and Loulie as they took seats on benches not far from the tables where the papers were to be signed. The room was quiet, as Clemenceau and his delegation entered the center doors, soon followed by Woodrow and the Americans, David Lloyd George and the British contingent, then Orlando and the Italians. Finally, the German delegation marched in, looking solemn and businesslike.

The four different sections of the treaty were signed by all the parties. Edith's heart leaped when she saw Woodrow use his gold wedding ring to press his monogram onto the document. She rubbed her own band, forged from the same nugget of gold. Within the hour, the ceremony was over. A cannon fired, and a great cheer went up. A thread of relief flowed through Edith. Soon they would be home, and all these months of trial and loss would be behind them.

After another red-carpet send-off, they were on their way. Edith looked forward to rest for herself, but especially for her husband on the *George Washington*. Indeed, he seemed in great need of it, as he stumbled a bit on the gangplank. Edith hoped no one else had noticed, as he would be humiliated. So she said nothing but moved along next to him, stopping to turn and wave at the ship's door.

While the president was in France brokering the peace, his nemesis, Henry Cabot Lodge, was busy sowing the seeds of doubt for tenets of the treaty. Woodrow made speech after speech to Congress, held meetings with leaders from all corners of the country, and pleaded his case to the press. The rest that Edith had long wished for him, and Dr. Grayson had urged him to take, was not to be found.

Edith knew the main arguments against ratification: Article X of the League of Nations Covenant, which pledged that each signatory nation would come to the aid of the others if they were threatened. Another was the decision to grant Japan the former German-controlled territory in China in Shantung, and the failure to address the long struggle of Ireland to be free of British rule. Secretary Lansing himself had not helped matters when it was leaked to the press that he thought the treaty severely flawed, in particular in being so harsh on Germany that another war was inevitable.

Edith raised these points with Woodrow, one at a time, at their brief lunch meetings. She rarely spoke in public, but if she was asked to defend his positions, she wanted to present his views. His answers were long and twisted, for all the decisions made had been the subject of great debate and compromise. But what she memorized was this: Article X was essential, for without it, the League would be a meaningless group of endless debaters. Furthermore, it was a moral obligation, not a legal one, and Congress would be the ultimate authority over any actions that could lead to war. Granting Shantung to Japan was the result of a secret agreement between Britain, France, and Japan, as a result of a long history that the United States was not party to. And grievances such as Ireland's were precisely the reason for the League, to finally have a negotiating body to settle disputes without taking up arms.

Edith planned long drives on Sundays, only to have them curtailed by urgent requests for Woodrow's attention. Sometimes she imagined blindfolding her husband, leading him to a private island, and holding him captive until he could properly rest and restore his health. Instead, she watched helplessly as he grew more gaunt, eating little and suffering from tremendous headaches.

He had a new routine in his study each evening after dinner. He would sit at his desk chair, with another straight-backed chair in front of him, and lean over with his forehead resting on the smaller chair as he dictated notes to his stenographer. He said it kept his headache at bay and helped him focus on the task at hand.

Woodrow had suffered from asthma as a child and mildly as an adult. The oppressive heat had worsened it and robbed him of precious sleep.

Edith summoned Grayson to find a way for him to get rest. It was an afternoon in late July, when dark-gray thunderclouds echoed the ominous feeling at the White House. Woodrow had suffered yet another humiliating trial by the press, with attacks on his positions and unyielding personality.

Grayson met with Edith in the second-floor oval room, whose windows afforded a view of the rain-soaked South Lawn.

"At least this may cool things off a bit." Edith pulled the window closed to keep out the pattering rain.

"I've thought about your request to somehow get some rest for the president. I'm afraid his condition is worse than an asthma attack. He has been stumbling in his speech, and the twitching in his face tells me he's had or is likely to have another small stroke."

A cold shudder passed through Edith, her vision narrowing as the world began to spin. "We must get him away then." She fought the alarm bells ringing in her head so that she could think clearly. How could they manage that? Obviously her fantasy of repairing to a deserted island wouldn't work. "Perhaps we could go up to the Homestead for a few days. He's so relaxed there, and it's cooler in the mountains."

Grayson shook his head. "Another long train ride, too far from a hospital. And leaving Washington will cause another round of suspicions." He joined Edith at the window. "The storm should clear up by tomorrow. How about a ride on the *Mayflower?*"

The idea appealed to Edith as easier to explain and more restful. "Ah, leave it to a navy admiral to suggest a boat ride."

The weekend trip down the Potomac was beset by unrelenting thunderstorms, but at least it served to get the president out of the city and away from its unrelenting demands. Edith and Grayson intercepted communications to the president that didn't require his immediate action, which were the great majority. When Tumulty came to their stateroom with yet another pile of telegrams, Edith would promise to get them to Woodrow. And she did, eventually. It worked. His speech became clearer and his breathing easier, and Grayson declared the crisis averted.

On a brutally hot day at the end of August, Woodrow called Edith, Joseph Tumulty, and Dr. Grayson to his study. He announced that Colonel

House was remaining in Paris for some time and that he wished for Tumulty to continue in the capacity as personal secretary and advisor, with the assistance of Dr. Grayson.

This was not unwelcome news, nor did it come as a surprise to Edith, who knew Woodrow was being diplomatic in saying House was stepping down as chief advisor. She had repeatedly advised her husband that House had let his ego get ahead of objectivity. While they were in France, a newspaper article had appeared that basically gave credit for the peace negotiations to House and reported that they had only started falling apart when Wilson returned. When Edith had confronted House on this, he meekly slipped away, muttering something about jealous persons spreading rumors.

The only jealous person concerned, she thought, was House himself. It was still unclear what damage he had done while he was Woodrow's emissary in Paris, but it was past time for him to go.

Edith loosened her top blouse button and adjusted an electric fan to oscillate on the group as Woodrow went on. How the men managed to carry on in suit and tie bewildered her.

"As you know, the Senate is in a stalemate and has not ratified the treaty. We need to take the message to the people to put pressure on them. I want to make a train trip across the United States, not unlike the campaigns. Of course you all will be with me, as well as the press and so on. Perhaps President Taft will join us. He's been quite supportive and people listen to him."

"Mr. President, I don't think that's wise." Grayson had been madly tapping his foot.

"I agree," Edith chimed in. "You never had time to recover from Europe and stepped into a frying pan here."

Tumulty sat silent, steepling his fingers. Woodrow calmly folded his arms and cast a look at him. "And you, Joe?"

Tumulty cleared his throat. "Although I see the doctor and Mrs. Wilson's concern, I think getting out to the people may be reviving to you, sir. Washington is not exactly a place of rest and restoration, is it? If it's scheduled well, with plenty of time between stops and speeches…"

"I'm sorry," Grayson said as he shot to his feet. "I have to heartily disagree. The president nearly succumbed to the grippe in France and needs rest and exercise. I hardly see that as possible on this proposed campaign." He paced. "The endless speeches, receptions, crowds, with nary a thought to rest or privacy." He stopped pacing as he reached Edith and stood behind her with his hands on the back of her chair, as if forming a team. "As a compromise, why don't we ask Taft to do it, and the president can join him in the most strategic places? As a former president, a Republican who supports the treaty, who better to convince his own party to come together on this?"

Edith pursed her lips. From the stony look on Woodrow's face, she knew his mind was made up. Even with Grayson solidly behind her, their team was going to lose.

"Thank you, gentlemen." Woodrow calmly wiped his eyeglasses. "Clear your schedules for the next five or so weeks. Joe, I'd like a proposed itinerary as soon as possible."

After Tumulty and Grayson left, Edith remained. "So much for listening to your doctor's advice. Or your wife, for that matter." She circled around behind Woodrow to massage his shoulders. "We're not just talking about a little fatigue here. You collapsed in France. You've had terrible headaches, which isn't a sign that all is well in there." She gave him a soft knock on his head.

He leaned back into her arms. "This is my duty. My health is not to be considered when the future peace and security of the country are at stake. I promised those boys, our soldiers, no less than my full commitment to make this a war to end all wars." He reached for the worn Bible the soldier had given him. "If this treaty isn't put into effect, all their sacrifices will be in vain. I must go."

Edith fought back tears as she envisioned the tough battle ahead. If he was still the man she'd married less than four years ago, she wouldn't have a concern. But the shoulder bones she felt poking through his shirt and the whiteness of his hair told her otherwise.

TWENTY-SIX

September 1919

Woodrow was right about one thing. The train trip very much resembled the campaign. The same crowds waiting at each stop, the mayors and dignitaries eager to meet and shake hands. The nights on the train during longer trips, the hotels in the bigger cities. Speech after speech, he was getting his message across, and the papers were abuzz with his words and the people's positive reaction to them. "A triumph!" headlines proclaimed. "Redemption!" said others.

Edith began to hope that her husband would make it through unscathed. That hope faded, however, after a speech in the blisteringly hot Mormon Tabernacle in Salt Lake City. The huge church was filled over capacity, and the doors shut tight to keep out the throngs still trying to get in. Woodrow was seated on a high platform. Edith, several feet below, had to use smelling salts to keep from fainting in the heat. She couldn't imagine how Woodrow could speak so clearly when it had to be even hotter where he was.

But speak he did, eloquently and with passion, though it seemed to take the last ounce of strength in him. Grayson and a Secret Service man helped him to the car and to his hotel room. There the butler and Edith peeled off his sweat-soaked suit coat and shirt and poured water down his throat.

On to Cheyenne, and Denver, and Pueblo. With each speech he seemed energized by the crowd, stronger in his conviction to fight on. At a huge gathering at the fairgrounds in Pueblo, he spoke of his commitment to the fallen. He described the American cemeteries in France, with row upon row of white crosses, lovingly tended and twined with flowers by the villagers. And how he "wished the men who are now opposing this settlement for which those men who died could visit that spot. I wish they could feel the moral obligation that rests upon us not to go back on those boys, but to see this thing through to the end and make good their redemption of the world."

Edith dabbed her eyes with a handkerchief, as most of the crowd did the same. There was a moment of silence; then a few clapped, then more and more, until the whole crowd was clapping or raising their arms in the air in support.

They were quickly escorted back to the train, which was scheduled to depart for Kansas. Woodrow did not make it through dinner, retiring to his cabin with a headache. Checking on him, she found him in the forehead-on-back-of-chair position she had come to know indicated severe pain. She tried all her usual comfort measures, but to no avail.

"Should I call Dr. Grayson?" She was going to, no matter what he said, but thankfully he nodded his head.

But the doctor's medication did not relieve the pain, and in agony Woodrow paced, unable to get any sleep. Around midnight, Edith told Dr. Grayson to go to bed, and she sat with her husband, speaking gently until he finally fell asleep, sitting straight up in a chair.

The next morning, she walked him to his bed, despite his protest that he needed to get ready for his talk in Wichita. His face had taken on a ghastly gray color, and he was sick to his stomach.

"It's over dear. We're going home."

"No, not yet. Just a few more cities to go." His voice was weak and tremulous, before he passed blessedly to sleep.

Exhausted herself, Edith returned to her cabin, where she summoned Tumulty and Grayson, who agreed with her decision.

"I'll make an announcement in Wichita that the speech has been canceled and have the train rerouted." Tumulty excused himself.

"We're doing the right thing." Half question, half statement, Edith just wanted to know she had Grayson on her side. She knew Woodrow wasn't.

"It's the only thing to do. Don't worry; I'll go tell him now and will take the full force of his wrath when he's well enough to give it."

Edith stayed at Woodrow's bedside through that night. As the train slowed approaching Wichita the next morning, she left him briefly. To her great surprise when she returned, he was up, dressed and shaved, sitting on his bed.

She sat next to him. "How is your headache?" she asked, although she could tell from his posture it was excruciating.

"It does no good to complain, so I won't. There's work to do."

"Do you remember what we talked about yesterday?" She kept her voice as gentle as possible.

He turned his head to her, an action that caused him to wince. "What's that?"

He didn't remember. She steeled her spine to break it to him. "The trip is over, dear. To go on now would only put you at severe risk, and we need you to live on to see this through. Your speeches have been effective. Let's leave them with the image of your forceful and passionate delivery of them."

It was one of the hardest things she ever had to say. Even as the sky pinked in the dawn of a new day, her insides crumpled, knowing their lives would never be the same. She had watched the slide into death of her grandmothers and father. She could feel the vitality oozing out of her husband's body, as sure as she had theirs. But she vowed to not let him know this. She must wear a mask for him and others... *All is calm, all is bright*.

She was relieved when he accepted the news calmly.

He nodded slightly. "Home then. We'll need to rest up. The battle in the Senate is still to be won."

⁓

The train sped back to Washington in two days' time. They rushed from the train to the waiting motorcars with scarcely a wave to the crowds assembled to greet them. Once back at the White House, Edith made sure Tumulty kept the president's calendar clear. For the most part, he did, and the Wilsons shared quiet family time, reading, playing card games, and watching movies.

The few days' rest seemed to be helping. Woodrow was eating again and able to read a Bible verse each night, as had been his habit during the war. Edith dared to hope this would continue. But the nights were the worst. Unable to sleep and sometimes nearly blinded by headaches, Woodrow paced the hall between their rooms. She tried to rest, while keeping an ear out in case he called out to her.

Early in the morning of October 2, she went to check on him. He was sitting on the side of his bed, trying in vain to reach his glass of water on the nightstand. She got it for him, noticing his left arm hanging limply on his side.

"My arm is numb. Can you rub it for me?"

She did, then helped him to the bathroom, with his weight heavily upon her. Alarm bells sounded in her mind; she had never seen him this weak. "I think I better call Dr. Grayson." With Woodrow safely seated on the commode, she ran to the private house phone in her adjoining room. No need to alert the gossipy switchboard.

With the doctor on the way, Edith rushed back. Rounding the corner, she heard a soft thud. She found Woodrow barely conscious on the bathroom floor. Her mind a blank, she acted automatically, as if some outside power had taken over to enable her to help him. She grabbed a pillow for his head and a blanket to keep him warm. Fighting the rising panic within, she soothed, telling him he'd be okay, Dr. Grayson was on his way.

She noticed Woodrow's face had finally relaxed. Was it because his headache had finally abated, or was he near death? Edith chased that thought from her mind and simply held her husband's cool hand.

When Grayson arrived, the two of them dragged and lifted Woodrow back into bed. After making him comfortable and giving him a brief examination, the doctor took her aside. "I'm afraid he's had a cerebral vascular accident—a stroke. Much more serious this time. It seems his left side is paralyzed, and he's drifting in and out of consciousness."

It didn't seem real. Edith felt as if she were looking down upon the scene from above. "Will he recover?" It was the only thing that mattered, she told herself. Not how ghastly he looked at the moment, but that there was hope she would get him back, as he had recovered before.

Grayson took a deep breath. "That is something only time will tell. We'll get specialists, of course, who can tell us more. A good sign is that he is lucid when he's awake and able to speak. That bodes well for his mental competence. I imagine with therapy he may regain use of his left arm and leg, but I have to tell you, Mrs. Wilson, it is doubtful he will have full strength in them. And his ongoing hypertension, well..." He glanced at their patient.

"I understand." Edith went to sit by her husband's side. "I'll do whatever it takes."

Soon the president's bedroom resembled a hospital room, with round-the-clock nurses and reconstruction aids in attendance. They started right away stretching and moving his left arm and leg and ensuring he was turned in bed every two hours. Edith wondered how he would get the rest he needed with all of this, but he seemed to fall right back to sleep. At least the headache had abated, and they were able to get him to drink small amounts when he awakened.

Colonel House had somehow gotten wind of the president's condition. He telegrammed and called and left messages with the switchboard staff, which infuriated Edith. She returned his call, after taking a moment to calm herself to some point of reason, as Woodrow had taught her to do.

"I understand your concern, *Mr.* House. But for the sake of the president's privacy and security needs of our country, please refrain from speaking to anyone, leaving messages, communicating with the press, however helpful you think that may be."

"If I can just see him for a few minutes, Mrs. Wilson. There are a few urgent matters—"

"You don't seem to understand. The only urgent matter right now is my husband's rest and recovery. Good day, Mr. House."

Of course the needs of the country did not abate, and there were continual calls from the press and Congress as to the situation. After a week with only slight improvement, Edith called for a meeting with Grayson, Tumulty, and Dr. Dercum, a specialist in the nervous system who had examined her husband. They met in Woodrow's study. It felt odd with him absent, but Edith wanted his presence to be felt as much as possible.

"I want the unvarnished truth," she said, "so that we, and the country, can move forward."

Dr. Dercum had set up poster-sized illustrations of the brain and bodily systems, giving Edith hope that she would learn enough to understand what Woodrow was going through and how best to help him.

The specialist was the first to speak. "It is still very early in the process, but I think we can be greatly encouraged by his progress so far. His mind is clear, and his will to live evident."

Tumulty joined in. "But his will to live is entirely focused on the work that lies ahead. Once he realizes he may not be able to continue it, I'm afraid it will evaporate."

Edith looked at Dr. Grayson. "You know him best. What do you think?"

"I agree with both of you. If there is a way for him to carry on, that is the best hope for the fullest recovery possible."

Edith was doubtful. She thought of elderly relatives who had suffered strokes. She had seen no such miraculous recoveries. "Can someone recover from this?"

Dr. Dercum replied. "Yes. Not all do, as much depends on motivation, as it is a long, arduous process, and depending on how much cognitive damage there is. But I think we have cause for hope." He stood next to a framed illustration of the brain, propped on an easel. "You see, the brain has redundant circulation, that is, the blood supply can flow from different vessels, should the need arise." He pointed to an area on the illustration that looked like a nest of thin red and blue tubes. "Here, at the base of the brain, is the circle of Willis. Four major arteries come through here, serving all parts of the brain. If there is a blockage somewhere, the blood can find another pathway to the brain. It's a built-in safety net, but it takes some time for all the new pathways to develop."

Edith's spirits lifted for the first time in days. "I read that Louis Pasteur had a similar event and recovered, doing some of his most important work afterward."

"Quite true," said Dr. Dercum. "But we don't know…"

"Woodrow's most important work lies ahead of him. We must do everything in our power to get him through this temporary setback." She would see her husband through this, and all his life's work would not come tumbling down in ruins. "How do we proceed?"

Again, Dr. Dercum took the lead. "We must give him absolute rest, and relief from his responsibilities at this time. No public appearances, nothing to take him away from his exercises and quiet."

Edith exchanged looks with Tumulty. "How will this be possible? The work of the president never ceases."

"That is not for me to say. What I can say is that the president cannot perform his duties at this moment, and you will have to either postpone them, allow the vice president to step in, or boil things down and present things as he improves and can attend to them. You will have to decide what is critical enough to bring to his attention and do all the follow-up for him." He looked pointedly at his audience. "The three of you, strong and healthy, should be able to share part of the load that has been on this one man."

So a plan was made. Grayson handled giving updates to the press on the president's improving condition. Tumulty met with the multitudes wanting to see the president, and when he wasn't able to, Edith did. Before dinner each night, Tumulty would present to Edith the items of the day needing the president's attention. Then, if she agreed that no one else could make the decision and it was urgent, she would find a moment to briefly state the problem to her husband and gain his answer.

Edith saw to it that no one other than herself, Woodrow's daughters, and Grayson saw Woodrow. They were his backup troops, his circle of Wilson. No one would get past them, and they would provide all that he needed. Too weak to protest, Woodrow cooperated, taking long naps in between therapies and consultations. Edith told herself that she was doing the right thing for her husband, as his best hope for recovery was to know his work on earth was still being done, that his promise to the doughboy soldiers was being kept.

But Edith knew something that Tumulty and Grayson either didn't know or didn't want to admit. Although Woodrow's thinking seemed clear, he wasn't the same man who had been elected president in 1912, or even 1916. She knew from others that his ability to reason, his ability to compromise, even his control over his emotions had changed, even before the recent devastating stroke. Although she hadn't recognized it at the time, blaming it on fatigue and stress, he wasn't the same after the last trip to France, when he became more fatigued and forgetful.

She considered her dilemma. Was what was best for her husband also best for the country? The world? She was grateful to have been involved in every step of his decisions, to have seen for herself the destruction of Europe and heard the passion of the countries for a lasting peace. He could guide her in decisions without saying a word. She knew without a doubt his opinions on all the major issues. One decision, one day at a time, and by the grace of God they could get through this.

Edith wrestled with seeking Colonel House's assistance. After herself, he was the person most knowledgeable regarding Woodrow's opinions. She debated whether to let him into the circle. One more person to inject opinions, one more person to leak untimely information to Congress or the public. She couldn't risk it, unless a decision was truly critical and not delayable. So far, he had adhered to her instructions not to interfere, but she knew he wouldn't be sidelined forever.

After several weeks of the new system, she decided to meet with Tumulty and Grayson to see if they still believed they were doing the right thing. This time they met in her rooms, no longer needing the illusion of Woodrow's presence.

"I'll get right to it. If we can, and we must, put the needs of the country first, are we doing the right thing?" She tapped a pile of newspapers on her desk. "There's talk of little ol' me acting as president. Or you, or you." She glanced at the men. "We're only acting on the president's say-so, of course, but others do not understand."

"What do you propose we do differently?" Tumulty fidgeted.

Edith thought of how he had five children to feed, and maybe his own interests played a part in his judgment. Grayson, a navy rear admiral, should have no such worry, but he was extremely loyal to the president.

"I wonder if it is time for the president to step down, even if temporarily, and let Vice President Marshall take over."

Both men sucked in a breath.

Tumulty took on his even, somewhat patronizing tone that Edith disliked. "Mrs. Wilson, what you need to understand is that such a move would be anything but temporary. It's like freeing a snake, then trying to get it back into its cage. And furthermore"—he looked at Grayson for concurrence—"the vice president has made it clear he wanted no part of it. He as much as said he would resign first."

"Explain to me, why is he in the office? Isn't he like an actor's understudy, ready to step in when necessary?"

Tumulty shook his head. "Not at all. He was on the ticket to balance it, to win the election. You know as well as we do that Marshall hasn't been kept in the fold. You know much more than he does about pretty much all national matters. You were in France for the peace talks. You got a daily briefing. Marshall would be starting in a position of great ignorance, at a time when we can't afford to lose ground. For the good of the country, we must continue to muddle through the best we can until the president is on his feet."

"If the vice president resigned, who would be next in line? The Speaker of the House? The secretary of state? Someone appointed?"

The men groaned. Tumulty mumbled, "Same problem."

Edith still had reservations, but without the support of these two, she would have to go to Henry Cabot Lodge. She shuddered at the thought. That would surely put her husband in his grave.

In early November, Edith received a letter from Colonel House. He had returned to the United States against Woodrow's specific instructions, and she considered tearing it up before even reading it. But her calmer self intervened. She had heard House had been quite ill, and perhaps this was a note to explain his intransigence.

The letter, however, was a cheerful note. He apologized for breaking the agreed communications embargo but trusted his letter was both critical and private. He wrote:

A dear friend has managed to persuade Lodge to temper his treaty reservations to a few changes in verbiage, which I believe the president will surely accept. Furthermore, the changes are significant to those opposed in the Senate, but yet not likely to raise any objections by the other signatories at Versailles...

It was an olive branch, he concluded, and one he earnestly saw as the only way the treaty was to be ratified and the United States to enter the League of Nations.

Edith dutifully read the letter to her husband. Whether or not he fully understood it wasn't clear, as his speech was particularly thick that day. What Edith did know was that he had steadfastly refused any changes to the document he and the others, including Germany, had signed. She tucked the letter away in the growing pile for Woodrow to review when he was stronger.

The vote in the Senate to ratify the treaty was scheduled for November 19, but it was a day like any other in the White House. Ike Hoover, the chief usher, had obtained a large rolling lounge chair that they could prop Woodrow up in and wheel him about the residence and, on mild days like that one, outside on the portico. Hoover was wheeling the president inside as it was already getting dark when Tumulty came to Edith, his face grave.

"The Senate has voted. Both the treaty as written and the treaty with Lodge's reservations have been defeated without the president's support."

This was not unexpected, but still Edith's face grew hot as she recalled House's unanswered letter with the proposed compromise on Lodge's reservations. It hadn't occurred to her that the bargaining wouldn't occur without Woodrow's direct support. "What does this mean then? For the treaty, for the League?"

"All the other allied nations have ratified it, so it will go into effect, as will the League. But I'm afraid that without the Americans' steady influence, it will have no teeth." He lowered his head. "I'm sorry, Mrs. Wilson. I feel I personally have failed. If only I could have gotten the president to compromise..."

"No." She sighed. "There was to be no compromising. He was firm about that. He felt we had no right to unilaterally change the agreement; it was a matter of honor. And I agree." But her words did not match her true opinion. She easily could have gotten Woodrow's nod, had she explained the plan to him. It was clear she would have to take a more active role, acting like House in helping Woodrow to see all sides of the issue, even if she had to take a guess as to his comprehension if it was one of his bad days.

She glanced down the hall, where Hoover was no doubt getting the president into bed and ready for dinner. She dreaded telling him the news, just one more thing to break his waning spirit.

Meetings with Tumulty each morning after breakfast became Edith's unwelcome routine. It wasn't that she disliked the fellow; it was the daily reminder that she had to step in and make decisions as to what rose in importance enough to trouble her husband. Grayson's adamant insistence that Woodrow's stress be kept to a minimum always tumbled in her head. On a morning in early December, she faced that very issue head on.

Tumulty had run through the daily developments, and Edith felt she could readily address all of them without consulting Woodrow.

"One more item, while I have you," Tumulty said as she tucked away her notepad. "The railroads are scheduled to return to their owners from federal control on December 31. The general director has written a letter urging for more time for the transition. He states the railroads have not yet gotten their leadership and finances in order, and we risk chaos in adhering to that arbitrarily established date. Will you please ask the president to extend the date?"

It seemed a very reasonable request. Edith couldn't think of a single reason not to do it. So it began as a simple request she made, almost as an afterthought as she cleared Woodrow's lunch tray.

"One more thing." She explained the railroad situation. "Will you permit some extra time while they make the transition back to private business?"

"No." His whisper was hoarse but emphatic.

"I don't understand. Tumulty says that this is what the department head himself recommends, and the railroads agree."

"That date was agreed." He swirled his hand around, the motion being his signal to get him a pen.

She got him a piece of lined paper and a pen, and he painstakingly wrote a note to Tumulty. *You must let me alone about the R.R.s. I've announced they go back to their owners January 1 and that cannot be altered.*

Edith pursed her lips. She felt sure he was making a mistake. But she recalled how adamant he was at the time that federal control would only be for a very specific time period. "I'll give this to him."

But Tumulty disregarded the note when she met with him the next morning. "I've taken the liberty of writing a press release for his approval."

Due to the railroad companies not being fully organized to receive and manage their properties by December 31 without raising serious financial and legal complications, the transfer of possession will be effective at 12:01 a.m., March 1, 1920. The release was stamped Woodrow Wilson.

"Now, just have him approve that, and the matter is resolved."

With a small pang of guilt, Edith took the note to Woodrow's room, where the aide was stretching his left arm.

"Oh, oh," Woodrow cried out, as his arm was moved over his head.

"Don't let me interrupt." Edith waved the press release. "The railroad companies have agreed to resume control on March 1."

"Yes, yes." Woodrow sighed as the aide returned his arm to his side. Whether he was expressing relief that his arm had been released or agreeing with the railroad settlement, Edith didn't linger to find out.

TWENTY-SEVEN

1920

By early January, it was clear that Woodrow wasn't going to recover quickly.

"Darling, you've hardly touched a thing." Edith nodded to Ike to take away her husband's breakfast tray. "How are you feeling today?" She pressed the back of her hand to his forehead, then gave him a little kiss.

He grasped her fingers with his still strong right hand. "Better," he said in a hoarse whisper, his mouth curled into a crooked smile, "now that you're here."

She piled pillows behind him to help him sit up. "Tumulty is already out in the hall. Will you see him today?"

Woodrow waved at his body, stretched across the bed, and slowly shook his head. "Not today. Maybe the girls?"

"You want me to telephone your daughters? Only Margaret is in town."

"Yes, Margaret."

"But what about Tumulty? What should I tell him?"

Woodrow became agitated, grabbing his breakfast tray back from Ike with a rattle of glasses and dishes. He pointed to the door.

"Easy does it, dear. Mind your blood pressure. I'll see what he wants for you."

She found the secretary sitting in a chair next to her desk down the hall, chatting with Rebecca.

"There she is," said Rebecca. "Mr. Tumulty requests an audience with the president straightaway."

"That's not going to be possible."

Tumulty slapped at a sheet of paper in his hand. "But, Mrs. Wilson, how am I to keep things running, if I can't talk to the boss?"

Edith took out her pad and paper. "Give me a list of the most pressing matters."

"How am I to know what is most pressing? International relations? Department head appointments? Bills to be signed into law? It's all pressing. Only the chief executive can decide what to sign, not to sign, push back to a committee..."

She nodded toward the paper in his hand. "What do you have there? Let's start with that."

"It's a letter I drew up for you, actually." He cleared his throat. "Please don't think I am trying to crowd you or to urge immediate action by the president..."

"Ahem. It seems that is exactly what you are doing. Give me that." She held out her hand for the letter. "Ah, a list."

"Yes, precisely. A list of all the critical appointments that need to be made. Without people in these positions, I'm afraid the government will come to a screeching halt."

Edith read on. "Secretary of agriculture, Secretary Lansing's recommendation for Holland, the heads of the Civil Service Commission, Federal Trade Commission, Interstate Commerce Commission, United States Shipping Board, United States Tariff Commission, war finance director, Waterways Commission, Rent Commission.

"Good gracious, why on earth would the president of the United States need to decide all this? Perhaps we need a commission to staff all these commissions. That is, if they're even necessary."

"If I can just talk to the president, ma'am. He has people he knows and trusts making good recommendations for these men and even knows a number of the candidates personally."

Edith ran her finger down the letter. "Diplomats in Bulgaria, China, Costa Rica, Italy, Netherlands, Salvador, Siam, Switzerland. You're telling me he knows all these people? And why are these countries all suddenly without an ambassador?"

"Various reasons—it's not just ambassadors, and there are resignations, reassignments, situational changes in these countries, and nothing's been done since... Ahem." He coughed, the words seemingly stuck in his throat. "Well, since early October."

He looked up at her, but getting no response, he continued, "We have dossiers on all of them, ma'am. There are many additional pressing matters, but if you can get that list to him today..."

Edith thought of her husband, currently napping in his four-poster bed. It would soon be time for his pureed lunch, which she would spoon-feed him. After that, she might get a nod in agreement for a few men on the list before he drifted off to sleep. She couldn't possibly get an answer for everyone on this list, and yet there was no end in sight to the decisions steadily mounting.

She would have to get some help in deciding these things more quickly. But whom could she trust?

There were risks for each person she allowed to see Woodrow. Risks to his health by disturbing his critical rest, and risk that word would spread about his condition, which could lead to calls for him to resign. With no reason to live, to fight for his beliefs, he would surely die.

But Grayson knew his condition better than anyone. He knew how to communicate with him. He had been with him in France and during many important events. He was a wise and loyal navy officer with flag rank. She needn't look outside for another advisor, since the Senate was no longer battling over the treaty. If she and Grayson had to make decisions for the president, based on their deep understanding of his positions, then so be it.

Inspiration hit her one morning as she listened to Tumulty drone on about the numerous requests for an audience with Woodrow. Secretary of State Lansing demanded to see the president to gain approval to sell wheat to the starving Russians.

"Why is the secretary in charge of selling wheat? Is there a problem sending food to the hungry? To our allies?"

"It's protocol for large sales to foreign states. This is nearly four million dollars' worth of grain. What if it depleted our supply?"

"Well, does it?"

"I guess not. We have a wheat director"—he shuffled through Lansing's message—"a Mr. Julien Barnes..."

Edith shook her head and sighed. "Tell Mr. Barnes to draw up the proper form of authorization and send it for the president's signature. Maybe if we leave the Cabinet members and agency heads alone to do their jobs, we'd see they are quite capable of making the decisions they habitually bring to the president. And tell Lansing to make a list of countries and products to be preapproved."

Tumulty scrunched his face. "I'm not sure how far we should go with this."

"It's quite simple. For now, the president decides the things that only the president can decide."

As Tumulty and Edith bounced back numerous items under the new policy, the requests became fewer, yet there were still mountains of items that did need the president's decision. Edith would take a pile of them to him when they had lunch and read them to him, taking his nod as approval. Sometimes she slipped a pen in his hand and guided it for a scrawled signature; sometimes he was able to sign on his own. She held in the back of her mind the knowledge that Tumulty could reproduce Woodrow's true signature in a way no one would detect. She never asked him to do it but wondered if he had on his own. Why else would he have perfected it so?

Negotiations with labor unions were trickier, and the threat of strikes in the railroad industry and amongst coal miners continued. Edith answered their calls for the president's action with a note saying he would deal with it when he was stronger. As much as she despised William McAdoo, he could be helpful in these areas. She made a mental note to forward union demands to him. In the meantime, they would just have to work it out themselves.

One other person Edith decided to bring into the circle, at least for advice, was Altrude. Edith invited her and her two children to the Residence for an informal tea. After a few minutes of playing with the babies, Rebecca whisked them away for a treat while she and Altrude settled into the Oval Sitting Room, the dreary winter day brightened by a roaring fire.

"Is there anything I can do for you and the president?" Altrude's cheeks seemed sunken, her eyes having lost their usual gleam.

"Kind of you, but all is in hand. It must be hard, caring for two very young children with your husband absent so much of the time. It is I who should be offering you help."

"Not at all."

"Well, there are a few things I'd like your opinion on, as you know the players well. First, how do you feel about bringing Colonel House back on board to help screen information to be presented to Mr. Wilson?"

Altrude cocked her head. "You have suddenly developed trust in him? More than others who are already 'on board,' as you say, and are capable?"

Edith chuckled. "I guess you have answered my question. The other person I think might be helpful in certain areas and can be trusted is William McAdoo. What do you think?"

"If it's something that William thinks will benefit William, he will do a fine job with it. So be careful."

"Agreed. This next concern is something that Woodrow and I have never fully agreed on. We are, of course, only acting as his voice and shouldn't take it as an opportunity to advance our own ideas."

Altrude leaned forward in her chair. "Hmm. I sense a crack in your resolve. I hope it's for something nefarious."

Edith gave her a one-eyed glare. "Nothing of the sort. You see, there are a great many appointments to be made—cabinet positions, assistants to the secretaries, on and on. It seems a never-ending merry-go-round of men cycling in and out of government positions as the winds of political parties change. There's been quite a bit of backlash regarding the racial makeup of people in these positions."

"Not to mention they're all men."

"Well yes, but one issue at a time. I've always believed in a merit-based system."

"And Woodrow doesn't?"

"He does, but in his mind, a good deal of merit comes from knowing and trusting an individual, and that's how he picks his senior leaders. He then leaves it up to them to choose the personnel to fill out the ranks of the various departments."

"And they pick more people like themselves. Wealthy white men. How do you propose changing this, while staying within Woodrow's wishes?"

"That's what I hoped you could help me with."

Altrude shook her head. "There are just things you have to accept that you cannot change. Why don't you focus on an issue that you might have a great deal of influence on and that would certainly be blessed by Woodrow?"

"Don't say hosting state dinners and coercing Republicans. As much as I love doing it..."

"No. It's time to move on. We're at the cusp of women finally, finally having the right to vote across the nation. Arizona, Oklahoma, even Woodrow's beloved New Jersey have ratified the Nineteenth Amendment. Only two or three more to go, I think."

"Well, that's good for the cause. But what on earth could I do?"

"The states that have rejected are primarily in the South. Let's put aside your lack of enthusiasm for this change and think about how you might guide the remaining states to ratify. It might all come down to Tennessee, and you grew up not far from its border. Maybe you could pay a visit and meet with some of the leaders."

"That doesn't sound like me."

Altrude shrugged. "You're probably right. I've never understood how you can be so protective of the rights of the Negroes and fail women. The two positions seem at odds with each other."

Edith tamped down the familiar anger that wanted to bubble over like overheated soup. "You know my reasoning on this."

"I do. And do you know why the Southern states have rejected the amendment? Because they don't want colored women to vote. Because that would mean they'd have to let colored men vote."

"I don't understand. The Fifteenth Amendment prohibits depriving citizens the right to vote based on race."

"Really. Is that so?" Altrude got up and sauntered over to the curved wall of windows. She pointed in the distance as Edith joined her. "Just there, right across the river, is Virginia. It's not illegal for colored men to vote there. But first they must pass a literacy test, prove they understand the Constitution, and pay a poll tax."

"That's true in many states."

"Many Southern states," Altrude corrected. "The same states who have rejected the Susan B. Anthony Amendment. Do you see a pattern?"

"You're implying the Southern states have those requirements because Negroes can't read or afford to pay a dollar tax?" Edit felt hot blood rise to her face. "Because that theory alone is rather disparaging of them."

But Altrude remained calm as she returned to her tea. "It shows in the decrease in registrations of African American voters when the law took effect. This has been the net effect. The desired effect."

Altrude's soft, almost patronizing tone irritated Edith like an errant undergarment. It seemed the girl no longer looked upon her as a mother figure and was now her formidable adult equal.

"I guess we have to evaluate whether it is unduly difficult for anyone to meet those requirements." Edith took a breath. She didn't like any of this, but what was she to do? "Fine. I accept your position. But I maintain that we need to work to see that women have their rights without destroying families and the very fabric of our society in the process." As she said the words, a feeling of peace washed over Edith. It wasn't either/or after all. Maybe the things she feared most would be less likely if all women had the vote.

A smile crept across Altrude's face. "Well, there you have it." She held up her teacup as if for a toast. "Your new role." She nibbled on a shortbread cookie. "Mmm. My compliments to your baker. This is almost as good as a Lorna Doone."

Edith had just said goodbye to Altrude and the littles and was looking forward to a quiet moment for herself when Helen Bones let herself into Edith's room. Surprised to see her, as she had been gone several months visiting family in Virginia, Edith let out a joyful screech.

Helen dropped the satchel from her hands and greeted Edith with a big hug. "Oh, sister, I have missed you."

"And I have missed you as well. I hope you've gotten all my letters. You understand how serious it is with Woodrow, don't you? I had to be careful. You never know who might steam open White House correspondence."

They spent some time catching up. Helen pulled some newspapers from her satchel. "I'm afraid what you're telling me doesn't quite match up with what I read. It seems the public has been misled."

"Surely more a sin of omission than commission. And the president does deserve a modicum of privacy."

Helen arched an eyebrow. "What about these claims—" She ruffled through some pages. "Here it says, 'We have a petticoat government,' and here 'The president is in hiding, while Mrs. Wilson runs the show...'"

"Have you seen him yet?"

"I did, but he had just taken to bed for his nap and we only had a few words."

"So you see he can still communicate. His mind is still sharp."

"Is it? Really, Edith, perhaps the presidency shouldn't be in his—or your—hands. The people deserve better."

Edith felt her defenses mounting like the doughboys in their trenches. "This is just temporary. And you know Woodrow. If we take away his role, right at the cusp of everything he's worked for, then he'll slip away."

Helen's crinkled brow revealed her doubt. "He would want what's best for the country."

"And who is to say what that is?"

"You, apparently." The color was rising in Helen's face as her eyes took in her surroundings. "I've heard my room has been taken over."

"Oh yes, we need it for a bit while your cousin needs round-the-clock care. If I'd known you were returning today, I would have..."

Helen waved aside the gesture. "You have bigger things on your plate." Helen took a deep breath, arranged her newspapers into a neat pile. "Edith, you know how much I love you and Woodrow..."

"Then you know that I would do anything to save him."

"And that, perhaps, is the problem."

Edith tossed and turned long into the night after Helen's visit. Was she doing the right thing for Woodrow? For the country? It seemed the women in her life felt she was failing in her duties, while the men urged her to maintain the charted path. Was one side too influenced by emotions? Was the other side seduced by power?

Just before she drifted off to sleep, her mind wandered to Woodrow returning to the apparently abandoned fishing village on the island in the Potomac. He knew the villagers were there, knew they were afraid and hiding. He had a sense about people, a gift for peeling away the layers of agendas and ambitions and stubbornness and finding the best solution for all.

Then she was riding in an open carriage, sitting next to a queen with flowers raining down on her—a parade in France for him, welcoming him as a hero who helped end a war. Next she was on the steps of the Capitol, looking out at the tens of thousands cramming the streets to cheer for the reelected president.

The reverie answered her questions. She must stay the course, do whatever it took to help him through this time, for he was the man the people elected.

There was no official entertaining, no open houses at the Residence. Truly, with the nasty things reported to the press by their detractors, Edith hardly missed having the never-ending rounds of receptions for people like Henry Cabot Lodge or Robert Lansing. But when it came to a long-standing invitation to the king and queen of Belgium, Edith relented.

Woodrow and Edith had been treated with such kindness and respect in Belgium so, knowing they would be discreet regarding the president's condition, she allowed them a brief visit. Although he could not rise from his sickbed, they enjoyed a lively conversation and served to raise Woodrow's spirits.

They brought lovely bone-china plates with scenes from their homeland, which Woodrow inspected with his magnifying glass. Edith recognized some cities she had visited before the war that now lay in ruins. It made her sad, for even though reconstruction had begun, those cities would never be the same.

"Such artistry. What a lovely gift," Woodrow said, his voice soft but clear.

With that simple remark, Edith began to feel her husband was returning to her. That was his true self, an admirer of beautiful things, hopeful for the future and appreciative of loyalty and friendship. She envisioned their retirement, filled with interesting people and reminiscing about their amazing experiences. She just had to protect him a while longer, until he could get up and walk. Already she could see that his face no longer drooped on its left side. He had shown great willpower to heal before and would do so again.

In March 1920, a year remained of Woodrow's term in office. Edith allowed Tumulty to have a rare visit with the president, on a day when he was especially refreshed and showing signs of his former jovial personality. She reasoned it was time to start in-person meetings, so Woodrow could be seen as the president a few more times. He was relearning how to walk with two canes and assistance, and soon, she thought, he might address Congress in person.

But that meeting came with a surprise. Tumulty came to her afterward, mopping his sweaty face on a cloth.

"You look like you were in a prizefight," she mused.

"I rather was. You're not going to believe this. He wants to run again."

Edith waved dismissively. "He's been saying that for months. He thinks with more time, he'll get the treaty ratified once and for all, get the railroads working again, and on and on. He's not running. I'll see to that."

"I'm relieved to hear you say that. These past few months have been a trial. We need to focus on his legacy, not a campaign. So I think it's time we allow a few more visitors."

Edith thought of her husband, who was making progress with a new reconstruction aid but hardly resembling his former self. "I agree, but only when absolutely necessary for very short visits, which we completely control. Whom do you have in mind?"

"I have a letter from a Miss Katharine Wright, sister to Orville and Wilbur, the aviation pioneers. I think the president would be very interested in this one."

Edith felt a wave of embarrassment. She had met Miss Wright briefly some months ago. It had been a hectic day of meetings and decisions and caring for Woodrow, and she had mistaken the woman for Maginel Wright, who had done the wonderful artwork for the Food Administration. When she discovered Katharine was the sister of the Wright brothers, now seeking Edith's support on suffrage, she had given her too hasty a response.

"Woodrow does love aeroplanes. What does this Miss Katharine want? Some sort of reward or recognition for them?"

"Not exactly. Back in 1914, we established the NACA, the National Advisory Committee for Aeronautics. She'd like Orville to be considered for a position on the committee."

Relieved, Edith saw a chance to redeem herself. And who better to serve on the important committee? "Oh, I think you can go ahead and approve that one for Woodrow. Next?"

"A really pressing issue is Mexico. If the president can meet with just two senators on the Foreign Relations Committee, it would send a signal that the president is on top of that. And Lord Grey, the British ambassador, has been waiting for months to see him. He's been blessed by King George himself, has a sterling reputation and very good relations with his people. I don't need to tell you how important it is that we explain to them why the treaty hasn't been ratified and the steps we're taking to rectify that."

"Fine. Set a date for the senators. And get more information on the ambassador. He's not to invade the sickroom with an entourage. Just him."

When Edith received the list of visitors, among the Ambassador Lord Grey's staff was a Major Craufurd-Stuart. She was horrified, as he was the indiscreet partygoer who had circulated tasteless jokes about her upon her engagement. In addition, along with the irascible Alice Roosevelt, he had been part of a spying episode on one of her dear friends. Her friend was completely innocent but suffered great embarrassment over the incident. Woodrow wouldn't do anything about it, but she was darned if she'd let that man remain in the country as an honored guest. She wrote Tumulty a note saying as much. There would be no presidential audience with the ambassador unless he sent this aide home.

Edith decided not to bother her husband with the British ambassador issue, as it didn't rise to the level of essential business that Grayson recommended. But a visit with a few senators should be an easy decision and would help Woodrow feel he was performing his duties.

She took his dinner tray to him herself and dismissed Hoover. She arranged Woodrow's utensils so he could reach them with his right hand and propped up his pillows. "Your aide tells me you stood on your own today. He says you're making great progress." She eyed the thinly sliced roast beef on his plate. The aide had been adamant that Woodrow was still learning to swallow properly, and until he did, he was at risk of choking. "I'll send this back to get pureed."

"No, no," Woodrow protested. He mimicked a knifing motion.

"You want me to cut it into small pieces? Do you promise to chew it thoroughly?" She hated that she had to speak to him as if he were a child, but it was for his own protection.

He responded by handing her the knife. She did as he requested, and he managed the meat quite well.

"A bit of business, if you're up to it."

His face lit up and his smile was only slightly lopsided. "About time."

"Will you meet with two senators on the Foreign Relations Committee? One Democrat, the other Republican."

"Yes."

"Will you meet with the British ambassador? There are many others in front of him in line." Edith decided to give herself an out, should the ambassador not cooperate with her request.

"Yes."

Edith ran through the rest of Tumulty's daily list of questions in her head. She decided to stop with her two positive answers rather than tiring him.

The reconstruction aide, who came every weekday morning, mentioned a problem that caused Edith to wonder if there was a common cause for her husband's digestive maladies. The therapist said that his exercises were frequently interrupted by the need for toileting.

Woodrow had always had poor digestion and a poor appetite. In addition, he had the eating habits of a toddler, with cookies and milk each evening and a tiny sandwich during the day. While she had grown up eating plenty of fruits and vegetables, he picked at his peas as if bugs had invaded his plate.

So she went to the kitchen and spoke to Chef Oliver. Wearing a crisp white jacket with a thermometer in the chest pocket, he seemed to have put some weight back on. The kitchen workers stopped what they were doing and stood at attention until Edith asked them to please carry on.

The chef pulled out a chair for her at a white enameled table.

"Chef, I'm concerned the president has lost much weight. Can you find ways to get more nutrition in him?"

"Oh, I wasn't aware. Most men dislike pureed foods, but if his teeth are better, perhaps we can give him a bit more to chew?"

Woodrow did have problems with his teeth, but of course that wasn't the true reason for the pureed food. "Yes, we can try some cooked vegetables and tender meats. I notice he often complains of a stomachache at bedtime, and well, his mornings are uncomfortable. Do you think his cookies and milk each evening could be the cause of it?"

"Have you consulted his physician on this?"

"Yes, but when I told him it seemed milk upset his stomach, he just said to cut back on his milk. But it's one of his few remaining pleasures and helps him sleep." She pulled a note card from her pocket. "Woodrow liked these when I made them during our courting days, an old family recipe for oatmeal cookies with blackstrap molasses. My mother swore they strengthened the blood."

The chef took the card. "Of course, we'll make them for him. And I will experiment with ways to make something resembling milk to go with them. Maybe coconut milk? And I'll dress up the vegetables for him. The notes I got were that he liked everything bland and steamed."

Edith scrunched her face. "That probably came from his daughters or Ellen. Those Presbyterians don't know how to eat. The president liked my cooking when we were courting, and I used plenty of herbs and spices." It was a bit of an exaggeration, she sheepishly admitted to herself. She could count on one hand the meals she had made for Woodrow.

Chef Oliver wrote some notes for himself, pausing to think while tapping his pencil on his front teeth. A kitchen worker holding a huge mixing bowl was eyeing them, while trying to be inconspicuous. Edith suspected she and the chef were sitting at the cook's accustomed work space.

She got up and pushed in her chair. "One more thing. As usual, the details of the private menus are to remain private. I don't want every dairy farmer in America pounding at the door in indignation. Thank you for your time, Chef. I look forward to your creations."

"No, thank *you*, Mrs. Wilson. We are here to serve you and Mr. President, and frankly I'm delighted for the opportunity to try new things. And of course..." He mimed buttoning his lips.

With a bit of grumbling, Woodrow accepted his new diet and actually ate more. His stomachaches disappeared, and Edith could tell he was getting stronger and more alert. Soon after, the aide called her to come see something. Woodrow was sitting in a proper chair, not the half-reclining rolling chair he had been using. And that wasn't all. The aide helped him to stand; then he took a step with his good right leg, then swung his left leg around for a second step.

Tears came to her eyes. "You're walking!"

The bedroom had a recent addition, the "Liberty rug." The center of it featured an image of the Statue of Liberty, in honor of its ceremonial illumination, surrounded by scenes from around the country.

Woodrow smiled. "Pretty good to walk over Niagara Falls. But I cheat." He pointed at his feet, which indeed had landed next to an image of the falls. "Show her."

The therapist lifted Woodrow's pant leg to reveal a hefty brace buckled around his lower leg and around his shoe.

"Well, I don't care how you're doing it, it's a miracle, and I know it's just the start." Edith helped the aide get him back into the chair. "I'm calling for some champagne. We must celebrate."

Cheered by her husband's progress, Edith went to the Drawer ready to plow through it. She tossed aside several letters from Colonel House unopened. A note from Tumulty advised that Lord Grey and his entourage had returned to Britain, having given up on a meeting with the president. *Good riddance*, she thought. A labor strike had been averted and the railroad conversion was going well. One report suggested a timetable for German reparation payments; another proposed upcoming legislation to prohibit the sale of alcohol.

She didn't even need to ask Woodrow his opinion on the latter. It was directly opposed to his policy of keeping federal government out of the lives of the people. If the states or a locality wanted to impose such a measure, they could do so at their level. Even that, he had told her, would be a bad idea; it would breed corruption and crime, as the people naturally would find ways to circumvent the law. *"The president says veto,"* she scrawled across Tumulty's note.

Feeling joyous, she made plans to visit Altrude and her new baby as well as her son, Gordon, now an inquisitive toddler. All seemed right with the world when she was holding a baby in her lap.

But her joy was short-lived, as Colonel House managed to talk or bribe his way past the guards and into the Oval Office in the West Wing. Of course Woodrow wasn't there, but Tumulty was and hurried over to the Residence to tell Edith.

Edith was at her desk writing letters when Tumulty came rushing into her office, his face ruddy and perspiration beading on his forehead. After telling her of House's unexpected visit, he proposed that Woodrow should see him.

"Absolutely not. You tell him he will be invited back when the president has the time and inclination, and not a moment before. And have the darned security detail with you so they know better next time."

"But, Mrs. Wilson, couldn't you come meet with him, just for a few minutes? We don't want him spreading rumors, and you know he has plenty of contacts in the press."

Edith put away her pen and letters and slammed her desk drawer shut. "Oh for God's sake, I'll send him away myself."

She freshened up first, more to make House wait than for any real need. Then she sauntered over to the West Wing with every intention of having the briefest of conversations.

House sat in a wingback armchair, one of two flanking the fireplace. The lovely Swedish ivy plant that sat on the mantel had withered to a tangle of dried stems. Apparently the housekeepers found little need to keep the office in its usual pristine state. Edith pushed aside her irritation at this and greeted House.

He stood upon seeing her but seemed to have shrunk in the several years since she had seen him. His white hair had thinned and his mustache grown more unruly.

After the usual pleasantries and inquiries regarding their spouses, they settled into the armchairs and House got right to business. "I have a pretty good idea of what is going on here. I don't blame you or anyone for covering up the president's true condition. But you are treading in dangerous territory, which could have profound effects on world peace. I know, and you know that Woodrow would want my counsel, as his most trusted ally."

"You seem to forget his anger with your handling of the treaty negotiations."

House opened and shut his mouth and wiped his eyes. "I'm sorry. It was such a misunderstanding. Later we discussed it and all was well—I thought. Did he not tell you?"

"No." Edith thought back on the duplicitous scheme during their engagement, and his strange reversal on the letter to the railroads. It would be beneficial to have his guidance, given his vast experience and usual good judgment, but could he be trusted?

"If I can just have a visit with him, we can let him decide what assistance I can provide."

There was something in his tone that made the hairs on the back of Edith's neck stand up. "Why do I get a sense that you are implying we need to do this or else?"

House wiped his snively nose. "Of course, as I said, there will be grave consequences if certain things are not handled carefully."

"Are you threatening me?" Edith stood up and caught the eye of the agent standing guard at the door.

House stood, held out a shaky hand. "Oh no, I'm afraid you misunderstand. I–I–I…"

"The guard will see you out." Edith turned on her heel. Half of her wanted to sort it out with the pathetic man, but she was too tired, too consumed with worry and mistrust to have the energy.

In a few weeks, Colonel House was a distant memory and so far it seemed hadn't gone blabbing to the press. He had his own reputation to protect, she supposed. Warm breezes were beginning to replace the bitter winds of winter, and Edith enjoyed her morning coffee on the portico, where Ike Hoover brought her some newspapers. The first thing she searched for was gossip regarding her husband's health. Finding none, she moved on to more pleasant topics.

"Oh I see they've plowed up the last of the victory gardens in Potomac Park for a golf course. Sad in a way; I don't see why we should give up on them. A good idea in wartime and in peace."

"Yes, ma'am. Will that be all then?" Hoover seemed in a hurry to get on with his duties. Woodrow should be done with his breakfast and wanting up in his chair.

"Yes, thank you. You might give the president an update on the victory garden. It was his idea."

"Oh, he'll see it in the paper I'm sure, but I'll point it out." Hoover turned to go inside.

"Wait a minute. What do you mean, he'll see it?"

"In the paper, ma'am. He's been asking for it, now that he's feeling better."

Edith popped up from her chair so quickly she knocked over the coffee. "No, no, no!"

"I'll get that," Hoover rushed to mop up the mess, but Edith was flying toward Woodrow's room.

Blood pounded in her ears as she rushed down the long hallway. She was sure she had given specific instructions. But of course, the president's wishes would have overridden them.

She found him in bed, his breakfast tray over his lap with a folded newspaper upon it.

"Good morning, dear." She removed the tray and its offending paper to the bedside table. "I trust you slept well."

"Don't take that." He pointed to the paper.

"Now we agreed, during your recovery you're not to get worked up about unnecessary things. And believe me, the paper is full of unnecessary things, and plenty of outright lies."

"Hmph. I'll be the judge of that."

"I'm sorry, but for now your doctor is the judge of that."

"Willful woman." He tried to twist himself away from her toward his newspaper but gave up in exhaustion. "Fine. Your report. What's going on with the treaty?"

"The Senate is going to vote again soon. We told you that. But nothing has changed."

"Hitchcock got the Republicans to agree with slight changes. Tell our side to vote for it. For God's sake, it's time."

Edith was bewildered. This was in direct opposition to his former instructions. Which was she to believe and act on?

"But dear, remember you worried about going back on your word, your honor, the agreement you signed at Versailles. You were quite emphatic that with the reservations, the treaty, the League, becomes meaningless."

"They should vote their conscience." With that, he closed his eyes, already worn out from the discussion.

Edith considered telling Tumulty about Woodrow's change of heart. Was there even enough time to put out the message? Would such a change of heart reflect poorly on her husband's judgment? She was desperately trying to represent her husband's wishes, but they sometimes changed from day to day. It seemed to her that senators should always be voting their conscience, so what would be the point of some last-minute presidential advice?

Indeed, the newspapers had been printing their suspicions, as if they were fact, that Edith Wilson was acting as an unelected president. She was referred to as Mrs. President, her presidency as the "tea table administration," after her habit of meeting officials over tea. If they only knew how she struggled to get through each day, the unrelenting demands on the president. How could one person, even in perfect health, have coped? This was why he had aged so much. This is why his body collapsed. All she could do was shepherd his beliefs. Fortunately, he had shared so much with her that she knew his standing on nearly all issues.

Still, she was greatly troubled by the issue of sanctioning reservations for the treaty. Woodrow had been so adamant about it when he was well. Had he truly had a change of heart, or was that a result of fogginess of brain? Helen Bones had warned her that his personality had changed after previous neurological incidents. He was more stubborn, less patient, less likely to explore all angles of a problem. But was that actually the result of maturing in the position? Should she swallow her pride and ask House for advice?

She decided to say nothing. Woodrow had made his decision at a time when he was more up to date, more familiar with the whims of the people involved. She took away most of the newspaper, leaving behind the society pages and the article on the victory garden.

TWENTY-EIGHT

I t was a glorious spring day and Edith was excited to escape the Residence. She was meeting with Altrude and her two children at Rock Creek Park. She had the limousine driver drop her off and nearly ran to meet them.

Altrude was already there, jiggling the handle of a pram while trying to corral Gordon, who was picking azalea blossoms.

"Oh, let me help." Edith scooped up Gordon and gave him a kiss on his chubby pink cheek. They walked and chatted about the lovely weather and how being in the park together was just like old times.

"But it's not, of course." Altrude was not her usual cheery self.

"You must be tired, with two babies to care for and with Cary spending nearly every minute with my husband. I'm so sorry. Are you getting some help? Can I do anything..."

"Oh, Edith, thank you. We're fine, and you have your own hands quite full."

A rabbit crossed their path, and Gordon scrambled from Edith's arms to chase it. She started to go after him, but Altrude grabbed her arm.

"Leave him be. He knows where to stop." Her voice was tight, something clearly bothering her. She stopped to adjust the blanket on the sleeping baby.

"What is it, my lovely girl? If something is bothering you, out with it."

They took several steps in silence. Whatever was bothering her was clearly difficult for Altrude to talk about.

"You know how dear you are to me. To Cary too, of course. So I want you to know I say this with love."

"Uh-oh." Edith swallowed. Nothing good ever followed that statement. "Well, go on."

"I know a bit more than does the public, from the bits and pieces that Cary does tell me. And he seems to verify what's in all the papers. That is, that you're acting as the president. Not just carrying messages back and forth, but making decisions, turning away anyone with bad news, problems, or whatever the president can't deal with."

"Oh, there's so much exaggeration…"

"Undoubtedly. But the fact remains, you are depriving the nation of true leadership. It is not enough to hobble through each day. You're courting disaster."

"Is this how Cary feels as well?"

"No! Listen to me! You are both much too close to the president to have any objectivity. You and he both need to stand down. But you won't, and I know why."

Fury was rising in Edith, but she didn't want to show it. She took a deep breath to remain calm and in control. "And that is?"

"Cary will be loyal to the president until his dying day. He sees his role as his healer, not as his political emissary. But you—"

"Am I not doing it out of love and loyalty as well?"

Altrude pursed her lips. Something hurtful was coming, so Edith braced herself.

"Of course you are. But there's something else. Don't forget, I knew you when you were a struggling jeweler's wife. I've heard your tales about having to leave school so your brothers could go, and about spending your days caring for your grandmother's canaries instead of learning science and math and history. The girl from the backwoods of Virginia."

Edith was trying to not take offense. After all, Altrude spoke the truth. "I am all that. I never said I was qualified for high office. I assure you, there are brilliant minds who do the thinking. Even Woodrow fully admits he uses not only the brains he has, but all that he can borrow."

Altrude nodded. "But that's not my issue. It's as if meeting kings and queens and being treated like royalty yourself isn't enough. Your image of yourself as the scrappy girl from the mountains keeps pushing you to prove something that doesn't need to be proved. Let it go, Edith. For the good of the country, let Woodrow step down."

Altrude's words did not fall on deaf ears, but still, Edith dismissed them. There was so much the young woman didn't understand, after all. She had barely seen Woodrow and couldn't know how they managed to get things done. It pained her to admit it, but Edith had to put some distance between herself and Altrude, at least for now. It seemed her young friend was stuck in days long forgotten.

Clear thinking couldn't dwell on childhood hurts.

The vote in the Senate once again failed to pass. The treaty, at least the American's part in it, was dead. With it went Woodrow's most important achievement, the very reason he hung on to life. Now it was time to turn to a new administration to salvage something from the ashes. Edith fervently hoped the Democrats would win the upcoming presidential election. Only then would her husband's legacy have a place of honor in history, where they could live out their days with their heads held high.

Of course, he was not able to actively campaign, but after the primaries that summer, she would help him endorse their chosen candidate. But would the candidate even want his endorsement? The realization that the party might not seek it hit Edith hard. In the months since Woodrow's stroke there had been deadlocks on important issues that needed the president's support. The defeat of the ratification of the treaty and the failure to join the League of Nations, the override of his veto on the Volstead Act all pointed to his diminished power. How far Woodrow's star had fallen was yet to be seen, but she only had to remember the Republicans turning on Teddy Roosevelt to know how ephemeral political popularity can be.

Sometimes when she allowed herself some self-pity, she shivered with guilty tears. If only she were stronger, wiser, and had paid more attention to all he had tried to teach her, his legacy would be untarnished. Edith could only hope that with time, Woodrow's achievements would outshine the failures, and he would be judged accordingly by history.

But by that summer, several crises grew and merged and threatened a conflagration like another Great War. The country's economy was struggling in a recession, and labor strikes had paralyzed many industries. Weakened by the war, with supplies of coal and oil depleted, some feared invasion from former enemies. The Russians were threatening Poland, Romania, and Bulgaria. Her beloved Armenian people were being massacred by the Turks, who were also locked in battle with Greece. Irish nationalists were fighting the Brits; Mexico was once again on the brink of civil war.

As Edith read the disheartening headlines, she came upon one issue she thought she could do something about. Thirty-five states had now ratified the Nineteenth Amendment. Seven had already rejected it, and it seemed the remaining ones would as well. The best hope lay in the lap of the Tennessee legislature. Scores of demonstrators for both sides were descending on Nashville to influence the vote. But the governor had yet to call a special session to address ratification.

Edith hurried over to the West Wing, where she knew she could find Tumulty. To her chagrin, she found him seated at the presidential desk.

"Oh, oh, I didn't expect you." Tumulty quickly came from around the desk and motioned to wing chairs by the fireplace.

"Clearly." But Edith quickly forgot her indignation and got to her point, explaining the situation in Tennessee.

"And what would you have me do?" He scratched his balding head.

"Draft a letter to Governor Roberts for the president's signature. Encourage him to set the special session for a vote and to support the amendment. He's a good Democrat. He won't go against the president."

"Hmm. He's up for reelection. That might not be a wise move for him. His party is pretty much against it. He could lose the primary."

"I don't care. I mean, the president won't care. He is fully on board with this issue."

"We could lose another governorship to the Republicans. Maybe if he simply waits until after the election…"

Edith's glare made him shut his mouth.

"Yes, ma'am. I'll write it up."

Edith took the drafted letter to Woodrow that afternoon. She also brought several newspapers, with all their bolded doomsday headlines. She was oh so tired of carrying this burden alone. It was time he addressed some of this himself.

To Edith's relief, Woodrow heartily approved the letter to the governor of Tennessee. Soon after, Edith received a phone call from Margaret.

"Hello, dear girl, how is life in Greenwich Village? Are you working on Cox's campaign?"

"In a way. I've got all my irons in the fire for the fight in Tennessee. We've been celebrating that Father finally got the governor to put ratification for the vote."

"Oh, you know about that?"

Margaret's voice lifted in ebullient praise. "Of course; it's all over the papers here, and all anyone talks about. I've a good mind to run out to Nashville for what I hope will be a massive celebration. Father will be recognized as a hero again."

A small ball of rebellion grew in the pit of Edith's stomach. Should she tell Margaret how this all truly came about? "Your father has always been a hero."

"Indeed. I hope the next time we speak, we will be discussing how the women's vote will ensure the Democrats remain in the White House. I know your heart is not fully with this cause, but I think this election will win you over."

❦

Edith followed the events in Nashville through the newspapers and updates from Tumulty. The two sides were clashing with protests that sometimes turned violent, and Edith worried that her worst fears about the movement would come true, But finally, on a scorching day in August, the news came.

Tennessee was the thirty-sixth state to ratify the Nineteenth Amendment. No state could now deny women the right to vote.

It was time for a meeting of the circle. With that issue finally settled, the presidential campaign would no doubt heat up, and there were so many critical issues to be addressed. Cary and Altrude, Tumulty, and Edith met in Woodrow's office in the Residence. But Edith had a surprise in mind for them.

After they served themselves coffee and tea from a tray, as Edith allowed no servants to be present during their meetings, they settled into the leather chairs. Edith asked Cary to give them an update on Woodrow's progress.

"I'm happy to report the president is nearly as fit as he was before the incident. Barring the physical weakness in his legs and some difficulty with expressive language, which I'm afraid is permanent, he is quite stable. His appetite and digestion have improved; he's put on some much-needed weight."

Edith had seen this with her own eyes but was happy to have the doctor's affirmation. "Then we can begin returning things to normal. Daily briefings, maybe a speech to Congress..."

Tumulty jumped in. "There have been calls for him to do some campaign speeches for Cox."

"Cox has utterly disregarded the president," Altrude said.

Edith nodded. "I'm not sure the campaign is the best use of his time. Rather more important to address the myriad of domestic and foreign problems, don't you think?"

Ike Hoover appeared in the doorway, caught Edith's eye. She wordlessly nodded her head to him.

The room erupted with everyone talking at once. Tumulty emphasized that if they didn't succeed in the November election, nothing else they did would matter, because it would all be undone. Cary was emphatic that they still needed to control the president's blood pressure, and this was more difficult without the ability to exercise as he had before.

Altrude argued against both of them. "It's simply time for him to step down. Enough is enough of this charade."

"Stop." Edith proclaimed. "Why don't we let the man decide for himself?"

Silence hung heavy in the room.

"This is the moment. Either we return the responsibilities back to the president, or we advise him to step down." Edith glanced at Altrude, whose coffee cup didn't quite conceal her small smile. Too late, Edith wished she had also invited Helen Bones to join them.

"That's not wise, not all at once." Cary had risen and was pacing the room.

The others seemed to agree. At least they didn't voice an objection. All eyes went to the door as there was a knock on it.

As Edith moved toward the door, she hastily made a plan. "Joseph, what are the three most pressing matters?"

"Today? I would say domestically the economy teetering on the verge of depression, and steel and coal workers' strikes threatening a collapse of many other industries. Foreign—undoubtedly Russia and her intent to swallow up Eastern Europe."

"That's quite enough to throw at him, don't you think?"

The group murmured, but there being no outright objections, Edith opened the door. There Woodrow sat in his rolling chair, his hair carefully groomed and wearing a suit for the first time since last October. Ike pushed him into the room. There were handshakes and awkward hugs as he greeted each of the members of the circle.

"We thought it time to bring you up to date on a few things." Edith dismissed the valet and wheeled Woodrow next to her seat. "Mr. Tumulty, why don't you start?"

Tumulty, his eyebrows still raised with the turn of events, sounded a bit hesitant at first, until his long experience and knowledge kicked in and he delivered a clear synopsis of his three top issues. He held nothing back, reciting the possible outcomes: a country in a severe depression, another war in Europe, global economic collapse. It was as bleak a speech as Edith had ever heard, delivered with the calculated coolness of a career political animal.

"I won't even go into the possible losses in the upcoming election. With the women voting, there's no predicting."

"Yes, yes, how about that." Woodrow smiled broadly. "We'll see what they do with it."

"Now that you've heard all this, what would you like to address first?" Edith tiptoed into the issue.

Woodrow chuckled. "What would you have me do, dear?"

Edith sucked in her breath. "Why, for example, do you want to speak to the heads of the labor unions, as you have before."

"I'm not sure what good that would do."

Altrude, who had been quiet, sat running a finger along the seams of her chair. "Maybe another trip to Europe is in order. Meet with Lenin and other Bolsheviks, the Armenians—you have friends there, no?"

The group gasped in unison.

"Sure, sure, why not?" Woodrow did not seem to be taking any of it seriously.

Edith tried another avenue. "Maybe we could work up to a trip like that. For now, how about an address to Congress, a public appearance?"

Woodrow instead motioned toward a signed baseball he kept on his desk. "Someone fetch that for me, will you?"

Tumulty did as he asked, and Woodrow rolled it around in his right hand. "Joe, you left out something important. I guess you thought it would upset me too much."

"What's that, Mr. President?"

"The White Sox scandal, of course. I'll never believe Shoeless Joe was in on it."

"He took the bribe. He's guilty." Cary suddenly seemed interested in the conversation.

"Nearly destroyed baseball, that crew. They should be thrown in jail for life."

"It's all crooked. Gangsters control anything. Just look at the mess they've made of Prohibition." Altrude unsuccessfully tried to steer the conversation back to politics.

The men stared at her for a bit, then went on, animatedly arguing over the 1919 World Series.

"Before they huddle over whiskey and cigars, what do you say we leave?" Altrude asked Edith.

The meeting was over, Edith realized. And nothing had been resolved. Woodrow wasn't ready, or was simply unwilling to make big decisions. The circle be darned; she would have to sort this out with Tumulty. As much as she loved Cary, his first and last thoughts would always be the president's health. Which she supposed was as it should be.

A new presidential limousine had arrived, and Edith saw the opportunity to get Woodrow out and divine his feelings, just as on the magical rides of the past. Indeed, Woodrow was as excited as a little boy going to the circus as the stately black vehicle pulled up in front of the Residence.

The leaves were just beginning to change, and the air had a hint of coolness, so welcome after the blistering summer. When the driver asked where they wanted to go, Woodrow answered, "Wherever you'd like to take us."

As they motored along the familiar streets, Edith marveled at the changes a few years had made. Many of the large ornate homes were gone, replaced with squarish apartment buildings that lacked any character. Thankfully, Rock Creek Park seemed much the same. If anything, the grounds were even more beautiful, with the graceful arch of tree limbs over the road.

"So, my dear, you didn't really give Tumulty much of an answer to his list of problems." Frustrated with that session, Edith didn't tiptoe into the conversation this time.

"I think he got my answer."

"Your answer? You said nothing."

"Sometimes that's all the answer there is."

"What are you saying? That you're not going to lift a finger for any of these things? Do you understand..."

"I understand. I read the papers. Do you know what a lame duck is?"

"You still have six months in office. Much can be accomplished."

"Cox is going to lose. It will be up to Harding."

A thundercloud of anger whipped through her. He was giving up. After all her sacrifice, everyone's sacrifices to get Woodrow healed so he could return to his duties. His dreams. His legacy. She never dreamed he would become so complacent. If she had known, she would have insisted he resign when he was too helpless to refuse.

"In that case, maybe you should just step down. Why fritter away the remaining months when someone else might do something? Like you were going to do if Judge Hughes won."

"No point; we're no longer at war. And announcing something like that would end any hope of Cox winning."

"After the election, then. Step down for whoever wins."

He stared out the window. "Is that what you want? Do you hate this life that much? Enough to set a precedent that perhaps isn't wise? Enough to humiliate all the people who have supported us? Worry the people unnecessarily?"

Edith had nothing to say. But a tear streaked down her face. There was no honor in either scenario. Oh, how she would like to talk it over with her wise father. Would he tell her she'd made a complete mess of things?

But as she watched the trees and houses float by, remembering the kids who came out to wave flags, the parades of people and carriages and even ships, she realized that so much of what they did was symbolic. It was tradition and respect for history and pride in being American. The British had their royal family primarily for that role, while Americans expected their political leaders to fulfill it.

Would another six months of an administration just stumbling along matter? If Woodrow was well, he would be consumed with the election anyway. This way, they could focus on the transition instead. Her husband was right. What would be the point in stepping down, and all the chaos that would create? It would be a selfish act when the country needed stability.

"No, dear. It will all work out." She patted her husband's hand and he leaned against her, just like in old times.

She turned her attention to finding a home for their retirement. Although they considered other cities, she couldn't bear to leave Washington, where she had lived all her adult life and where her mother, brother, and sister resided as well. But finding a proper home in a fine neighborhood with some privacy proved difficult with their modest budget. She hired a real estate expert, and together they scouted suitable homes for months.

Finally, a wonderful property with some acreage and a modest but comfortable house became available. It offered outstanding privacy yet was still within the District, everything she could hope for.

Excited, she rushed back to tell Woodrow about it. "It's remarkably well priced, within our budget," she enthused. She spread out a map of the city for him to inspect. "Look, close to everything we could need. Just a few steps from..."

"Hold on." He peered at the map through his magnifying glass and stabbed a forefinger on the location. "Next to the Bureau of Standards."

"Perfect, isn't it?" Edith wondered if it was too late in the day to submit an offer. "You loved that place, as I recall. And now you can go visit whenever you want without breaking in through a window." She laughed, but Woodrow did not join her.

"We can't buy that. The Bureau of Standards needs to expand. That lot's the best place, without having to pick up and move."

Edith's heart sank. But she was used to a fight. "It's not public land, and the owner has every right to sell it to whomever he pleases."

"It isn't right, knowing what I know. And what if the government takes it after we've settled? Iminet..emmmit..." He struggled with the word but gave up. "Why it's selling at a good price."

"Eminent domain. We'll cross that bridge then. Really, dear, you're being ridiculous. This is Washington, DC, and I've been looking for months. This is perfect and you know it."

"You buy it then. I'll have nothing to do with it." He folded the map and tossed it aside.

Edith was crushed. She set her teeth and tried to tamp down her anger. After all they had given for this country, to have fewer choices than any other ordinary citizen. Somewhere beneath the anger, she knew he was right. She remembered the important although little-known work the Bureau of Standards did. She remembered the comical face of the commerce secretary as he fretted about the missed appointment and the excitement of sneaking in anyway. It would have to remain a good memory and not the start of a new life.

Her search continued, until finally a lovely home on S Street became available. It didn't have the privacy of acreage like the Bureau of Standards property, but it was situated in a leafy neighborhood near Rock Creek Park and even had an elevator already installed, one less thing to have to modify.

With that settled, they limped through the remaining days of his administration. Warren G. Harding, the Republican candidate, won the presidential election in a landslide. Harding had barely mentioned Cox in his campaign. Instead he focused on the failings of Woodrow and a call to return to normalcy. She feared the new administration would undo much of their hard work.

Perhaps that was for the best, Edith thought. Bright, shiny ideas sometimes led to too much change too soon. It took others to pull back, and then some sort of equilibrium could be restored. Perhaps the new Republican administration could succeed where Woodrow had failed and pick up the broken pieces of the League of Nations. Perhaps they could get rid of the abominable Prohibition law and stabilize the postwar economy.

The White House transition team assured her that she and Woodrow need not pack a thing. Everything was to stay in place until the very end of their administration. When all parties were at the inauguration, dozens of workers would flock in and replace the Wilsons' belongings with the Hardings'.

She understood. Who wouldn't want to hold on to the moment until the last second? But a person needed time to process such an immense change. If there was no packing up, how did one let go of the old? So she made rounds of the Residence, saying goodbye to all the wonderful staff, saying goodbye to five years of her life. She hugged Ike Hoover as he inspected Woodrow's suit and gave him a letter with her personal thanks. She did the same for the housekeepers and maintenance men. She couldn't help wondering if their tearful farewells were sincere. How was she to be remembered?

Would her efforts to bring comfort to soldiers be thought of? Her support for her husband during such difficult times? Her efforts to preserve the history of the mansion and its furnishings, such as the presidential china? The strong relationships she had developed with the leaders and royalty of Europe?

But most of all, she wondered if she had contributed enough, or perhaps had overstepped what a reasonable, responsible person should do. There was still so much left undone, but now it was in someone else's hands. It seemed the answers to her questions wouldn't be known for many years to come.

There was one last room Edith wanted to visit. She went down to the ground floor and retraced her long-ago steps to the cloakroom. The long and narrow room with its dark paneled walls and fancy light sconces was empty, as usual. She stepped to the spot where her wrap had hung, where Woodrow had placed it around her shoulders. It was here that she started to fall in love with him, when she finally got a moment alone with him. Just a man, not the president, not someone who belonged to the millions.

Now that she would be moving on to a quiet life with him, she considered she had never known him as anyone else but the president. Would they be able to adapt to life as an ordinary married couple? And of course, he was no longer the hale and hearty man she had met. In many ways, he was still a patient. She shuddered, fearing the worst, that she would regret leaving the comfortable, free life she had back in 1914. She worried that she would be hounded as the woman who had usurped the presidency and be scorned by the very people she had tried to serve.

There was talk of changing the cloakroom into a movie theater featuring a real screen, a modern projector, and, some day, even talking pictures. She imagined a happy crowd around a future president, their faces illuminated in the flickering light, music and voices overcoming the clicking of the projector.

She didn't want to be with them, she realized. She *did* want the life she and Woodrow had long dreamed of. It was a new decade, full of the promise of peace and prosperity. Women's fashions seem to reflect that as they rapidly changed from dresses that somehow managed to be both restrictive and cumbersome to breezy affairs with shorter hemlines. Edith looked forward to attending a whirl of social events in comfort. That is, if they were invited to them.

On March 20, 1921, Edith and Woodrow had their final ride in the presidential limousine. A sense of calm filled Edith as they pulled up to their four-story brick home, three Palladian windows dominating its facade. A truck with all their worldly possessions followed, including some very special rugs and a lovely painting of a hopeful little girl. Edith was ready to spend whatever time she had left with the love of her life in the first home of their own.

TWENTY-NINE

December 1946
Hot Springs, VA

After dropping off the heavy room key with the clerk, Edith headed out to the golf course. A light dusting of snow had fallen overnight, so no one was playing. *Ha!* she thought. The cold and wet would not have stopped Woodrow and Cary, may they rest in peace. She walked up the first link, which had a fine view of the sprawling hotel and the surrounding hills.

In her pocket were two envelopes, the contents of which had sent her to the Homestead in order to reflect on their meaning. She hoped that here, on the very grounds she had walked with him, she could feel Woodrow's spirit and have him tell her it was not her fault. She pulled out the first one, a carbon copy of a letter written by Colonel House back in 1919. It was full of advice on how to overcome Congress's objection to the Treaty of Versailles. He advised telling the Democrat delegation to vote for the treaty with Lodge's reservations. He wrote:

The compromise would be infinitely better than no treaty or League. The Allies are desperate for the U.S. to join the League of Nations, you wouldn't be going back on your word, as all parties knew the Treaty still needed to be debated in the U.S., but we now leave it up to the Europeans to accept these small necessary changes in the terms.

The letter was addressed to Edith. She tried to clear the fog of her memory but could not recall ever receiving it. Surely she would have acted on it if she had. By then, Woodrow had been amenable to most reasonable suggestions and was desolate over the failure of Congress to ratify.

Edith's heart sank to the place it had inhabited throughout both wars. Woodrow's most dire predictions, and those of others as well, had come true. Without the strong, steady hand of the League, the same anger and issues had boiled up, made even worse by the suffering of the vanquished nations.

Perhaps the second World War was inevitable, the animosities too bitter, the economic and cultural pressures too great for any agreement to amend, no matter how fairly and thoughtfully laid out. It was tempting to play what-if, yet one little letter wouldn't have changed the world, she assured herself.

But then there was the second letter.

This letter had also been forwarded and was a copy of a private note from Lord Grey, the ambassador from Britain who had refused to fire his unctuous aide. The letter outlined the message he was meant to give to the American president, from the prime minister and king of the United Kingdom. It said that the European Allies were most anxious for the American ratification of the treaty, and that without them, the League of Nations would fail in its mission. He acknowledged the American hesitancy in the wording of specifically Article X of the Covenant and advised that the Allies would accept the reservations in order to move forward. They recognized the very purpose of the League was to work out future disagreements.

Why had the ambassador not gone to someone else, knowing of the president's ill health at the time? Why, why, why? Had she been foolish to send him away due to a silly personal hurt? It had been a matter of principle to her, that guests of the country, especially in a high, visible position, needed to behave properly. And the ambassador had been stubborn when he alone knew of the importance of his message.

Edith walked along, the wind stinging her face. She stuffed the letters back into her pocket. She would burn them when she got back to her room.

Up ahead of her on the pebbled path were two figures who seemed familiar. The young man had his arm around the young lady, and they walked in step with the easy cadence of a couple in love. It seemed he limped a bit, leaning ever so gently on the woman. Edith caught a whiff of a perfume—Shalimar. It was the couple from the line at the concierge desk. They stopped for a kiss, and Edith came upon them and tried to politely and silently pass.

"Well, hello there. Lovely grounds, aren't they?" the young man said.

"Indeed they are. Is this your first visit?" Edith replied.

"Yes, we're on our honeymoon."

"Ah, congratulations. I too spent my honeymoon here. Many years ago."

The woman held out her kid-gloved hand to shake. "It's wonderful, isn't it? I'm Janet, and this is my husband, Barry."

Barry held out his hand as well. "And if I'm not mistaken, you are Mrs. Woodrow Wilson."

Did everyone know her on sight? She shook both of their hands. "I have that honor."

"I have the honor of being your husband's fellow alumnus."

"Oh, did you go to Princeton?" Edith pulled her coat tighter and started walking again to warm herself.

"No, Johns Hopkins. Everyone associates him with Princeton, but he earned his PhD at Hopkins. They have a wonderful collection—I studied his papers. His history books, essays, even watched a film of one of his speeches. Quite moving." Barry took Janet's hand and they walked alongside Edith. "Do you mind if I ask you a question? Something I've wondered about for a long time."

"Anything. But you might not like the answer."

He chuckled nervously. "I know Mr. Wilson's main concern at the end of World War I was preventing another. He wrote extensively, obsessively some would say, about it. He pushed hard for the League of Nations. Yet another war broke out, exactly as he and others had predicted. All this you know, of course."

Edith braced herself for what was coming next. Would it be the same question she was asking herself? "Yes. So what is your question?"

"Do you think he actually believed, given the intense animosities, the horror inflicted in the Great War, the history of conflict, that there was any possibility that we could have avoided another one? Or did he just do his best to postpone the inevitable?"

His question surprised her. She had never for a moment doubted that Woodrow believed a lasting peace was possible. "Yes, he did believe it. And I did too. Working toward that end drove him to an early death."

Janet said, "And we managed to get twenty years of peace. We can thank him for that, God rest his soul." She stopped walking and turned to Barry. "Is your foot bothering you? Do you want to turn back?" To Edith, she said, "My husband is a war veteran."

"Thank you for your service. Were you wounded?"

"Not by enemy fire. But I lost part of my foot to frostbite during the Battle of the Bulge."

Edith felt sorry for her impatience with them earlier. "Well, don't let me keep you. Enjoy your honeymoon."

Alone on the path once again, she contemplated. Could she alone have stopped the chain of events that resulted in the deadliest war the world had ever seen? She shook off the thought as presumptuous for this girl from the backwoods of Virginia. Everything she did, she did out of love. Love of her country, love of her husband. If Barry's opinion reflected the truth, that unescapable evil forces had for a time prevailed, the second world war was not something she could have prevented.

But had her love blinded her to an unwelcome truth? Had protecting her husband resulted in great suffering in the country, in the world? Had Altrude been right, and she had let her own feelings of inadequacy affect her decisions?

If life offered a second chance, knowing future outcomes, she would have told Woodrow in no uncertain times that he needed to resign for the good of the country. And he would have complied. In fact, he was so ill at first, he could not have objected. The Constitution provided for that, even named a successor. But, failing the president's own admission of noncompetence, there was no solution. It was left in the hands of people so close to the president as to be utterly incapable of making such a decision.

And if fingers were to be pointed, she would stab one right into the chest of Henry Cabot Lodge. At his door lay the wreckage of human hopes and the peril that afflicted mankind. It was time to forgive herself. It was time for healing for her and for all the nations of the world. She would spend the rest of her days protecting Woodrow's honor, sharing his deep love and dedication to the country, a man who had stood up for a cause but was no match for the evil that spread like a cancer. But now, just as he predicted, peace finally prevailed.

EPILOGUE

At eighty-nine years old, Edith felt as if her body was trying to tell her it was time to give up this life and move on to the next. She had lost her precious Altrude a few months before and had been going to the Rock Creek Cemetery to leave flowers whenever she could. The week before, she had kissed the granite headstone in farewell. "Ah, my dear friend, you have gone to be with Cary. My time is coming."

But there was an important event she had been anticipating for years. The long-planned Woodrow Wilson Bridge, spanning the Potomac just to the south of the District, was to officially open that day.

She hobbled over to her desk and paged through the diagrams, now curled and smudged with age. It would be a critical bridge, carrying traffic from the rapidly spreading suburbs in Virginia to those on the Maryland side.

Oh, how proud and pleased Woodrow would have been!

Also on her desk was her engraved invitation to the opening ceremonies that afternoon. She was to be the guest of honor. The end of December was an unforgiving time to hold a long outdoor ceremony, but when the timing worked out, she had agreed that holding it on Woodrow's birthday would add to the celebration of his life.

She would wear her fur coat and a smart wool cloche.

"The bright-blue one," she heard her husband say. "It brings out your eyes."

Thirty-seven years gone, and still she heard his voice as clearly as if he were sitting in his favorite leather chair, always a book in his hands. Sun streamed in from the arched front window. Just like the ones at the Homestead. Just like the ones at Mount Vernon, home of Woodrow's beloved George Washington, and in the most important rooms of the White House. Margaret's grand piano took the full width of the room. After they'd given it up while residing at the White House, it had been rescued by Woodrow's loyal friends. Margaret had played it here, while singing her warbly soprano that had made Woodrow so happy. Margaret was gone now too, as was sweet Jessie. Edith let the sunlight warm her as it wrapped her in the memories of all she had loved.

The whole house was a memorial to the wonderful family that God and fate had somehow allowed Edith to be part of. She hadn't changed a thing since Woodrow died. His Bible and books of poetry still sat on his bedside table; his toiletries remained neatly arranged in his bath. They gave her comfort somehow, visual reminders of the part of her heart that was forever his.

She sat in her husband's chair, something she never did, the dent from his own weight being too sacred. But she felt closer to him now. The event invitation still in her hand, she asked him, "What do you think, darling? It might be the death of me to go on this blustery day. How I would rather stay warm and cozy in this home we shared."

Or better, she thought, she should go to be with him. She closed her eyes, and he was teaching her a dance, a scratchy song coming from the Victrola. Then they were riding horses through Rock Creek Park. The next moment they were on the South Portico, and he, on bended knee, was asking her to be his wife. She did not fall out of bed in surprise but laughed at the old joke.

She waved to the happy crowds of Europe as showers of flowers landed in their carriage. And suddenly they were in his White House bedroom, the Liberty rug spread across the floor. He was in the poster bed, dictating while she madly scribbled notes on the backs of envelopes and anything else she could find, his brilliant, brilliant mind held captive by a failing body.

But then he was no longer frail in her vision. He was whole and healthy. A smile beamed on his face and he beckoned her.

"Come, my love. It's time we're together once more. Leave this life on the date of my birth, for only when you are with me again is my life complete."

She imagined the workers setting up bandstands and bleachers at the new bridge. Red, white, and blue bunting spread on every available space. The people filing in, perhaps sharing their story of meeting the great Woodrow Wilson.

Edith set the invitation on the small side table and nestled deeper into the worn leather chair. She pulled up the soft afghan she had knit for him and closed her eyes to see what she most wanted to see. The crowds, then the motorcars, then the carriages faded away. She walked the halls of the White House one last time, the Armenian girl and presidents in the portraits nodding down to her.

Soon, all that was also gone, and only one vision remained. Her husband, dressed in an impeccable dark-blue suit and white shirt, stood tall in a blazing light. Woodrow held out his hand and she walked toward him, then took his warm hand in hers, trusting his love to guide her into the next world, just as he'd done before.

AUTHOR'S NOTE

I am often asked how and why I choose the subjects and characters for my novels. For this book, it was a combination of interesting and controversial historical persons, geographic locations in which I have knowledge and interest, and current events that relate to the historical persons and events in the novel's time frame.

The two main characters—Edith and Woodrow Wilson—have been in the news lately due to several factors. Woodrow's legacy has been tarnished by his perceived racist views (to the point that previous honors bestowed on him such as named buildings and organizations have been changed); his movement toward building the size, power, and control of the federal government; and his questionable leadership and decision-making after several debilitating strokes.

Edith has been less scrutinized, which is one of the reasons I chose to focus on her. I think the central question of the book—*Did her actions contribute to the causes of WWII?*—is worthy of examination, especially in light of current concern over presidents' ages and possible failing mental acuities.

It is tempting to judge history through the lens of modern ideals. A primary goal in this work is to try to view the events and decisions through the point of view of the characters of that time without our benefit of hindsight, without our more global understanding, and without access to instant (and sometimes erroneous) information.

Indeed, a review of his writings would indicate that President Wilson did not think of himself as a racist. But his actions, by today's definitions, would give him this label. And as a child of the South during the Civil War, he was acutely aware of the importance of states' rights and was not, in theory, in favor of a more powerful federal government. Yet it seems his actions, such as forming the Federal Reserve, creating a federal income tax, and others such as federalizing the railroads, fly in the face of those opinions.

So I submit that the actions and opinions of my characters don't reflect how I or any other modern person might judge them but instead how I imagine the characters themselves would have viewed them, based on their own intent and efforts at making the best decisions they could with the knowledge and ability they had at the time.

Central to this novel is a love story, based on the well-documented relationship between Woodrow and Edith. Indeed, the profoundly romantic letters between them were one of the reasons I became enamored with their story and chose to write about it. I think the power and trust of their bond are so intertwined with Edith's decisions that one must understand them in order to understand what she did. I also wanted to examine Edith's background and the ways it may have influenced her decisions.

In my research, I found that Edith's actions following the president's stroke didn't come from the uninformed position that I, and I'm sure many others, presumed. Rather, she was involved in his presidency from day one of their marriage. For the above reasons, I chose to explore those tumultuous times from 1916 to 1919 in more detail than the final year and a half of his presidency, which frankly suffered more from inaction than action.

There are lessons to be learned from examining the access to information, power, and influence of unelected friends and family of our leaders. For example, the Twenty-Fifth Amendment to the Constitution, outlining the succession of power should the president and/or vice president be unable to continue their duties, was only enacted after the assassination of John F. Kennedy. It may be time to reexamine this legislation to ensure it encompasses the many possible scenarios.

I hope this book will lead to lively discussions and deeper thought and understanding regarding the pressures and frailties of those in high positions and those they love and depend on.

A note on fictitious versus real characters: All of the main characters and many of the minor characters take their names and positions from real persons. Their thoughts and dialogue, however, except for published works, are as I imagine them. Entirely fictional characters are Rebecca, Henri Dimidjian, and Chef Oliver, although they are named after some beloved characters in my own life.

Tracey Enerson Wood
November 2022

DON'T MISS MORE MUST-READ HISTORICAL FICTION FROM TRACEY ENERSON WOOD!

ONE

T he light, sweet honey scent of burning candles did not quite mask the odor of blood and sweat in the makeshift ballroom. Not far from the White House, the room was tucked inside a military hospital, itself a repurposed clothing factory. Noise echoed in the vast space, with cots, machinery, and great rolls of cotton neatly stacked against the walls. Tall windows let in slanted rectangles of light upon women in dark uniforms setting out flower arrangements. I too felt out of place. Dressed in a ball gown, I was like a fresh flower in a room meant for working men.

Double doors opened from an anteroom, and chattering guests tumbled in. An orchestra hummed, tuning up as men clad in sharp Union dress uniforms gathered in conversation groups with women in their finery. Nearer to me, a line of men on crutches and in rolling chairs aligned themselves along a wall, each of them missing a limb or two or otherwise too broken to join the healthier soldiers.

I nodded my greetings, hesitant at first. Like most young women in my small town of Cold Spring, New York, other than a glimpse of a few limping, bedraggled returned soldiers, I had been sheltered from the consequences of war. Here, the wounded men clambered over one another, some in hospital pajamas, some half in uniform, reaching out to me, seeking to be included despite their infirmities.

I ignored the bloody gauze wrapped around heads and the stench of healing flesh as I shook their hands, right or left, bandaged or missing fingers, making my way down the line. One after the other, they thanked me for coming and begged me to dance and enjoy myself.

In the letter that had accompanied the invitation to the event, my brother had been clear: *The ball is intended to be a celebration of life, a brief interlude for men who have seen too much, and the last frivolity for too many others.* It pained me to look into their eyes, wondering who amongst them were enjoying their last pleasure on this earth.

"So pleased to meet you. I'm Emily." I offered my hand to a soldier with one brown eye, his face cobbled by burns.

He held my hand in both of his. "Miss Emily, you remind me there is still some joy in life."

I smiled. "Will you find me when it is time to dance?"

The soldier laughed.

My face flushed. It was too forward for a lady to ask a gentleman to dance. And perhaps he was unable.

"You can't tell from my pajamas, but I've earned my sergeant's stripes." He tapped his upper arm. "I won't be joining the butter bars."

The term *butter bars* rather derogatorily referred to the insignia of newly minted lieutenants. Belatedly, I recalled my invitation was to the *Officers'* Ball, and the sergeant had apparently come to watch. My cheeks warmed. I had gaffed thrice with one sentence. Not an auspicious beginning, considering my goals for the evening.

More women filtered in, each on the arm of an officer. In contrast to the men against the wall, the exuberance and freshly scrubbed skin of these officers made me doubt they'd seen battle. I felt rather out to sea. I had insisted on arriving without a chaperone, as I had expected to be escorted by my brother, but he was nowhere to be seen.

His last letter had said the fighting had slowed during the winter months, but that could change at any moment. Even if it hadn't, he was a target. I shook the image of a sniper out of my head. Surely, if something terrible had happened, they wouldn't still be setting up for a ball.

The soldier still had a firm hold on my hand. I pasted a smile on my face and peeked about the room. Was it more awkward to mingle with the others, all in couples, or rude not to?

The sergeant jutted his jaw toward the center of the ballroom. "Go now. We'll be watching."

I nodded and slipped my hand from his, resisting a peek at my white silk gloves to see if they'd been soiled. My ball gown showcased the latest fashion: magenta silk, the skirt full in the back and more fitted in the front. My evening boots echoed the profile; with an open vamp and high heel, they reminded me of Saint Nicholas's sleigh. I smoothed the gown's travel creases and mulled its merits. *Comfort: adequate. Usefulness: very good, considering its purpose was to please the eyes of young men.* Mother had disapproved of the deeply scooped neckline, but she had sheltered me long enough. I was now twenty years old and craved amusement.

The handsome dress uniforms and elaborate gowns each guest wore suggested formality and elegance, but raucous laughter shattered the tranquility of the elegant piano music. Clusters of young men erupted in challenges and cheers, guzzling whiskey and fueling their spirits.

I stepped closer to a particularly animated group in which a tall, handsome captain held court among a dozen lieutenants. Perhaps he could advise me as to where I could find my brother.

"What will you do after the war?" someone asked.

"Rather the same thing as before. Build bridges. Blow them up." The captain raised his glass, and the others followed, laughing and cheering.

A bespectacled, earnest-looking young man asked, "Sir, why would you blow up bridges in times of peace?"

The captain's smile faded, and he leaned into the group as if sharing a great conspiracy. "There are only so many places to build a bridge, and sometimes we have to blow up an old, rickety bridge to make room for a new one."

I stepped back, feeling awkward for eavesdropping.

The captain continued his lesson. "I'll be helping the country to heal, connecting Kentucky and Ohio with a long-abandoned project. And then we'll be doing the impossible. Connecting New York and Brooklyn with an even grander bridge. It will become one enormous city. If you want a job after the war, boys, come see me."

I shook my head. The captain didn't lack for hubris. But just as I was about to approach to inquire about my brother, he excused himself and hurried off.

❧

Twilight had faded, and the candles and gas lamps burned brightly, as if the assembly's energy had leached out and lit the room. All the women seemed thoroughly engaged, so I wandered about, my worry for my brother steadily increasing. A tiny glass of golden liquid was thrust at me, and I took a sip, the burning in my throat a pleasant sensation.

The orchestra played a fanfare, and a deep voice rang out. "Ladies and gentlemen, the commander of Second Corps, Major General Gouverneur Kemble Warren—the hero of Little Round Top."

Relief ran through me like a cool breeze on a hot day. I should have known that the commander of thousands would need to make an entrance. Officers snapped to attention and saluted the colors as they passed, then held their position for my brother. My heart fluttered when I saw him, taller than most, shaking hands as he made his way through the crowd. Our family called him GK, as Gouverneur was a most awkward name. Thirteen years my senior, he was now in his thirties, with sleek black hair and a mustache that met the sides of his jaw.

After months of worry and cryptic letters from which I could only gather that his troops had won a major battle in northern Virginia, seeing my brother lifted me two feet off the ground. I waved as he scanned the room, his eyes finally finding me.

GK had been more surrogate father than older brother, our father having passed away several years previously. He was the closest to me amongst all our surviving siblings, no matter the time or distance that separated us. As he edged closer, my smile faded at the sight of his gaunt frame, the strain of war reflected in the streak of gray in his hair and the slump of his shoulders.

The young officer following behind my brother glanced my way. I looked, then looked again—GK's aide was the same captain who had been boasting about healing the country with bridges. His eyes landed on me for the briefest moment, then scanned the room as if the enemy might leap from the shadows.

I coughed to cover a laugh. While he tried to appear vigilant, his gaze returned to me again and again. Perhaps he had seen me eavesdropping.

I squeezed past the knots of guests toward GK, but the crowd was thick around him. He greeted the wounded men, exchanging a few words and shaking hands down the line. Next, he worked his way into the larger crowd, and I was pushed back by officers surging toward him as they jockeyed for his attention.

"Men of the Second Corps." GK's booming voice filled the room as if to assure them that he could be heard over the firing of cannons. "Let us welcome these fine ladies and thank them for honoring us with their presence."

He signaled the orchestra, and hundreds of young men in dark blue began to dance, their shoulders shimmering with gold-fringed epaulets, like an oasis after years in the desert. I danced with one handsome lieutenant, then another and another, each spinning me into the arms of the next in line. When at last I paused, gasping for breath, the officers gathered around me, helping me to tuck back the long ribbons that were losing the battle to contain my curls. While the other women sniffed their disdain at my exuberant dancing and frequent change of partners, the men laughed and vied for me. No matter about the women. I meant to keep my promise to my brother by providing amusement for his men.

A lieutenant came by with a tray of drinks, whiskey for the men, tea for the ladies, he said, although it was difficult to tell them apart. The guests emptied the tray save two. The lieutenant handed one of the glasses, filled nearly to the brim, to me. "For you, Miss...?"

"Just Emily." He needn't know I shared a surname with the general.

"For you, Miss Just Emily," he said, loudly enough to elicit chuckles from the crowd.

I took the glass and sipped. It was whiskey.

"No, all wrong." He took the last glass, swirled the amber liquid, and took a deep whiff of its aroma. Then he downed it in several gulps.

I poured the whiskey down my throat and held up my empty glass, pressing my lips together to stifle a cough. The group cheered and my spirits lifted, sailing on fumes of whiskey. I was no longer a fresh flower in an old factory. I was their queen.

The crowd grew louder, but this time, it wasn't me they were rooting for. A short, broadly built officer leaped into the air and landed with his legs split. The throng whistled and yelled "Just Emily!" for my response.

The group clapped a drumbeat, encouraging me. My competitive spirit outweighed my sense of decorum, and I spun, each step in synchrony with the clap, faster and faster until my dress lifted. Then I slid down into a split, one arm raised dramatically, my ball gown splaying in a circle of magenta folds around me.

As several officers helped me up, the crowd parted, revealing GK and his aide. My brother raised one eyebrow in warning, and the younger officer gaped at me. Heat rose in my face, but this time, it wasn't the whiskey.

"Moths to the flame." GK gave his aide a slap on the shoulder.

The aide then closed his mouth, his Adam's apple bobbing above his blue uniform collar. "Shall I escort the young lady from the dance, sir?"

My opinion of him matched that of the booing crowd.

GK rubbed his chin. "A generous offer."

The aide flashed a conspiratorial grin, but his smile faded when GK added, "But that won't be necessary."

Even though the captain had seemed a presumptuous young man, I was chagrined that GK was teasing him. GK slung his arm across my shoulders and led me away from the group.

"Emily, I trust you are enjoying yourself?" GK's face showed a mix of tenderness and disappointment. I wanted to curl up like a pill bug.

"Quite. It is my pleasure to offer a small bit of entertainment." I crossed my arms across my middle, feigning boldness. It had been a full year since I had seen my dear brother, and I wanted to show him how grown up I was and how much I cared about our soldiers. But despite my good intentions, I was a bit late to realize that my actions might reflect poorly on him.

One of the men called out, "Aww, let her stay and dance with us, sir."

"Not now. The lady needs a rest." GK maintained a grip on my arm, firm enough to tell me I was most certainly out of line.

The aide glanced wide-eyed from GK to me. His thick hair and neatly trimmed mustache were the color of honey, and his expressive eyes reminded me of the crystal water that filled the quarry at home.

"Miss Emily Warren, allow me to introduce Captain Washington Roebling." GK lifted my gloved right hand and offered it to his aide. "I owe my life to this captain and my sense of purpose to this charming sprite. It is only fitting the two of you meet."

The captain cleared his throat. "You—your wife? I thought she was unable to—"

"Gracious no." GK laughed. "My sister. She and my wife happen to share a name. Now then, will you be so kind as to guard the honor of *Miss* Emily Warren?"

I felt sorry for the poor man; his eyes took me in, from escaping curls to rumpled hem, as he reconciled my identity. Perhaps trying to oust his commander's sister from the event was only slightly less humiliating than ousting his wife. My presented hand hung awkwardly in the air until the captain regained his composure and took it in his own.

"It will be my pleasure, sir." Then his first words to me: "Miss Warren, Captain Roebling, at your service."

"Very well then." GK gave a last glance, a small tilt of the head to remind me to act with decorum. He went back to his hosting duties, signaling the orchestra to resume and coaxing the officers back to the dance floor.

My new guardian took my hand and kissed the air just above it, then regarded me for several uncomfortable moments. My hand warmed from his touch despite my silk glove. Sensible of his gaze, I smoothed my hair and adjusted my dress.

I was no delicate beauty. A lifetime of riding horses and chasing—and being chased by—my siblings had afforded me a robust constitution, so I appreciated a sturdy man. The captain certainly appeared stalwart; it was doubtful I could break his arm in a bit of horseplay, as had happened to one of my more unfortunate suitors.

Unlike most men, he towered several inches over me. Many accoutrements adorned his perfectly kept uniform: a sword and scabbard, red sash, gold braid, and the gold epaulets. GK had taught me to read a uniform:

Branch: Engineers; Rank: Captain; Position: Aide de camp; Appearance: Outstanding. That last observation would be considered quite unofficial.

Still, I needed no honor guard, and this man had seemed insufferable. "You don't need to escort me all evening," I said. "I'm afraid my brother has put you in a rather unrewarding position."

"There are worse duties."

Biting my tongue at his inelegant reply, I caught the eye of an officer behind him. "It was lovely to meet you, Captain Roebling, but I'll make my own way."

His jaw dropped—in surprise, relief, or panic, I wasn't sure which.

"Please don't concern yourself. I'll put in a good report for you with General Warren." I turned on my heel to flee, but the captain gently caught my elbow.

"Wait."

"Yes?" I wrinkled my brow at his offending hand, and he withdrew it.

The orchestra played a slow waltz.

"I believe the general expects us to set the example. May I have the honor of a dance, Miss Warren?"

I nodded my acceptance. It wouldn't be good form to refuse.

The captain led me to the dance floor where he was light on his feet, his hand gentle across my back, guiding me in graceful circles. "I'll let you in on a little secret."

"Oh?"

His eyes held mine; there was something quite endearing about them.

"The general caught me sneaking peeks at you."

A sympathetic soul—who admitted to watching *me*. The orchestra stopped, and other dancers retreated from the floor. Captain Roebling had a presence about him, a confidence I first took as hubris. Other officers called to him, but his eyes never left mine. Those ice-blue eyes seemed to see everything yet give nothing away.

The muscles knotting my neck softened as the shame from embarrassing my brother ebbed. My instinct to flee had disappeared, replaced with a desire to learn more about this curious man. "Why does the general say he owes his life to you?"

"Perhaps that's a story for another day. Or never." His hand went to his neck, and he absently fingered his collar.

The room grew quiet as couples dispersed for refreshments, and I worried I had spoiled the captain's mood, speaking of the war that GK was trying to put aside for just one evening.

The pianist played Liszt's "Liebestraum No. 3 (Love's Dream)." Candles flickered soft shadows into the golden light.

"May I have the pleasure of another dance, Miss Warren?" His hand, warm and firm, lifted mine.

"Please, just Emily."

He drew me close and whispered in my ear. "So I've heard. I am Washington. And for you only, just Wash."

We danced again, heedless of sustaining a respectable gap between us. The wool of his jacket smelled of earth, rubbing pleasantly against my cheek. I couldn't resist laughing at the other officers whistling and calling our names. That was, until Wash gently placed a finger under my chin and turned my face toward him as he swirled me around the ballroom. Had any other man done that, it would have felt disrespectful. But the way he held me—like a treasured gift—enchanted me.

All others faded away that night as we danced and talked, learning about each other's big families and bigger dreams. While I hoped to join in the effort to gain the right to vote for women, he was planning to forever change our nation's largest cities with the bridges he would build. His breath smelled like an exotic concoction of anise and cinnamon, and even as the light-headedness from the whiskey faded, I floated on a scented cloud, just listening to him. When it was time to go, I yearned to hold on to him and to the evening.

It seemed he felt the same. "It was my very great pleasure to meet you, Emily. I hope we will meet again soon."

"My pleasure as well, Captain Roebling. I mean, Just Wash."

READING GROUP GUIDE

1. Edith is swept into an intense, and often tumultuous, romance with Woodrow, but despite her love for him, she has continual reservations about the direction of their relationship. What are some things that Edith worries about when it comes to her romance with the president? How does it affect his presidency? Are her worries valid?

2. Edith is a hardworking and successful businesswoman, who fears she will lose her identity by becoming a First Lady. How does Edith handle this fear? Is she able to keep her beliefs intact?

3. How did you feel when you found out that Woodrow hid his affair from Edith? Would you have reacted differently than her? Why or why not?

4. Edith is not only a romantic confidant to Woodrow but a political one as well. How does Edith's feeling about being a sounding board for the president change throughout the novel, and what power does she have in the president's decision-making? How would you feel if you were as involved with the decisions of the president as she was?

5. One of Edith's main concerns is how she will be remembered as a First Lady. What kind of First Lady do you think she was? What kind of First Lady would you want to be?

6.   Edith makes it clear that she is against women's suffrage, though her reasoning is complex. Discuss the many reasons why Edith was not in favor of the Nineteenth Amendment. Do you agree with some of her points? Did her views make you think of her differently?

7.   World War I is the intense backdrop to Edith and Woodrow's story. How did each of the characters feel about entering the war? How did their opinions about it differ?

8.   After Woodrow's stroke, Edith continues the presidency in the shadows. How do you think she handles the emotional toil of her situation, and what do her actions say about her as a person? How would you handle such a devastating situation?

9.   At the end of the novel, we learn that much of Edith's guilt about the world wars stems from her decision to keep Woodrow in office after his stroke. What does she feel she should have done differently? Do you think different actions on her part would have changed the course of history?

A CONVERSATION WITH THE AUTHOR

Of all the First Ladies in United States history, why Edith Wilson? What drew you to her story?

Two main reasons. I think we are at the cusp of finally having a female president. And when we do, I thoroughly hope she is chosen as the person most fit for the job, not just for her gender, for if she flounders due to inexperience or incompetence, it will set back the cause for women attaining positions of power. Of all the women in power in our history, I believe the unelected Edith Wilson has come closest to the position of president, so she should be studied for both the positive and negative things she did and the lessons we can learn from that.

Secondly, there is an irresistible love story. Woodrow Wilson, often thought as having a rather stuffy and professorial nature, was completely different in private, as the multitude of his love letters attest. I relished this dichotomy and enjoyed exploring their complex and entertaining relationship.

The story you tell is based on the lives of real people. Was it difficult writing a novel about such complex historical figures? How did you balance fiction and fact?

It is the complexity of exploring real people and imagining scenes that would demonstrate their assumed thought processes that I find most rewarding when writing historical fiction. For it is those scenes that bring history to life.

I have a few rules concerning fact versus fiction. My stories are true, or could be true, as far as I am able to determine. In other words, I use the facts that I research and imagine the parts that aren't documented. I don't claim to have done exhaustive research and vetted every fact as done in nonfiction, hence my caveat of "as far as I can determine."

There is one instance when I knowingly misrepresented an inconsequential historical fact: a timeline change to create a more dramatic arc and to simplify a complex event. This was the timing of the British equerry Craufurd-Stuart's offensive remarks that so angered Edith. His transgressions actually occurred in 1918 and 1919.

Since many of the things we enjoy in fiction—such as emotions, relationships, dialogue, inner wounds, and private thoughts—are not documented, I imagine those things, with careful thought put into matching the imagined things with the facts we do know. In this way, history is entertaining and has more emotional impact.

Not many people know about the things that Edith Wilson did for the U.S. government during her marriage to Woodrow Wilson. Why do you think it's important to tell stories such as Edith's?

I agree that little is known about Edith's contributions to the country.

With our most recent presidents being well into their seventies, the Twenty-Fifth Amendment (which deals with accession of power in the event of death or incapacity for the office of the president or vice president) has been much discussed. Although the most compelling reason for the adoption of the amendment was the assassination of John F. Kennedy, the legislation was in no doubt also influenced by the incapacitation of President Wilson, and Garfield and W. H. Harrison before him. I hope shedding light on this history will encourage knowledge and analysis of the Twenty-Fifth Amendment. Does it need tweaking?

What are you reading these days?

Things Fall Apart by Chinua Achebe, *The Light of Luna Park* by Addison Armstrong, and *The Wright Brothers* by David McCullough for research.

ACKNOWLEDGMENTS

Writing a book is a journey, one that begins with the first spark of an idea and continues long after publication. Along the way there are innumerable people, pets, and places that inspire, guide, and cheer on an author. Here, we capture just a snapshot of those; rest assured there are many more, who may be quite unaware of their contributions.

First, my everlasting gratitude to my friends and family, who have been with me every step of the way. To my beloved husband, Dave, who understands that although my body may be sitting next to him at the dinner table, my mind is somewhere in 1917. To Mary Elizabeth Riffle, thank you for being my partner in crime, for adjusting my crumpled blouse before I speak in front of an audience of readers, for driving me to three events in three different cities in a day while I deal with family emergencies on the phone, and for being fun and cheerful the whole time. I love you, Louise.

To my adult children and grandchildren, I love you beyond measure. Being with you is my favorite thing in the world. I'm sure you will find little bits and pieces of yourselves in my characters, little Easter eggs for you to discover.

To my publicists, Kathie Bennett and Cristina Arreola, thank you for making me get out there to talk about my books and helping them find their audience, when I'd really rather be home with my coffee and laptop. My eternal thanks to my agent, Lucy Cleland, who once again championed me and my book, making it all possible.

To my team at Sourcebooks, especially my editor, Anna Michels, and production editor, Jessica Thelander, I am so grateful for your guiding hands and sage advice. Once again, the book cover blew me away, so kudos and thanks to James Iacobelli and the design team for their talent and hard work.

Research is a critical part of writing historical fiction, and one I particularly enjoy. For this book, I traveled to Paris and the surrounding countryside of France; Washington, DC; and the Shenandoah Valley. Particularly helpful were Hunter Hanger of the Woodrow Wilson Presidential Library and Museum in Staunton, Virginia, who is perhaps as obsessed with the 1920 Pierce-Arrow as I am; Scott Gower at the National Defense University and CDR Scott Riffle for information on the Hains Island War Garden; and Elizabeth Karcher, executive director of the President Woodrow Wilson House in Washington, DC, who gave an amazing and informative tour. The wonderful people of Wytheville welcomed my grandchildren to their Halloween street festival, making research for Edith's hometown a fun family event.

And once again, to my early readers, especially Anne Lipton, this book is vastly improved from your insight. I frequently advise budding authors to find their tribe to review their work, for the best writing comes from learning how your words are interpreted by others.

Finally, to my dog, Violet, who quietly lays her head on my lap when she'd rather be playing fetch, for she somehow understands the words must come first.

Tracey Enerson Wood
November 2022

ABOUT THE AUTHOR

© Katie Beyer Photography

Tracey Enerson Wood loves discovering amazing women whose stories have been lost to history and bringing them to life for today's readers.

Her debut novel, *The Engineer's Wife*, the story of the woman who saw to the completion of the Brooklyn Bridge, is an international and *USA Today* bestseller. Her sophomore novel, *The War Nurse*, tells the unforgettable tale of Julia Stimson and her nurses in WWI France. Both novels are published by Sourcebooks.

Her coauthored anthology/cookbook, *Homefront Cooking, American Veterans Share Recipes, Wit, and Wisdom*, was released by Skyhorse Publishing and all authors' profits are donated to organizations that support veterans. *Life Hacks for Military Spouses* is her latest nonfiction release, also an anthology from Skyhorse.

Tracey has always had a writing bug. While working as a registered nurse, starting her own interior design company, raising two children, and bouncing around the world as a military wife, she indulged in her passion as a playwright, screenwriter, and novelist. She has authored magazine columns and other pieces of nonfiction and written and directed plays of all lengths, including *Grits*, *Fleas and Carrots*, *Rocks and Other Hard Places*, *Alone*, and *Fog*. Her screenplays include *Strike Three* and *Roebling's Bridge*.

Other passions include food and cooking, and honoring military heroes. A New Jersey native, she now lives with her family in Florida.